The World In-between

The World In-between Series
Book 1

IE Castellano

Laurel
Highlands
Publishing

Cover by JosDCreations

Laurel Highlands Publishing
Mount Pleasant, PA
USA

http://LaurelHighlandsPublishing.com

ISBN-13: 978-1-941087-02-2
ISBN-10: 1941087027

This book is a work of fiction. Names, characters, places, and
incidents either are products of the author's imagination or are used
fictitiously. Any resemblance to actual persons, living or dead,
events, or locales is entirely coincidental.

To my parents and brother, with love

Chapter One
A Knock on the Door

"Turn right," said the cool, female voice of the on dash navigator. The car turned right, slowly riding on the tree-lined street. Its driver peered out the windows at the old homes. From what the driver's eyes could see through the thick trunks of the mature trees, each home had a well-kept, restored feel. Separated from one another by a long, narrow driveway, all the homes seemed to have been built roughly during the same era. An elaborate Victorian house nestled next to an ostentatious Italianate home, which stately stood near a cozier Tutor-styled abode. The styles changed from house to house, but the well-to-do feel remained ever present.

"You have arrived at your destination," the machine said. Pulling up to the curb, the car rolled to a stop. The hum of the engine was silenced. Taking one last peek out the windows, the driver grabbed the strap of the wide, canvas shoulder bag that lay on the passenger seat and opened the car door. The smell of autumn found his nostrils even though summer was desperately trying to linger.

Standing in the space made by his open car door and the car, his hands smoothed his wrinkle-free khaki chinos and checked to make sure that his blue pinstriped button-down shirt was flat and that his sleeves were rolled up evenly. Carefully resting his shoulder strap on his shoulder so that it did not make his collar askew, he took a deep breath of the warm, late summer air before closing the car door. His feet followed the cement sidewalk to a large covered porch that surrounded a stained glass door belonging to a modest looking Victorian house.

In his left hand, he held a small piece of paper with a scribble of an address not in his handwriting, which he checked twice. His eyes glanced to the right and saw the brass numbers, 727, against light blue wood siding while his right index finger pressed the doorbell.

Somewhere inside, a chime rang. He fidgeted with the paper as he waited for a few moments before he could see an outline of a person grow larger in the multicolored glass. His ears heard a click. The stained glass door opened to reveal a strikingly, pleasant looking face of a woman. He was instantly face to face with wild, short, dark red hair. Looking down, he gazed into intense, yet soft, brown eyes. Her whole persona gave a delicately strong vibe.

Almost forgetting why he was standing on her porch, his heart beat hard and fast while his lungs filled with air. "Hi, my name is Berty Chase," he said. "I am from the Post..."

"Yes, of course. Please come in," she said. Berty stepped over the threshold. He found himself in a dark wood paneled foyer with a modest crystal and brass chandelier hanging from the ceiling. An ancient wool carpet softened the footsteps as the woman led him through a pair of beveled glass pocket doors to his left.

"I am Silvia," she said. "Please, have a seat." She extended her arm towards a dining room chair. Not sure what to expect, Berty sat on the carved wooden chair nearest the door while Silvia took the seat across the table.

He carefully placed his bag on the floral Oriental rug, then extracted his flip top notebook, pen and recorder. Opening his notebook to a blank page, his eyes absorbed every detail of the antique dining room. In his notebook, he scribbled details concerning the crisp, white linen tablecloth, the ornate stone and wood fireplace on the opposite wall, the large brass chandelier with six matching wall sconces scattered around the room and the silver teapot on the Victorian styled sideboard. When he finished noting the room, he scribbled the details concerning Silvia—her claret blouse, dark washed jeans, leather heeled boots, silver teardrop earrings with matching necklace pendant, and no rings or bracelets.

Rereading what he had written, he wondered why he was sent since everything seemed normal, so far. Berty looked up from his notebook, saying, "Sorry, it helps me create a mood."

Silvia simply pleasantly replied, "Coffee? Cookies?"

"Thank you." His pen hovered over the page. "Could you spell your name for me, please?"

"Of course," she said as she poured him a cup of coffee from a silver coffeepot that sat on a silver tray. "S-I-L-V-I-A."

"Last name?"

Placing a plate of cookies between them, Silvia said, "No last name."

"Okay." Berty started to get a sinking feeling in his stomach. Interviews where the interviewee refused to answer the basics never boded well for him. "Age?"

"Your mother taught you better than that, Mr. Chase."

Hoping to salvage the interview, he smiled at Silvia, then grabbed a cookie. "Please, call me Berty."

She returned his smile. "Is Berty short for Albert or Bertwin?"

"Hubert, actually." Berty blushed. His stomach could not help but sink further.

"Your editor was quite excited when he contacted me to set up this interview." Silvia sipped her coffee. Putting down her cup, her eyes carefully scrutinized him. She asked, "Low man on the totem pole, Berty?"

"I write human interest stories for the paper," answered Berty. His mind rushed back to his un-office, as he liked to call his desk sitting in the corner of the open newsroom surrounded by other desks and some cubicles, where he sat typing stories about happenings at the zoo or how some old lady's cat was rescued from a drain pipe.

In his un-office is where he was sitting when the stern voice of his section's editor called, "Chase, go up to the fourteenth floor, editor-in-chief wants a word. Now." Berty saved his work, then stumbled off his chair. In the elevator, he wiped sweat off his face and smoothed his dark hair and shirt.

When he found his way to the assistant's desk, he managed to say, "Berty Chase here to see…"

The woman behind the desk said, "He's expecting you. Go right in."

Berty walked cautiously through the open door to the corner office. The silver-haired man sat in a large, leather armchair behind a handsome cherry desk.

"Close the door behind you, Chase," he bellowed. Berty did as he was told. "I am sure you are wondering why you are here. Well, I have a special assignment for you."

The sound of a passing car brought Berty back to the foreign dining room. He glanced at Silvia. She raised an eyebrow. "I could be doing worse," he said. As he sat across from her, he could feel his heart beating strongly enough to almost make his shirt move. Not wanting to let her see his nerves, he ignored his shirt, begging, "Enough about me. I am here to interview you."

"Fair enough," she conceded. The intensity of her gaze relaxed. "I will not deprive you of your interview any longer."

Berty's fingers fumbled as they switched on his recorder. He took a soothing sip of his coffee, then asked, "What do you do for a living?"

"I do not wish to divulge that information."

Berty did not realize that his stomach could sink any further as he promptly turned off his recorder. "Off the record?"

Silvia's eyes seemed to penetrate into his soul. Trying to stifle a burgeoning panic attack, Berty's mind tucked away his editor-in-chief's intimidating voice that told him to have a story for Halloween. He noticed how the midmorning sunlight captured the red in her hair. She turned her head to look out the window. "I have a job, which I really enjoy." Turning to face Berty, she said, "Forgive me if I do not trust you to keep it off the record."

Berty swallowed hard. "I understand." Hoping to salvage something, his fingers clumsily switched on the recorder. "So," he continued, "can I call it a hobby?"

4

Both of her hands held the coffee cup to her lips. Peering through the steam, she said, "If it makes you feel better."

"What sort of tools or instruments or whatever do you use?" asked Berty.

"Tools for what?"

He forgot to breathe for a moment. "For your hobby." Berty hated when interviewees answered a question with a question. "Do you have a special room or space? I brought a camera, if that is okay with you."

Smiling, Silvia shook her head.

A sickness in his stomach thoroughly moved throughout his body. He was feeling very confused. He knew that this attempt at an article set by his editor-in-chief would bomb completely, making sure he would never leave his un-office. Thinking that he could possibly lose his job because of this, Berty pleaded with her. "My editor said you would show me everything."

"And I shall, if you are ready."

"Okay," he said, feeling somewhat relieved.

Silvia picked up the cups and the plate of cookies off the tablecloth, then placed them on the tray. When she stood, Berty asked, "Where are we going?"

"Out," Silvia stated.

While Berty gathered his things and picked up his bag, Silvia carried the silver tray through a swinging door that Berty assumed took her into the kitchen. He waited for her in her wood paneled foyer, wondering what she was going to show him.

Berty watched her slender shape saunter down the hall into the foyer and opened a door disguised as a panel behind which she extracted a dark gray cloth bag with a shoulder strap. When she threw her bag over her shoulder, he imitated her.

"Would you like to leave your bag in the closet, Berty?" Silvia asked.

"No, thank you. I'd rather take it with me."

"I am sorry," said Silvia, "but you are going to have to leave it here, as well as your cell phone and car keys."

"But what if I need something?" implored Berty.

"I have everything that we will need," she assured him while patting her bag.

"But—"

"Did Martin not tell you my conditions?" Silvia asked.

"Martin?"

"Martin Hunter, your editor."

"Oh. He told me to go along with whatever you wanted," answered Berty.

"I want you to leave your things in the closet," Silvia said.

Exasperated, but somewhat hopeful, Berty reluctantly placed his bag in the closet. As she closed the panel, he felt a strange mixture of separation anxiety and anxiousness swimming in his stomach.

"Thank you." Silvia opened the stained glass door, ushering Berty out onto the porch. Following her lead, the two of them walked down the sidewalk from her porch, then turned to walk down the tree-lined street.

Two houses later, as the neighbors were meticulously mowing their green grass, she turned to Berty. "I am curious. What did Martin mention about me?"

"He said that he had a story for Halloween time and that writing a story about you would be a magical experience," Berty recounted.

Laughing, Silvia said, "Martin likes a tabula rasa. Nothing like starting an adventure bathed in ignorance." She laughed again. "So, you think that I am a Witch?"

Feeling like he might have been the butt of a joke, Berty opened his mouth, but no sound escaped. He promptly closed it.

"It is all right. I am not a Witch by any stretch of the imagination. That does not mean you will not have a magical experience." His face showed an expression of blank confusion. "I will show you what I mean. But first," Silvia continued, "I want you to remove any thoughts of common magical stereotypes from your head. No pointy hats, no broomsticks, no dark clothes and no pentagrams to be found."

Wanting to continue the interview and figure out what the purpose was of sending him to see Silvia, Berty asked, "Do you use magic?"

"In a sense," Silvia vaguely answered. The last side street before the abrupt dead end passed without Silvia making a turn.

Attempting to get into her mind, he asked, "What is magic?"

The street ended where the woods began. Silvia stopped at the edge of the two, looked hard at the forest enticing her to enter, then answered, "What isn't?"

Berty's eyes darted from her to the trees, then back again. Keeping the questions flowing, he asked, "Would wands and spell books be stereotypical as well?"

Silvia's face turned towards him. Berty noticed a wild sparkle in her brown eyes and the gentle manner in the way her lips curved when she smiled. She stepped off the pavement. Her feet found a path through the woods that only they knew. His feet followed while his mind was trying not to think about arriving at some sort of stone or wood circle with a fire pit at the center.

When they finally stopped, Berty was a bit surprised to find himself on the bank of a brook. The air was chillier in the shadow of the canopy where the leaves began their multicolored show. His body began to shiver and goose bumps briefly appeared on his arms.

Crossing his arms in front of his torso, he watched Silvia with her back to the brook, facing the hill. Berty did not know at what she was looking, but he did know that she showed no signs of chilliness. Finally turning around, she removed her bag from her shoulder.

"Autumn has seemed to have arrived early in this part of the woods. We are walking even further and it will not get much warmer. Here, put this on. It will keep you warm." Silvia extracted a dark gray cloth bundle from her bag, then handed it to Berty.

"Thank you." He was so busy trying to unravel his bundle that he did not notice that Silvia came over to help him until her soft hand was on top of his. His hands let go of the wad of charcoal gray cloth. Her delicate hands gently shook the mass of gray to reveal a cloak. Sheepishly, Berty swung the cloak over his shoulders. He instantly felt warm. She stood in front of him as he watched her dainty fingers delicately fasten his cloak.

"Must have been the chill," muttered Berty. Silvia's lips grinned while her head nodded slightly. As she turned from him, he noticed that she was wearing a similar cloak. "Where is your bag?"

"I am wearing it. Come." Berty trudged up the hill after her.

Silvia stopped halfway up the hill before a three-foot space between two oak trees.

"Are you ready?" she asked.

Wondering what was going to happen next, he answered, "As ready as I will ever be." His shoulder brushed hers as he leaned over to answer.

Her left hand stretched between them, palm up. "Place your hand in mine," instructed Silvia.

Resigned to the fact that in order to keep his job he must proceed blindly, his right hand dutifully slid on top of hers. Soft, delicate fingers pushed through the spaces between stronger fingers, clasping his hand tightly. Strong fingers returned the grip.

"Follow my lead and do not let go," Silvia warned. Her foot stepped forward and her body's strength led him between the two oak trees.

Chapter Two
A Tale or Two

Berty was not sure what to expect. A chill trickled down his spine while his eyes registered a loss of light. Looking around, he realized that they walked into a small grove of tall pines. The cloaked figure before him made for an opening in the trees and a rarely used path. A couple of steps free of the pine grove, the light returned. His companion dropped his hand.

"Best to keep your hood up while traveling, my Lady. The weather is not being cooperative," said a low gruff voice beside them. From behind a bush emerged a creature unlike Berty had ever seen. It stood about four and a half feet tall, had long arms and legs with a short torso and its face resembled an upside down triangle.

Silvia turned to it, saying, "Thank you very much, kind sir."

The creature removed his hat, revealing dark blond curls. He bowed while saying, "It is an honor, my Lady." Hat still in his hand, he straightened his body. "Good travels." He disappeared behind the bush.

Silvia raised the hood over her head, then motioned to Berty to do the same.

A couple of minutes later, the unused path brought them to a wide, dirt road. She turned right onto the road. Following, Berty saw that the forest encroached into the road with vines, ground cover and other greenery growing towards its center.

Squirrels scurried across branches. He heard the caws of birds over the sound of their feet softly crushing the earth. Being a journalist, a million pointed questions had already been forming in Berty's mind, but in his experience, he had always thought it best to start simple. "Where are we?"

"This is the perimeter road. It has also been called the portal road. It is not as widely used anymore, but it allows us to find a secure spot to make camp," Silvia explained.

"Camp?" Berty was glad his editor did not give him a rigid deadline.

"Yes," said Silvia. "We need to find a secluded spot. If we run into anyone, tell no one our real names. If anyone asks from where we have come, say the South Lake."

"Why?" Nerves started to flutter in his stomach.

"I will explain later," she whispered. "We have a long way to go and it will be starting to get dark in a few hours."

He hoped that some sense of security would find its way into his mind. Walking closer to her, Berty softly asked, "What was that creature back there?"

"A Troll." Seeing the stunned look on his face, Silvia explained, "Trolls take care of the borders and watch the portals here."

Not knowing whether or not he could believe her, Berty asked, "Where is here exactly?"

"The Land of Sages."

Berty wracked his brain. "I have never heard of it."

"Of course you haven't," said Silvia. "If we were to travel this entire road it would take us to the different portals that are connected to the different corners of the world. A long time ago, that was how the Sages traveled from place to place without having to cross oceans or traverse mountain ranges."

Looking at the wide trunks of the old trees that surrounded them, Berty knew that he was no longer in the woods on the outskirts of Silvia's neighborhood. Although he was finding it hard to believe, he yearned to know more. "What is beyond the border?"

"The Dragonlands."

"Dragons?" After seeing the Troll, Berty was not sure what to believe.

"Yes."

"Like in the stories? Flying, scaly beasts that breathe fire?"

Silvia sighed. "So they say."

"Have you ever seen one?" he asked.

"No."

"How do you know they exist?"

"That's a fair question," she answered. Deep in thought, her eyes focused on a distant point. At first, Berty thought she was thinking about her Dragon knowledge, but then he saw the subject of her focus—movement in the distance. Her eyes quickly scanned the road's edge. Silvia nudged him to walk along another rarely used path.

They followed the path in silence. The further they walked helped ease the intense trepidation and loosen the knots in Berty's stomach. When he could no longer see the road, Berty whispered, "What is going on? Who or what was that?"

Silvia whispered back, "I do not know, but," her voice left a whisper, "we should find a place to camp soon.

"Going back to the subject of Dragons, the Sages' Tales talk about Dragons that existed a long time ago. I do not see why Dragons would not still exist today," continued Silvia. "Legend has it that a son of a great warrior wished to be an even greater warrior than his father in order to prove that he was worthy to lead his people. Every day, he would go deep into the forest to train in private. One day, the boy heard a great roar and he followed the sound to see what kind of creature made that roar. Expecting to find a great bear, he instead found a clan of Dragons. Foregoing his training, he went back to this place every day and watched the Dragons. On a particularly cold evening, he lost track of time. As evening was fast approaching, the Dragons collected some wood to build a fire. The boy watched in awe when who he figured was the head Dragon breathed fire on the pile of wood for an instant, roaring fire.

"Up there." Silvia pointed to a spot a bit uphill from the path. Berty followed her to a hidden clearing behind boulders and trees.

"How did you know this was here?" he asked.

She smiled slyly, simply saying, "Luck."

After clearing some brush and gathering an ample amount of

wood for a fire to prepare for their night's stay, Silvia and Berty sat on a low rock. They faced the fire pit to have a limited view of the path below them.

"Now only if we had some food," said Berty.

From inside her cloak, Silvia handed him a small, soft leather bag, then placed an identical bag in her lap.

"What is this?" he asked, taking the bag.

"Beef jerky, granola, chocolate chip cookies with walnuts, and a canteen of water," she explained.

Berty smiled. "Thank you." He expected her to extract a nice wad of dryer lint for kindling and a waterproof book of matches from her cloak.

Watching her curiously, Silvia opened her left palm facing the fire pit, then raised it about three inches. Instantly, a fire rose from the pile of wood. Berty's jaw dropped in awe. "This is just between you and me, understand?"

The act of nodding closed his mouth.

"As I was saying before," Silvia said, continuing with her story, "the Dragons had lit the fire with their breath and the boy was still watching. The intensity of the fire brightened the surrounding trees and the boy's hiding place. One of the Dragons saw him and beckoned him closer. As he walked towards the fire, the Dragons realized that he was merely a boy. They offered him a place to sleep for the evening and some food to eat. He would journey back to his people in the morning. To the boy's surprise, the evening was filled with good conversation and laughter. When dawn broke the following morning, the boy awoke and found that the Dragons were awake and laid out food for his journey. The boy thanked his hosts for their hospitality and asked if he could return someday. They told him that he would always be welcome in their midsts.

"Upon the boy's return to his people, his family questioned him about his absence. He told them about meeting the Dragons. However, he changed a few details to make himself to be the brave survivor of his encounter. No one ever questioned him because Dragons were feared.

"I should say that Dragons, as well as the Dragonlands themselves, are still feared, but that's neither here nor there.

"Many years later, he rose to be the brave leader of his people that he had always hoped he would become. His Dragon story was retold many times by storytellers who embellished and stretched for entertainment value. These tales inspired legions of Dragon slayers hoping to prove their worth. Finally, this now King who was known as the one delivered from the Dragons, had enough of the madness.

"He returned to the Dragons to ask for help, for guidance, in stopping the slayers. The Dragons, however, were not so helpful. They blamed him for the deaths of the slain. The King pleaded and tried to explain that he did not want any of this. They called him a liar. He wanted to know what he could do to prove what was in his heart. Unfortunately, unbeknownst to the King, his young daughter followed him.

"The Dragons saw the young girl peering behind a tree not unlike her father did many years before. Once again, they beckoned the child into the clearing. The Dragons told the King that if he gave them his daughter, then they would know what his heart held."

"The King did not give his daughter to the Dragons?" asked Berty.

"Oh yes, he did."

"What happened to the girl?"

Silvia shook her head. "I do not know. The Dragons eventually retreated to the Dragonlands, where to this day, they stay very reclusive. No one has seen a Dragon in ages, but no one seeks to find one either."

Before Berty had time to decide whether or not she was just an extremely good storyteller, Silvia's head turned sharply to the left. Her whole body stiffened as to be able to run at any moment. Her tense trepidation poured into Berty. He, too, cautiously waited for a sign to run.

"Here's the place," shouted a voice behind the rocks. "Gloria, I

13

found it!"

A silver haired, stout man stumbled between the rocks, then stopped behind the fire. Berty clearly saw the look of surprise on the man's face.

"Sorry," said the man. "I did not know anyone was here." A woman and a lanky younger man appeared behind him.

"It's all right," Silvia said, smiling. "The site is big enough for all of us."

"Thank you, ma'am," said the man, looking relieved. "It is getting too dark to find another place, especially with the thieves around."

"Safety in numbers," Silvia said while motioning for them to sit around the fire.

"Gloria, why don't you sit and let us men get our stuff," the man said to the woman.

The woman sat and smiled at Silvia and Berty while she removed her hood. The fire danced in the silver of her hair. "Thank you again," said she. "We have been traveling all day. I am Gloria and I believe you have already met my husband, Simeon. The young man is our son, Michael."

"I am Leigh and this is my companion, Marcus." Berty kept silent, not wanting to mess up the lie. "What brings you and your family on the road?" Silvia asked.

"We are traveling for a wedding," Gloria said with a gleam in her eyes, "my son's wedding. Tradition dictates that the groom's family goes to collect the bride's family from their home and bring them back to the groom's home for the wedding. Not everyone abides by tradition anymore. Simeon and I find that keeping traditions such as this to be very important."

When the two men returned to the fire, a third man, older and a head shorter than Michael accompanied them. Berty eyed this man as suspiciously as the man eyed him and Silvia. Not liking the way the man's gaze lingered on Silvia, Berty scrutinized the man's every feature. The light from the fire illuminated the man's cold, gray eyes, flat nose and straight, black hair.

"This is Sean," Gloria explained. "He joined our party just a little ways out from our village."

"Since we were headed the same way," Sean said, "it's safer to travel together." Berty did not like the breathy, mouse like sound of his voice nor did he like the way Sean always glanced in Silvia's direction.

Berty thought that Silvia was just as uncomfortable as he was with Sean for she was securing her food bag to the inside of her cloak. He followed her lead, securing the bag she gave him to the inside of his cloak as Simeon spoke.

"Did I hear you telling a Sage Tale when we arrived, Leigh?"

"Yes, you did," answered Silvia.

"Please, don't let us stop you."

Silvia smiled, saying, "I had already finished when you had arrived."

"Which one did you tell?" asked Michael eagerly.

"The Story of the Dragons."

"Is it true that the girl in the story became the first Empress?" Michael asked. His eyes were wide with excitement.

"Michael," Gloria exclaimed, "behave yourself."

"It is natural to be curious about certain things," Silvia assured her.

Turning to Michael, she said, "Legend has it that the Empire was started by the Seven High Sages when they crafted the scepter, long, long ago."

"What does the scepter look like?" interjected Michael.

"Supposedly," Silvia answered, "it was crafted out of some type of white metal and a single, large, white crystal, which is visible at the top."

"How did they make it?" Michael ignored the disapproving looks from his mother.

"They used magic."

"Wow," he said softly.

"Once the scepter was in place inside the Empire Tree," continued Silvia, "the scepter chose the first child that was born in the Empire, who happened to be female, to become the first Empress."

"How do you know so many of the Sages' Tales so well?" Michael's curiosity was endless. Berty thought that he would make a good journalist.

Michael reminded Berty of himself during his first semester of college. He had an annoying combination of extreme curiosity and eagerness. When he was a writer for his University's Independent Press, his editor would always yell at him for asking too many seemingly useless questions. Four years of writing well-researched and thorough articles helped him land his current job.

In all the years he had been working there, he had only been slowly rising through the channels. Berty had hoped that receiving an assignment from the editor-in-chief was a big break for him. Sitting around the fire, he had no idea what was in store for him, in the Land of Sages or in his job.

"It is obvious; is it not?" said Sean, glaring at Silvia with the utmost contempt.

"What is obvious?" Berty finally broke his silence.

"That we have the Empress in our midst," answered Sean. Wide-eyed Simeon and Gloria gasped. "I thought you looked familiar."

Silvia said nothing. Her actions neither affirmed nor denied this claim.

"Unarmed and without your guard," said Sean. "This is almost too easy."

"What is too easy?" Silvia asked.

"Capturing and killing you." With one fluid motion, Sean stood, withdrawing a sword. Berty and Silvia quickly jumped to their feet. Frightened, Simeon's family withdrew to the edges of the enclave. Only the fire separated Sean from his prey.

"You assume too much," said Silvia. Her voice was calm and cool.

Berty's hands frantically searched the pockets inside his cloak for anything that could help. From one pocket, he withdrew what felt like a smooth, short stick. He raised it in front of himself. In the bright light of the flickering flames, he realized that it looked like a wand that he had seen in popular movies.

Sean took a step backwards. "A Watcher."

The fire grew larger. Berty knew that it was not his doing. Silvia grabbed his free hand and squeezed hard. Her pressure meant that he needed to follow her at a moment's notice. The fire extinguished in a cloud of smoke that enveloped Sean. Pulling Berty's hand with hers, Berty followed Silvia as she ran into the darkness.

They weaved in-between trees and leapt over fallen logs. For an hour, they did not stop nor look back. When Silvia found a large tree, she pulled Berty inside its hollow trunk.

She pushed her back into the side of the hollow, grabbing him tightly next to her. He could feel Silvia's heart beating hard and fast against his chest and her hot breath rhythmically shooting onto his neck. His nose caught the familiar scent of his mother's end of summer mixed berry pie, which she made when he was a child, emitting from Silvia's hair. His head became light and dizzy as if he were intoxicated.

Before his mind could register the cold, damp wood and moss smell from within the trunk of the tree, he felt his feet leave the ground. The next thing he saw was a thick branch stemming from another opening in the trunk. When he looked at Silvia, she pressed a finger to her lips, then pointed to a spot behind him outside of the hollow.

Some twenty feet below them were a group of what Berty perceived to be thieves. About a half a dozen men and women rested around a central fire. Outside of the fire sat canvas tents. The group laughed while passing around items for inspection as well as a bottle or two of drink. Leaning against logs and rocks were swords and crossbows. One man emerged from a lighted tent boasting about the abundant week's earnings, and saying that their bounty would be split the usual way in the morning. A claoked figure pointing a sword at the group walked into the firelight.

"What's the meaning of this?" one of the men bellowed. Others grabbed their swords and crossbows.

"Have you seen two people, a man and a woman, around?" asked a voice that Berty recognized to be Sean's.

"Like I'd tell you," taunted the man.

"Seen any magic in the area?" Sean asked.

Some of the swords lowered. "Are you telling us that there are Watchers nearby?"

Sean sheathed his sword. He left the group discussing leaving their spot. After they agreed that leaving was imperative, they quickly packed their sacks and deconstructed their tents. Berty watched them throw dirt on the fire, extinguishing the roaring light. Carrying heavy sacks and flickering lanterns, they silently slipped away from the tree. Berty and Silvia waited in the hollow until after the thieves were well out of hearing range before emerging from their perch.

Silvia pulled Berty's hood further over his head, throwing his face further into the shadows. After doing the same with her own hood, Silvia tiptoed onto the branch, guiding Berty to do the same.

Feeling him waiver, she stretched to whisper in his ear, "We will not fall, just look straight ahead."

In the moonless night, they crept along the branches, hand in hand, from tree to tree, going in all sorts of directions at varying heights. Berty heeded Silvia's advice and only looked ahead. He had an inkling that their feet were not touching the branches of different thicknesses, but he dared not look down to see. Over Silvia's head, Berty could see dark shapes form as they approached yet another tree trunk.

Chapter Three
High in the Empire Tree

As the black sky began to lighten at the horizon, Berty's feet ached. His weary body wished to relax. Every muscle protested for sleep. Berty had not done crazy all night things since college, and usually, with the aid of lots of caffeine.

In the strange light that proceeds daybreak, Berty thought that his eyes deceived him. What he saw ahead looked like a wall made of live growing trees. The trees seemed to have grown together, making one wide trunk. Branches did not grow out from the wall. All the branches grew from above the wall, creating a leafy canopy. As intimidating as Berty found the wall of trees, he was sure that anyone approaching from the ground would find the wall formidable. He noticed a narrow crack in one of the tree trunks.

The branches of the forest kept a wide distance between them and the wall. Yet somehow, Silvia walked on something seemingly invisible towards the small crack within the wall. Reaching that crack, Berty knew that Silvia, although small, could not fit through it, let alone him.

Silvia threw her arms tightly around him as if to give him a bear hug. To his bewildered surprise, she rolled both of them through the crack.

Inside the wall, they landed on a plank platform supported by the trees' branches, like a tree house. When Silvia released him, Berty noticed a man in strange, leather armor standing off to the side with a bow. The man immediately bowed to Silvia.

"My Lady," the man said, "let me escort you to the Empire Tree." Berty took in his pale complexion and tall, lanky gait.

"That will not be necessary. It is best to stay at your post. Make sure we were not followed. Send a report an hour after the sun rises," Silvia instructed.

"Of course." The man nodded, then stood by the crack.

Berty followed Silvia onto a narrow, plank and rope bridge. "I apologize about the labyrinth of branches I dragged you through," Silvia said. "I did not want to be seen or followed."

"I understand," said Berty. "Where are we now?"

"We are in the Sages' Grove and are heading towards the Empire Tree." Silvia stopped walking, then took Berty's arm.

"Are you really the Empress?" Berty asked.

"Yes." As she pulled on a nearby rope, they ascended to another bridge, walking around the tree instead of directly towards it.

"The man at the wall?"

"A guard," she explained. "He is an Elf. Elves are the best archers in the Empire."

Berty nodded before asking, "Why did that man, Sean, want to kill you?"

"Hopefully, we shall discover that soon enough."

Berty followed Silvia through a window sized opening into what appeared to be an extremely leafy bunch of small branches. Astonished, he found himself inside a rather normal looking, although round, room. The circular room's walls were covered with books and strange objects made of metals and woods sitting on shelves. In the center of the room was a circular staircase. At its side sat a desk. Silvia pulled on an ornate sash, like an old-fashioned doorbell.

A minute later, an elderly man descended the spiral staircase. His wild, gray hair and his coarse, gray beard held onto remnants of red.

"Empress," said the man, bowing his head. "What is it?"

"There is a man who wishes to kill me. I was told his name is Sean. Mid-adult looking, straight black hair, gray eyes, average height and he wields a sword." Silvia paused to look into the man's eyes. "Leif, gather as much information about this man and his cause as you can."

"Of course, my Lady," said Leif. "May I inquire about your

companion?"

"He is a Watcher."

"Shall I take him—"

"No." Silvia's firm tone resonated throughout the room. "He is my Watcher."

"My Lady...." Leif stood behind his desk.

"He will require a chamber close to mine," Silvia said.

"My Lady," implored Leif, "the Pixies—"

Silvia cut him off, raising her voice. "I know about the Pixies!" Leaning towards Leif, she slammed her fists on his desk. Taking a deep breath, she regained her composure. "We must do what we can to prepare ourselves. We will be in my study."

"Yes, absolutely, Empress." Leif bowed his head once more, but Berty could not shake the feeling that something deeply troubled the old man.

Berty and Silvia left using what Berty thought was the real entrance. More bridges connected all of the various limbs. Silvia led Berty onto a bridge that ascended to yet a higher level.

When they entered another mass of leaves through an arched doorway, Berty again stood in a circular room. Bookshelves covered the curved wall behind a large, wooden desk off to one side. A small, burled wood topped coffee table separated two yellow couches in a sitting area on the other side of the room. On the back wall was a large, wooden carved relief of a tree.

"Welcome to my chambers. Please, have a seat." Silvia sat down on a couch facing the door, so Berty sat on the couch facing her. She looked weary.

"Leif is my most trusted advisor," she began.

"Is he an Elf as well?" Berty remembered how tall he was.

"No. The Elf on the Advisory Council is also the Captain of the Empire Guard."

"Are there any Pixies on the Advisory Council?" Berty asked.

"No, Pixies do not get involved with the business of the Empire. The Advisory Council," Silvia explained, "consists of different posts within the Empire and tends to include one of each peoples who dwell mainly in the Land of Sages including Dwarves, Fairies and Trolls." She paused, looking at Berty. "The newest member of the Council is you."

"Me? Why me?"

"Because you are my Watcher." Berty thought he heard the faint clinking of wind chimes.

"What is a Watcher?" asked Berty. "And why does that upset Leif?"

"I will explain in a minute," She said in hushed tones. Raising her voice, Silvia said, "Come in."

In through the door walked a small woman, roughly five feet tall with waist long, strawberry blonde hair and freckles. She looked from Berty to Silvia before saying, "Breakfast, Empress."

"Millicent," Silvia said, "why are you carrying a tray?"

"I had to speak to you, my Lady," explained Millicent, "and Theodore is tending to his," she glanced at Berty, "chambers."

"Thank you. Please sit," instructed Silvia. Standing, Berty took the tray from Millicent. While he placed it on the coffee table between the couches, Millicent threw him a quizzical look before sitting on the couch beside him.

After he sat, Silvia spoke. "Millicent, I would like you to meet Hubert, my Watcher." Millicent said nothing, just nodded politely. Silvia addressed Berty. "Millicent is the Empire's Historian and is a member of the Advisory Council. I can only suppose that the reason why she is upset to see you is because the Council told the Watchers' Guild that no Watcher is allowed to go near the Empress."

"Why did you accept him, my Lady?" Millicent interjected.

"Please tell everyone who talks behind my back," said Silvia sternly, "that Hubert is not from the Land of Sages." Millicent's face showed an expression between shock and guilt. "He is an outsider and neither one of us had any knowledge of him being a Watcher until we were confronted by a sword."

Thoroughly ashamed, Millicent leaned forward towards Silvia to plead, "My Lady, I beg your forgiveness." She turned to Berty.

"Sir, and yours as well."

"Sometimes we forget the world in which we are betwixt." Silvia's eyes were full of kindness and understanding. "Is there anything else of which you wished to speak, Millicent?"

"Yes." Millicent looked grateful. "Leif told me about the would be assassin. I thought it might be best to send some Watchers, for they would have an advantage. The problem lies in the fact that the Guild is angry with us. The Council, I mean."

"I see," said Silvia, deep in thought. "Perhaps, I should speak to them. Assemble the Council to meet in two hours. That should give me enough time. And tell Theodore he is allowed to come in."

"Thank you, Empress." Standing, Millicent bowed before she left.

Berty watched her leave while trying to figure out what the crumpled shades of blue and purple were on her back. He stared at the door for a few moments after she walked through it.

When he turned back around, Silvia was smiling. "They are wings, folded. Millicent is a Fairy."

He knew that fatigue had set in because his head spun.

"Eat," she encouraged, "we have had a long night."

Picking up his bowl of porridge, Berty began to eat. Energy flowed through his body, reaching his tired limbs. Feeling returned to his feet.

Silvia swallowed a spoonful before saying, "Theodore should be here soon to take you to your chambers. I want you to go with him, let him show you around. After he leaves, change your clothes into whatever you find in your wardrobe. Then, wait for me in your study. Whatever you do, I implore you not to leave." Bowl in hand, Silvia stood, and so did Berty.

"We have many things to discuss," continued Silvia, "but first, I must change. Please sit and wait for him in my absence." Berty watched her walk still wearing her charcoal cloak to the back of her room, disappearing behind the carved tree relief.

As soon as Berty sat on the couch, he heard the wind chimes. "Come in," he said.

"You must be Hubert," said a rather young looking man, walking into the room. Standing barely three feet tall, Berty believed him to be a Dwarf. "I am Theodore. Your chambers are ready."

"Yes, of course," said Berty, standing.

"Is the Empress not joining us?"

"No, she wanted me to see them first."

"The Empress is truly great," declared Theodore. "Follow me."

Taking his bowl, Berty walked with him through the door. Outside of Silvia's chambers. Berty followed Theodore across a short bridge to yet another mass of leaves.

"Here we are, just as the Empress wanted," Theodore said. "Place your hand there." Theodore pointed to a small twig nestled in the mass of twigs and leaves at Berty's right.

Instinctively, Berty placed his hand on the twig, wrapped his fingers around the smooth wood and pushed it down. A few branches disappeared into the surrounding mass to reveal an arched entryway.

Upon entering the circular room, he was pleased to see that it did not differ much from Silvia's. He had a wooden desk with a mostly empty bookcase behind it, a sitting area with some chairs and a spiral staircase in the center of the room.

"Upstairs are your sleeping quarters," Theodore stated. "If there is nothing else, I'll leave you to it."

"Nothing. Thank you, Theodore."

The Dwarf smiled at Berty, then said, "Welcome to the Empire Tree, sir."

Alone for the first time since he knocked on Silvia's door, Berty tried to digest all that had happened. Everything that he knew of what was real and what was fantasy had been thrown out the window. At first, he thought that what bothered him the most about the portals, magic, even the would-be assassin, Sean, and the fact that Silvia, as Empress, lives in a massive tree with Elves, Fairies and Dwarves was how comfortable he felt in the Land of

Sages and the Empire Tree. Berty figured that any normal person would have demanded to leave if not awakened from the nightmare. Then, he thought, he was chosen to come. He began to wonder if his destiny lay in the strange land straight out of fairytales.

Looking around the first floor, he decided to explore what waited for him just up the spiral stairs. He placed his hand on the smooth, light wood railing and stepped onto the first curved wooden step. When he reached the top step, he smiled as he gazed upon his big bed, his wardrobe and a door off to the side that enticed him to peek behind. Poking his head inside the doorway, he saw a nice looking bathroom. Smiling, he thought that he had the coolest tree house.

The bed beckoned him to try its softness, but he knew that if he sat on his bed, he would not be able to get up without closing his eyes for a little nap. Opening his wardrobe, he found a claret cloak, dark brown trousers, a tan shirt, and a pair of dark brown leather boots. Not knowing if he needed everything, he spread it all on the bed. After he quickly showered and dressed, he ran downstairs to explore his study. As Berty walked over to the desk, a wind chime rang.

Chapter Four
Finding the Time

Hastily throwing his cloak over a chair, he said, "Come in." Silvia glowed in a pale blue cloak. "May we sit?" she asked.

"Of course," Berty said, hurrying to help Silvia remove her cloak. Seeing a cloak tree near the door, he hung both cloaks. Silvia took a seat in one of his leather club chairs dressed in a royal blue gown with gold trim.

As he sat in one of his chairs, Silvia looked around his study, asking, "Do you like it?"

"Yes, it is very nice. Thank you." Berty smiled, glancing around the room once more.

"Before we go to the Watchers' Guild, you need to know more about the Land of Sages," Silvia began. "Where would you like to start?"

"Well," said Berty thoughtfully, "how did I become a Watcher?"

"You extracted a wand from your cloak."

"Did you place it there?" Berty asked.

"No. A Watcher finds a wand of his own placing."

"How?"

"Magic," replied Silvia.

"How many other Watchers are there?" Berty asked.

"Many."

Berty thought for a moment. "Why did you call me your Watcher?"

"Because you found and extruded your wand in the attempt to defend me." Silvia continued, "This also means you should stay near me." She looked away from Berty. "I know you did not ask for this," she said in a small voice.

"I chose to come," said Berty reassuringly. "I could have

turned back at anytime. And I could have not looked for something to help defend you." Berty watched her eyes well and her eyelids blink back any attempt of cascading tears. Reaching over, he placed his hands on hers. Her misty, brown eyes found his. "Don't worry, I will stay near you."

When Silvia smiled at him, Berty saw infinite gratitude in her eyes. "Thank you," she said.

Feeling way too much softness in his palms, he removed his hands. Her enticing eyes were a rich shade of brown. He tore his gaze before any awkwardness developed, then he quickly changed the subject. "What Leif said about the Pixies... was he talking about Millicent?"

With a wrinkled brow, Silvia said, "Millicent is a Fairy."

"Fairies and Pixies are different?" asked Berty.

"Very much so. Fairies integrate with everyone more," Silvia explained. "They have excellent memories and are usually storytellers and historians. You have undoubtedly heard the term 'Fairytale.'" Berty nodded. "Pixies, on the other hand, tend to keep to themselves more. They often speak in riddles and sometimes not in a language anyone can even understand."

"Since Fairies are not the tiny troublemakers of lore, then Pixies get mistaken for Fairies?" Berty deduced.

"No. What you are thinking about are actually called Knownots. People often mistake Knownots for Fairies and Pixies, because they can change shape and often portray tiny versions of Fairies or Pixies. But Knownots are the mischief-makers. They are the ones who hide your keys or take just one sock. Knownots are banned from the Sages' Grove unless in special circumstances."

"How do people not know about the Knownots? How do people not know about all this?"

Silvia sighed. "Because people are taught that certain things are real and certain things are fantastical. I find that in-between what is perceived as reality and what is perceived as fantasy, lies the truth."

Berty took a minute to internalize her words before

continuing with another question. "Then, what did Leif mean when he mentioned the Pixies?"

Silvia took a deep breath. "During a new moon, the Pixie High Priestess will sometimes venture into the world and make a prophecy," she explained. "If she speaks to you, you had better listen."

"So, she made a prophecy about you having a Watcher?"

"Her exact words were:

> Empress watches over all
> High in the Empire Tree
> Finding the time 'fore will fall
> Watcher watches over thee

"Most have interpreted her song as when I get a Watcher, the Empire will collapse."

"That explains my ill reception," said Berty. "Who are the four who will fall?"

"What four?"

"'Finding the time, four will fall,'" recited Berty.

He saw Silvia's mind working. "That makes sense. It was always interpreted to mean 'before.' It will have to be brought to the attention of the Advisory Council."

Silvia paused for a moment. "Now, we must go to the Watchers' Guild. We must convince them that they need to discover more about that man, Sean, and his agenda."

Berty helped Silvia with her cloak. He swung his cloak over his shoulders. For the second time he had worn a cloak, Berty made sure that he could fasten the tree shaped clasp himself.

Donning their cloaks, they crossed another rope and plank bridge that brought them to a relatively tiny opening in the enormously wide trunk of the Empire Tree. Looking up, Berty could not see the top. When he looked down, he did not see the bottom. Inside the tree, a dark passageway led to the right. To the left, a staircase was hewn into the trunk of the tree.

"That passageway leads to the Watching Rooms and the Star Gazing Area," Silvia explained. "This staircase and that passageway are for our use only. It brings us to every room in the trunk except one." As they descended, Silvia told Berty what had lain on each level. "The next level is the room that holds the scepter. Then, there is the Roundtable Room."

"Like King Arthur and his Knights of the Roundtable?" asked Berty.

"You do not think Arthur came up with that Roundtable idea on his own?"

Berty laughed.

"The Mage, who you know as Merlin, sat at our Roundtable long before Arthur ever became a king." They walked down a few more steps. "Next, we have the Reception Room where the stairs end. On the ground level is the Receiving Room."

Berty followed Silvia out of the private staircase onto a dais. Emerging from a small area behind a long, heavy, purple drape that framed an extremely ornately carved throne, the Reception Room opened up before him. Berty's gaze wandered off the dais into a large round room. Multiple gold toned chandeliers with too many candles to count hung from the high, smooth, wood ceiling. They walked between the back wall and the throne when Berty stopped.

A large tree was expertly carved into the wooden wall. Its many branches held individually carved leaves. Berty noticed how the grain of the wall made the tree look as if it were moving. The tree's roots were carved in such a fashion that they could have been growing into the floor.

Carved into the tree were seven circles that started from the top and continued in a line down to the roots. Each circle had a different design that Berty did not recognize.

Two steps down from the dais, Silvia turned. "That is the Sages' Seal," she said.

"This is carved into the wall of your study."

"Yes," said Silvia. "It is the Empire Tree and each circle represents one of the Seven High Sages."

"It almost looks like someone superimposed a chakra chart

onto the Tree of Life," Berty said.

Silvia did not reply. She simply moved towards the top of another flight of stairs. Berty hastened to her side. Together, they descended to a lower level.

Before emerging from the dark staircase, Silvia raised her hood. They walked behind a large, square desk where at different stations, attendants took care of people who were coming to request appointments to see one of the Advisors, to file registrations or conduct other sorts of Empire business. As they approached the sun flooded opening where the double wooden doors stood wide open, Berty raised his hood as well.

Outside, he expected to see more tree houses or wooden houses on stilts, but instead, all the buildings surrounding the tree were made of cob and painted white with thatched roofs. While following Silvia around the tree on the dirt paths, Berty watched merchants at their wooden stalls. While some had wheels, all had canvas awnings. They sold their wares to all sorts of people.

The Sages' Grove had a quaint village feel, although the variety of goods and people reminded him more of a metropolitan city. He turned to Silvia so that he could inquire more about it when Silvia knocked on a plain, wooden door. Berty noticed a small, wooden sign on the right side of the doorframe. The primitive, round sign had an open eye in the center of what looked like a six-pointed star.

They waited no more than a few moments before a bald boy, no older than fourteen dressed in what looked like a red monk's robe tied around the middle with a simple rope, opened the door.

"May I help you?" asked the boy.

"We wish to see your Guild Master," Silvia said.

The boy looked hard at Silvia, then at Berty before allowing them to enter. He led them through a dark, narrow hallway to a main room full of hard, wooden chairs. The walls were made from dark planks of wood that reminded Berty of the paneling in his parent's basement. Painted in gold on one wall, Berty saw an enlarged version of the same Watcher's symbol that he found on the sign.

"Please wait here," said the boy. "Who may I tell the Guild Master is calling?"

"We are who we are," said Silvia. Nodding, the boy left, using an entrance that Berty did not notice at first.

"Empress, what an honor it is to have you in our Guild," said an elderly man. His long, white beard grew well past his waist. Walking into the room, he bowed.

"Thank you for that kind welcome, Guild Master," Silvia said, shaking his hands.

"How may the Watchers' Guild be of service to the Empress?" asked the Guild Master.

"We need information," Silvia vaguely answered.

"Perhaps if the Empress would be more specific," said the Guild Master, bowing his head. Berty watched the lights from the lanterns dance on his bald head.

Silvia looked away from the Guild Master's direction and began to walk towards the symbol on the wall. Stopping a few feet from the wall, she said, "I know that the Guild has not been on the best terms with my Advisory Council. I would like to remind the Guild Master that everyone is capable of mistakes in this world and that no one is infallible."

The Guild Master closed his eyes, taking a deep breath. When he opened his eyes, he walked next to Silvia.

"What type of information do you require?" the Guild Master inquired, keeping his eyes on the wall.

"The type that is discovered," answered Silvia. She turned to look at Berty. "Guild Master, I do not believe you have met my Watcher."

The Guild Master turned to look at Berty as well. "He is not of the Guild."

"I know." Silvia turned towards the Guild Master. "There is a man who desires me dead."

"You have guards, Empress."

"We need to know more about him and his reasoning."

31

"Who are we to seek a killer's heart?"

"You mean what business is it of the Guild's?" Silvia asked shrewdly as she held her gaze.

The guilt and reluctance on the Guild Master's face disgusted Berty.

"Well," said the Guild Master, looking away and swallowing hard, "what gain—?"

"You make me sick," interjected Berty. "What is to be gained is the ability to keep the life you are used to living."

"The Watchers' Guild is not a toy of the Empire Tree," shouted the Guild Master, taking a few steps towards Berty.

"Yet you live beneath its branches," said Berty, "and the treed wall perpetuates your very existence."

The Guild Master hung his head.

"The Advisory Council does not embody the Empress," Berty continued, "nor does the Empress embody the Advisory Council."

The three of them stood in silence for a few moments. Both Silvia and Berty kept their eyes on the Guild Master as he fidgeted with his beard, looking everywhere except at them. Finally, the Guild Master looked at Silvia, saying, "Empress, I am truly sorry. I let my anger cloud my better judgement. You would not have come to see me if it were not of great importance. Of course, the Guild will help. What is already known about this man?"

Silvia recounted every detail of their encounter with Sean including his exchange with the thieves.

"Empress," said the Guild Master, "before you go, there is something that I want to give you." He left the room for a moment. When he returned, he carried a small, dark wooden box in his hands. The old man flipped open the box on its hinge to reveal a large, golden locket with an opened eye inside of a six pointed star imbedded on the front, resting on a bed of red satin. Picking the locket up by its golden chain, he said, "I would like you to use this for direct communication with the Watchers' Guild. All you need to do is open it and use the clasp's rod to write a message and it will show on mine." He gently lowered the locket into

Silvia's hand.

She turned it over in her hand, saying, "Thank you, Guild Master, for everything." He smiled at them both while Silvia placed the locket into a pocket on the inside of her cloak.

The boy showed them out of the Watchers' Guild. They retraced their steps up the dirt path into the Empire Tree. Walking unnoticed up the stairs from the Receiving Room, they returned to their private staircase hidden behind the Sages' Seal.

Up a flight of steps, they stopped on a side platform in front of a door that allowed private entry into the Roundtable Room. Before walking through that door for a meeting with the Advisory Council, Silvia smiled at Berty. "Thank you for your help in the Watchers' Guild. The Advisory Council should not need such intense persuasion."

Entering the room behind Silvia, Berty discovered that the Advisory Council members were already sitting around the large Roundtable. Their conversation abruptly ended. The shine of the table's finish perfectly reflected every detail of Leif's wild mane, Millicent's soft curls, the Troll's pointed light brown beard, the Dwarf's thick, vivid red, Yosemite Sam-esque facial hair, and the Elf's distinguished graying temples of his otherwise dark hair. Every member stood as Silvia approached her carved, throne like chair.

"As you all are aware," Silvia addressed them in a business like manner, "this is Hubert, my Watcher." She raised an arm in Berty's direction. "Now, we have important matters to discuss." She swept her cloak over her shoulders like a cape, then sat. Everyone promptly took seats, waiting with bated breath for her to speak again.

Silvia turned to Berty, who sat in the empty chair on her left, saying, "A brief introduction, starting at my right. Leif is the resident Scholar. Millicent is the Historian. Hatcher is the Sages' Grove Head Gatekeeper. Colvin is the Head of Construction and Alvar is the Captain of the Empire Guard." Each one nodded their heads in turn to Berty as she called out their names.

"Hubert and I visited the Watchers' Guild. They have consented to find more information. They will report directly to me. Alvar, your report please."

"There was no sign of you being followed, my Lady," said the stoic Elf. Alvar towered over Berty even when sitting. "We also think it is prudent to increase the guards at the wall and at the entrances of not only the Sages' Grove, but the Empire Tree as well."

Silvia nodded. "Colvin."

"All mining tunnels to the Empire Tree should be sealed, my Lady." The Dwarf was resolute.

"Hatcher."

"The gates to the Sages' Grove shall open from one hour after dawn and close one hour before dusk, my Lady," said the Troll.

"Millicent."

"If history tells us anything it is that one thing is clear, there will always be an Empress, my Lady," said the young Fairy. "The scepter makes sure of that."

"Leif."

"We need to institute a curfew within the Empire Tree," the old man stated, "and no one will be allowed beyond the Receiving Room."

Silvia's eyes examined each chair's occupant. The table pulsed with a nervous energy. Her gaze landed on Berty.

"Hubert," she said, "your thoughts."

"Until we have more information," said Berty, "there is little we can do except be prisoners in this tree. We are making ourselves sitting ducks while someone may be planning to lay siege to the Sages' Grove. Everyone suffers."

"I agree." Silvia paused to look at the council before continuing. "We are unaware of what this man is capable of doing. Alvar, increase wall security immediately. Colvin, can we keep a few tunnels open in case of evacuation, heavily guarded?"

"Yes, my Lady," answered Colvin.

"Hatcher," Silvia continued, "the gates will stay open from full daybreak to sunset. An hour after the gates open, the Empire Tree will open, and an hour before the gates close, the tree will close. Leif, more security in the Receiving Room as well. In addition, I want an evacuation plan for the Sages' Grove's inhabitants, including those of us in the Empire Tree. Any questions?"

The table murmured a collective, "No."

"Very good," said Silvia, standing. The council hastily stood also. She looked at Berty with meaning before she walked crisply towards the door. He quickly walked after her.

Stopping at the entrance of the private stairs, Silvia addressed the table once more, "We wish to not be disturbed for the remainder of the day." The Advisory Council did not have time to acknowledge her command before she and Berty disappeared over the threshold. Climbing the staircase, they crossed the bridge.

Outside of Berty's chambers, Silvia said, "Change back into your other clothes and meet me in my study."

Nodding, Berty watched her walk across the short bridge to her chambers before entering his own.

Chapter Five
A Tapestry and a Feather

He did not realize how tired he was until he climbed his spiral staircase, gazing longingly at his bed. Per Silvia's request, Berty carefully hung his new shirt and pants on the bar and set his boots on the floor of the wardrobe. He picked up his other clothes off the bed, resisting the urge to lie down. His fingers fumbled, trying to push the buttons through the buttonholes on his shirt. It took him a few tries to align the buttons and holes correctly. Finally, he tucked his shirttails into his khakis and tied the laces of his shoes. Berty securely placed his wand into the pocket of his pants before he trudged out of his chambers and across the short bridge to ring Silvia's wind chimes.

"Come in." Her voice sounded as tired as he felt. Upon entering her study, Berty found Silvia standing towards the back of her room wearing her jeans and red blouse.

"Do you have your wand?" she asked.

"Yes."

"Good. Follow me."

Berty followed Silvia behind the Sages' Seal and up a flight of curved stairs. At the top, he found a nicely appointed room with a large bed, a wardrobe, a door, and a colorful tapestry depicting a stag in a woodland scene.

"Nice room." He could not think of anything else to say because he had no idea why he was there.

"Ready?" asked Silvia.

"For?"

"A journey back," replied Silvia.

"Oh," said Berty, feeling a little hurt, "I thought I had to stay near you."

Silvia smiled, "You will see." Holding out her delicate hand,

Berty relished in her soft touch. Winking at him, she led him through the tapestry into a dim Victorian bedroom.

"Where are we?" Berty asked.

"Back inside my house," Silvia answered. "This is my bedroom."

Turning around, Berty expected to see the tapestry. "Did we just come through your fireplace?"

"It really is the best spot to hide a portal," she said. "Shall we retrieve your bag?"

Nodding, Berty followed Silvia into the dark hall. He barely took two steps when he heard a soft whoosh and the dark wood paneled staircase was illuminated. Descending the stairs, he noticed the flickering brass chandelier in the foyer.

"You have gas lights," remarked Berty as he landed on one of the wool rugs of the foyer.

Extracting his bag from behind the panel, Silvia said, "The house was last updated in the mid to late 1800s."

"Thank you," he said as he took his bag from Silvia. He extracted his cell phone. After clearing the messages stating that he had missed five calls and six unread text messages, he focused on the date and time.

"How is it," Berty asked, "we have only been gone for twelve hours?"

"Time is funny that way," shrugged Silvia. "Go get some rest. Be back here seven in the morning tomorrow. You can use the driveway, too."

"Okay, I shall," said Berty, smiling.

Berty found his way home from Silvia's house in no time. Entering his small apartment, he placed his bag on the floor by the door and his keys and cell phone on the coffee table. He threw something frozen in the oven for dinner before collapsing on his couch.

His mind rewound the day he spent with Silvia. What a day, he thought. "How am I going to write an article about this?" Berty wondered aloud. His thoughts wandered to Silvia—her dark red hair, the sparkle in her brown eyes, the softness of her hand in his. He lay on his couch with a smile on his face until a strange, buzzing sound brought him back to his apartment. Automatically, his hand reached for the table, picking up his glowing, dancing cell phone.

"Hello?" Berty answered the phone without glancing at the caller id.

"Where have you been?" accused a woman's voice. "I've been trying to reach you all day."

"Jenny?" He had no intentions of telling her exactly where he had been. "I just got home."

"Nice of you to return your phone calls," Jenny snapped. "Anyway, I made reservations at that little restaurant on the river. You know the one that we always talk about going to. We will be going out at seven-thirty tomorrow evening."

"What restaurant? Why?"

"Oh, you tired, little puppy," said Jenny in a cutesy, baby voice that made Berty cringe. "You know the place. It's to celebrate our one month anniversary."

"Celebrate our what?" Berty could not believe his ears.

"We've been together a whole month tomorrow. We should celebrate."

Dumbfounded, Berty asked Jenny, "Who celebrates after dating for a month?"

"We do." Jenny's voice sounded hurt.

"No, we don't, because that's asinine. And you can't call it an anniversary because that technically means year-marker. Besides, a couple only celebrates them when they are married."

"Just because you had a long day doesn't mean you have to get nasty to me."

"You assume a lot." Berty tried to keep his voice calm.

"I had to," said Jenny. "You weren't answering your phone."

"Of course, I didn't answer my phone. I was working." Blood pulsed through his veins in his temples so hard it made his head pound.

"Oh, so work is more important than me. I see how it is."

"Than I," Berty corrected her grammar while trying to keep his voice level. "And yes, it is."

"I thought we had something special." Jenny sounded as though she were holding back tears.

Berty's head spun. He remembered their last date. They went out to dinner at a cozy little hole in the wall place before wandering into a jazz bar. Jenny was jovial, vibrant and vivacious. He wondered when she turned psycho, but he was glad that she was showing her true self sooner rather than later.

"Wow," said Berty. "You know what? You and I should not celebrate anything except our separation."

"How can you say that?" She punctuated each word with sharp intakes of breath.

"I cannot be with someone who butchers the English language like you do." Berty could hear her sobs through the receiver. "Plus," he continued, ignoring the crying, "I need someone with more."

"More what?" Jenny sobbed.

"More everything—integrity, understanding, compassion, passion." Berty stopped rattling off words that popped into his mind. "I am sorry, Jenny, but you deserve someone... more like you."

The phone beeped, telling him that Jenny had hung up on him, but he did not care. Snapping the phone shut, he threw it back on the coffee table. He checked the oven just to get off the couch.

With still a lot more time on the oven timer, Berty wandered to his laminate covered pressed board and plastic desk, then sat, staring at his black computer screen. His mind drifted back a few days to when he was standing in Martin Hunter's corner office.

"Here is the address," Martin said as he walked out from behind his desk, handing Berty a small slip of paper. "I want you to conduct a thorough interview and let her take you to see everything." He leaned against his desk. "Send me something whenever you get the chance, but hopefully before our Halloween printing." Martin chuckled. "I want to see something fresh and exciting. Don't look so scared," he said as he clapped Berty on the shoulder. "It will be a magical experience."

Martin was right about that, Berty thought, as his screen came back into focus. Technology intruded into his life. Opening a drawer, he extracted an old spiral notebook, then placed it on the desk. His hands robotically turned the pages as his eyes merely glanced at his handwriting. Poems and unfinished short stories passed with a crinkle.

Finally, the pages stopped turning. Berty grabbed a pen from an old, chipped coffee mug that he had been using as a pen and pencil holder since his college roommate knocked it off a shelf on the top of his desk freshman year. With a pen in his hand, he hesitated above the blank page for only a second before writing, *the Adventures of Leigh and Marcus*. Through his pen, Berty retold his day with Silvia as fate-met wandering adventurers in a far away land in another time.

He placed his pen down as his oven timer beeped. After pushing the button depicting the circle with the line on his computer tower, he walked two steps into the kitchen, fixing himself a plate of food. Returning to his desk, food in hand, he began to type his newly penned story. In an email to his editor, Berty wrote that Mister Hunter could break up the story any way he saw fit and that he should expect another installment sometime in the near future. After clicking send, Berty wondered if his somewhat fictitious account of his day qualified as "fresh and exciting."

To ease his mind, Berty tidied his apartment before he crawled into bed, wondering what tomorrow would bring.

In the morning, Berty filled his bag with his old notebook, a pen, some snacks, and a plastic zip bag encasing his cell phone. He drove back to Silvia's house, pulling into her driveway ten minutes earlier than she had told him to be there. She must have anticipated that he would be early because she was waiting on her front porch for him, smiling while holding a large mug. Mug in hand, Silvia gestured to Berty to drive behind the house.

He parked in front of the old, two-story garage. Opening the car door, the crisp morning air hurried to sting his face, but Silvia's smile chased away the chill. She greeted him at the back door, pressing a generous mug of coffee into his hands as he entered her old-fashioned kitchen.

White subway tile lined the walls while old, painted wooden cabinets covered the rest. In the center of the room, a small, French press coffeemaker stood alone on a plank table. Taking a sip, his eyes registered an antique stove and large farmhouse sink. Her kitchen was pleasantly devoid of small appliances like a microwave, toaster or blender. However, he noticed that there was one big item missing.

"Do you not have a refrigerator?" Berty asked.

"No. Those run on electricity," Silvia said. "And there is no electric in this house."

"Why don't you have electricity?" asked Berty.

"It tends to interfere with magic," replied Silvia, "so you live without it. Besides, that is one less bill that needs to be paid."

"You have to worry about money?"

"I would not say worry. All I pay are taxes, gas and water," Silvia explained. "Though I need to make money to pay those in a way that does not interfere with being Empress."

"How do you do that?" Berty inquired.

"A combination of part-time selling and investing," answered Silvia.

"What do you sell?" His interest was piqued.

"A little of this and a little of that. Shall we go?"

"Sure." Berty knew she was ignoring the subject of money, but he did not care because he was anxious to return to the Land of Sages. "What shall I do with my mug?"

"I will take care of it." With a swipe of her hand, the mugs and coffeemaker disappeared.

Berty removed the plastic bag holding his cell phone from his shoulder bag, placed his car keys in it, then handed it to Silvia.

Smiling, she put the plastic bag in another hidden cupboard, masquerading as a panel, in the hall just outside the kitchen door.

Opening a nearby paneled door with a crystal doorknob, Silvia motioned for Berty to enter. Berty ascended a dark, narrow back staircase. When he reached a landing with a door, Silvia told him to open it.

Berty opened the door, following Silvia into the much wider upstairs hallway. Walking into her bedroom, Berty glanced at the large, cherry, four poster bed before standing next to her in-between the two wing chairs that flanked the fireplace. He was able to see the fireplace more clearly than the previous evening.

A dark wooden mantle surrounded the stone fireplace. Above the mantle, the same dark wood framed a large mirror that reflected the vases and figurines that rested in front of it. Wooden columns majestically flanked the stone and brick firebox. On the back wall of the fireplace, he saw an intricate, stone carving of the same stag in a woodland scene that was depicted on her tapestry.

She held out her hand. He took her soft hand in his. Together, they stepped through the fireplace, returning to Silvia's chambers in the Empire Tree.

"Why didn't we go this way the first time, Silvia?"

She smiled. "Would you have come?"

"You have a point," he conceded. "What do we do now?"

"Dinner in your study," Silvia said. "Please change into the clothes in your wardrobe. I will be there shortly."

Leaving Silvia's chambers, Berty crossed the bridge with a smile on his face. He was glad to be back. Walking up the stairs to his bedroom, Berty did not know what challenges laid ahead. All he knew was that being in the Land of Sages made him feel more alive than anywhere he had ever been. Something inside of him awakened.

In his wardrobe, he found a set of clothes into which he changed. Downstairs, he hung his cloak on the hook in his study when the wind chimes rang.

Silvia stood in the doorway, wearing a blue gown with her

cloak draped over her arm. While he hung her cloak, she walked to an empty area in the back of his study. Berty walked over to join her and discovered a small, plain, wooden dining table and two plain, ladder back chairs that were not there prior.

"Looks suitable for a meal," she said when the wind chimes rang for a second time since his return.

"Come in," said Berty.

Theodore walked into the room, carrying a rather large tray. "Good evening, my Lady and sir. I hope you rested well."

"Yes, very well, Theodore. Thank you," Silvia said.

"Very good, my Lady," said Theodore as he placed the tray on the dining table. After Theodore set the table, he asked, "Will you be needing anything else?"

"We will be working late this evening," Silvia said. "Would you be able to bring each of us a small basket of food later?"

"Of course, my Lady," Theodore said.

"Thank you, just place them outside the doors. We will find them."

Bowing, Theodore left.

"What are we doing after we eat?" Berty asked Silvia.

"You will see," Silvia replied with a sly smile.

Berty helped Silvia into a chair. He sat in the chair across from her.

"Berty, tell me, do you have any siblings?"

He liked it when she said his nickname. "I have a younger brother."

"And your parents are doing what?"

"Now that my parents have retired, they have been spending a lot of time with my brother, his wife and their daughter. My parents love spending time with and money on my niece," Berty said. "What about your family?"

"We can talk about mine later," said Silvia, cutting her pork chop. "Has anyone in your family ever been considered odd?"

Berty placed a piece of roasted potato in his mouth and thought while he chewed. Swallowing he said, "I want to say yes because I know that my grandfather told us some strange stories when I was a child, but you would have to ask my dad about it."

Silvia nodded, then took a sip from her goblet.

When they finished their meal, Silvia said, "I have a place that I want to take you."

A rush of excitement filled Berty's body. Donning their cloaks, they placed the tray outside of Berty's door. After traipsing across the bridge to the trunk, Berty expected them to go down their stairs. Instead, Silvia began to walk along the path to the right.

"Where are we going?" whispered Berty, following her closely.

Silvia answered by grabbing Berty's arm and pulling him through what he thought was a solid wall. Berty thought they were inside the wall itself for the darkness was compressing. Then he heard Silvia inhale sharply through her nose and forcefully blow out her mouth. At least twenty candles sparked to life on shelves and hanging lanterns. The lighted candles revealed a circular room without doors or windows. Inside the room were plain wooden chairs, a small table, at least a half a dozen trunks of different sizes, and a plethora of shelves with books, scrolls and boxes.

"This is the Sorcery Room. We are standing in the very core of the Empire Tree. No one else knows about this room and no one else can enter," explained Silvia as she dropped his arm. "My mother brought me here so that I could learn to hone my gifts when I was growing up." As she held out her open hand in front of her, Berty watched as one of the flames floated away from its wick to sit in Silvia's palm. She spread her fingers. With a pulse of her hand, one flame sitting in the center of her palm became five flames at her fingertips. Gently, she blew on her hand. Five flames converged into one as the flame returned to its candle.

"It is time you learned how to use your wand, Berty."

Extracting his wand from his pocket, Berty held it out before him. "What do I do?"

"I can honestly say that I have never used a wand before, but I am going to guess that the concept is the same," said Silvia, contemplating the wand. "Though I think we should start with something less dangerous than fire."

Taking a small rectangular wooden box off of a nearby shelf, she placed it on the table, flipping the top open. Showing Berty the contents, she said, "Feathers are what I used to start."

"Okay," said Berty, nervously examining the long, quill-like feathers sitting in the box. "What do I do?"

"Look at the feather," Silvia said. "Concentrate on the feather and what you want it to do." As she explained, a brown feather with white spots rose out of the box, hovering in mid air. "Your turn." The feather dropped to the table.

Berty looked at the feather on the table. He wanted that feather to stand on its quill. After a few minutes of staring, he thought it would have been better if he wanted to bore a hole in it. Trying a different approach, he pointed his wand directly at the feather. It exploded, making him jump while leaving a lingering singed smell.

Silvia laughed. "You got frustrated after a while, did you not?"

"I did. How did you know?"

"Let me show you the scorch marks from my first feather." Berty looked where Silvia pointed on the tabletop. Seeing a black explosion mark, he laughed, too.

Laughing made Berty feel much more relaxed. For his second attempt, he pointed his wand at a new feather, coaxing the feather upwards while slowly moving his wand upwards as well.

As the feather stood on its end, Silvia said, "Good, now lift it off the table."

Berty raised his arm slightly and the feather hovered over the table about six inches.

"Bring it towards you," Silvia instructed.

The first thing that entered Berty's mind was to have the wand suck the feather towards it like a vacuum hose would. The silvery blue feather moved very rapidly across the room, striking him in the center of his forehead.

Lowering his wand, he peeled the feather off his head. "Good thing those are light," said Berty.

"Interesting," remarked Silvia while watching Berty rub his head.

"What is?"

"You did not use the wand," Silvia explained. "Watchers are lost without their wands. He or she can only perform magic by channeling any surrounding magic through the wand."

"Does that mean that I am not a Watcher," asked Berty, confused.

Silvia ran a slim finger across her lips before allowing it to rest on her chin. "Though you may not be *a* Watcher, you remain *my* Watcher." Berty thought she was looking at him through new eyes. "It seems that my Watcher is a True Sorcerer."

"What is a True Sorcerer?"

"A man who performs True Sorcery," Silvia winked at him, smiling. "All magic stems from the mind. It can be channeled through your hands or a wand. Some can only use magic channeled in either one of those ways. Others need the help of spoken incantations. Then, there are those who only need to think it and it happens."

Suddenly, the room was gone. In its place was a heavily wooded forest, full of thick trees and ample underbrush.

"Where are we?" asked Berty, looking around.

"I used to play here as a child," Silvia said as she slowly walked a few steps. "We did not go anywhere, I simply transformed our surroundings to reflect the woods I remember."

When the forest disappeared, Berty was once again standing in the candlelit room.

"True Sorcery," Silvia continued saying as she turned to face Berty, "is heavily guarded. Not many can do it. In fact, it is so rare that many people believe that True Sorcery is a myth. You and I must never mention it to anyone. Everyone assumes you are magical because of your wand and Watcher status. I would advise you to let everyone continue that assumption."

"Why? Is magic feared?" asked Berty.

"I believe it can be. There are those who fear it and there are those who revere it," said Silvia. "Remember young Michael by the fire, he was enamored with magic. I was taught to keep it secret, to keep it hidden, because even though some people use it, those in positions of power, who have magic, are thought to be able to do anything. The people would start making demands for magic to be used everywhere and for everything." Silvia gazed into the candlelight. "The more I think about it, the more I am beginning to realize that being taught to hide magic kept Empresses not only safe, but also in check, so that we did not abuse our power. I guess being taught true responsibility would not have worked because people, as a whole, do not understand magic.

"However, history tells us that the Empress only has magical powers within the Sages' Grove itself because that is the limit of the scepter. Magic is bestowed upon the Empress by the scepter, but any magic is limited and cannot be used outside the wall."

"So," said Berty, "no one knows, not even the Advisory Council?"

Silvia shook her head. "There are certain things that the Advisory Council does not fully understand."

"Such as?"

"Why there is an Empress," explained Silvia. "The Council thinks that the Empress is simply to keep order in the Empire. The Empress' real role is to guard the secrets of the Sages and of the Empire."

"Why does the Advisory Council not know this? Especially someone like Millicent," asked Berty.

"If they were meant to know everything, then they would be able to enter this room," Silvia said.

"You mean all these books and scrolls," Berty said as he looked around the room, "hold the secrets?"

"Yes."

"Have you read everything?"

"I have," Silvia said, "for knowledge is the key to true understanding."

Chapter Six
Leif

Berty looked at the wand in his hand, then placed it on the table. Taking a deep breath, he stepped away from the table to concentrate on the feathers in the box. After only a minute of concentration, twenty-eight feathers marched in a line out of their box, circled around Berty, then stacked themselves onto the table.

"Very good," said Silvia, laughing jovially. "Now, that is progress." She collected the feathers placing them back into their box. After she returned the box to its shelf, Silvia handed Berty his wand.

"There is one other place that I want to take you tonight," she said, extending her hand towards him. Stowing his wand in his pocket, Berty grabbed Silvia's outstretched hand. In one fluid motion, the candles were extinguished and they stepped into the hallway.

Smiling, Silvia tugged on Berty's hand as she led him further down the dark hallway to a plain, closed door. "On the other side of this door is where our private access ends. It connects to the passages used by the other inhabitants of the Empire Tree," she explained.

Before Berty could place his hand on the doorknob, they stepped through the door. His eyes had a hard time adjusting to the brighter hallway. As he blinked, he could see the smooth, wood grained walls that lined the wide hall. Turning around, he noticed that the other side of the door was simply a wall, completely seamless, blending with the rest of the hall. Wrought iron sconces lighted the public passageways well. Letting go of Berty's hand, Silvia moved towards an intersecting dark corridor.

A lone torch like sconce illuminated the first few steps ascending to yet another level of the tree. With each step they climbed, the light faded as the cool night air whipped their faces.

Berty raised his hood to shield against the chill.

Reaching the top, they stepped onto an open platform above the forest canopy where the night sky opened up before them. The top leaves of the surrounding trees rustled in sequence as the cool, early autumn breeze caressed each tree. Listening further, Berty could hear crickets in the background trying to extend their season. Night hunting birds and bats swooped between branches. Over it all, the stars performed a mesmerizing sparkly show.

"Now, this place is magical," Silvia whispered, smiling at Berty. Her eyes reflected the stars' sparkle. Berty watched her glowing blue cloak trail in front of him as she walked towards the railing.

Joining her, Berty whispered, "Can you hear that?"

"Hear what?"

"The night music."

She listened to the sounds of the forest. "Yes," she giggled.

Berty held out his hand, "May I have this dance?"

Taking it, she smiled while softly nodding. He thought he had even caught her blush a little. Berty placed his other hand in the small of her back. Silvia rested her free hand on his arm near his shoulder. Guiding her back on the first step, he pulled her close, then twirled her around the platform. With each rotation, the space between them lessened. The scent of berry pie found his nose when his cheek grazed her hair.

Berty lost track of his box step, so he pulled her closer and smiled. Silvia smiling back prompted Berty to lower his head, getting closer. Breathing in the intoxicating scent of berries, he could no longer move. He slowly slid his hand to the middle of her back. Her dress felt like silk. He moved his head in closer, dropping her hand. His newly free hand grazed her warm cheek, finally resting in her soft hair. Their noses were less than an inch apart when part of her cloak began to vibrate.

Startled, Silvia stepped out of Berty's embrace. The chill of the crisp night air stung his senses. She extracted the large, golden locket that the Watchers' Guild Master gave her from her cloak. He watched the eye on the locket glow in her hand.

Opening it, she read in hushed tones to Berty, "Empress, we request an audience to discuss our findings. Will two hours after the sun rises please you? Respectfully, the Guild Master."

As per the Guild Master's instructions, Silvia took the rod part of the chain's clasp and wrote while telling Berty her reply, "That will be fine. I will have someone meet you in the Receiving Room. —The Empress." Closing the locket, she placed it back inside her cloak.

Realizing that the moment was lost, Berty said, "We should go."

Silvia merely nodded, turned away from him quickly, then led him back down the stairs. When she grabbed his hand, his heart fluttered as they stepped into their private hallway. Dropping his hand quickly, they walked in silence down the passage and out of the trunk.

Trying all he could to think of anything but the Star Gazing Area, halfway across the bridge Berty finally asked, "What exactly is a Watcher?"

Stopping, Silvia turned around to face him. "What do you mean?"

"Everyone seems to assume that they are just magic users with their wands. However, I do not think that they are merely channeling magic from their surroundings," Berty deduced. "They are called 'Watchers' for a reason. What do they really do? What do they watch?"

Smiling satisfactorily, Silvia said, "Watchers see what is really there, things that others cannot. For example, a Watcher is the only one who knows what a portal looks like."

"Interesting," said Berty. "For what do they use their wands?"

"One could compare a wand to a divining rod," Silvia explained, "but instead of water, it finds magical disturbances. If they use their wands for magic, then any magic performed with the wand is usually weak. Of course how weak depends upon the strength of the surrounding magic."

"Magical disturbances," repeated Berty. "They know if magic is being used. Has one ever found you?"

"It does not work quite that way." Silvia continued walking. "They can find portals and magical concealment. The magic has to be in constant use, not just for a fleeting moment."

"So," said Berty following, "their wands are like magic magnets, thus their own magic is limited."

"Exactly." Stopping in front of Berty's door, Silvia maintained eye contact. "Please try to get some rest. You should be awake at dawn. I shall collect you a half an hour before we meet with the Guild Master." Berty nodded. "Goodnight, Berty."

"Goodnight, Silvia." Silvia looked at him intensely for a moment, then turned. Berty watched her walk across her bridge. He longed to walk after her, but he knew other things had to come first. When she was no longer in sight, he picked up the basket of food, then entered his study.

Not feeling remotely hungry, he placed the basket on the table and hung his cloak. Berty removed his old writing notebook and a pen from his shoulder bag that rested next to his bookcase, setting them on his desk. For an hour and a half, he wrote another chapter of the *Adventures of Leigh and Marcus*. After closing his notebook, he climbed his spiral staircase.

The first bright gold rays of the rising sun shone through his window, directly onto the backs of his eyelids. The brightness awakened Berty. He squinted as soon as his eyes opened. Moving quickly to find a reprieve from the direct sunlight, he stumbled into his bathroom. His stomach growled while he showered. After he dressed into a new set of clothes that magically appeared in his wardrobe, he walked downstairs to peer into his basket. Inside it, he found some cheese, bread and fruit. Grabbing an apricot, he walked around his study, biting into its soft, sweet flesh.

For the first time, Berty was able to inspect the bookshelves behind his desk. Opening boxes, he found pens, ink, and paper. He found some boxes empty, waiting to be filled. His meager book collection included a copy of the *History of the Empire*, *Secrets of*

Trees and a blank book.

Removing the blank book off the shelf, he opened the cover to find an inscription:

Berty—

> *I give you these pages so that you may fill them with whatever comes to mind.*
>
> *—Silvia*

He stared at Silvia's words written with her own hand. He could not help but smile. His fingers traced the loops in every one of her words. The sound of the wind chimes made him snap the book shut, returning it to its shelf.

"Come in," said Berty.

Silvia walked in, cloaked in light blue. "Shall we?"

Nodding, Berty fastened his claret cloak. Walking through the tree, Berty felt Silvia's anxiousness. Her trepidation increased with each step closer to the Roundtable Room. Before entering the Roundtable Room, they removed their cloaks and hung them on the hooks outside of the door. Berty watched Silvia's hands shake as she secured her cloak.

"Are you okay?" Berty asked.

"I have never dreaded a meeting more," replied Silvia. She inhaled deeply. With the stature of an Empress, she entered the room.

Walking behind her, Berty noticed a large silhouette pacing on the other side of the room. Two pairs of footsteps announced their arrival. Leif turned his head sharply, then crossed the room to greet them.

"Empress, may I inquire about the nature of this meeting?" Leif asked.

"The Watchers' Guild Master will be joining us momentarily," explained Silvia. "Theodore is escorting."

A door on the other side of the room opened. Theodore entered, saying, "The Guild Master has arrived, Empress."

"He is early, good," said Silvia. "Bring him in."

"The Guild Master brought accompaniment," Theodore said.

"What shall I do with them?"

"How many in his party?"

"Just two, my Lady."

"They all may come." Theodore bowed before closing the door behind him. "Leif," Silvia said, "you are here representing the ears of the Advisory Council only." Leif scowled. Berty smirked, knowing that the Advisor was not happy knowing that he was not allowed to speak.

When the door opened, Theodore announced, "The Watchers' Guild Master and company."

The Guild Master and his men entered. Silvia walked a few steps towards them with her emerald green gown floating around her. They walked the rest of the way to greet her.

"Welcome to the Roundtable," Silvia said, extending her hand.

The Guild Master took her hand, kissing it. "Empress, it is truly an honor being allowed at your Roundtable," he said. "May I present two senior Guild members, Brian and Kevin."

"Gentlemen," Silvia said, making eye contact with all three of them, "if you would join me." Gliding to the table, she sat in her chair. Following closely, Berty sat at her left while Leif sat at her right. The Guild Master chose a chair directly across the table from her, then his men flanked him. Silvia watched the Guild Master with intense apprehension as he opened his mouth to speak.

"We have found that the man called Sean is roaming the Southern Villages. After ditching the family with whom he was traveling, he apparently has become quite vocal since that night in the woods. In addition to this Sean telling anyone who will listen about how magic has been disappearing from these lands, he has fabricated a story about how you are in league with the thieves that hide in the woods and tried to have them kill him."

Berty noticed how the news strengthened Silvia. She drew herself straighter in her chair while raising her head higher. "Have people been listening?" asked Silvia.

"Oh yes," answered the Guild Master. The faces of his men

mimicked the horror and disgust on the old man's face. "People want magic back in their lives. They remember the stories of the abundant magic of their ancestors. People seem to want to know where all the magic has gone. Sean gives people a place to direct their blame."

"Me," interjected Silvia.

"Sadly, yes," said the Guild Master. Taking a deep breath, he tried not to wince at the poisonous words that were escaping from his mouth. "Sean seems to be convinced that you in all your evil ways have, in a sense, sucked the magic out of the world and into the scepter. My men have heard him tell people that you use the magic in the scepter to expand your own powers so that you can control and connive. Somehow, he believes that by killing you and claiming the scepter for himself, not only will he become Emperor, but the stolen magic stored in the scepter will return."

"How many has he gathered?" Silvia asked.

The Guild Master lowered his head. "Over a hundred strong. Many believe that if the magic is restored, then their lives will be enriched because crops will not fail, sickness will be healed, and overwhelming prosperity will be throughout, making everyone richer than they could possibly imagine.

"One of our own has volunteered to infiltrate the cause. He will send messages to me when he can. As far as we know, their plan is to be here in a couple of weeks' time and to either lay siege to the Sages' Grove or fight their way inside the Empire Tree."

"I see. Can you trust this man?"

"Yes, my Lady."

"Is he a true Watcher?" Silvia inquired.

The Guild Master straightened in his chair. "The Guild only admits those who can see. But you are asking, how do I know if he has not joined or will not join?" Silvia nodded. "Of that I cannot be sure. However, the manner in which we communicate is incapable of transmitting lies. Therefore, I know what I receive from him is the truth."

"Very well," said Silvia. "Thank you, Guild Master." She

turned to address Leif. "Call the Heads to the Empire Tree."

"My Lady," Leif said, "I do not think that it is wise to entertain the Heads in advance of a coming war."

"Do you contradict me?"

"My Lady, I must intercede."

"Leif," said Silvia in a voice so stern Berty thought the tree would crack, "I would like to remind you that *I* am Empress and that *I* have sole authority in the Empire. Your role is simply to advise. You have said your piece and I have made my decision. Shall I send someone else?"

"No, Empress." Leif looked mortified as he rose out of his chair. Dejected, he left the table and walked out the door.

After watching Leif leave, Silvia turned her attention back to the Guild Master. "I apologize for my Advisor. Culminating war is not easy to digest. I would like for you to be the first to know that I am evacuating the Sages' Grove. My advice would be for all of you to go into hiding as soon as possible, and do not let your Watcher status be known. You will all be certainly targeted as magic users."

"Truly sage advice that will be heeded," the Guild Master said. "Thank you, Empress."

Nodding, Silvia said, "Theodore will see you out. Good luck. I hope we meet again."

The trio of Watchers stood and bowed before Theodore ushered them out of the room. As one door closed, another opened.

"The Heads have been contacted," said Leif, entering the room.

"Good," said Silvia. "Call the Council." With a bow, Leif disappeared through the door.

Berty and Silvia sat in silence for a few minutes. She glanced quickly at Berty before looking away. In those few seconds, he found determination in her richly colored eyes. Taking a deep breath, Silvia locked her gaze straight ahead as the Advisory Council quietly filled their places around the table. When the last council member was seated, Silvia broke the silence.

"I trust Leif has told you about the coming war," Silvia began. "I have already advised the Watchers to go into hiding. Anyone with magical prowess will be condemned and perhaps hunted." A shutter circled around the table. "I also am going to ask that everyone else who resides in the Sages' Grove to be evacuated. Colvin and Hatcher, I entrust those tasks to you." Both Dwarf and Troll solemnly nodded their heads.

"My Lady," said Alvar, "how will we prepare for battle?"

"My battle plan is thus," answered Silvia. "The guards will ensure the safety of the inhabitants of the Sages' Grove, including the Empire Tree, as they find safe shelter elsewhere. Because you can fight, you will be the last to leave."

"We are not staying?" asked Alvar, not believing his ears.

"None of you will be staying."

A look of comprehension, then horror flashed across Leif's face. "You intend to stay here alone? To surrender to these usurpers?"

"My intention," Silvia said calmly, "is for no one to be harmed."

"Leif," said Millicent, putting a small hand on his large forearm, "the scepter will not allow the Empress to be taken. Once this man strikes and takes the scepter, he will die in her place. There is no heir and the Empire must have an Empress."

"Yes, that is all well and good, Millie," Leif exasperated while shaking off her hand, "but have we forgotten the Pixie Prophecy— 'Finding the time, 'fore will fall?'"

"One has already fallen," stated Berty as he looked into the wild expression on Leif's face that matched his wild mane.

"About what are you speaking?" asked Leif. His tone was short.

"That line of the prophecy," Berty said calmly, "it means the number four, not the word before."

"How do you know, Watcher?" asked Leif. He said that last word with the utmost contempt. His eyes narrowed as he stared at

Berty. "You are not of these lands." Leif spoke through clenched teeth.

"It makes sense. And what does it matter from where I hail?" Berty retorted. His breathing quickened.

"I have served under three Empresses," said Leif, poking himself in his chest, his voice rising. He addressed Silvia. "Neither your mother nor your grandmother scoffed at my advice."

"She did not scoff at your advice," Berty shouted.

Leif did not hear him. "My advice means nothing now that *he* is here." Leif pointed at Berty. "You have let silly childish romantic fantasies about an outsider blind you to the reality of running this Empire. I will not have it!"

Leif pushed his chair backward with his calves as he attempted to stand, but Alvar stood much more quickly, knocking his chair over in the process. Unsheathing his sword, Alvar reached across the table effortlessly, pointing it at Leif. Leif looked down at the sharp point inches away from his chest. "Watch yourself, Leif," warned Alvar.

"Enough," said Silvia disgusted. Alvar retracted his sword. Picking up his chair, the Elf returned to his seat. As if his legs were glued to his chair, Leif did not move. "Like generations of Empresses before me, I understand all too well the struggles and achievements of this Empire and my duties as Empress. Unlike my recent predecessors, I face a looming war. Better than all of you, I know what must be done and I need not give any of you full disclosure. After everyone has left, make sure the gates are locked and the tunnels are sealed. I alone will stay in the Empire Tree. As Empress, I will let no one be harmed by ignorant thoughts or foolish hearts. You have your orders. You are henceforth dismissed."

Silently enraged, the only noise Leif made as he stormed out of the room were huffs of disgust. With her face etched with wetness and her eyes red and puffy, Millicent ran out the open door.

Berty watched both Hatcher and Colvin stand and say something about not disappointing either the Empress or the

Empire, but Berty could not focus. His mind kept switching between thoughts of what could he do to help, because he knew that he was staying no matter what Silvia said. He also knew that the Advisory Council was the second to fall. He wondered who the last two would be and when the last two would fall. Thoughts clouded his mind so much that he barely noticed Alvar pledging his allegiance to the Empire and to the Empress.

Feeling a familiar, warm, soft hand on his hand, Berty's eyes focused on the small, feminine hand. His eyes followed the arm, draped in green, up to a warm smile and kind, brown eyes that searched into his own.

Berty watched soft lips form the words, "It will be okay. You are with me." His ears caught the sound that paired with the last four words. His head replayed them as the empty room reformed around him. The smooth, light wood, circular walls returned. He felt his body resting on a hard, wooden chair. His one hand was finally releasing its grip on the edge of the smooth table. A vision of beautiful strength sat next to him. A new fire seemed to emit from her dark red hair.

"There is something I want to show you," Silvia said, standing. "Come with me."

Rising out of his chair, he walked with Silvia to their private staircase. As they ascended to the next level, Berty replayed the last Advisory Council meeting in his mind. "Why is Leif so upset with you? He has seemed bothered since my arrival."

"Leif has been upset with me for a while before I met you." She sighed. "It has been building inside of him. All of the developments of the past few days have brought it all to the forefront." Silvia stopped at the landing they always pass. "Here we are, the Scepter Room."

Berty followed Silvia through the dark doorway into a windowless and seemingly doorless round room. The only light in the room came from flameless sconces. At closer inspection, Berty realized that the sconces were crystals held onto the walls by facets of white metal like a gemstone secured in a piece of jewelry.

They threw off an almost florescent type of light. The usual, soft looking, wood grained walls looked harsh and intimidating in the strange light.

Halfway between the wall and the center of the room, seven carved wooden columns formed an inner circle. Each of the columns seemed different, but carved in the same style. The different carvings consisted of pictures arranged like family crests, characters that looked to be ancient runes and words that Berty thought could be a very old version of English or German.

In the very center of the room, Berty saw what had to be the scepter. A very large, multidimensional, glowing white crystal fused onto a cylindrical, silvery-white metal staff was inserted into a similarly carved wooden pillar a third of the height of the surrounding columns.

"The scepter," said Silvia, standing next to Berty, "is shrouded in mystery. It fills minds with misunderstanding and misconceptions. It sits at the very core of not only the Empire Tree, thus the Empire itself, but of Leif's anger and Sean's desire.

"Leif was only a teenage boy, barely out of his age of learning, when my grandmother appointed him to replace the retiring scholar. He proved to be a brilliant boy with fresh ideas and keen insight. My grandmother, first thought to be crazy in her appointment, was hailed as an excellent judge of character after Leif proved himself.

"As a small girl, my mother would find this new appointee spending hours just sitting and staring at the scepter. At first, she thought nothing of it because the scepter is a fascinating object. After a few years, Leif still spent a good amount of time in the Scepter Room. My mother became concerned with what she called an obsession of Leif's. Whether or not she brought it to the attention of my grandmother, I do not know.

"When my grandmother passed the scepter to my mother, she confronted Leif privately about his obsession with the scepter. He assured her that his interest was purely scholastic. Not entirely convinced, she told him stories about how the scepter can make men go mad, and that how she was concerned about him catching the madness. Touched, Leif thanked my mother for her concern. To her knowledge, he did not return to the Scepter Room.

"In fact, Leif fully immersed himself in all other scholarly matters. One could say that his scepter obsession morphed into an obsession of being indispensable. When I was a little girl, our Astronomer retired. Talented astronomers were scarce, so my mother chose not to replace him because Leif had learned astronomy well. Leif now had duel roles. A few years before my mother passed the scepter to me, my mother granted the Historian's wish to return to his people. Leif applied for the role of Historian as well. At the insistence of the King and Queen of the Fairies, she gave Leif the Historian's job. The Fairies did not have a properly trained Historian and needed a little while longer.

"When I became Empress, only four advisors were left. For the first few years, everything ran smoothly. Then the Pixie Priestess arrived. She sang for not only me, but for the Advisory Council as well, as we all gathered to hear her song in the Reception Room. Immediately after hearing the news, the Fairies sent me Millicent. Leif vehemently protested her appointment. He told me that she was not needed and that I should send her away. I had to tell him, needed or not, that she could not leave. If I had sent Millicent home, then I would have insulted and alienated the Fairies, and that was not the job of a good Empress.

"Although Leif was annoyed, he understood. Or, at least, he led me to believe that he had understood. As time passed, he grew very fond of Millicent, and took her under his wing. They stood together on all issues. Unbeknownst to me, together and without the rest of the Advisory Council, they told the Watchers' Guild to steer clear of me.

"When I had found out what they had done, I was livid. In a meeting that I had called, Millicent seemed to be under the impression that I had approved the decision. Leif did not see why his decision had upset me, and proceeded to tell me that I was naïve, amongst other things." Silvia sighed. "Their relationship was never the same after that."

"And he blamed you," said Berty.

"He did," agreed Silvia. "Although, he had never outwardly stated that. Afterwards, he criticized almost everything I did or said."

"His pompous arrogance clashed with your sensibility," Berty reasoned. "Leif probably did not realize there was anything that he did not know."

Silvia nodded. "I agree. I believe he thought of himself as the one really in charge of the Empire because he felt that *he* told the Empress what to do." She looked at the blinding crystal of the scepter. "One who claims to know everything, knows nothing."

As Berty mulled over Silvia's words, he thought about how the scepter sat at the core of everything. Staring at the scepter, he asked, "Silvia, does the scepter bring out the evil in men? Is that why there has never been an Emperor?"

"The evil of which you speak manifests in women as well as men," Silvia said. "The scepter does nothing of the sort. It no more brings out the evil in people than money does. The thoughts that swim in a person's mind are merely coaxed to the forefront by the possibilities that these objects may hold.

"The reason why there has never been an Emperor is because the scepter has never chosen a male to rule. The scepter looks for certain criterion to choose a ruler, which has always manifested in a female in the family. Unlike mainstream royal delineation, an Empress is not always the first born. She can be the second or third born. Sometimes Empress-ship has skipped a generation, but it has always remained in the maternal bloodline of the first Empress."

Berty saw a hard determination beyond the reflection of the crystal in her eyes. "You are going to defend the Empire Tree yourself and with everyone gone," he said, "no one will know."

"That is my plan, but not everyone will be gone," said Silvia. "Some will choose to lurk in the shadows and just beyond the trees. But, no one will die for me."

"Are you scared?" Berty asked.

"Not anymore." She lingered for a moment gazing into Berty's eyes, then turned to walk back through the door.

Caught by surprise, Berty hurried to follow Silvia down the steps. "Where are you going?"

"The kitchen."

"Why?"

"Lunch."

"You are hungry?" asked Berty incredulously.

"We must eat," Silvia said as she turned to face Berty. "Starving ourselves will not stop them from coming."

Chapter Seven
Rewards

Silvia floated down the next flights of stairs into the Receiving Room. Wanting to keep an eye on her, Berty followed closely. The room was completely empty with the exception of Silvia's throne standing alone on the dais. As they walked through the room, the sounds of people on the move around the Empire Tree bounced off the curved walls.

She led Berty through another door onto a much wider bridge than those Berty had been walking on above. Taking a few steps forward, Berty saw a maze of rope and plank bridges in all sizes heading in every direction. All sorts of people, Dwarves, Fairies, Elves and Humans, destinations unknown, hurried about on every one.

"Empress!" shrieked the familiar voice of Theodore. Berty saw him walking onto the wide bridge from a narrow bridge above them. All movement halted. "Is there a problem, my Lady?" he asked while trying to keep his voice steady.

"No," said Silvia, "no problem." The busyness of the bridges recommenced. "We fancied a bite, so we are heading to the kitchen."

"I can bring you food," said Theodore. "Where would you like to eat?"

"That is very kind of you, Theodore," Silvia said, "but I will not take you away from your preparations."

"Preparations for what, my Lady?" asked Theodore. "Chambers for all the Heads are ready, if they so desire them."

"Very good, Theodore, thank you," Silvia said, "but have you not made preparations to leave yet?"

"No, my Lady," said Theodore, bowing his head. Straightening his body to his full height, he said, "I have no need to prepare to leave for I serve the Empire Tree, my Lady, you."

Looking at the proud man standing before her, tears welled in Silvia's eyes. With great stature and poise she said, "You are truly a noble man with a very noble soul. I am deeply honored to have such a man in my midst." Theodore beamed while his chest swelled with pride and his eyes blinked furiously. "We will be at the Roundtable," she announced. Bowing, he walked away, wiping his face with his sleeve.

As the two of them made their way up the stairs to the Roundtable Room, Berty asked Silvia, "You are allowing him to stay?"

"Loyalty and honor are virtues that cannot be lost," said Silvia. "I will not punish them."

"But why Theodore and not Alvar?"

"As Captain of the Guard, Alvar will be targeted," Silvia explained as they walked into the room. "Theodore, a servant, will not, and is better able to stay safe within the Empire Tree. Therefore, I reward Theodore by honoring his decision, and I reward Alvar by allowing him to do his duty without a bull's-eye on his back."

"Brilliant," Berty exclaimed, taking a seat at the table.

"Thank you," said Silvia, joining him.

A side door opened and in walked Theodore, carrying an extra large tray. When he placed it on the table, Silvia said, "Thank you, Theodore. If you would sit with us for a moment." She gestured for him to sit in the nearest chair.

Surprise flashed across his face. "Thank you, my Lady." Theodore climbed in the chair, sitting proudly.

"I wish to speak to you about what will be happening this week," Silvia began. "As the Heads arrive, you are to greet them and bring them into the Reception Room. Have refreshments for them and any that wish to stay, show them to their lodgings. When I am ready, you will bring them here. Do you have any questions?"

"Not a question, per se, my Lady."

"Okay."

"I... I wish to help," stammered Theodore, "help fight for the Empire Tree."

"Are you trained in fighting?" asked Silvia.

"No. But," he leaned in close, whispering, "I can do magic." He looked at Silvia and Berty with scared eyes. Berty knew that Theodore had never told anyone.

Silvia smiled. "A demonstration please."

Instantly, Theodore relaxed, then said something that sounded like, "place a deer um." All the plates, bowls, platters, goblets and flasks flew off the tray. They landed on the table neatly and ready for Silvia's and Berty's lunch.

"Very impressive, you have the makings of a Mage." Theodore beamed at Silvia's compliment. "Allow me time to assess. In the meantime, keep your talent only between the three of us."

"I will, Empress," said Theodore. "Thank you, Empress." Climbing off the chair, he skipped out of the room.

Taking some food, Berty marveled at Silvia's diplomacy and tact. With her goblet paused at her lips, she extracted the glowing, golden locket from the Watchers' Guild Master.

Opening it, she said, "Another message from the Guild Master. It turns out that the embedded Watcher is on our side. He has enacted the locket in such a way that we can now see and hear everything the Watcher can."

Closing the locket, Silvia used the rod from the clasp to push the very center of the eye on the front of the locket, so that the pupil and iris looked depressed like on ancient Greek and Roman statues. When she opened the locket again, the side where messages were sent and written became an oval television screen while sounds emitted from the other side. Silvia passed her hand over the open locket. In the middle of the table, both picture and sound magnified for Berty and Silvia to see and hear.

In the enlarged view, Berty saw the shaft of an arrow as it was being pulled back on a string. The back of the arrowhead stayed close to the curve of the bow for a few seconds. He watched as it released. The arrow sliced through the air, hitting the center of its target.

"Nice shot," said a mouse like, breathy voice that Berty vaguely recognized.

"Thanks," said the voice of the archer, keeping his eyes on the yellow and red cloth covered straw target. The view changed quickly to the source of the compliment.

From a nearby tree against which they were leaning, three men approached the viewer. The man on the right was tall and lean with a dark complexion and a coarse beard. The man on the left was shorter and stocky with a lighter complexion and long, dirty, blond hair that hung limply on either side of his round face. The center man had straight, black hair and a flat nose. Berty could make out his cold, gray eyes as he walked closer.

"I do not believe that we have met," said the center man, "I am Sean." He extended a hand towards the viewer.

"Declan," said the archer while shaking Sean's hand. Berty's stomach turned and lunch did not settle in his stomach well.

"Where did you learn archery, Declan?" asked Sean.

"From my grandfather," answered Declan. "He was quite a woodsman. He used to craft bows and arrows."

Berty only turned away from the scene when a door opened, distracted him. Theodore showed a tall, thin Empire Guard through the door. He stopped a few feet from the Roundtable, standing still like a statue. "Empress," said the guard only moving his mouth, "Captain Alvar has sent me—"

Silvia held up her hand to cut him off, without turning her head to look at the Elf. With his mouth closed, she motioned for him to sit down at the table. The guard promptly sat in the nearest chair, waiting.

Berty, distracted by the guard's arrival, missed a part of the exchange between the men in the image, and he hastily paid attention.

"What is that around your neck?" Sean asked.

Declan's head tilted downwards. His hand gently grabbed a small, plain, gold locket. "It is how I take my family with me, wherever I go, for I am here to better my family."

Declan raised his head to find Sean smiling at him. Smiling did not improve Sean's rat like demeanor. Sean clapped Declan on the shoulder. "We are glad that you are here," Sean said. "The return of magic will better your family and everyone's families across the Empire." Sean stood proudly, like a peacock showing off his exquisite plumage to the surrounding fawning peahens. "We will let you return to your archery practice. You will need it when you face those entranced Empire Guards." He smiled once more. Turning to the two men flanking him, he said, "Come, men." Sean and his two companions rejoined the rather large encampment of mostly men and some women.

When Declan returned his focus to his bow and arrows, Silvia finally broke her gaze from the hovering image in the center of the table to look at the intruding guard who seemed mesmerized while looking at the image. "A gift from the Watchers' Guild, very useful," she said. "Continue."

With disgust written all over his face, the Elf acknowledged Silvia by nodding. He stood in his previous statue like stance, shaking the appalled look off his face from what he just saw. "Yes," he said, "Captain Alvar sent me to tell you that preparations for the evacuations are going rather smoothly. He gathers that everyone will be starting to leave by mid-afternoon tomorrow. The Captain would like to know if there are any additional instructions, my Lady."

"And you are?" asked Silvia.

"Lieutenant Edwin, Empress."

"Lieutenant Edwin," said Silvia, "I wish for you to share your opinion about the exchange we just saw."

Edwin's stony face melted to show a mixture of surprise and excitement. "That man we saw—the one who is trying to destroy you—acts like he is doing everyone a great favor. He pretends that he is doing all of this for the entire world and not for himself."

"And you believe he is doing this for merely personal gain?"

"Yes, I do," answered Edwin. "He does not care about magic,

only about gathering followers and being Emperor."

"Thank you, Lieutenant," said Silvia. "As for further instruction, I wish you to only share what you have seen with Captain Alvar. Also, tell your Captain to keep things going as planned."

"Yes, Empress." Bowing, Edwin left.

"Berty, do you feel the same way as Edwin?" Silvia asked.

"Well," answered Berty slowly, "there is something that I do not understand." He watched Declan release an arrow before he continued. "If he truly felt that the lack of magic within the Empire was a problem, then why does he have to resort to violent means to resolve the problem? Why has he not tried to find any reasoning behind the problem so he could find the actual answer?"

"So you think that being Emperor is his goal?"

"Pretty much. I think that he has contrived the solution to a problem about which he has heard people complain. He believes that if he has hold of the scepter, then he will become Emperor. He cannot walk into the Empire Tree and take the scepter unnoticed. So, Sean concocts a story about how the scepter is holding all the magic and that way he can lead everyday people to their deaths for his own selfish means," said Berty, utterly disgusted. "Classic case of good verses evil."

Silvia studied Berty for a minute. "I am not so sure about wanting to be Emperor is his true goal. Sure, he lied and manipulated. He chased us into the forest. How would he have claimed the scepter if he had killed me that night? Do you think that Sean knows that he is the evil party?"

Berty opened, then shut his mouth without emitting a sound.

"You are right about his case being classic, but wrong about it being good verses evil." Berty shot Silvia a puzzled look. "The proverbial battle between good and evil, seen often in stories throughout time, tends to make situations seem simple and clean. It justifies people's behavior and eases any guilt, no matter who is on the winning or losing side. That classic conflict is fabricated by man. It was one of the first complex tools invented to make life easier. That tool was and is used to teach, placate and control." Silvia looked at Berty's shocked face. "Do not get me wrong. Yes, there are opposing forces always at work in this world, but the classic battle is simply to live. Take the owl and the mouse, for example, one is not good or evil simply because one is prey and the other is a predator. The owl hunts the mouse as food that it needs to survive."

"A person does not need magic to survive," said Berty.

"Technically, no, but it does make life more convenient," reasoned Silvia. "Answer me this, in the non-magical world in which you have been living, if you took away things like electricity, running water or gasoline from a person, could he survive?"

"Eventually, he would figure out a way to be able to live without them," Berty answered, thinking rationally. "But, he would remember a time when he had those things that used to make life easier for him."

"And," Silvia said, "would he fight one way or another to have those things returned?"

"Yes, I suppose he would," said Berty. He paused to look at Declan removing his arrows from the target. "What I cannot comprehend, is how this Sean guy came to his conclusion about you stealing the magic if his first goal was not to be Emperor."

"He found no answers when he came to the Sages' Grove and perhaps even to the Empire Tree itself to investigate," said Silvia. "And like you said, good verses evil. It was the only conclusion he surmised."

"How do you know he came to the Sages' Grove?"

"Remember back to that night around the fire. He recognized me as the Empress," answered Silvia. "It is the only way."

She returned to her plate of food, eating in silence. Berty ate his food while watching her think and Declan practice.

Chapter Eight
Oversight

Chewing his food helped his mind reformulate ideas about the world. So far, during his career as a journalist, as well as in his life, Berty had never formed conclusions, especially in his writings, without questioning and questioning again every possible angle. However, he had found himself jumping to conclusions without realizing other possibilities. He had let this scum, Sean, rattle him under his skin. Or had he? Berty looked over at Silvia as she tore a piece of bread and buttered it.

He drank in every detail of her appearance. He liked the way her gold trimmed sleeve swayed as her arms moved. Her short, dark red hair curled slightly around her face. Momentarily mesmerized by her eyelashes batting as she blinked, his eyes blinked, too, which allowed them to follow the gentle slope of her nose. As he watched her lips part to accept the buttered piece of bread, he realized that it was not Sean who had gotten under his skin, clouding some of his clear judgement. Tearing his eyes away from Silvia's profile, Berty's left hand clasped over his mouth.

Everything Silvia had been doing in preparation made sense to Berty. The dismissals, the evacuations, the allowances, they all made sense in some twisted, logical way. Finally, calmness settled in his mind and body.

Removing his hand from his mouth, he picked up his goblet to take a drink, but found it empty. Catching sight of the pitcher across the table, Berty concentrated hard. After a few moments of concentration, the pitcher rose off the table, floating towards his goblet. It tipped itself to fill the goblet, then returned to its place on the table. Taking a sip, he had never felt more proud of himself.

"I am glad you are learning to control so quickly," said Silvia, smiling.

Berty smiled back, looking into her soft, brown eyes. Her eyes said to him that anything was possible.

A door opened, breaking their eye contact. Theodore said, "My Lady, the Lord of the Goblins has just arrived. I brought him to the Reception Room."

"Bring him here," instructed Silvia. Theodore left to retrieve the Goblin Lord.

Rising from her chair, Silvia stood between the table and the door, waiting to greet her guest. Berty stood beside her, yet kept behind her shoulder. When the door opened, Theodore led into the room the most peculiar looking creature Berty had ever seen. Roughly two feet tall, the Goblin Lord had a small, but hearty, build, greenish-gray skin, dark hair, dark, beady eyes and an unapproachable, forbidding look on his face.

"Empress," said the Goblin in an uncharacteristic squeaky voice that made Berty jump, "what an honor it is to be at the Roundtable."

"Lord Darnell," said Silvia, "Hubert, my Watcher."

Darnell's eyes opened wide. "It is true."

Silvia ignored both his comment and his obvious staring at Berty. "Let us sit."

The Goblin Lord took the popular seat across the table from Silvia's chair. After sitting, Darnell's gaze moved from Berty to the image at the center of the table. In the image, Declan still practiced his archery. He was using his system of separating broken arrows from the good arrows as an excuse to watch the people in the encampment. Darnell opened his mouth to speak, but seemed to change his mind for no squeaks escaped. Then after a few seconds, he said without taking his eyes off the image, "The Troll at the gates told me that if I had arrived one minute later, I would have been forced to spend the night outside."

"Security has increased," Silvia stated, "but for you, special arrangements would have been made. May I offer you something to eat or drink?"

"The group that gathers in the South woods," said Darnell,

lowering his head to look at Silvia underneath the picture, "are mad." Silvia waited for him to explain. "They speak of diminishing magic." Darnell shook his head. "While magic is not as widely used anymore by all peoples, that does not mean that the Empress hoards it. They have not thought that perhaps people have forgotten how to use it, or just do not see it anymore," he paused, rubbing his index finger on his chin, "or maybe an unknown source is taking it."

"Lord Darnell, I need to ask a favor," Silvia said.

"Anything, my Lady."

"It is imperative that what is hidden stays hidden, especially in the central woods around the Sages' Grove," said Silvia.

"It will be done," said Darnell.

"Thank you," Silvia said. "I am sure you would like to relax after your long journey."

"Yes, my Lady."

"Theodore will show you to your lodgings and get you anything else you need." The door opened and Theodore stood ready to guide Darnell through the Empire Tree.

Darnell bowed his head, then jumped off the chair. Halfway to the door, he said, "The one known as Leif has been seen in the Dragonlands this afternoon, alone. He heads towards God Mountain." Turning, he walked out the door.

"It is good to know that Leif has not joined the anti-Empress club," said Berty.

"Indeed, but we cannot worry about the betrayal of Leif at the moment," Silvia said. "We have more pressing issues." She turned her head to watch Declan as he gathered his arrows to head back to the encampment.

Walking past a rather large tent, Declan heard a raspy voice saying, "Do you think we can pick up the pace? They are going to know we are coming." Declan slowed.

"If we travel at night," said a deeper voice, "then we could arrive in a week."

"Would these men be ready in a week?" asked the voice of

Sean. Declan dropped his quiver, spilling both his good and broken arrows on the ground. As he knelt to pick them up, the men in the tent continued their conversation.

"It would give us the element of surprise," said the man with the raspy voice.

"I agree with Wagner," said the deeper voice. "It would be exactly what we need."

"Sean, you are not saying much," said Wagner. "We would like to know what you think."

"There are only a handful of us who would stand a chance against the guards," Sean said. "Everyone else needs more training."

"But, if we take them by surprise, we could get through without much training," said Wagner.

"You might be right. Because unfortunately, I do not think our numbers will improve if we wait too much longer. We will take only a handful of chosen men. So far, I want to bring with us Jarvis, Lester and that archer, Declan. Let us get ready to move at daybreak and no stopping for more than a couple of hours at a time."

Quickly gathering his arrows, Declan walked into the food line. Berty blinked. Seeing the chair opposite him, he realized that Silvia had closed the locket.

"Theodore," said Silvia.

Moments later, the Dwarf emerged from behind a door. "Yes, my Lady."

"I wish to see Colvin, Hatcher and Alvar in the Reception Room immediately."

Bowing, Theodore hurried out the door.

Berty followed Silvia down the stairs to the Reception Room. She sat regally on the throne and told Berty to stand next to her. Soon after they were in place, the Dwarf marched into the room with Colvin, Hatcher and Alvar on his heels.

"Empress," they said in unison, bowing. Theodore began to leave, but Silvia put her arm up, stopping him.

"You may stay, Theodore," said Silvia. "It has come to my attention that Sean and his men will be here within a week's time. Evacuations are to commence immediately and continue into the night. The other Heads should be arriving tomorrow and will leave as soon as possible, if they so choose. That is all."

Bowing, the four men left to do their duties.

Standing, Silvia said to Berty, "Time for oversight."

He followed her as she disappeared behind the Sages' Seal. Stopping only to put on their cloaks, they climbed up the stairs with only the sounds of their footsteps on wood filling their ears. When the stairs finally ended, Berty followed Silvia into the dark hallway, past the Sorcery Room, and through the one sided door into the wide public passage. Berty followed her down the well-lighted hallway. She opened an arched shaped, curved door, entering one of the rooms.

"This is called a Watching Room," said Silvia. "From here, we can see what is going on in the Sages' Grove."

The entire room was narrow and curved with the trunk of the Empire Tree. Mostly empty with the exception of some plain chairs, Berty wandered away from Silvia to look out of the long window of the arc shaped room. Darkness was fast approaching, making his view of the ground below was limited.

"Not as much can be seen from there as from here," said Silvia as she lit the sconces on the walls with the magic of her thoughts. They illuminated a miniature model of the Sages' Grove. Every thatched roofed building and wooden stall that existed between the wall and the Empire Tree were all depicted.

Once Berty walked away from the window, Silvia took a deep breath, then breathed into the hollow center of the miniature Empire Tree. As her breath spread throughout the stalls and buildings, the Sages' Grove model came to life. Tiny people appeared, walking out of buildings, carrying belongings and loading carts. When the people walked through the gates of the Sages' Grove, their images disappeared.

"Wow," Berty exclaimed softly as he watched the figure of a

guard help a family tie their things to the bed of a cart. "We cannot hear what they are saying?"

"No," said Silvia. "We are merely watching, not spying."

Berty was pleased to see that the people were evacuating sooner rather than later. His attention was drawn to a group of people who were traveling light with only a few small bags and no carts like most of the people. An elderly man hung a lantern on the crook of his staff. As he led the group of people towards the gates, the lantern dimmed. When Silvia pointed her finger at the lantern, the illumination grew. A look of relief spread on the man's face. Looking out the window, Berty could see the elderly man leading his group with a strongly lighted lantern hanging from his staff's crook.

For over an hour, they watched the inhabitants of the Sages' Grove help each other secure their possessions and homes. Every so often, Silvia would magically help the struggling by giving them light or strengthening their ropes.

When darkness completely enveloped the Sages' Grove, the number of people leaving dwindled. Most of those who stayed behind for the night had everything ready to be able to leave at first light. Silvia breathed in the hollow of the mini Empire Tree again. The model of the Sages' Grove was still.

"We should rest," said Silvia. "We need to be in the Reception Room at day break." Berty nodded. He walked with Silvia through the passageways and across their bridge. Stopping on Berty's platform, Silvia said, "Theodore will have breakfast waiting for us. Sleep well." He watched her walk across her bridge, clutching the locket in her hand.

When she was out of sight, Berty entered his study and fell into one of his chairs. Putting his feet on the table, his mind replayed the day. Before he forgot the details and became too sleepy, he sat at his desk. Opening his old notebook to a new page, he wrote another installment of the Adventures of Leigh and Marcus.

Chapter Nine
The Heads

Waking with the morning still draped in darkness never appealed to Berty. He had always tried to avoid early morning appointments whenever possible. It was a major reason for him not having that nine to five, which really meant eight to seven-thirty, job like his peers. He felt that waking while the morning was being bathed in sunlight energized his soul. Begrudgingly, he left his comfortable bed to head into the shower.

After he dressed, Berty stumbled across the bridge and down the stairs, hoping that his longing for a steaming cup of coffee would be fulfilled. Emerging from behind the carved wall, he walked over to join Silvia at a long buffet table. His hopes rose when he saw that she was pouring something hot into a cup.

"Would you like a cup?" Silvia asked.

Berty peered into her cup. Through the rising steam, he saw a murky brown liquid sitting in the ceramic. Catching a whiff, the odd, earthy aroma told him that this was nothing remotely similar to coffee.

"What is it?" asked Berty.

Silvia hesitated. "An infusion of certain roots and barks."

"No coffee?" Berty glanced at the pitchers and carafes on the table. Deep down he felt that only coffee could quench his thirst.

Grabbing a new cup off the table, Silvia poured another cup of the infusion. Handing it to Berty, she whispered, "Change it. You know how."

She left him standing next to the buffet table looking into his cup of murky, earthy smelling infusion. Grasping the cup with his one hand, he thought hard. Berty placed his other hand over the top of the cup. When he removed it, the liquid was much darker. His nose caught the warm, rich, coffee aroma wafting from the cup. As he brought the cup to his lips, his hand tipped the liquid into his mouth. The warm liquid embraced his tongue. When he swallowed, he thought that it was the best coffee he had ever tasted. Satisfied, Berty loaded a plate with food, then sat with Silvia at a nearby table.

"Sean made the announcement last night," said Silvia in a casual, conversational tone. "His group was poised to move this morning well before dawn. I expect them to arrive early to midmorning within two days with only a small group of hand picked elite, of which our Watcher is one. The rest should arrive later in the afternoon that same day." Without worry, Silvia spread some sort of jam onto her oatcakes. "When we finish eating, I want to walk through the Sages' Grove."

Berty watched her closely as they ate their breakfast. Silvia showed no signs of feeling scared or even concerned with the fact that a madman was marching through the forest towards them as they sat eating, intent upon destroying the life that she grew up knowing.

After they ate, Silvia and Berty walked through the empty Receiving Room and into the almost empty Sages' Grove. The few who stayed the night secured any last minute items before being checked out by the guards. As they meandered down the winding dirt path through the empty picturesque village, Berty felt a sense of lifelessness that made him uneasy.

Hidden behind the Empire Tree, a lone lighted windowpane stood out among the dark panes of the surrounding white buildings. Someone in his or her haste forgot to extinguish a lantern, thought Berty. He was about to ask Silvia what they were going to do about the lantern when something else caught his eye. Shadowy movement in the window made him stop in his tracks. He was relieved to know that Silvia noticed the movement, too, so it was not a figment of his imagination from getting out of bed way too early.

Berty followed Silvia as she navigated through the emptiness towards the house to which the lighted window belonged. The white cob house looked much older than the surrounding homes.

The thatched roof was not as neatly thatched as the others were. Supposing it had many more repairs than the others, Berty looked away. They stood in silence as Silvia's knuckles rapped on the old, wooden door. About a minute passed before the slow shuffle of feet and the rhythmic clunking of wood on wood could be heard. Slowly, the door squeaked opened to partially reveal an elderly woman being supported by her wooden cane.

"We apologize for the intrusion, madam," Silvia said, smiling. "We just wanted to see if you needed anything."

The old woman looked at Silvia with surprise. "Please, come in," she said, shuffling away from the open door. Silvia and Berty crossed the threshold. The house was one large room with wooden steps that led to a loft area for sleeping. Under the stairs, hid a lumpy, unmade bed. Mismatched chairs furnished the room. Some had broken spindles that needed to be fixed. In the dim light cast by the lone lantern, the old woman's feeble attempts to make breakfast sprawled over the small plank table and spilled onto the floor. "It is such an honor to have the Empress in my family's humble home," she said.

Silvia smiled, saying, "What is your name?"

"Leena," answered the woman.

"Please do not stand on my account, Leena," Silvia said. Leena sat on the nearest chair with some difficulty. When she sat, her long, white hair glistened in the sunlight as it inched through the grimy windows.

"I am sorry that there are not many other places to sit. What can I offer you, Empress?" Leena sat as straight as she could.

"Thank you, Leena," said Silvia, "but we are fine."

Berty looked around at the mostly empty shelves. If he did not know someone was in the house, he would have thought it had been vacated. Silvia must have noticed as well for she asked, "When did your family leave?"

"Last night," said Leena. "I forced them to go without me. I would have only impaired their journey." She looked across the room at a plain wooden box near the bed under the stairs. "Young man, could you bring me that box? My legs are not what they used to be." Berty, smiling at being called a young man, retrieved the box for Leena. "Thank you." Leena looked up at Silvia. "This must be passed to my granddaughter, once she leaves the age of discovery. She will need it for her re-naming ceremony."

"Re-naming," said Silvia surprised.

"Oh yes," said Leena. "She has shown the signs. I could not give it to her beforehand for she will still be in the age of discovery for a few more years. I know what tradition dictates. I can only entrust this to you, Empress, so that you can give this to her in my absence."

"What is your granddaughter's name?" asked Silvia.

"Alina," the old woman said proudly. "Her new name will be Kalina."

"Have you had breakfast yet, Leena?" Silvia asked.

"Not yet, no," answered Leena. "I was just about to make some."

"Have breakfast in the Empire Tree and bring your grandmother's box," said Silvia, smiling.

Leena was speechless.

"Come, we will accompany you," Silvia said, extending her hand.

With gratefulness in her eyes, Leena took Silvia's hand and with Silvia's magical assistance stood without difficulty. Box in hand, she walked in between Silvia and Berty up the winding path to the Empire Tree.

"My grandmother," said Leena while holding onto Berty's arm, "would tell us kids stories about being in the Empire Tree and talking with the Empress, scholars and astronomers. She even met the Queen of the Fairies once. Who would have ever thought that one day, I, too, would be ascending into the Empire Tree."

With magical assistance, Leena climbed the stairs to the Reception Room between Silvia and Berty. When the three of them reached the top of the stairs, they found the room occupied.

Three occupants were helping themselves to the food on the

buffet table. Chatting, they did not notice anyone entering the room. Berty saw the backs of the three. On the left, stood a tall, thin man with short, dark hair streaked with silver, wearing a long, green, robe like garment tied with a matching sash around his middle. To his right, a much shorter woman with short, light brown hair in a ruby gown talked animatedly, and on the far right was a slightly taller man with dark hair, wearing an orange flowing shirt and pant ensemble. Both of the latter had bluish purple, folded wings on their backs. Letting go of Leena's hand, Silvia said to Leena, "Please, sit at the table while we get you something to eat."

At the sound of Silvia's voice, the three strangers stopped. Putting down their plates, they walked over to greet her.

"Empress," said the very tall, older man who Berty confirmed to be an Elf, "I wish this visit was less serious and more social." He bowed and kissed her hand.

"High Elf Alfred, King Elrick and Queen Lida of the Fairies," said Silvia, "so good of you to come on such short notice." The trio nodded their heads. "May I introduce Hubert, my Watcher, and Leena of the family of Rowan. Please, continue to get some food. You must be famished from your journeys."

The Elf and Fairies resumed their places at the buffet table while Berty helped Leena into a seat. Silvia poured a cup of the infusion while Berty fixed Leena a plate a food.

"I met your grandmother, Kalina, once," said Alfred as he joined Leena at the table. "I was in the age of learning and accompanied my father during his more routine pilgrimages to the Empire Tree. Needless to say, on that particular visit, I, thinking I was so very smart, did something stupid and Kalina was there to patch my injuries. She was one of the best Witches I have ever encountered. Your family must be very honored, Leena."

Leena sat proudly. "Thank you, High Elf. Our family will be honored once more for my young granddaughter is showing the signs."

"Has she found what is to be found yet?" asked Lida. Both she and her husband took seats across from each other.

"Not as of yet," answered Leena, "but I am confident she will now that she has been able to leave the Sages' Grove."

"She has never left the Sages' Grove?" asked Elrick in disbelief. "Have her parents not seen the signs?"

"Her mother would not allow it," Leena said, rolling her eyes. "She would say that such things are not necessary. I argued with her, but my son's wife started shouting about how all Alina would be is a Witch. As if there was something wrong with being only a Witch. Of course my son, barely home because he is working so often, does not take part in the discussion and leaves it all up to his wife." Leena scowled disapprovingly.

Lida shook her head. "Abandoning magic because it is only something or other. I have seen that attitude before."

"I thought people wanted magic in their lives," said Berty, sitting to join the discussion. Silvia made her way to the staircase behind the Sages' Seal unnoticed by everyone except Berty. She motioned for him to stay before she disappeared.

"They do," said Alfred.

"Then why not allow her to become a Witch?" Berty asked.

"Because," answered Alfred, "people seem to only want magic without so-called limitations."

"There was a time," Lida began, "when magic flourished throughout the Empire in all manners of ways. Every village and town had a resident Witch or Wizard, and Mages with different specialties roamed the lands. Once in a long while, a True Sorcerer or Sorceress would come along to help where they could. People liked the specialization and variety of magic that abounded."

"Then," continued Elrick, "people became unhappy with different types of magic. They got tired of having to seek out the specialists that they needed. A movement swept throughout the Empire where people wanted to expand their magical abilities, even if they lacked any magical talent. They experimented with all sorts of things from stones to toxic concoctions. Needless to say, the people failed in their endeavors. The results of their experimentation were as mild as numbing of their minds and hallucinations or as extreme as experiencing violent seizures and even sudden death."

"People abandoned their attempts," said Lida. "And instead of accepting and embracing what limited magic they had, they rejected it."

"Generations after," added Elrick, "were also unsatisfied with just some magic so they turned their backs on all of it because of what they saw as limiting magic and even discouraged magical abilities in their children. Nowadays, you will have to travel far and wide to be able to find any bit of magic. Most people displaying any sort of magical prowess have been banished from their villages."

"They want all or nothing," said Berty.

"Yes," said Alfred, "and it seems that this attack-the-Empress scheme is just another fruitless attempt to have magical equality."

"But not everyone is good at everything," exclaimed Berty. "Some people excel at business or in art and some are even better at those things than others who share the same propensities. Why should people have the same skills as everyone else? Doing so would make everyone mediocre. Mediocrity does not help societies progress and grow. Those who have tried it have failed, miserably. Having the same skill sets as everyone else completely undermines how societies work and how people work together to ensure our very survival."

"Precisely," Alfred said.

"Hubert, sir," said Theodore, interrupting the conversation, "the Empress would like to see you in the Roundtable Room."

"Thank you, Theodore. Excuse me," said Berty as he rose out of his chair. Berty nodded to everyone at the table and walked towards the staircase as Theodore started speaking to Leena.

"The Empress would like you to stay in the Empire Tree," said Theodore, "until your family returns. If you have finished eating, I can show you to your lodgings." Tears finally began to cascade down the old woman's cheeks. Leena mumbled inaudibly to the young Dwarf. "Whatever you require from your family's house, I will be able to retrieve for you." Climbing the stairs, Berty smiled as Theodore's voice trailed away.

When Berty reached the Roundtable Room, he noticed that Silvia was not alone. Seated across the table from Silvia was an old Troll. The Troll's red felt hat was placed on the table, revealing silvery-white curls on the top of the inverted triangular head. The characteristic pointy chin was covered with a rather long, curly, silvery-white beard.

"Chief Miercia," announced Silvia as Berty walked closer to the Roundtable, "I would like you to meet Hubert, my Watcher."

"Ah yes," said Miercia in a strangely soft and high pitched, almost feminine voice. Taking in every detail of Berty's appearance, the Troll continued, "He was the man who accompanied you through that portal."

Silvia looked at Berty, saying, "Join us. Chief Miercia was just about to tell me about the problems they have been having with the portals." The Troll Chief waited until Berty sat next to Silvia at the table before speaking.

"More and more people are traveling through the portals on our side, and then they cannot seem to return," said Miercia. "It is quite a problem for the Counters. Sometimes, we find them on the other side, wandering about the area trying to find the return portal. Many times, we are able to guide them to the portal without being seen, but , there are the rare occasions where we must make our presence known, so that they can find their way back to the Land of Sages."

"And other times?" inquired Silvia.

"We do not find them at all." Miercia's head lowered in shame.

"Why are the Goblins not helping you find these people?" asked Silvia, clearly upset.

"They feel that it is not their duty to help correct waywardness," Miercia answered, looking distraught.

"I see," said an agitated Silvia. "Why do you think that people cannot find the return portals?"

"People have complained about the portals not being clearly marked on the other side," explained Miercia. "They seemed to have lost their sense. We Trolls are thinking about reinstating the portal tests."

"That is a good idea," Silvia said. "In the meantime, keep your eyes peeled for waywardness. I will talk with the Goblins."

"Thank you, Empress," said Miercia. Standing, the Troll picked up the hat, placing it on the silvery-white curls. "Good luck." Miercia walked out the door where Theodore waited to accompany the Troll Chief out of the Sages' Grove.

"Why was he not downstairs with the other Heads," asked Berty.

"She," corrected Silvia.

"She?"

"Trolls are more androgynous than the rest of us," Silvia explained. "Chief Miercia cannot stay for any length of time with us. She needs to get back to her duties and oversight to make sure that the portals are not compromised by the magic haters, as she calls them. It is honestly best for her to stay away from the Empire Tree at this time. Trolls like her are not suited for any amount of combat. Besides, she has told us more, perhaps the most important bit of information, than she is even aware of telling."

"Which part was the most important bit of information?" Berty asked. Confused, he reviewed what the Troll Chief had just told them.

Chapter Ten
Four Will Fall

"The fourth has fallen," Silvia stated.

"What was the fourth?" asked Berty. He knew that the dismissal of the Empire Guards marked the third to fall.

"The Hidden Treaty," answered Silvia. "Goblins and Trolls have never gotten along. They can barely live in peace. You saw Lord Darnell's dislike for Hatcher when he came. No Goblin will be a part of the Advisory Council as long as there is a Troll on board. However, they are still loyal to the Empress and the Empire Tree. Goblins understand that Empresses must work with everyone."

Berty nodded.

Sighing, Silvia said, "Since the beginning of time, Goblins and Trolls have been at each other's throats. Anytime they would get close to one another or each other's holdings a skirmish would ensue. A very long time ago, there was a skirmish where the violence between Goblins and Trolls escalated to an all out war that affected the goings on of the Empire. People could not get close enough to a portal to use it. Whole areas of the Empire had to be circumvented because of the fighting. When the fighting spilled over into towns from the countryside, the Third Empress had to intervene. Along with the Heads, she drew up a treaty, giving them distinct areas with clear borders and rules for interaction and working both separately and together. Included in the lines of this treaty was a certain stipulation. That stipulation said that for the good of the Empire, they must put their differences aside to work together and help each other."

"Meaning the Goblins must help the Trolls find the missing people," said Berty.

"Exactly. Not doing so voided the Hidden Treaty signed by their ancestors." Silvia shook her head. "Theodore," she called.

The young Dwarf entered. "Yes, Empress."

"Have all the Heads arrived?" Silvia asked.

"Yes, Empress."

"What is the news regarding Leena?"

"She decided to stay in the Empire Tree," Theodore said. "I have already retrieved her things. While I was in her house, I tidied everything."

Berty knew that the Dwarf was talking about Leena's breakfast that she spilled everywhere.

"The chairs?" asked Silvia.

"All fixed," Theodore answered. "As well as the roof. I could not allow myself to leave those things in that house in such disrepair."

"You have gone above and beyond," said Silvia, "and I would not expect any less from you." He smiled proudly at Silvia. "You may bring the Heads now." Bowing, Theodore walked out the door.

As soon as the young Dwarf was gone, thoughts raced through Berty's mind. He wondered that if the four have already fallen, then what would come next. His mind recited the Pixies' song, *Finding the time four will fall, Watcher watches over thee.* He pondered the meaning of the last two lines. Did the Pixie Priestess mean Declan or himself? Before Berty could pose that question to a very contemplative Silvia, Theodore opened the main door, announcing the new arrivals.

Silvia stayed seated while Theodore called, "High Elf Alfred, Queen Lida of the Fairies, King Elrick of the Fairies, and Prince Goscislaw of the Dwarves." Theodore bowed low as the Heads cautiously approached the Roundtable. Berty watched the newcomer trail behind the other three. The Dwarf Prince stood at least a head lower than the Fairies, but prouder than the others with his bald head, short white beard, dark brown pants, tan blouse like shirt and a dark brown cape.

"Honored guests," said Silvia with her arms outstretched, "please, sit." She watched while each one found a seat around the table. Once everyone had stopped fidgeting with his or her chairs and cloaks, she said, "The Pixie Prophecy has finally come to pass. In a couple of days from now, ignorance will be knocking at the gates of the Sages' Grove. If you wish to stay, you may lodge in the Empire Tree. If you wish to leave, I suggest you do so this afternoon. Please know that your honor will not be tarnished. I will do my best to not allow the ignorance to spread among the Empire, so that it does not knock on the gates of your peoples." Silvia paused to look at each face. "Before I leave you, you must know that the Hidden Treaty has been violated. When this is over, it can and should be redrawn."

Without saying another word, the Empress stood and walked to the private stairway. Turning his head, Berty saw the hem of her light blue cloak disappear in the shadow.

The four Heads watched the door through which she left as if she may return any second for a couple of minutes. Looking at the shocked faces surrounding the table, Berty hoped that his own face did not reflect such shock. Eventually, the four of them turned their heads away from the door, and just looked at each other while the silence pounded in Berty's ears. Prince Goscislaw's low growl broke the silence.

"Of course, I am staying," said the wizened Dwarf. "There is nothing more important than solidarity when utter madness attacks the Empire, especially its heart—the Empire Tree itself."

"You are absolutely correct, Goscislaw," said Elrick, emboldened by Goscislaw's words. "We are staying. If we defeat them, what a tale that will tell."

"The odds are against us," said Lida. "That will make all the difference."

"I am staying as well. We shall wait for the Empress' return to discuss a battle plan," Alfred said.

"Her plan does not include us." Berty spoke at last. The four Heads looked at Berty as if they had forgotten that he was sitting at the table. Berty sat up straighter in his chair. "Well, not directly. The Empress is allowing them to come unobstructed."

"Which would give them a false sense of security," growled

Goscislaw.

"Giving us the advantage because of the element of surprise," said Alfred. "They will be expecting Empire Guards and instead..."

"They will find us," completed Berty. "We are a complete unknown to them. While they have calculated the strength and ability of the Empire Guard, they have not calculated what we know or our capabilities."

"So we wait?" inquired Lida.

"So we wait," answered Berty.

The Heads looked at Berty with an earned respect. Ignoring their stares, he focused on his new found clarity. Berty knew that Silvia's first priority was to defend the scepter. She would be in the Scepter Room waiting for Sean. He also knew that in order for her to do her job properly, it was their job to make sure that no one else found a way to the Scepter Room. Lost in his thoughts and forgetting that others were sitting at the Roundtable with him, Berty stood and began to walk away from the table.

"Where are you going?" asked Alfred.

"To form a plan," Berty answered. Alfred gave him a calculated look, then nodded. While the other three wore confused looks on their faces, the Elf seemed to understand that Berty had a mission.

All afternoon, Berty walked the deserted, unfamiliar passageways and bridges throughout the Empire Tree and its many branches. Learning the Empire Tree inside and out was imperative. Silvia depended on him to do so. He knew exactly what she had planned—defend the Empire Tree with everything she has, even her life—for that is what he would do.

As darkness crept across the sky, Berty found himself in the Reception Room while Theodore arranged a spread of cured meats and fish, cheese, bread, and fruit on a buffet table. Automatically, Berty grabbed a plate, filling it with food. Soon after he sat down, the others joined him at the table.

Spearing a sardine, Alfred asked, "What is the plan?"

Berty felt four pairs of eyes boring into his head. Tearing his eyes away from his plate, he returned the intensity of each pair's stare in turn.

"The Empress will position herself in the Scepter Room to defend the scepter," began Berty. "Each one of us must stop all but one from entering that room from every possible way. We shall hide in strategic places throughout the Empire Tree that will take advantage of each of our strengths. Then, we will either advance or retreat to the Scepter Room, just in case. I would suggest becoming more familiar with the Empire Tree's passageways and finding that hiding place by tomorrow evening. By the break of dawn the following day, we should all be in position in our hiding spots."

"Excellent," said Goscislaw with relish. Gobbling his food, he quickly left to begin preparing his hiding place. Elrick and Lida followed soon after the Dwarf Prince left the table, leaving Alfred alone with Berty.

"Hubert," said the wizened Elf, "you are a good man. We believe in you." The High Elf gave Berty a fatherly smile, then disappeared down a corridor.

He gazed around the large, round room. Silvia's throne, high on the dais, sparkled in the candlelight of the lone, lit chandelier. Behind her throne, stood the Sages' Seal carved into the wall. Her throne did not cast any shadows onto the carving. He knew it held a deep meaning, but he could not think about what it could be. Nonetheless, looking at it made him feel optimistic from which he pulled strength. Paying attention to his food, Berty drew more strength from both the unwavering solidarity of the Heads and his ever-increasing solitude.

As he finished his meal, Theodore walked over to the table. "Sir," he said, "Leena is comfortable. Is there anything that you will need me to do this evening before I get ready for bed?"

"Have you spoken with the Empress?" asked Berty.

"Yes. She told me to take instructions from you now, as she needed to prepare and cannot be disturbed," said the young Dwarf.

Looking at Theodore, Berty saw a flicker of fear in his eyes. "Place a basket of food and drink outside of everyone's chambers, including the Empress and myself this evening. Make sure Leena has enough food to last both you and her for a while, just in case. When dawn approaches, do not worry about providing breakfast. Refill the baskets in the afternoon tomorrow, if need be." Berty paused to look around the Reception Room. "Tomorrow, fill this room with tables and chairs. I want to be able to slow them down on their way through. After that, your only job is to keep Leena safe until this has passed." Berty spoke with authority that only he knew Silvia to have.

"Yes, sir." Theodore bowed, then began to clear the tables. As Berty rose out of his chair and approached the private doorway, Theodore called out to him. "Good luck, sir."

Nodding, Berty said, "You, too." The Dwarf smiled as Berty walked up the stairs.

Chapter Eleven
The Supposed Calm before the Storm

Alone with only the sounds of his footsteps to accompany him, Berty felt a strange sense of abandonment. He was not used to walking along the private staircase without Silvia. Silvia's guidance within the Land of Sages gave him strength to deal with whatever he encountered. Although he knew that she needed him to be alone, Berty did not like being without her.

Reaching a landing, he paused, then walked through the doorway. Berty paced around the windowless, round room. He noticed that the crystal sconces did not allow the carved wooden pillars to cast any shadows on the floor. As he walked towards the shining white crystal of the scepter, he also noticed that he did not cast any shadow either.

Gazing at the large multifaceted crystal, Berty's mind went blank. All thoughts about the men who camped in the forest exited. In the back of his eyes, he saw the figure of a man strolling through a forest, wearing a long garment like Alfred's covered by a claret cloak like his own. Blinking broke his gaze, and he lost the figure in his mind's eye. Deciding that he was much too tired, he left the Scepter Room and went to bed.

Berty awoke with an ever-increasing sense of foreboding. Looking out his window, he gazed upon the first rays of sunshine peeking over the horizon. He wished that they eased his unsettledness. The sky became lighter with each passing moment as Berty lay motionless in his bed, staring at his dark wood ceiling.

While his eyes followed the intricate branch like pattern on his ceiling, his mind retraced the labyrinth of passageways that he had walked the day before. Searching for a place to hide, the hallways and bridges faded from his thoughts. They were replaced with another memory from yesterday.

The forest was lush with greenery and the canopy of green

leaves filtered the sunlight, keeping the forest floor cool in the summer heat. A man with dark hair wearing a dark red robe with a matching sash tied around his waist under a darker red cloak that floated behind him, strolled through the underbrush. He stopped to close his eyes. Inhaling deeply, he smelled the freshness of the leaves. The man smiled before opening his eyes. Seeing the medium brown irises of the man's eyes, Berty shook his head, then climbed out of bed.

After his shower, he opened his wardrobe and was glad to find brown pants and a blue shirt without any robes or sashes. Looking at himself in the mirror, Berty examined his dark hair, then gazed into the depths of his own eyes that were a medium shade of brown. Taking in his entire appearance, he mumbled, "Why would I want to wear the male version of a dress?" When Berty walked downstairs, the reality of what was lurking in the woods and heading towards the Empire Tree sneaked back into his head to haunt his thoughts.

Outside his chambers, Berty found the basket of food that Theodore placed there overnight. He set it on his table. Figuring that he should eat, he dug inside the basket, pulling out some bread and cheese. Not wanting to sit at his table alone, he sat on one of his club chairs. Forcing the makeshift cheese sandwich into his mouth, he had to think hard about chewing and swallowing, so that he would actually eat.

After his meager breakfast, he walked into the crisp, morning air. Taking a whiff, he figured autumn would last well through the next month. He also knew that Halloween should be right around the corner. Berty had hoped that Mister Hunter, his editor-in-chief, had accepted his creative endeavor installment. In his haste to return to the Land of Sages, Berty had neglected to check his email to see if Mister Hunter had responded. "Too late now," he said quietly to himself, "because he is getting another installment when this is over whether he likes it or not." Smiling, Berty crossed the bridge, entering the trunk of the Empire Tree.

He looked into the dark, narrow hallway, then looked down

the staircase. Deciding which way to go on a whim, Berty turned right. He walked down the hallway, pausing when he reached the door. Taking a deep breath, he stepped through the door into the wide passageway. Berty looked around. Seeing no one, he walked down the stairs that took him to the Scepter Room.

Berty peeked in as he passed, finding it devoid of people. The next landing down was much wider because more than one corridor met at the entrance of the Roundtable Room. Peering through the door, Berty saw Prince Goscislaw unrolling paper over the top of the Roundtable. The Dwarf looked up to see Berty in the doorway.

"Hubert," said Goscislaw in his low growl, "come in and see what I have been working on."

Surprised to be invited to spend time with the Prince, Berty cautiously walked into the room. As he approached the paper covered table, Goscislaw flashed him a smile. Sprawled across the tabletop were what looked liked an architect's blueprints except the paper was an off white and the ink was brown.

"Is this the Empire Tree?" Berty asked.

"Yes. I put it together last night."

Berty gazed at all the passages and bridges marked on the plans. "Just from walking around the Empire Tree?"

"It is just thrown together from memory. Usually, I take exact measurements, but there was not time for that," said Goscislaw. "But I got all the passageways, even the Tenders' passageways."

Berty noticed that he did not have the Empress' private passages anywhere on the blueprints.

"Now, I was thinking about hiding here," Goscislaw said, pointing to a small bridge nestled in the middle of a bunch of other bridges. "I will have the advantage over all of these passages and can use the pulley system to distract and confuse." The Prince pointed to other bridges, then produced yet another piece of paper depicting the pulleys. "What do you think?"

Stunned, it took Berty a second to reply. "I think that it is a great idea."

Rubbing his hands together, Goscislaw gritted his teeth while growling. He was obviously pleased with his plan. Berty walked back out to the landing, hearing the Dwarf Prince say, "Gotcha!"

Down another flight of stairs, Berty finally reached the end of the staircase. He walked through the Reception Room to find Theodore magically filling the room with tables and chairs. The young Dwarf stood in the center of the room, conducting tables and chairs that floated out of storage areas around the round room. Smiling, Berty nodded at Theodore as he passed to the next staircase.

At the bottom of the stairs, the empty Receiving Room was dark. Through the darkness, Berty maneuvered his way to the large doors. Finding them locked, he thought about having the doors opened. Instantly, he heard a series of clicks, then the doors opened before him, flooding the room with sunlight.

Berty stepped onto the sunlit dirt path. He breathed in deeply, filling his lungs with the chilly, autumn air. His nose could smell the different colored leaves that had fallen on the still warm earth. Feeling grounded, he strolled down the deserted path. Approaching the gates, he noticed the former Empire Guards queuing to leave the Sages' Grove.

"Hubert, wait," called Alvar. Stopping, Berty waited for the Elf as he jogged up the path. Alvar wore a brown shirt and pants. Berty almost did not recognize Alvar without his leather armor. When Alvar reached Berty, he looked over his shoulder at the men leaving the gates, saying, "Let us walk."

Berty walked with Alvar who towered over him, making Berty feel like a child. After a few paces, Alvar said, "I know that there is no longer an Empire Guard or an Advisory Council. But I feel the need to report to someone and share what has happened." Berty did not know what to make of the Elf's declaration, so he stayed silent, waiting for Alvar to continue speaking. "Every building in the Sages' Grove is vacant. My men did a final check this morning. All the excess weapons and armor are securely hidden. The Goblins hold the keys to the storage areas." He stopped walking and looked out into the empty Sages' Grove. "Is the Empress doing well?"

"Yes."

"She is a strong woman. I have never met anyone like her," said Alvar, still gazing ahead of him. "When the Pixie Priestess sang her song making the prophecy, I thought that she would collapse under the strain. I was wrong. The next day, she emerged stronger and more resolute than ever." He chuckled. "I never saw her unleash more anger than when she discovered that Leif and Millicent had conspired behind her back. I am sure you heard about that."

"Yes, I did."

Alvar chuckled again, then looked at Berty with a softness in his stoic face. "I respect her highly, not just as an Empress, but as a person." The Elf sighed. "I will abide by her orders to leave the Sages' Grove even if I do not like it."

Berty looked at Alvar, who seemed lost in his thoughts. "She respects you a great deal as well," Berty said. "Her orders are to keep you and your men as safe as possible."

Alvar looked out into the lifeless village. "She puts others before herself. I would not be surprised if she sacrificed herself to save the Empire. Such is the duty of an Empress, I suppose." Alvar stood, gazing at the gleaming white, sunlit buildings for a few moments before glancing at Berty. The Elf gave him a sharp nod. Berty watched Alvar join the other dispatched Empire Guards waiting to exit through the Sages' Grove's gates.

Berty continued his stroll through the Sages' Grove. The winding, dirt path took him past more white cob buildings with highly pitched thatched roofs. Every now and then, dormers would peek through the thatching, giving the houses what appeared to be eyes watching over the vacant village. Berty wandered off the main path through the homes and storefronts. Reaching the wall, he was surprised to find it so thick. He walked along the wall, passing doors that allowed entry into the fortifications.

Finding his way to the barracks, he noticed that its windows were mere narrow slits. Berty walked past the massive wooden doors, then stopped. He stood among the empty buildings, looking around. Off to one side, he could see straw archery targets. In another direction, he had a clear view of the gates of the Sages' Grove. Looking above, Berty could barely make out rope and plank bridges that connected the outer edges to the Empire Tree at the very center.

Even though everyone had gone, Berty felt comfortable as if he had come home. He was filled with a sense of belonging that he had never felt before. The growling of his stomach brought his thoughts out of the abstract. Berty remembered what Silvia had said about how Sean and his men were coming whether they ate or not. Deciding that he needed to eat, he walked towards the doors of the Empire Tree.

Back on the main path, Hatcher came running up to Berty. "Hubert," said the Troll in a panic, "will any of the Heads be leaving before...?" He could not finish the sentence.

"No," Berty answered. "Everyone is where they are going to be."

Hatcher looked at Berty in disbelief. "Everyone has been evacuated. I will be locking the gates after I leave, which will be very soon." He looked away for a moment, then said, "Tell the Empress that I will be ready to return whenever she is ready."

"I will."

"Good luck," said Hatcher. He did not wait for Berty to respond before he hurried down the path out of the Sages' Grove.

Hearing a series of clicks, Berty knew that Hatcher had magically locked the gates to the Sages' Grove. Inside the Empire Tree, Berty waited until he was on the stairs before he made the doors close and lock themselves. After he was plunged into darkness, he carefully climbed the stairs to the Reception Room.

At the top of the stairs, Berty met Elrick staring at the Reception Room littered with tables and chairs. "Hello, Hubert," said Elrick, not turning his head.

"Hello," Berty answered back.

"Tell me something," said Elrick. He squinted, making calculations. "If you were coming through here, intent on reaching the Empress, which path would you use?"

Berty stared at the maze. "Well, if I walked onto the dais, then I would have an unobstructed path. But, that would make me more visible to an attacker." Elrick nodded. "So," Berty continued, "I would weave through the tables to be able to use them as a cover. I would also make sure that I went very slowly so that I did not hit into anything, announcing my presence."

"Good observation," said Elrick. "I see why the Empress trusts you implicitly." The Fairy King turned to look at Berty. "Do you think it would be better to lure them into a false sense of security?"

Berty stared at him. "Lida and I are deciding between a couple of different spots," Elrick explained.

"I think that when they leave the Reception Room, they will split among the different routes. It will be easier to pick off a divided group. Did Prince Goscislaw tell you where he will be?" asked Berty.

"Yes. And I agree with your evaluation," Elrick replied. "Lida and I will fight over the first spot." He chuckled. "I will not allow my wife to be on the front lines, so to speak. Well, I must get back to her. See you soon." The Fairy King took a few steps forward before his purplish blue wings unfolded off his back. His wings spread twice as wide as his body and about a foot longer. The top pointed gently, then gradually widened to create a bulbous area before tapering inward towards his legs. They skirted out with flare to another rounded point at the bottom. Elrick flapped his wings gracefully, like a butterfly, ascending over the tables. The candlelight from the chandeliers glistened in the multifaceted sparkle of the purples and blues as if mother of pearl glitter covered his wings. Berty watched him bob ever so slightly up and down as he flew to the other end of the room.

Berty's stomach growled again as he climbed the steps of the dais. Choosing to use the private staircase, he disappeared behind the Sages' Seal. When he reached the next landing, he glanced into the Roundtable Room. Berty saw Alfred, alone in the room, muttering to himself in a language that Berty could not discern as he moved around the table. Not wanting to spy, Berty kept walking up the stairs and across the bridge.

Outside his door, rested a small parcel wrapped in a cloth. He placed the parcel on his desk as he hung his cloak. Untying the knot on the top, the cloth fell away to reveal a small platter of extra food and drink. Berty smiled as he picked up the platter placing it on his table. He sat at his table, alone, to begin eating a large lunch.

Refusing to eat alone at his table seemed silly to Berty. Silvia wanted him to eat. She counted on him to keep his strength. He could not let her down. His mind recounted the morning as he ate. Berty still felt weird about how both Alvar and Hatcher had to report to him. He also thought it strange that Goscislaw and Elrick had asked him for advice.

Berty was not used to being in some sort of authoritative position. He spent the majority of his life following orders from one newspaper or another. Here he was in the Land of Sages because he had followed orders from his editor-in-chief. Now, he was suddenly plunged into being a leader. As weirdly inexplicable as he felt, he could not help but notice how easily he slid into the role. Smiling, Berty finished his lunch.

Chapter Twelve
Strength Within

With his stomach full, Berty had no reason to stay in his study all afternoon. Not having a destination in mind, he stepped onto the sun filled bridge leading into the Empire Tree. As he walked, he could not believe that anything foreboding was on the horizon. It was a perfect autumn afternoon where the sun warmed his face only to be cooled by the occasional breeze.

Entering the trunk, Berty hesitated for only a second before he turned right, strolling down the narrow passageway. An impulse made him turn suddenly and step through the wall. Darkness surrounded him. Immediately, he thought about lighting the candles in the room. All at once, flames danced over melted wax tapers. Berty stood alone in the flickering candlelight in the middle of the small round room. He looked at all the scrolls and old faded bindings of tomes he was sure that Silvia had read years ago. Turning his head away from the shelves, he examined the old wooden table that was loaded with scorch marks. For the first time, he noticed a handful of old, wooden chairs. His fingers ran over the smooth looking tabletop, feeling the slight bumps and divots in the rich, warm wood. Sitting in one of the chairs, his eyes glanced around the room once more. The room did not look like a place to practice sorcery. He found it to be a cozy place to do work or study.

The candlelight illuminated the chairs around the room. Berty counted six chairs that were all the same. He turned to look at the chair on which he sat, noticing that it matched the other six. "Seven chairs," he breathed. He looked around the room once more. "Odd," he said. Chuckling at the unintended pun, Berty remembered what Silvia said around the fire about how the Seven High Sages crafted the scepter. "What happened to them?" Standing, Berty took a last look around, deciding that he should be practicing his magic in the open. Thinking about extinguishing the candles, he was plunged back into darkness before he stepped through the wall.

In the narrow passage, he walked towards the private staircase. Down the steps, he paused at the first landing, then walked through the door. The Scepter Room looked the same as before. Berty wondered if the room had ever changed since the creation of the scepter. The eerie florescent like light thrown by the crystal sconces made him uneasy. Walking through the room to the other door, he searched for his shadow, but found none. He paused at the doorway, turning around. Staring at the large crystal of the scepter, Berty felt that perhaps nothing had changed, but it was just a matter of time before change came to the Scepter Room.

Berty galloped down the common stairs to the next landing. He peeked into the Roundtable Room, finding it empty. Deciding that it was too nice to stay within the trunk, Berty stepped onto the bridge that led to the Advisory Council's chambers. Halfway across the bridge, he stopped. Looking down at the bridges below, he saw Alfred and Goscislaw walking, deep in discussion. Berty wondered if either Head felt nervous, scared or intense trepidation about the coming onslaught. None of those had completely sunk into his head. He figured that his body and mind were numb from everything that had happened over the past few days.

However, the numbness did not come with fear. He did not know why. Never had he experienced anything remotely life threatening. The closest he had ever come to being scared for his life was when he just started driving as a teenager. A few months after getting his driver's license, Berty was driving his friends home from a fun night. To get everyone home by curfew, he took a shortcut that he knew well. It had snowed earlier that day and the wind began to pick up during the evening. His friends were chatting exuberantly about their evening.

Listening to the conversation, he kept his eyes on the dark, windy, mountain road. The car's headlights were never as strong as he would have liked, but he did not complain because at least he had a car. Pulling back the small, plastic stick behind the steering wheel, the high beams illuminated the sparkling branches that reached over the road, giving it a tunnel feel. Berty had wondered when the ice glazed the trees, but the thought was pushed from his mind when someone asked him a question from the backseat. He glanced into the rearview mirror. By the time his eyes' gaze found the road again, the tires began to lose their grip on the road.

The car spun out of control. Berty held tightly onto the steering wheel. Somewhere in the background, he could hear the screams of his friends. In the forefront, he heard metal scraping metal. Looking into the side view mirror, he saw a series of dents in the guardrail. Every time he turned the steering wheel to try to straighten out the car, ice caused the car to overcompensate.

Down the hill they slid on the ice covered road. Berty was helpless to stop the inertia. He threw the car into a lower gear and pumped his brakes, but the car only slid faster. The light of the high beams revealed a car sized hole in the metal guardrail. The road curved sharply to the left, but they were traveling too fast to make the turn. Berty frantically turned the wheel. Luckily, the car was able to stay on the road. His passengers were shaken when rubber finally found pavement once they rounded the curve.

Standing on the bridge, Berty tried to remember how much luck was on his side that night. His mind brought him back to the driver's seat seconds before the car approached the gaping hole in the guardrail. His friend in the passenger seat was screaming about there being a hole and how they were going to wind up down the steep hill. Trying to ignore the hysteria, his right foot was still trying to pump the brakes. Both of his hands were tightly grasping the leather steering wheel. In his mind, he was saying, "Stay on the road. Come on car, stay on the road." His grip slacked. The wheel spun left on its own accord. The back end of the car stopped sliding mid-fishtail. The car cut the corner close to the inside. As soon as the front tires found pavement, the low gear kicked in, slowing the car.

The Elf and Dwarf came back into focus as Berty whispered to himself, "I willed the car to stay on the road. I used magic back then and never even realized...."

When he first discovered that he could do magic, he thought it was because he was in the Land of Sages, a magical place. He realized that he had magic all along. Coming to the Land of Sages helped him recognize his magical potential.

Looking away from the two men below, his gaze rested among the reds and yellows of the leaves. In his mind, he thanked Silvia for bringing him to this world. Berty closed his eyes. He saw Silvia's face glittered with tears. Opening his eyes, he walked back inside the trunk of the Empire Tree.

Berty slowly descended the steps. His mind replayed the image of Silvia's tear streaked face. He wondered why he thought of her crying. Reaching the bottom of the steps, he walked into the Reception Room, then sat on the lowest step of the dais. He looked out at the sea of chairs and tables, picturing Silvia's face.

Silvia seemed so strong to Berty. Nothing could shake her or break her spirit. He could not imagine anything that would make her forlorn. Then he thought of Sean's conspiracy against her. Berty closed his eyes, trying to imagine why Silvia, so strong, would cry. He saw Silvia sitting on one of her yellow couches in her study, looking at a picture. The black and white picture showed a happy couple with two small children in front of Silvia's Victorian house. The woman was thin with dark hair. The man looked like a younger version of his editor, Mister Hunter with light hair. The mother was holding the hand of the small girl who had dark ringlets covering her head. Holding the father's hand, the boy was older and seemed to enjoy picture taking with his family.

"I'm so sorry," Silvia whispered. A new tear streaked down her face. "Why didn't I see the signs?" She wiped her face dry with a lace edged handkerchief. "What could I have done to stop it?" Her fingers ran over the picture. "Perhaps it was meant to come. Perhaps this is what the Empire needs." She placed the picture on her table, then walked away.

Opening his eyes, Berty marveled at the vividness of his imagination. Playing the scene over in his head, he figured that disappointing her family would be devastating. Silvia came from a long line of Empresses who have always been the keepers of the secrets of the Empire. "To be on the edge of losing that, Silvia would feel as though she could not live up to the rest of her family," Berty murmured.

Staring at the sea of tables and chairs, memories that he would had hoped to have forgotten forever flooded into his mind. His mind's eye saw the disappointed look on his father's face when Berty told him that he wanted to become a journalist instead of following in his father's footsteps. Berty was between junior and senior year in high school, pouring over different college booklets. They were spread all over the kitchen table when his father walked into the room and began to pick up a few.

"Did you send away for all of these?" asked his father.

"No," Berty replied. "They came because of my SAT scores."

His father perused one. "This place looks like it has a great engineering program," he said as he pushed it towards his son.

Berty looked at it, saying, "I'm not looking for an engineering program."

"What do you mean?"

Berty's eyes found his father's eyes. "I want to go to a place with a good liberal arts college or school of journalism."

His father's eyes flashed. "You want to waste your time writing?"

Berty could say nothing, but his father continued raising his voice.

"I thought this writing thing was just a fad or something that you could use in the business somehow. But you actually want to throw your life away, writing."

A thousand replies entered Berty's young mind. He wanted to answer that he would not be throwing his life away or that he loved the way words created magic on the page. However, Berty sat there silently, looking at his father standing beside the table, breathing hard.

His mother entered the kitchen. The smile on her faced faded when she saw her husband's face. "What's the matter?" she asked.

"He does well in school," Berty's father answered. "He does well on his college entrance exams and what does he want to do with his life? Write his life away!"

"George," said Berty's mother, "were you not the one who always said that you have to love what you do?"

"What's not to love, Kate?" George looked at his son, saying, "What a waste." Shaking his head, he walked away.

Kate walked over to her son as he sat dumbstruck at the kitchen table and comforted the young Berty.

The Reception Room came back into focus. His mind rewound further back. As a boy, Berty remembered how his father was never home. He was always out, selling to and servicing for his clients. Kate was left home with Berty and his younger brother while George traipsed around the country. Every few days, George would hop another plane to somewhere. When his father was home, Berty barely saw him. George would spend the majority of his free time at his plant, overseeing its operations.

Most nights were spent at the same kitchen table either with the three of them eating or with his mother helping them with their homework. While Berty was in the fifth grade, the teacher assigned a writing project. Kate was busy helping his brother as Berty placed a blank piece of lined paper on the table. He picked up the pencil. When he touched the graphite to the paper, words flowed out of the point into the spaces between the thin, blue lines. As a feeling of euphoria washed over him, a smile stretched across his young face. When he finished his assignment, George walked into the kitchen, looking weary. He slumped into a chair, and Kate rose out of her chair to retrieve her husband's lukewarm dinner. She placed it in front of George, then leaned over Berty to check his work.

"That's very good, Berty," Kate exclaimed.

"Thanks, Mom."

"George, read what your son wrote," said Kate.

George looked up from his dinner. "What? Oh, in a minute."

Kate looked at Berty again. "Do you have any other homework?"

Berty shook his head.

She glanced over at her husband, then said to Berty, "Why don't you leave your work here so that your father can read it when he's done with his dinner and you can go get ready for bed."

"Okay, Mom." Berty jumped off his chair. After kissing his parents goodnight, he followed his brother's path to bed.

As soon as the swinging kitchen door swung closed behind him, he heard his father's voice. "Why do I have to read what he wrote?"

"Because it is good," said Kate. "He's got a burgeoning talent."

Berty tiptoed back to the kitchen door to listen.

"What does it matter?" George asked. "It isn't like writing talent can get him anywhere."

"George, being able to write is important."

"I know it is, Kate, but math and science are more so." During a pause, Berty's breath stopped. "Don't encourage it Kate. I don't want some namby-pamby writer for a son."

Berty's heart sank to his knees and he trudged up the stairs. He never forgot how great it felt when he placed words on paper. However, Berty always made sure that he did as well in math and science as he did in English throughout his schooling.

Berty's eyes glazed over as he stared at the flickering flames of the chandelier. Growing up, Berty knew that his father was building his business so that he and his brother could have a better life. However, it was not something that he wanted for himself. The workings of machines did not interest him. The workings of words captured him. His brother joined his father in the business. In time, his father forgave him and accepted his decision even if his father did not understand it.

His mind flashed back to the day he graduated from college. Dressed in his black cap and gown, Berty and his family entered the arena in which the graduation ceremony was being held. Like other families in the vestibule, Kate hugged her son as she fought back tears. A sign told graduates to head down the hall to the right and their guests to the left.

"We're so proud of you," said Kate.

Berty's brother touched his mother's shoulder. "We'll see Berty soon," he said. "We need to grab our seats."

"You are right, Jon," said Kate. She adjusted Berty's golden honor sash and smiled at her son before turning down the hall.

"I'll be with you two in a minute," George said. Reaching in his pocket, he handed two tickets to Jon. "Here are your tickets so that you can get inside." He put his arm on Berty's back to steer him down the graduate's hall.

Other parents also escorted their sons and daughters to stand in their lines. For a few minutes, all Berty could focus on was the clicking sound of their dress shoes on the cement floor. The clicking ceased. George stopped walking. Looking at his father, Berty was surprised to see his eyes filled with tears.

"I could have not been prouder of you, Berty. I know I gave you a hard time about wanting to write growing up," George said. "But you stuck with it, no matter what. You have proved to be stronger than I ever could have imagined. Stronger than I was at your age or any age. Such fortitude does not come without its trials and life will be full of them. I won't have to worry about you because you have an inner strength that you tap, which is truly amazing."

"A through C line up here," bellowed a voice down the hall.

"That's me, Dad."

George smiled at Berty, giving his son a hug. Berty walked into alphabetical order, holding his head high with tears in his eyes and a smile on his face.

Staring at the flames, Berty had to blink a few times before his eyes registered that the sun was setting. Taking a deep breath, he looked around the room. The reds and golds streaming through the windows and doors reflected upon the shiny walls, bouncing around the room. Berty sat, bathed in the warm glow, remembering walking through the portal between the trees in the woods. He recalled drawing the wand from his cloak pocket. His hand dove into his pocket, clutching the smooth wood. Sean's cold gray eyes, full of malice, swam into his mind. "Inner strength," Berty whispered.

Standing on the step upon which he had been sitting, Berty looked at the orderly mess of chairs and tables. With two swipes of his hands, it became a less orderly mess. Berty smiled, knowing that it was going to be much harder for Sean and his men to traverse the room undetected. Satisfied, he turned to walk onto the dais. His eyes glanced at the empty throne and an uneasy feeling filled the pit of his stomach. He closed his eyes, took a deep breath, then continued walking.

Berty's body followed his feet, as they clearly knew the way. Opening his eyes, he found himself walking up the private staircase. With each step, his head became more clear and his thoughts more focused. He saw Sean's cold, accusing, gray eyes clearly in the forefront of his mind. Berty knew what he needed to do. When the stairs ended, his feet led him down the dark, narrow hallway, through the door, across the wide, public passageway, and up the stairs to the Star Gazing Area.

Berty walked over to the railing, resting his hands on the smooth, round wood. As he gazed upon the treetops glistening in the moonlight, he raised his hood. Thoughts of Silvia and the gold Watcher's Locket entered his mind. A soft breeze rippled across the forest, making the leaves flutter and blowing off his hood. In the corner of his eye, he caught a glimpse of a glowing figure coming to a halt behind him. He turned.

"Silvia," Berty said, "are you—?"

"I am fine," Silvia interrupted. The moonlight illuminated a hard, blazing fire in her eyes. "A faction of two dozen will be arriving first on horseback." With Berty's eyes captured in the moonlight that danced in her hair, she thrust the large, gold locket into his hand. "Take this. You know how to use it. Watch through Declan's eyes." His hands registered the warm metal on his cool skin. Silvia pressed both her hands on his and closed her eyes. Berty relished her touch. "It will be okay," she said, opening her eyes. Her brown eyes found his, lingering for a moment. Without another word, she released his hands and backed away from him. While he watched her hair and eyes gleam in the moonlight, Silvia quickly turned. Her shining light blue cloak billowed around her as she descended into the Empire Tree.

Berty's eyes transfixed on the empty space where Silvia's shining cloak disappeared. The moonlight and the darkness kept the light blue image in the front of his sight. His hand clutched onto the hard, warm metal as the glittering gold chain swayed in the chilly, autumn breeze. When the shiny blue imprint finally faded to darkness, his eyes looked away to find the next shining object.

Lifting his hand to waist level, Berty unclenched his fingers around the oblong, metal object. Turning the locket over in his hand, the eye within the Watcher's symbol gleamed in the moonlight. Listening intently, he pushed into the background the sounds of the nocturnal creatures of the forest, and brought to the forefront the sounds coming from inside the Empire Tree. After a minute of hearing nothing, Berty glanced around, making sure that he was alone. Without hesitation, he sat on the floor, prodding the eye with the rod clasp. When it depressed, Berty opened the locket, just like he had seen Silvia do.

When a picture appeared on the one side of the locket, he knew that he did everything correctly. Passing his hand over the locket the campfire around which Declan and the others sat, burst to life in front of Berty. His ears could hear the logs crackle and pop while they produced large flames, which danced before his eyes. The high reaching tongues of reddish orange illuminated the faces of the men who appeared to huddle around the fire with him.

Berty did not recognize any of the dozen or so men but two.

Sitting on the other side of the flames was Sean. It was as if he were back in the clearing surrounded by large stones while Silvia told her stories. The fire separated them then as it separated Sean from Declan now. He could clearly see how Sean's flat nose and dark, straight hair framed his beady, gray eyes. Berty's breath quickened. Tearing his eyes from the face he despised, he looked at the lank, stringy, light hair of Sean's henchman sitting beside him. The man's blue eyes looked at Sean with reverence. The other men, Berty was relieved to see, did not mimic his reverence. He felt as if he could touch these men and tell them to run from Sean's selfish guidance. However, as close as everyone around the fire seemed to Berty, none of the flames' warmth reached his hands or face.

"Men," said Sean from across the fire, breaking through the silence with his breathy, mouse like voice, "we are approaching the pinnacle of our mission. As far away as we are to the Empire Tree, the morning's approach must be slow and quiet. We do not want to give the Empire Guard time to assemble. Now, there is only one entrance to the Sages' Grove and likewise, only one entrance to the Empire Tree. The entrances are not in line with one another, so we must calculate our moves carefully.

"You have all been provided with a rough map of the Sage's Grove. I hope you have been studying it closely. It will be difficult to traverse the relatively short distance from the gates to the door of the Empire Tree. Once a good number of us, although I would prefer all of us, get inside the Empire Tree, two of us must close and secure the doors. While two are keeping watch on the doors, the rest of us must fight our way to the upper levels. The scepter is kept at or around the top of the Empire Tree. Our goal is to reach the scepter so that the magic stored within its crystal can be released."

"Surely we cannot release the magic from the scepter ourselves," said a doubting voice next to Declan.

"No," answered Sean. "You must guard it. Whoever finds the Empress, must bring her to the scepter."

"Then we force her to release the magic?" asked the same voice.

"Yes," said Sean with a gleam in his gray eyes, "but leave that to me."

The men sat silently around the fire, apparently contemplating Sean's words and the day ahead. In the shadows, the taller of Sean's two accomplices walked outside the circle of men, stopping to lean against a tree behind Sean. The dying fire crackled and sputtered through the silence. Declan's eyes followed each man as he left his seat around the fire and went into his tent for the night. As the fire died, Sean and his companion got up to go into their much larger tent, which they shared.

Declan checked his arrows in the fading light. After watching Declan for a moment, the dark man leaning in the shadows entered the tent. Declan glimpsed a lock of dirty, blond hair hanging limply in the tent's entrance. The dying fire illuminated Wagner's eye as he spied on Declan. In response, Declan continued his performance of gathering his arrows. He did not have to look directly at Sean's tent to see Wagner spying on him.

Entering his tent, Declan noisily placed his quiver on the ground. After he blew out his lantern, he crept into bed.

"All clear," said the raspy voice of Wagner through the darkness. "Everyone is in bed."

"Good," Sean's voice said. His soft voice carried through the tents.

"Killing the Empress still in the plans?" asked Wagner.

"Of course."

"Then why didn't you say anything?"

"These men do not need to know all the details," Sean answered. "If I had told them, I do not know if they would have the courage to storm the Sages' Grove and penetrate the Empire Tree."

"Without these men, we would not be able to get inside anything," said the third man's deep voice. "Use your head." Hearing a hand slapping a skull, Berty knew that Wagner was reprimanded for his stupidity.

Berty did not need to hear anymore. Shutting the locket, he proceeded into the warmth of the Empire Tree. What bothered Berty the most was that Sean had asked these men to risk their very lives to help restore the magic without telling them the one crucial detail. Would any of them have agreed to go along with Sean had they known Sean's assassination plot? Berty hoped the answer was no. Deep in thought as he descended the stairs into the wide common passageway, he walked into Goscislaw, also deep in thought.

"I am so sorry," said Berty.

"It is okay, Hubert," growled the Dwarf. "Nothing like a nighttime stroll to get the mind moving."

"Yes," Berty agreed. Looking at the wizened Dwarf, he realized that he needed to know. "Goscislaw, you know that Sean has every intention of killing the Empress?"

"Yes, of course."

"What you do not know, is that Sean has not informed his men of his intention."

A look of shock washed over Goscislaw's face. "That makes him much more despicable." His eyes narrowed. "He cares not for anyone but himself."

"Only two of his men know the full extent of his plan," said Berty.

"Two does not make it any better," Goscislaw said in disgust. "Does the Empress know this?"

Berty answered, "Yes." He did not know how he was so certain of his answer. "The ones who do not know are Alfred, Elrick and Lida."

"I will inform them of this selfish treachery. Thank you for telling me." The Dwarf started to walk down the passageway.

"Goscislaw," Berty called, not knowing what made him get a sudden wave of inspiration, "I think that it would be best for everyone involved if we do our best to try to avoid seriously harming these people that unwittingly help Sean attempt to achieve his dastardly deeds."

"That will not be easy for us to do." Goscislaw thought hard for a moment. "But I agree that it would be the best thing to do if we can help it."

Berty watched the Dwarf Prince walk into the shadows between the sconces as he determinedly walked down the wide hallway. When he disappeared from view, Berty stepped through the wall, emerging in the dark, private hallway. He let his eyes adjust briefly to the lack of light before continuing. After taking a few steps, he stopped, realizing that he was outside the hidden entrance to the Sorcery Room. His mind drifted to thoughts of Silvia, and he wondered if she was inside. His foot made an involuntary movement towards the wall. Stopping it, he figured that she wanted to be alone, but then he hoped that maybe she would not mind if he joined her. Berty stood in the dark hallway, placed his hand on the wall and began to close his eyes. The sound of echoing footsteps snapped open his eye lids. Quickly stepping away from the room's entrance, he continued to walk down the dark, narrow hall. By the doorway to the bridge, he met Silvia who had just ascended from the stairway.

They both stopped at the doorway. She smiled warmly at him as her hand reached for his hand. Gazing into her warm, brown eyes, Berty gently collapsed his hand around hers. He could feel nothing except Silvia's soft hand. His thumb lightly stroked the back of her hand. A single tear escaped from her eyes, flowing down her cheek. With his free hand, Berty barely touched her cheek while he delicately wiped it away. Lingering at the curve of her cheekbone, his fingers reveled in the softness of her skin, longing to know the silkiness of her hair. As his hand slid further back and caressed her hair, Silvia closed her eyes. A soft smile appeared on her lips while her breath deepened. Berty took a step closer, inhaling the smell of berries, then whispered, "I will not let anything happen to you."

Opening her eyes, she looked up at Berty, merely inches away from her face, then breathed, "I know." With an intake of breath, she stepped backwards. Silvia delicately pulled her hand out of his, saying, "You will be able to get through the portal without me." Looking away from him, she ran across the bridge, leaving a confused Berty in her wake.

Wondering what exactly she meant, he watched her light blue cloak disappear from view. Slowly, Berty crossed the bridge, feeling the crisp, autumnal breeze sting his face. When he reached his door, he glanced longingly towards Silvia's chambers before grabbing his basket and walking inside.

Casting his cloak aside, Berty placed the basket of food on his table. He noticed a note on the top. Hastening to open it, he recognized Silvia's handwriting. He read:

> *My dearest Berty,*
>
> *The short time spent with you has been an enthralling experience, even given the circumstances. I want to thank you for trusting me and for believing in me. Your support has meant everything to me and from it I have been able to gather strength.*
>
> *Whatever happens, I want you to write about it and give it to your editor, Martin Hunter. You will be able to get back to the house through the portal in my chambers without me, if need be. Please continue to practice and use your magic.*
>
> *Eternally Yours,*
>
> *Silvia*

Finally understanding what she said at the bridge crossing, he read her words a few more times, then walked over to his desk. Tucking the note into his bag, Berty opened his notebook to write another chapter of the *Adventures of Leigh and Marcus* before going to sleep.

Chapter Thirteen
The Storm in All Her Fury

Berty startled awake. He sat up in the semi-darkness as the moonlight crept across his bed. Following the moonlight, he looked out the window, knowing that dawn was nowhere near approaching. Looking away from the moon, his eyes searched his room in the darkness. As his eyes allowed objects within his room to form, Berty's eyes caught the shining, gold Watcher's locket on his bedside table. Instinct told him that he should see what was happening. Grabbing the locket off the table, he stared at the eye within the six-pointed star. His curiosity took hold as he depressed the eye, opening the locket.

Declan's eyes stared into the inside of his dark tent, but his ears were listening to the surrounding conversation.

"Wagner," said Sean's mousy voice, cutting through the darkness, "wake everyone. We need to move within the hour if we wish to arrive at the Empire Tree by daybreak."

Declan closed his eyes, waiting to be awakened by Wagner.

Placing the open locket on his night table, Berty climbed out of bed. During his quick shower, he wondered if he was ready to face them. After he pulled on his brown clothes, he grabbed the open locket. Peering into the window, Declan packed his belongings. Suppressing a queasy feeling deep inside, he took a deep breath and proceeded down his spiral staircase to force some food into his stomach.

Searching his basket, Berty found a flask of juice and easy to carry food. He drank some juice to moisten his mouth and throat, but to no avail. Scratching the roof of his mouth with his tongue, Berty placed a couple of rolls and a few pieces of fruit into his pockets. Checking the locket's window, Declan was still packing. Berty threw his cloak over his shoulders. Carefully clutching the open locket in hand, he made sure that his wand was tucked safely in his cloak. Berty took a last glance around his study before he walked into the crisp, early morning air.

The sun still had not risen, but the dark sky had begun to lighten to navy blue. Looking at the bridge in front of him, the cool air caressed his face, melting any queasiness. With a newly found strength, he crossed the bridge and descended the stairs until he reached the Reception Room. Not a sound found his ears except the rustling of Declan's tent.

Emerging from behind the Sages' Seal, Berty sat on the edge of the dais. He glanced at the clutter of chairs and tables. Removing a piece of fruit from his pocket, he held it in his teeth while his hand passed over the open locket, watching through the Watcher's eyes.

Berty chewed his food as he watched Declan secure his belongings to his horse. The Fairy King and Queen emerged from the side corridor. Lida turned to walk up the main stairs, but Elrick stopped, staring at the scene playing in front of Berty.

"What is that?" he asked.

Berty briefly tore his gaze away from Declan's preparations to see Elrick captivated by the scene. Before Berty could answer the Fairy, Goscislaw and Alfred materialized from the same corridor, talking in hurried voices until the Dwarf Prince almost walked into the Fairy King. The almost collision brought the scene to both the Dwarf's and Elf's attention.

"We are seeing through the eyes of a Watcher," Berty answered, knowing that every eye looked in his direction.

"Fascinating," exclaimed Alfred. He walked towards the holographic image of Declan helping the others secure their packs to their horses. "I have never seen such magic in use before."

Declan checked his bow and quiver before mounting his horse. Once he was securely seated in his saddle, Sean and his men mounted their horses a few feet in front of Declan. Berty's eyes narrowed as loathing enveloped him. "See that man," said Berty with clear disgust in his voice, "with the dark hair. He is the leader. Sean is his name."

"So that is the filthy usurper?" growled Goscislaw.

"Yes," Berty answered. "Those two men who flank him are the only two who know Sean's true intentions."

The Dwarf spat on the ground.

"We will be able to know when they are upon us," said Alfred. "May we sit and wait?"

"Yes, of course," Berty replied.

Elrick pulled two chairs from the staged melee. Joining her husband, Lida sat on one and he on the other. Goscislaw sat on the bottom step on Berty's left. On Berty's right, Alfred climbed to the top step and sat next to him. The four Heads and Berty huddled around the hologram, watching in silence as the men rode through the ever lightening forest. The carpet and the canopy of the forest muffled the clomping of the horses' hooves. Sean was careful to keep the horses at a friendly, trotting pace. Sunlight had fully crept along the sky when Declan's eyes rested on the treed wall of the Sages' Grove. The circle of voyeurs stiffened when Sean raised a hand to stop the following men.

Sean paused for a moment to stare at the wall. He turned his body to his men saying, "We need a look out. Any volunteers?"

"I will go," said Declan. "As a trained archer, I have an advantage. It will be easy for me. At any sign of trouble, I will shoot an arrow this way."

"Good man," said Sean. "We will await word here." Declan dismounted, securing his horse to a nearby tree. With his bow in his hand and quiver on his back, the Watcher sneaked into the surrounding forest towards the Sages' Grove.

Declan cautiously weaved through the trees. Looking over his shoulder, Sean and the others could no longer see him. He threw his arm over his back and removed his quiver. His right hand delved deep inside, pushing the arrows aside. When it emerged, a long, thin, wooden wand extended from his fingers. Declan slung his quiver over his back, then proceeded through the forest with the wand clutched tightly in his hand.

The woods through which he walked had an eerie stillness. It was as if the birds had already flown south for the onset of winter and the squirrels and rabbits had already climbed into their hidey-holes for hibernation. The closer that he walked to the wall of trees that surrounded the Sages' Grove, the more unnaturally quiet the forest became. With the gates to the Sages' Grove in sight, Declan climbed a nearby tree with catlike precision.

Resting on a thick limb, his eyes searched both the trees around the area and the Sages' Grove's wall of trees. His scan found nothing. Signs of life were nowhere. As his eyes continued to scan the area, Declan's breath quickened. Berty knew that the Watcher could sense something out of place. The wand in his hand twitched slightly as he turned to face towards the trunk of the tree.

A slight thud-like noise in the tree made his hand clutch both his wand and his bow more tightly. Declan stood, watching an Elf materialize from thin air while approaching his position. Berty recognized the Elf to be Lieutenant Edwin.

"I have no intentions of harming you," whispered Edwin. His palms were open and empty. He glanced quickly at the large, golden locket hanging from Declan's neck. "You are the Watcher?"

"I am." The wand and bow lowered from view.

"The Captain of the Empire Guard thanks you for your bravery, Watcher. Your information has been very useful. Perhaps a little more would not go amiss. How many men approach with you?" Edwin asked.

"There are about two dozen now," answered Declan. "We are to be followed by about one hundred and fifty soon after."

"Thank you. I think it may be best if you do not let your true nature be shown," said Edwin. "We will not expose you. When you approach again, you will not see us. Perhaps you should go back and report. They will wonder where you have gone."

Declan watched Edwin disappear back into the tree. After climbing down the tree, he hid his wand deep in his quiver before carefully making his way back to the waiting men.

"Well?" asked Sean as Declan emerged from the wood.

"I saw nothing," Declan answered. "However, the gates to the Sages' Grove are closed."

"I have heard that they have begun to keep the gates closed more often," said Sean. "At any rate we approach carefully. You have done well, Declan."

Declan nodded in thanks, walking towards his horse.

Tearing his eyes away from the scene, Berty looked at the others sitting beside him. Their gazes were still fixated on the hologram. "It is time," he said. Each Head focused on Berty in turn while slowly nodding. One by one, they rose walking away to take their positions.

The sound of the Heads' footsteps faded. Berty found himself alone again. He passed his hand over the open locket in reverse. The picture resumed its play inside the confines of the oval while the sound emitted only from the other side of the open locket. Walking behind the Sages' Seal, Berty sat on the steps, watched and waited.

Sean and his men slowly rode their horses closer to the wall of trees. A few yards from the expansive gap between the forest and the wall, he raised his hand, signaling them to stop. Declan's eyes quickly scanned the trees for movement, but everything was still. Sean waived his hand for everyone to follow, and carefully made his horse turn, walking into a dense thicket of trees off to the side.

Once they all had entered the thicket, Sean dismounted, allowing the reins of his horse to fall. He motioned for them to follow his lead. After all the men dismounted, Sean whispered, "Gather your weapons and keep them in reach just beneath your cloaks." He took a few steps towards the edge of the thicket. Turning, he whispered, "Hoods raised, men."

Declan walked behind the group of brown and gray hooded figures. They emerged from the thicket with Sean in the lead. He turned around to see the closely-knit mass.

"Break into smaller groups of three, four, or five," suggested Sean. "That way, we do not look like an advancing army." A small smile slipped onto his face.

Sean and his two loyal men formed the front group. As the others followed suit, Declan kept with a group near the back. The groups of men marched casually closer to Sean's prey. From the Watcher's position behind the pack, Berty watched them advance cautiously towards the gates.

The men seemed uneasy as they approached on foot. "Be careful, men," whispered Sean. "This could be a trap."

Berty was pleased to hear trepidation in Sean's voice. The groups kept their slow pace as they walked towards the gates, careful to keep their cloaks covering their weapons. When no one was watching, Declan's eyes quickly scanned the trees for signs of Elves, but saw nothing.

Within six feet from the closed gates, one of the men in Declan's group looked behind him. "Sean," said the man, "look."

Sean turned. The worry on his face melted. Declan sharply turned his head. In the distance, a large faction of their men approached on horseback.

Sean raised a hand to stop the groups of men, then whispered to the blond haired Wagner. After receiving his instructions, Wagner ran towards the approaching men.

After a long few minutes, Wagner returned to Sean's side. He whispered into his boss' ear. Sean mumbled, "Excellent."

Sean's hand beckoned the groups forward. Everyone stopped within a couple of feet of the gates. Sean whispered into his other companion's ear. The man looked at Sean imploringly.

Sean nodded at his tall, bearded companion. Lowering his hood, the man stood up straight, walking to the closed gates. His hand gave a gentle nudge to the one gate to see if it budged. The gate remained unyielding. The man's large knuckles rapped determinedly on the wooden gate.

A low voice boomed from behind the gates. "Who knocks upon these gates?"

"We are men from the villages of the Land of Sages," answered the deep voice of the man who knocked.

"State your business inside the Sages' Grove, men from the villages," said the booming voice.

The man looked shiftily at Sean. After receiving whispered instructions, he said, "We wish to have an audience with the Empress."

"I regret to inform you that the Empress is not receiving audiences at this time," answered the voice.

Sean whispered in his ear again. "Then perhaps we can speak to someone else," said the tall man.

"To what does this business pertain?" asked the voice.

With a sickening smile on his face, Sean hurriedly whispered into the man's ear. When Sean backed away, the tall man said, "We wish to discuss matters of magical natures."

"There is a chance that someone will be able to receive you," said the voice. "However, there are conditions to which you must agree before you enter these gates."

"What are the conditions?" asked the man.

The voice boomed sternly. "No weapons of any kind are allowed beyond the gates of the Sages' Grove. Upon entering, every one of you must submit to a search. All weapons will be confiscated from you and will be returned to you when you leave. Do you agree to such terms?"

Sean nodded to his henchman. The man said in his deep voice, "We agree."

With a wave of his hand, Sean motioned to all the men to huddle close to him. "Once we're inside," he whispered, "you are to never surrender your weapons. When I give the signal, we will run through the buildings of the Sages' Grove and if we must, fight our way to the Empire Tree. Do not worry about anything except getting inside the doors to the Empire Tree. Behind us, seventy-five men will be following us inside the gates to help."

Slowly, one gate opened. Berty watched with heightened anticipation to see what Silvia had planned next.

Two guards dressed in blue gray armor from head to toe waited on the other side of the gate. Their faces were completely

121

covered and they had swords sheathed at their sides. When the sunlight fell onto the metal, the armor shone like multifaceted crystals. Berty wondered how they existed as he gazed at their appearances through Declan's eyes. One of the armored men beckoned the tall, bearded man forward for inspection.

As he walked forward, the rest of the group inched inside the gate. The Sages' Grove appeared to be empty with the exception of the two guards wearing crystal armor. Sean kept looking at the two armored guards as if he were waiting for something. The guard inspecting the one man removed the man's sword, then handed it to the other guard. While the second guard turned to place the sword behind him, the first guard began to pat the man down, looking for more weapons. With both guards distracted, Sean yelled, "Go! Now!"

The group of men started to scatter into the Sage's Grove between buildings, but were soon impeded by more armored guards that materialized out of nowhere.

Unsheathing gleaming, crystal swords, the guards blocked the paths to the Empire Tree. Sean's men produced swords as well, lunging forward. Berty heard the scraping of metal against crystal. In between the dull clangs of the metal swords and the sharp rings of the crystal swords ran Sean and his two cronies, not even raising a sword to help.

Only possessing a bow and arrows, Declan scrambled on top of a thatched roof for a bird's-eye view of the fray. Sean's handpicked group of men were woefully outnumbered by the armored guards. As Silvia's guards pushed the men backwards, even Sean and his two loyal men had to join the fight. Not shooting an arrow into the fight, Declan kept a close eye on Sean.

Berty's eyes narrowed when he saw the smug look on Sean's face as he was being pushed towards the wall of trees. Wielding swords and battleaxes, the large group of seventy-five men poured through the open gate. The fight was renewed as Sean and his men pushed through the crystal bearing guards. With the doors of the Empire Tree in sight, Sean fought with a wild look of glee in his eyes. His sparkle faded as more armored guards materialized and a number of Empire Guards followed the men into the Sages' Grove.

Berty had never seen such a melee. Sean's followers' flanks were split, fighting both Empire and crystal sword-wielding Guards. Berty watched in amazement as one of the crystal swords sliced effortlessly through a metal sword, leaving a blunt metal stump. With a shocked and scared look on his face, the man holding the stump quickly ran as far away as he could get from the crystal armor guard only to be detained by Edwin at sword point. The man dropped his stump of a sword while his head shook as if he were pleading with the Lieutenant.

Declan turned his attention back to the general fight in his search for the elusive Sean. Sparkling in the filtered sunlight, the armored guards with the crystal swords fought with grace and mercy, disarming their opponents instead of killing them. On more than one occasion, a crystal sword-wielding guard appeared out of nowhere, intervening to save the life of either an Empire Guard or one of Sean's men. Whenever a weapon struck the crystal armor, the weapon would shatter instead of the armor being crushed, making the armored guards indestructible.

Marveling at Silvia's magic, Berty closed his eyes, hearing the grunts and screams of the fray through the locket. Behind his eyelids, he saw Silvia in the Scepter Room dressed in bright gold. With her eyes opened, but unfocused, she danced around the room, making gracefully strange movements with her arms. She pirouetted, playing puppeteer to her armor clad warriors. Every so often, she lunged in different directions or threw her body across the room as if she were blocking an attack.

Hearing a loud thud from the open locket, Berty opened his eyes. Declan jumped off the roof on which he was perched to follow Sean and a small handful of men running to the doors of the Empire Tree. Someone in front of Declan shouted, "Open those doors! Quickly!" Berty held his breath as he watched them push and pry open the doors of the Empire Tree only a floor below.

The men quickly filed in the dark Receiving Room, rushing to close the doors. Wagner and the tall, bearded man secured the doors with large chairs and other furniture in the room. Sean looked around the room, evaluating the situation. "Declan, Wagner," said Sean, "you two stay here and keep watch. The rest of us will explore the Empire Tree."

Declan merely nodded while Wagner answered, "No problem. We've got it." Wagner moved over to the side of the room with his hand on his sword. Declan positioned himself behind a desk with his bow and arrow in his view. Pleased, Sean motioned to the rest of the group to follow him up the stairs.

Berty quietly closed the locket, listening intently. The sounds of shuffling feet entered Berty's ears. His breathing almost stopped. Securing the locket inside his cloak, he extracted his wand and raised his hood. Along with the shuffling of feet, Berty heard the scraping of wood against wood. Trying not to laugh, he smiled satisfactorily, knowing that they were having problems crossing the room within the sea of tables and chairs. He could imagine the dirty look on Sean's face as more than one person bumped into the furniture. Not wanting to reveal himself and lure them into a false sense of security, he waited on the stairs for someone to approach. Berty could hear the men scattering around the Reception Room, trying to move while unsuccessfully touching as little as possible, searching for a bigger trap.

"All clear," breathed a deep voice. Berty pictured a tall man with a dark complexion and a scruffy beard. "Which way?"

"There is the main way and there is the servant's way," answered Sean. "We go through this passageway, then on the large bridge we will split."

Berty was relieved that Sean did not know about the Empress' private staircase. Thinking that he would pick them off from behind, another thought entered his mind. He wondered if Sean was just telling his men one thing while knowing another, making his relief short-lived. After the shuffling sounds of the men faded, Berty waited to see if Sean was going to double back to use the stairs on which he stood.

In the distance, the silence gave way to muffled screams. Berty knew that Sean and his men were being ambushed. He could not help but smile. His smile quickly faded as Berty's ears caught a new sound. He heard a soft, cat-like stepping of feet climbing the few steps onto the dais. The soft steps crossed behind Silvia's throne, and then were muffled by the large, purple drapes that framed either side of the dais. Knowing that someone was near, Berty clutched his wand tightly, ready to face a foe.

Stepping into Berty's view was a slender, sandy haired man also clutching a wand. His other hand held a gracefully curved bow, which Berty knew he had seen before. Peeking through the parting of the man's cloak, Berty saw a rather large, plain, gold locket.

Catching a glimpse of Berty's wand, the man lowered his wand, whispering, "You must be the Empress' Watcher. The Guild Master told me that he had met you."

Lowering his wand as well, Berty whispered, "You must be Declan."

The man nodded, whispering, "I am."

With his free hand, Berty reached beyond the magical border to Declan. Declan grabbed it and Berty pulled Declan onto the stairs.

"Thank you," said Declan. "I could see you through the haze, but I could not reach you."

"What haze?"

"Magic has a haze," answered Declan. "Surely you see that as well."

Berty shook his head.

"Oh." Declan looked puzzled, then said, "It is like watching heat radiate off of something. At least to me, anyway." He shrugged.

"What happened to that man who was with you downstairs?" asked Berty.

"Wagner?" Declan smiled slyly. "He is bound, gagged and

blindfolded." He chuckled. "Never saw it coming."

"Did you unblock the doors?" Berty asked.

"No," answered Declan. "There would be no way to be sure that the Empire Guards would enter and not Sean's sheep. After encountering those armored guards that I have never seen before in the Sages' Grove, I figured the Empire Tree has a few hidden tricks as well. By finding you, I know I was right. Better safe than sorry, I think."

Berty nodded in agreement. "Let us go up."

Tightly clutching their wands, Berty and Declan crept, stair by stair, up to the next level. Reaching the landing to the Roundtable Room, Berty glanced inside to see Goscislaw burst through the door with two men chasing after him. Berty turned to Declan who nodded. Both of them charged across the room to the Dwarf's aid.

Goscislaw had his back to a chair when the first man swung his sword. Moving quickly for a Dwarf of his age, he dodged the strike so fast that the man's blade became imbedded into the back of the chair. The second man lunged with his sword at the rolling Dwarf. Goscislaw growled an incantation. A length of rope sprung out of nowhere. The man tripped over the rope, allowing Goscislaw to roll away. Declan furthered the Dwarf's work, making the rope wrap around the man's ankles. The other man struggled to remove his sword from the wood. Berty thought the timing was perfect. He was about to take aim with his wand when Alfred and another tall man crashed into the room.

Taking a good chunk of wood out of the chair, the man extracted his sword to run after Alfred. Afraid that he was going to hurt someone, Berty did the first thing that popped into his mind. He pointed his wand at Alfred's would be attacker and the man's sword melted into a useless lump of metal.

"A Watcher," someone called. "Get his wand!"

The tall man who Alfred had slammed into the wall was the same man who knocked on the gates of the Sages' Grove. He ran across the room, charging at Berty. Without warning, the tall, bearded man swung his sword, slicing Berty's wand in two.

Shocked at the sound of the small piece of wood clinking to the floor, Berty looked for Declan. Alongside Goscislaw, the Watcher fought a man who kept calling Declan a traitor. Berty's hand rubbed the smooth useless stick, then cast it aside. It rolled across the floor, joining the rest of the debris.

The tall man flicked his sword. It was inches from Berty's neck when he said in his deep voice, "What are you going to do without your wand now, Watcher?" The man laughed.

Looking into the man's cold, yet maniacal, eyes repulsed Berty. Wanting to push the threatening man away, Berty placed both hands, palms out, in front of his body. His hands pulsed slightly. The tall, bearded man flew backwards, hitting his head on Silvia's exquisite chair. He slumped motionless to the floor with his head under the table.

"Help me," said a frantic man's voice from the corridor, "she's deranged." A tall, blond man scurried into the room, disrupting the battles.

"Get back here you cowardly toad," a woman's voice shrieked. "I will teach you to mess with my husband."

Lida flew into the room with a fury unlike Berty had ever seen. Her rage juxtaposed the beauty of a Fairy in flight. Lida balled her delicate fist, slowly raising it above her head.

Realizing what she was doing, Alfred's face showed horror. He yelled to Berty, Goscislaw and Declan, "Cover your faces and run! Fairy Dust!" Covering his face with a piece of his cloak, Berty ran with the others into the corridor. Pausing on the landing, a couple of Sean's followers followed the four of them, trying to escape Lida's wrath.

Out of range of her Fairy Dust, Sean's two men recommenced the fight to the Scepter Room. Each man took on Alfred and Goscislaw. Attempting to come to the Heads' aid, Declan almost tripped over an injured Elrick who moaned in great pain. Berty looked down to see the Fairy King collapsed against the wall. Blood oozed from multiple places.

Declan squatted next to Elrick and examined his wounds. "I

will stay here with the Fairy," Declan said to Berty. "I am learned in the art of healing."

Berty patted Declan on the shoulder. Weaponless, he ran up the stairs after the escaped men who were screaming, "The Scepter Room must be around here somewhere."

Another voice called, "Hurry up! They are on our heels."

Over the sounds of scurrying feet, Berty tried to listen to the strange language in which Alfred spoke. Berty thought that the words sounded guttural, perhaps Germanic, and he wondered what Alfred was doing.

As Berty caught up to Goscislaw, a loud thud resonated in the staircase. Someone shouted, "The Elf is using magic against us."

"Perhaps," Goscislaw shouted back as he rushed up the steps, "you will not be so quick to turn your nose up to any amount of magic that comes your way next time."

"Magic thieves!" shouted a man. Sword pointed high, he charged the Dwarf Prince. Goscislaw ducked quickly, evading the enraged man's sword. Confused at first from the disappearance of the Dwarf, the man then saw Berty further down the steps and began his charge again.

Concentrating on the shiny steel, Berty simply stood in the man's line of fire while he watched the sword fall over limp in the man's hand like a deflated balloon.

"Wha... what the," stammered the man. He looked at Berty, then at his useless sword. Berty could see fear manifesting in the man's eyes. He scrambled down the stairs away from Berty and the others.

Reaching the landing to the Scepter Room, Berty saw Goscislaw reinforcing magical bindings on the man Alfred knocked unconscious. On Berty's right, Alfred stood under the doorway lintel of the Scepter Room. As Berty approached, Alfred pressed a finger to his lips. Peeking in, Berty did not see carved wooden columns, crystal sconces, or the pillar holding the large, crystal scepter. Instead, Berty gazed upon many tree trunks and lush green undergrowth. Silvia had transformed the Scepter Room into her familiar forest.

"My patience wears thin, Empress," said a thoroughly disgusted Sean, emerging from behind a tree. Berty clenched his fists and inched closer. Alfred pressed a hand onto Berty's chest, cautioning him about entering the fray.

Sean held his sword out in front of him. "Come out and face me," Sean said, looking around. "You can't hide among the trees forever, Empress."

"Can't I?" said Silvia. Her voice resonated throughout the room so no one knew from where it came.

"A battle rages at your feet, Empress, outside of the Empire Tree," taunted Sean.

"That battle is over, Seanlaoch," said Silvia's cool voice. "Your followers have surrendered."

"You couldn't know. How did you know? Unless...," said Sean, his voice trailing off. With a confused look on his face, his sword lowered a tiny bit.

"There are things that you do not understand," Silvia said.

"Like magic?" asked Sean, raising his sword again. "Is that why you keep it from us, because you don't feel that poor, peasant minds can comprehend magic?"

"It seems to be no secret that you, Seanlaoch, are ignorant in the arts of magic," Silvia retorted, still keeping her whereabouts elusive.

"My great-grandfather was a Mage," shouted Sean.

"A Warrior Mage, to be exact," said Silvia. Her voice sounded calm and cool as if she were having a casual conversation.

"Yes, and there hasn't been another one since," Sean said angrily. He kept searching the trees for Silvia.

Berty finally understood Sean's violent quest. Sean was angry that he did not become a Warrior Mage like his ancestor. Because he had not been blessed with magical gifts, he was taking his anger out on Silvia.

"Why do you suppose that is?" asked Silvia.

"Because you stole it all," screamed Sean as he waved his

sword. "You stole all the magic, including my great-grandfather's staff."

The forest disappeared to reveal the carved wooden columns and glowing white crystal of the scepter sitting serenely in the middle of the room. Though Sean seemed to have walked extensively between and around trees, he stood in a space between the smooth wall and wood column. Silvia glided from behind a carved wooden column in the back of the room, shining and radiant in her golden gown.

"What need would I have for the magic or for your great-grandfather's staff?" Silvia asked in her cool, calm voice. She walked out into the open space slowly and deliberately, keeping her sights on Sean while also keeping the scepter between them.

"How does one rationalize madness?" Sean answered.

Silvia stopped walking. The distance between her and Sean was not insurmountable, but he seemed too leery to approach any closer. "It is nice to see you are finally looking inside yourself for the answers," said Silvia, smiling.

Sean's eyes narrowed while his hand gripped the handle of his sword more tightly. In a surge of fury, Sean began to take a step towards Silvia, but his legs were unable to move another step as if his feet became stuck to the wooden floor.

"Release me," he demanded while he swung his sword wildly with both hands.

"No," said Silvia, staring serenely at Sean. His sword flew out of his hands, crashing into the smooth wall, then sliding to the floor on the far side of the room.

"You can take my sword, but you cannot control me," Sean said defiantly. "The scepter should not be used that way."

"I do not use the scepter," said Silvia. She glanced at the glowing, white crystal. "I have never used the scepter."

Sean looked confused. "The scepter," Silvia explained, "is not at the disposal of an Empress. For generations, the only times an Empress has ever touched the scepter is at the beginning and ending of her reign."

"So you don't touch it," Sean exasperated. "There are other ways you can steal the magic with it."

"How would I do that precisely?" asked Silvia.

"You know how," Sean sneered.

Silvia chuckled. "You assume much, Seanlaoch. The bond between Empress and scepter is not like that."

"I don't care," Sean shouted, struggling against his bonds. His hands were bound to his sides. "Release me, woman!"

"You should care," said Silvia softly, yet clearly, "and again, no."

Alfred removed his hand from Berty's chest and stepped through the doorway into the Scepter Room. "What you do not understand, Seanlaoch," he said calmly, "can kill you." He stopped walking before he reached the wood columns.

Sean switched his focus from Silvia to Alfred. Sean's eyes moved up and down as they took in the High Elf's tall, thin gait, which was emphasized by his dark green robe, and asked, "What do you mean?"

"If anyone but the Empress even barely touches the scepter, that person dies instantly," explained Alfred. "Even after an Empress' death."

Sean moved his lingering gaze from Alfred to the crystal scepter, then to Silvia. His gaze passed over the three again and again until finally it rested on the scepter. Berty could tell that Sean was remembering something when his eyes lost their intense focus. After a moment of silence, Sean said, "I am not listening to anything you have to say, Elf. You would not tell me the truth, especially being in cahoots with her."

Alfred shook his head while Silvia said, "That is your choice to make." She sounded disappointed.

Distracted by the exchange between Silvia, Alfred, and Sean inside the Scepter Room, Berty barely noticed Elrick and Lida join them in the doorway.

"How are you feeling, Elrick?" asked Goscislaw in a whisper.

"Not too badly. That Watcher, Declan, is quite the healer,"

Elrick whispered back.

"Where is he?" asked the Dwarf, looking around.

"Opening the doors so the Empire Guards can collect the other prisoners and sweep through the Empire Tree," answered Lida.

While he listened to the conversation beside him, Berty watched Sean struggle against his bonds. He wondered what Silvia was planning to do with him.

Berty propelled forcefully into the Scepter Room with the others. The unsteadiness of the four pairs of feet forced the Dwarf Prince to knock into Alfred. Collapsing in a tangled heap on the floor, the five of them struggled with each other to stand.

"Sean, get a move on it!" shouted a familiar deep voice from behind the mass on the floor. "The Empire Guards have infiltrated."

Trying to untangle himself from Elrick and Lida without injuring the Fairy King, Berty had his back to the man. However, he had a shrewd idea that the deep voice belonged to the tall man who Berty sent crashing into the roundtable.

"You, Watcher," said the man to Berty's back, "I owe."

Chapter Fourteen
Watches over Thee

Berty knew that tall, bearded man had come for him. Every muscle in his body tightened. As if it were made of lead, he arduously raised his head. His eyes had a clear view of Silvia still looking radiant in her gown of gold.

His heavy body moved languidly. To him, it seemed as if everyone in the room moved in slow motion. Berty's eyes finally focused, catching Silvia raising a hand towards the man looming behind Berty. With a slight closure and reopening of her fingers, Silvia forcefully pushed the man out of the room. The dull thuds of his body falling down the stairs echoed inside the Scepter Room.

Out of the corner of his eye, Berty saw Sean's shadow move. Sean reached inside his cloak. He extracted a small, silver dagger. Sean had eyes only for Silvia.

His hand snapped forward. The silver dagger sliced through the air. The dagger's trajectory led directly to Silvia.

Berty's immediate thought was to stop the dagger, but his magic could not touch the silver object. Silvia's magic created a strong barrier.

The silver dagger shone in the crystal sconces' florescent-like light. It struck Silvia in the center of her body. The dagger deeply penetrated her abdomen.

All breath exited his lungs as his eyes helplessly beheld Silvia as she stumbled backwards. With her arms outstretched, she crumpled gracefully onto the smooth, wooden floor.

Finding air in his lungs, Berty screamed. "No!" He jumped over people jumbled on the floor.

A momentary look of triumph flashed across Sean's face. Disgusted and angry, Berty ignored him. Kneeling beside her bloodstained body, he grasped the cold, silver handle. With a gentle tug, Berty removed the dagger.

Setting the weapon aside, Berty stroked her soft, dark red hair, muttering, "No. This was not supposed to happen. No." He gazed into her soft, brown eyes, which struggled to keep their warmth. Tears leaked from Berty's eyes as he leaned closer, whispering, "Silvia, don't leave me."

He clasped Silvia's soft, limp, cold hand in his and shouted, "No!"

The Scepter Room plunged into semi-darkness. Afraid to let go of Silvia's hand, Berty held it more tightly. The only light crept in from the stairway landing through the open door. The large crystal in the scepter along with all the crystal sconces around the room stopped glowing.

His ears heard Lida ask, "Elrick, what does this mean?"

His eyes saw Sean slinking away against the wall, mumbling, "What have I done?"

His hands dropped Silvia's hand as his body stood. Automatically, his feet took him to the center of the room. He reached for the dark, colorless scepter. Grasping its cold white metal staff, he said, "My life for hers."

Berty removed the scepter from its carved wooden holder. He raised it. "I give the Empress my life."

The crystal remained dark. In the dim light, he vaguely made out the silhouettes of five people, four of which stood in a group helpless. Her body draped in bloodstained gold remained motionless on the floor.

Berty knelt beside Silvia's peaceful body. Gently, he picked up her hand that he abandoned for the scepter. He wrapped her delicate fingers around the cold, white metal of the scepter. He held them there so that both Silvia and Berty touched the metal staff. Berty took one, last, lingering gaze into Silvia's face, closed his eyes, then said, "I give you my life."

After uttering those words, the white metal under his hand warmed. Berty reluctantly opened his eyes to see the dark crystal glow. The crystal glowed red, not white.

The deep, bright red glow of the large crystal grew brighter and brighter until it's red hue encompassed them both. Berty thought he heard gasps from behind him. He could no longer see anything beyond red. Closing his eyes, he allowed the red warmth to overcome him.

From behind his eyelids, Berty could tell that the bright redness was fading into the crystal. Per the legend, he expected his lungs to stop drawing in and expelling air and his heart to cease beating. He was acutely aware that neither had happened, so he opened his eyes.

Light from its fluorescent glowing sconces filled the Scepter Room. The light revealed Silvia's golden gown without the scarlet bloodstain. The dagger-sized slit might never had existed. Berty tightly held onto the scepter.

As the glow fully receded and became contained within the crystal, Silvia took an intake of breath. Berty's eyes found her face as her grip around the scepter tightened. She looked up at him, smiling with her warm, brown eyes.

Silvia's eyes moved from Berty's face to glance at the scepter's crystal. Softly, she said, "Crimson." The large crystal had kept the deep red color.

Her soft, brown eyes found Berty's once more. Looking at him warmly, Silvia smiled, saying, "Thank you, Emperor."

A confused Berty grabbed her free hand, helping her to her feet while he asked, "Why did you call me Emperor?"

"Because that is who you now are," answered Silvia. She removed her hand from the scepter and let go of Berty's helping hand. The Heads and Sean watched their every move.

"And you?" Berty asked tentatively.

"Are no longer Empress," Silvia stated. She walked backward a few steps, turned to the others, then said, "May I present, your Emperor." Silvia nodded to Berty while the Heads bowed.

Sean sheepishly raised his eyes. Still on the floor, Sean did not bow to Berty. While Berty's gaze swept the room, he saw Sean staring at him with jealousy, loathing and contempt.

"My Lord," said Alfred. The formal address captured Berty's

attention. "What are your instructions?" Alfred glanced in Sean's direction. The Elf wanted to know what to do with the murderer slinking in the corner.

Little clinking noises echoed throughout the room. "Do nothing yet," Berty instructed.

"Very well," said Alfred, bowing. The High Elf turned to Silvia. "How does the former Empress wish to be addressed?"

Elrick nudged his wife. "Lida, can it be? After all this time, does the Empire have...?"

"An Elder," finished a bewildered Lida. Whispered gasps resonated around the room. All eyes roved from Berty to Silvia.

Silvia smiled, then said, "I wish to be addressed as Elder Hunter."

Berty's eyebrows raised. The name, Hunter, rang familiar in his ears, like a ghost from a previous life.

"Of course, wise one," said Alfred with the utmost respect. "May we be privy to your council, Elder Hunter?"

"You may," Silvia answered. "As the Emperor is aware, each of the seven wooden columns have deposited a crystal. If everyone would please take one."

She looked at each of the other six people in the room. When none of them moved, Silvia stepped forward. Everyone's eyes followed her as she walked over to a column to remove her crystal. Each column's crystal was completely void of color and deposited at different heights. Glancing around the room, he found that three were at Human height, one at Elf height, two at Fairy height, and one at Dwarf height.

Knowing that he had to take a crystal, he hesitated, wondering which of the remaining two columns held his crystal. Taking a deep breath, Berty's feet seemed to know from which column he should collect his crystal. When he reached the wood column, Berty did not take the time to look at the carvings. He just gathered his crystal and walked back to stand next to Silvia, still clutching the scepter in his other hand. After he took his crystal, the four Heads, somewhat hesitantly, retrieved theirs. Only one crystal remained in its column.

"Seanlaoch," said Silvia in her calm manner, "you did not collect your crystal." All eyes rested on the dark mass trying to blend in with the surroundings. Still crouching on the floor, Sean cowered against the wall. His eyes looked from Silvia to the others standing around the Scepter Room. Finally he stood, slunk towards the column and removed the last remaining crystal.

"Good. If everyone will place their crystal into the palm of their hands, thusly," Silvia instructed. She held her crystal in her left hand for everyone to see. Once they had followed her instructions, she said, "Now, close your hand around the crystal."

Lida and Elrick exchanged nervous glances. Goscislaw watched his crystal curiously. Sean stood near the wall with great apprehension. Only Alfred looked calm, as if he regularly received a crystal from the Empire Tree. Finally, everyone wrapped his or her fingers around the crystals as she instructed.

Berty's hand examined his crystal. He felt no sharp edges on the roughly three inch long, cool crystal. The thin crystal had a comfortable and almost familiar, but clearly defined, presence in his palm. Once Silvia clasped her fingers around her crystal, Berty felt his crystal grow hot in his hand for a few moments.

Once the crystal had cooled, Silvia said, "Open your hands."

The looks of shock gave way to looks of confusion. In each hand, laid a colorless crystal bound to the same kind of white metal of the scepter strung on a dark brown leather cord.

"These crystals," Silvia explained, "bind all of us to the scepter and to the Empire Tree. They are to be worn at all times." She draped hers around her neck. After a bit of hesitation from the Fairies, the Dwarf and Sean, everyone followed suit. "This bond," continued Silvia while some examined the crystal around their necks, "requires us to return to the Empire Tree at some point determined by the crystal.

"As for you, Seanlaoch," Silvia walked towards the retreating Sean, "your crystal binds you to the Empire Tree differently. Because of your deeds here today, you are bound in service to the

Empire Tree and to the Emperor. Unless you accompany the Emperor, you are forbidden to step foot beyond the treed wall that surrounds the Sages' Grove."

Sean did not answer nor look at Silvia. Instead, he nodded at a place on the floor.

"Alfred," said Silvia as she turned away from Sean, "would you be so kind to present the Emperor?"

"Of course, Elder Hunter," said Alfred. Turning to Berty, he bowed. "Emperor, when you are ready."

Berty glanced at Alfred, then at the scepter in his hand, then at the crystal around his neck. His mind repeated Alfred's words, *"Emperor, when you are ready."* Being Emperor seemed almost surreal to him. He did not know if he was ready or not. Taking a deep breath, he finally looked at Silvia, asking, "Will you be there with me?"

Silvia smiled her familiar warm smile at him, saying, "Only for the announcement, then I must collect my cloak and be on my way."

"To where are you going, Elder Hunter?" asked Goscislaw.

"It is my duty, dear Prince, as an Elder to travel beyond these walls, bestowing knowledge and wisdom upon those in the Empire who are of need," Silvia explained.

Listening to Silvia's words, Berty could not believe his ears. He did not want to imagine a world in-between anywhere without Silvia near him. Surely, he thought, that as Emperor he would be in need of her knowledge and wisdom. But he knew that crystal required her to go beyond the wall of trees that surrounded the Sages' Grove. Recognizing that he had to take a more solitary journey, Berty took a deep breath, then said, "I am ready. We *all* shall go." He looked pointedly at Sean.

Goscislaw immediately walked over to Sean, growling, "You are coming with me and just in case you get any ideas...." The Dwarf held out his hand towards Sean's feet and muttered something indistinct to Berty's ears. When Goscislaw moved to Sean's side, Berty saw metal shackles on each of Sean's ankles with a chain connection. "I get even a whiff of trouble," the Dwarf growled to Sean, "and you get a matching pair on your wrists."

Berty took a few steps towards the main door. Silvia followed his lead as Alfred stepped in line beside her. Elrick and Lida took their positions behind them while Goscislaw nudged Sean along in the rear. With Alfred and Silvia by his side, Berty processed down the stairs until they reached the Reception Room.

The massive gathering of tables and chairs occupying the room parted, coming to rest near the walls as he strode forwards. He halted in the center of the Reception Room. Berty gazed at his throne on the dais, then turned to face the opposite wall.

The six other crystal wearers surrounded him in an arc with Goscislaw keeping a close eye on the sulking, shackled Sean. Berty walked towards the wall with the crimson scepter tightly in his grasp. Part of the wall melted to reveal a balcony from which he could see the Sages' Grove. The unarmored Empire Guards patrolled makeshift jails in which held Sean's followers.

When Berty walked out onto the balcony, the crimson crystal of the scepter pulsed. Everyone looked up at the balcony. Alfred's smooth voice resonated through the Sages' Grove, saying, "Behold, the Emperor." The people knelt, making waves across the village. As Berty held the scepter high over his head, the people rose to their feet. Lowering the scepter, somehow he knew that it was not the time for speech making and that he should not stand on that balcony for long.

After what seemed like an appropriate time, Berty turned, walking through the temporary opening into the Reception Room. The wall reformed behind him. Looking at the arc of witnesses, he found that Silvia had left the group. Addressing the Heads, he said, "It has been a rough day, Theodore will tend to you."

"My Lord," growled Goscislaw, "what is to be done with this?" He motioned towards Sean.

"I believe Alvar has a special holding cell for him, away from the others," Berty answered. "He will be dealt with later." Goscislaw bowed his head.

Theodore appeared in the doorway, bowed, saying, "Yes, my Lord."

"You and Leena have faired well?" Berty asked.

"I fought one off, my Lord," said a proud Theodore. "The Empire Guards have collected him."

Berty smiled at him. "Good man. If you would be so kind to please tend to everyone here. I will have further instructions for you later. Right now, I must return the scepter." Theodore began to pull a table and some chairs from the sides of the room.

As soon as he was out of view, Berty ran up the stairs, his cloak billowing behind him. Walking into the Scepter Room, he placed the crimson scepter into its pillar. He took two steps at a time up the private staircase, hoping that he had not missed Silvia. Racing across the bridge, he found Silvia cloaked in her usual light blue, waiting for him beside his chamber door.

When he approached, Silvia smiled at him. "Silvia," Berty said, "must you leave?"

She nodded. "You know that I must. Berty, the chambers across the bridge that were mine are now yours. The house on the other side of the portal belongs to you as well." She held out a piece of paper. "Here is a letter that you must deliver, in person, to your editor."

"My editor," repeated Berty. As if he remembered a dream, he put things together that he could not while in the Scepter Room. "Mister Hunter. Are you two—?"

"Related," answered Silvia with a smile. "You must tell him that you are to be moving into the house. While in the house, you will find that you will not have to change much. Martin should be able to explain." She placed the letter in his hand. "I must go now."

"Allow me to walk you to the gates," said Berty, placing the letter in his pocket.

As he held out his hand, she placed her hand in his. Berty's hand felt the softness of Silvia's delicate fingers intertwined with his. He relished in the gentleness of her touch. He did not know when he would feel it again.

Hand in hand, they strolled across the bridge and down the private stairway. When they reached the Reception Room, Berty helped her down the steps of the dais. Alone in the room, the Heads were sitting around a table, chatting. Lida noticed Berty and Silvia entering the room and the four Heads walked over to wish her well.

"My Lord," said Theodore while entering the Reception Room from the lower staircase. Berty walked over to the young Dwarf. "Captain Alvar has that man detained and wishes to have a word with you."

"He will have to wait until after I see Elder Hunter out of the Sages' Grove," said Berty. Bowing, Theodore hurried out of the room.

After receiving many hugs, Silvia rejoined Berty who stood near the stairs. "Are you ready?" he asked.

"As ready as I will ever be," she answered.

Taking her hand, Berty led Silvia down the stairs towards the open doors. Silvia paused before the light flooding inside reached her cloak. Dropping Berty's hand, she smiled her warm smile, then raised her hood over her dark red hair. She stepped forward into the light and out the doors with Berty by her side. In the Sages' Grove, Empire Guards and prisoners alike watched them as they proceeded towards the gates.

"Elder Hunter," called a very familiar voice. Both Berty and Silvia stopped to turn while Theodore ran towards them, carrying a large stick. When he reached them, he said, "A gift from the Empire Tree, Elder Hunter, to help you on your way."

"I graciously accept this gift," Silvia said. She received the walking stick from the Dwarf. "Thank the Empire Tree for me." Theodore nodded to Silvia and bowed to Berty before heading back up the dirt path.

In silence, the two of them traversed the few more yards to the open gate. Arriving at the gate, they stopped. Silvia turned to face Berty. He gazed into her warm, soft, brown eyes.

"Will I be able to see you again?" asked Berty.

Silvia smiled. "If you seek me, then you will find me." Clasping her hands on Berty's, she kissed him on the cheek.

Turning from him, she walked beyond the gates and out from under the protecting, reaching branches of the Empire Tree. Berty stood at the edge of the Sages' Grove, watching as Silvia and her walking stick disappeared into the early evening fog that shrouded the surrounding woods.

Chapter Fifteen
A New Beginning

Berty stood behind the opened gates, gathering his claret cloak around him as he tried to see into the dense fog. His eyes saw shadowy shapes that turned out to be only trees.

Finally turning away, he said to the nearest guard, "Close these gates and allow no one through without permission."

The guard bowed, "Yes, my Lord."

Walking up the dirt path, Berty looked up at the majestic Empire Tree whose branches were many. He felt a sense of fulfillment and of being home, yet a terrible emptiness filled the pit in his stomach. He wondered how it could be home without her.

Pushing his thoughts aside, he pressed onwards. He trudged passed the empty, white cob buildings with their quaint thatched roofs. Reaching the dark wooden doors to the Empire Tree, he took a deep breath of the sharp, evening air before stepping inside. He resolutely walked around the empty desks and up the stairs. The thing that he desired most of all was to be alone, but when he reached the top of the stairs, the smooth walled Reception Room was full of people.

Brass chandeliers flickered to life in the increasing darkness, illuminating the large amount of tables and chairs that still pressed against the walls. His eyes glanced at the ornate throne that sat on top of the dais. Looking away, he found a lone table around which four people sat. A Dwarf, two Fairies and an Elf watched him in silence. As he stepped away from the stairs, the Elf rose from his chair, approaching him.

"Emperor," said Alfred, bowing his tall, thin body exposing his mostly gray head, "Is there anything that you need?"

He wanted to answer solitude, but Berty knew that his duty must come first. "Is the Roundtable Room empty?" he asked.

"Yes, my Lord," the aged Elf answered. "However, it is still," he paused, "a wreck."

"No matter," he answered, "that is where I will be. Have Theodore send Alvar." He had begun to turn away from the Elf and the others who sat around the table. Stopping, he said, "Alfred, the four of you must be tired, please get some rest."

Alfred bowed. Berty climbed the steps to the dais, walking past the carved relief of a large tree with seven circles superimposed on its trunk from its highest branch to its lowest roots. He remembered when she told him that the carving was called the Sages' Seal. Feeling a pang in his pit, he disappeared through the hidden entrance behind the seal and plodded up his private staircase.

Reaching the Roundtable Room, signs of the battle remained. Overturned chairs were scattered around the room. The Roundtable itself was pushed off center from him knocking the tall, bearded man into it. Where the man hit the side, the shiny tabletop dulled. Walking around the room, Berty's fingers felt the notch in a chair made by the sword whose jab missed Goscislaw. The walls still echoed with yells as Lida pursued a man into the room for injuring Elrick. His ears could still hear Alfred's screams to run as Lida raised her fist to unleash Fairy Dust.

After circling the room, he waived both arms in front of his body. The Roundtable Room returned to its pre-melee state. Taking a deep breath, he approached the shiny Roundtable with many high-backed, carved chairs. When he reached the largest and most ornate of the chairs, his feet stopped. He sat in the large, throne like chair, feeling queasy as if he were overstepping a boundary. Sitting in what used to be her chair seemed strange to him, but it was something that he must get used to, he thought, for he was Emperor while she, the former Empress, wandered the Land of Sages.

A door opened, interrupting his thoughts. A young Dwarf entered. He announced, "Alvar is here to see you, my Lord."

"Thank you, Theodore," he said.

A tall, middle aged Elf dressed in brown leather walked into the room, proud, but exhausted. "Emperor," he said, "everything and everyone is secure."

"Thank you, Alvar," said Berty. "You and your men have done well. Please, have a seat." Alvar sat in the chair in which he used to sit when he was a part of her Advisory Council. "I would like to commend you and your men's loyalty to the Empire Tree," he continued. "I understand that you were waiting in the trees surrounding the Sages' Grove for the would be usurper, Sean, and his followers even though the former Empress disbanded the Empire Guard."

"We did, my Lord," said Alvar. "Our duty to the Empire Tree resides in our hearts."

"A most honorable quality," Berty noted. "I hereby reinstate the Empire Guard and you as its Captain."

"Thank you, my Lord." Alvar paused. "What shall we do about the gates and the prisoners?"

"Have your men monitor the gates until Hatcher either returns or is replaced as Gate Keeper," said Berty. "The gates will remain closed. The only people allowed entry are Heads and residents of the Sages' Grove who wish to return to their homes. Everyone else must get permission.

"The prisoners will be given food and other necessities throughout the night. In the morning, I will have them questioned and either sentenced or released."

"Very well, Emperor," said Alvar, nodding.

"Before you go, Alvar," Berty said, "I am forming another Advisory Council and I would like very much for you to be on the council. What say you?"

Alvar's face glowed as he sat even straighter. "It would be an honor to be an Advisor on your Advisory Council, my Lord."

"You bestow much honor on the Empire Tree," said Berty, extending his hand. Alvar shook his hand. "Welcome to the Advisory Council, Captain Alvar."

Alvar smiled. When Berty released his hand, the Elf rose,

bowed, then said, "We are lucky to have such a noble Emperor." He walked proudly out of the room, leaving Berty in momentary solitude.

His thoughts regressed to the time when he first sat at the Roundtable. He sat in the chair to his left during her Advisory Council meeting. He remembered the shocked looks on some of her members' faces when she turned to him, asking, "Hubert, your thoughts?" Smiling, his thoughts were interrupted when the door opened again.

Theodore made his way to the table, saying, "The Heads would like a word, my Lord."

Berty nodded, saying, "Send them in." Theodore turned to go when Berty said, "Theodore, wait."

Facing Berty, the Dwarf said, "Yes, Emperor?"

"I would like a word with you first." Berty motioned for Theodore to sit. The young Dwarf walked as fast as he could to sit proudly in a chair. "Your loyalty and courage must be rewarded." Theodore looked at him with great anticipation. "You are being promoted," Berty continued, "to Head Tender." Theodore almost fell off his chair in elation. "Your orders come only from me. You have the important task of staffing the Empire Tree and finding trustworthy people to tend to the Advisory Council. Also, you and I are the only people who are allowed access to my chambers unless I invite someone."

Theodore nodded.

"Leena is still in your care until her family returns to the Sages' Grove. At such time, I wish to be notified," said Berty. "There is one other thing. Sean. As punishment for his misdeeds, he is required to serve the Empire Tree. I am placing this man under your jurisdiction for I trust you can handle him and perhaps find him useful in some way. I want you to know that since he is responsible for all that has happened, I do not trust him. It would be advisable for you to excise caution and be on guard around him. Do you accept your new duties?"

"Yes, my Lord," said an exuberant Theodore.

"Also," Berty said in a lighter tone, "please continue to practice and use your magic, even in the open. Now, you may send the Heads."

"Thank you, Emperor." Theodore climbed off the chair, bowed and quickly left to retrieve the Heads.

Berty stood to receive the Heads of the Empire. As they entered, each one greeted him as Emperor. He motioned for the four Heads to sit around the table.

Sitting in his chair to join them, he noticed everyone's crystal pendants, which had been obtained from the seven carved wooden columns that surrounded the scepter in the Scepter Room. When they originally hung the crystals around their necks per the former Empress' instructions, the crystals were colorless. Now, each crystal had a different color. Around Goscislaw's neck hung a dark brown crystal. Hanging on Lida's neck was a bright yellow crystal. On her husband, Elrick had a crystal of a golden orange. A forest green crystal adorned Alfred's neck. Glancing down at his own crystal, Berty noticed that his crystal had changed to a deep red.

Before he allowed his mind to wonder about what color crystal Silvia had, he asked, "Elrick, how are you feeling?"

"Much better, thank you," said Elrick, smiling. "Nothing that a good night's rest could not cure."

"I am glad," said Berty. "You are all welcome to stay for as long as you would like."

"That is very generous, my Lord," Lida said.

"Emperor," said Alfred in a more serious tone, "what are your plans for reinstating the Advisory Council?"

"I am not reinstating it," Berty answered. "I am forming a new Advisory Council."

"May I inquire about whom you had in mind for the scholar position?" asked Alfred.

"Would you like to submit a name for consideration?"

"I would like to be considered for the scholar position," said Alfred.

147

Berty watched the High Elf sit in his chair nobly for a moment. "Alfred, you would be excellent as a member of my Advisory Council. But what of your people?"

"My successor is ready to lead," explained Alfred. "I had been planning to step down soon. Now would be an appropriate time."

Berty pretended to consider Alfred's offer. Finally, he smiled, saying, "Welcome to the Advisory Council, Alfred."

Goscislaw, Elrick and Lida congratulated Alfred on his new position. Turning to Berty, Elrick said, "Lida and I would like to offer a more suitable Historian for your council, Emperor."

"I will accept anyone who you wish to send me," Berty said.

"My Lord," said Goscislaw in his low growl, "would Colvin be accepted? I know that he served on the former Empress' Advisory Council, but he is very loyal to the Empire Tree."

"I am well aware of his loyalty, Goscislaw," said Berty. "He would be most welcome."

"Excellent," replied the Dwarf. "I would like to discuss another matter, my Lord—your celebratory dinner this evening."

Lida read the look of apprehension on Berty's face, saying, "We know that it will be a bittersweet affair."

"But it is a tradition," Elrick added. "And traditions should be upheld."

A door opened. Theodore entered the room. "Pardon the intrusion, my Lord, but I have come to inform you that Hatcher has returned and wishes to resume his post. What shall I do with him?"

"Invite him to the celebratory dinner this evening. I will speak with him then," replied Berty. "Also extend invitations to Captain Alvar, Lieutenant Edwin, and the Watcher, Declan."

"Excellent," growled Goscislaw. "It will have all the important people as well."

"And," added Berty, "make sure Leena is included as well." That is what Silvia would have done, he thought.

"Very good, my Lord," Theodore said. "There is one other thing." The young Dwarf paused, fidgeting with his hands. "He,

Sean, would like to request an audience with the Emperor."

Berty's nostrils flared and the room got quiet. "I decline his request on the grounds of the fact that he is not in the position to make such requests. Remind him that his actions have lost him his freedom and tell him that his presence is required in the Reception Room at daybreak tomorrow."

"Yes, my Lord," Theodore said, bowing. He quickly left the room.

Berty looked at the silent Heads sitting in shock around the table. "If there is nothing else," he tried to sound pleasant, "then I will join you downstairs shortly."

Everyone bowed his or her head. The only noise was the sound of wooden chairs scraping the wooden floor as the Heads left Berty alone.

His eyes unfocused, and in his mind, he saw a stained glass door at which he waited for the subject of his next newspaper article to answer. When it opened, he introduced himself as Berty Chase. The woman on the other side of the threshold introduced herself as simply Silvia.

Silvia, who brought him through the portal, knew all the answers. He wondered how he was going to live in the Empire Tree without her. Berty recollected her warm smile, her kind, soft, brown eyes, and the way the light danced in her short, dark red hair. He wished that she could attend tonight's dinner, but Silvia was Elder Hunter and had to wander the Empire.

Feeling empty, Berty focused his eyes. He rose from his chair, knowing that any food would not fill him. As he walked towards the door to his private staircase, he saw a small, brown object on the floor. He bent down for a closer look to find his wand whole once again. Picking it up, he smiled, placing it in the pocket of his cloak. Berty descended the stairs, ready to be a part of the night's festivities at least in body.

At the bottom of the stairs, he took a deep breath before he emerged from behind the Sages' Seal with a smile plastered on his face. His guests bowed as he stood on the dais. When he sat at the long table filled with food and drink, they jovially raised their glasses toasting their new Emperor. Drinking with them, he graciously accepted their compliments and gifts.

"My Lord," said a rather short creature with messy, dark blond curls framing a triangular face. "I hope you remember me. My name is Hatcher and I was Gatekeeper." Berty remembered the Troll who stayed loyal to Silvia. "As soon as I heard that the battle was won, I hurried back to the Empire Tree to see if I could be of service to you."

Considering the humble Troll, Berty said, "I know of your service and of your loyalty to the Empire Tree. Tomorrow morning you can resume your post as Gatekeeper."

Smiling, Hatcher said with a bow, "Thank you, my Lord."

"Would you honor this Empire by reestablishing your seat on my Advisory Council?" Berty asked.

"I know of no higher honor, Emperor," said Hatcher, bowing low.

After Hatcher resumed his place at the dinner table, Berty's eyes searched for the other person to whom he wished to speak. Finding the thin, sandy haired man, he asked, "Declan, may I have a word?"

"Of course, Emperor," said Declan. He followed Berty to a relatively private section of the room.

"You have shown outstanding courage," said Berty, "and for that I thank you."

"My Lord," Declan said, "I wish I could tell you that I pledge my endless loyalty to the Empire Tree and to the Empire, but I do not believe in being loyal to an institution. Loyalty, I believe, is given only to people." Declan paused. "I was in the Watchers' Guild the day you and Elder Hunter came to see the Guild Master. It is to you and Elder Hunter in which I pledge my loyalty."

"Because of your loyalty to me," said Berty, "I would like you to have a place on my Advisory Council."

Declan's eyes opened wide. "My Lord, what an honor it would be to be considered one of your advisors."

150

Berty shook Declan's hand, welcoming him to the Advisory Council. While the two men walked back to the table, Berty asked, "Do you need lodgings for tonight, Declan?"

"No thank you," he answered. "I figured I'd stay in the Watchers' Guild tonight and return to the Empire Tree in the morning." Declan stopped walking. Berty stopped as well, looking at the sandy haired Watcher. "This might sound like a stupid question, my Lord," said Declan, lowering his voice. "When I arrive tomorrow, where do I go?"

Smiling, Berty clapped Declan on the shoulder, saying, "Breakfast will be served in here tomorrow. Come for breakfast and afterwards Theodore will show you to your chambers."

Looking relieved, Declan returned to his seat. Berty returned to the table as well, hoping that he could retire after a few more toasts. As he looked around the long table, seeing happy faces, he heard a mousy voice in his ear. "You must accompany me outside the Sages' Grove."

Berty turned his head to see Sean, still in his shackles, crouched next to his chair.

"Who are you to tell me what I must do?" asked Berty loudly. Everyone around the table froze.

"I need to see my parents," said Sean, "tell them how I am."

"You should have thought of that before you threw your dagger into the former Empress," Berty said coldly. "Write them a letter."

"Someone is enjoying his power," said Sean as he stood. "And look at how I am thanked."

"And why should you be thanked?" asked Berty.

"Because I made you Emperor," shouted Sean, pointing at his own chest.

"Unlike you," Berty said calmly, "I never wanted to be Emperor."

"You were happy being nothing but a two-bit Watcher?" taunted Sean. "I heard your wand was sliced in two. Boo hoo. Can't do anything without it." Theodore appeared in the doorway, looking horrified that his charge had escaped.

"This wand?" Berty extracted the repaired wand from his cloak pocket. Standing, he pointed its tip at Sean's neck. "Do not tempt me. Before I see you here tomorrow at daybreak, you had better learn how to tell the truth or I will use it." Berty held his stance for a second before placing his wand back into the folds of his cloak. Staring Sean down, Berty's eyes followed him as he sulked into the servant's corridor. Berty's eyes met Theodore's.

"I am so sorry, my Lord," apologized the young Dwarf. "It will not happen again."

"It is all right, Theodore," Berty soothed. Theodore bowed before charging after Sean.

"My Lord," said Alvar, "I will be here at daybreak to escort you outside."

Berty turned his head to face the table, then nodded. "It has been a long day," he said. "I am going to retire now. Thank you all for coming." Walking up the dais with his cloak sweeping behind him, he found solace in the relative solitude of his private staircase.

With each step, he thought of his large bed. Mindlessly, he stepped out of the trunk, crossing the long rope and plank bridge. Reaching the cluster of branches whose leaves had a combination of yellows and oranges, he stepped through the arched entryway into his study.

Hanging his cloak near the door, Berty realized that he was too riled to sleep. Looking around the round room, he gazed at his club chairs, his spiral staircase that led to his bedroom, and the carved wooden desk. He walked over to his desk, noticing that his old notebook sat open. Sitting in the chair, he turned the page and wrote the next chapter of *the Adventures of Leigh and Marcus.*

When he had finished writing, he put down his pen and sighed, knowing that he would have to go back to his other life tomorrow. Per Silvia's instructions, he had to see his editor-in-chief who Silvia admitted was her relative, Martin Hunter. Packing his notebook in his shoulder bag, he remembered that she gave him a letter to give to Martin. Berty retrieved the letter from a pocket in his cloak, packed it, then went to bed.

Chapter Sixteen
Dissonance

Berty opened his eyes to complete darkness. Today was the last day, he thought, that he was going to awaken before the crack of dawn. Begrudgingly, he climbed out of bed, then stood in the shower. Wearing fresh clothes felt better. When he bent down to tie his boots, he noticed the gold trim on his clothing like Silvia's used to have. Even his boots were different. The new clothes made being Emperor more of a reality.

After securing his cloak, he stepped into the cool, morning air. He breathed deeply. He smelled the leaves changing color. Crossing the bridge, Berty drew strength to deal with the one whom he loathed.

The route from his chambers to the Reception Room seemed to have gotten shorter, the more he traveled it. A stoic Elf waited for him in the otherwise empty round room.

"Emperor," said Alvar, bowing. "He has yet to arrive."

Berty nodded, saying, "Theodore."

"Good morning, Emperor," said the young Dwarf as he entered the room.

"Where is Sean?" Berty asked.

"On my heels," replied Theodore. He looked behind him. Seeing no one, Theodore snapped his fingers. Sean stumbled into the room, half dressed.

"I'd wish you would stop doing that," mumbled Sean. He continued to tuck in his shirt as his shackles jangled.

"When you learn some respect," said Theodore, clearly enjoying himself.

"Theodore," Berty said, "are the chambers ready for the Advisory Council members to occupy?"

"Everything will be ready by breakfast, my Lord."

"Excellent." Berty turned to Alvar and said, "It is time."

Alvar nodded. Theodore muttered a few words under his breath and Sean's shackles disappeared. Alvar took Sean's arm to guide him outside. Sean tried to wrestle his arm out of the Elf's firm grasp.

"This is ridiculous," exasperated Sean. "It is not like I can go anywhere."

Berty faced Sean. "You have two options. Either let Captain Alvar guide you or you wear the shackles. Which will it be?"

Sean's cold, gray eyes narrowed. "What am I, a prisoner?"

Berty walked within inches of Sean. "Yes. In case you were not aware, you committed crimes against the Empire Tree. Conspiracy to assassinate a sitting Empress. Attempting a coup d'état. Then there is the part where you actually killed the Empress."

"But I have a crystal, just as you do," shouted Sean, thrusting his silvery gray crystal in Berty's face. "Besides, the Empress lived."

Gritting his teeth, Berty breathed deeply through his nose. "That does not make you any less of a prisoner," he said. Turning, he walked down the stairs. Alvar followed clutching Sean.

Berty magically opened the doors that led to the Sages' Grove. A cold, autumn breeze thrashed around his cloak. They walked down the dirt path, past thatched white buildings until they met guards in front of a few makeshift paddocks full of disheartened men.

Lieutenant Edwin met Berty. "Emperor, we await your instructions."

Berty lowered his hood to address the prisoners. "Men, the information that you were given was wrong. It seems as though this person may have misinformed you for more sinister reasons. I believe that you should be told the truth."

Standing aside, Berty watched Alvar push Sean towards the prisoners. Sean looked at the men who listened to him and who were now packed into cells. He glanced at his feet, then back at the men before he spoke.

"I have told you that the reason magic had been disappearing was because the Empress stole it and stored it in the scepter," began Sean. "I was wrong. Did I believe it? Yes. I also thought that not only could I restore the magic, but that I could become Emperor as well. Neither of these things happened. The Empress could not restore any magic because she never stole any magic. When I struck her," Sean saw horrified looks on the men's faces when he said that. "Yes, I struck her. That was part of my plan, which I never told the majority of you." He looked down at his feet again before he continued. "When I struck her, the scepter stopped glowing. This man," he pointed at Berty, "restored the crystal's glow and became Emperor in the process." Sean paused to take a deep breath. "I have no idea why the magic has been diminishing and neither does the Emperor nor anyone else for that matter. I am sorry."

An awkward silence ushered in the full light of the morning. Berty broke that silence by saying, "Thank you for being honest." He nodded to Alvar who escorted Sean back inside the Empire Tree.

"Men of the Empire," addressed Berty, "I believe you to have families and lives that you are missing." A general murmur of agreement swept through the prisoners. "I understand your desire to have magic back in your lives, but all that you can do is live your lives the best that you can and accept any magic that comes. Know that all has been forgiven. In the future, shall any conflict or concern arise, seek first a diplomatic solution. You are all free to return home to your families." Berty nodded at Edwin who began to have the paddocks opened.

As the men filed out, Berty saw Declan talking to the Guild Master of the Watchers' Guild, so he walked over to greet them.

"Guild Master," Berty said, "so nice to see you have returned to the Sages' Grove already."

"Emperor," said the Guild Master, bowing. "Declan had messaged me, telling me that it was safe to return. I arrived just before you entered the Sages' Grove." The Guild Master turned a large, gold locket over in his hand to show the Watcher's Seal, comprising of an opened eye inside a six pointed star. "Declan has also informed me that you have decided to have a Watcher on your Advisory Council. Very wise, my Lord. There has not been a Watcher on an Advisory Council in generations."

"I am glad you approve," Berty said. He lowered his voice, asking, "Is there a more private place to talk?"

"I do approve," said the Guild Master, keeping his tone light. "Your choice of Watcher could not have been better. Please, honor us by coming in for some tea."

"Why thank you, I shall," Berty said while walking inside the Watchers' Guild after the elderly Guild Master.

The Guild Master said, "In here," and guided Berty into a small room to the left of the door. "Declan, come in and shut the door behind you." Declan walked into the room, closing the door in case other guild members returned. "With what can I help?" asked the old man.

"This locket," said Berty. "He extracted a large, gold locket with the Watcher's Seal from the pocket of his cloak. "You never mentioned when you wanted it returned."

The Guild Master's eyes welled with tears. Closing his eyes, he sat in the nearest chair. "I never thought I would live to see...," he said to himself more than to the others. Lifting his head, he opened his eyes, saying, "You will bring hope back to this land. Your predecessor tried, but as Empress she could not quite do so. She was still a remnant of the old way. To be reborn anew is how...." The old man glanced at Declan. "Emperor, the locket is our gift to you. Let it be a symbol of our unity."

"Thank you, Guild Master," said Berty. "It is an honor to receive such a gift." Regaining his composure, the Guild Master stood. "With this locket," Berty asked, "will I be able to communicate with Declan?"

"Yes. The locket will allow you to communicate with both mine and Declan's lockets," he explained.

"Does it only work within the Land of Sages?"

"Anywhere in the world," answered the Guild Master.

After Berty thanked the Guild Master for his time, he and Declan walked to the Empire Tree. Reaching the Reception Room, they found others already eating breakfast. Declan fixed himself a plate of food while Berty found Alfred.

"Good Morning, Emperor," said the Elf.

"Morning," Berty replied. "I would like a quick word." The two men walked out of earshot. "There are things that I need to do away from the Empire Tree," explained Berty. "I shall not be gone long. Can you manage things in my absence?"

"Of course, my Lord," answered Alfred. "Those in your position have always straddled the worlds. Is there anything in particular you wished for us to do?"

"First, make sure Declan gets his bearings. Second, can you look at the Hidden Treaty that was written during the time of the Third Empress and see how it can be improved so that the Trolls and Goblins can be civil to each other?"

"Consider it done, my Lord," said Alfred, bowing.

"Very good. Your council level chambers should be ready after breakfast."

Alfred sat to eat. Strolling by the food table, Berty picked up some fruit and bread before disappearing behind the Sages' Seal.

He ate as he climbed the stairs, thinking about all that he has to do. His first order of business was to see his editor-in-chief.

Crossing the rope and wood bridge to his chambers, he noticed that although the sun was rising, the temperatures were not. Berty entered his study and saw his bag sitting on a chair, ready to go. Removing his wand and the locket pockets from the pockets of his cloak, he placed them in his bag. He quickly changed into the jeans and sweater that he wore to Silvia's house on his second trip through the portal.

Berty ran downstairs, threw his bag over his shoulder and donned his deep red cloak. Feeling a little weird, he stepped out of his door, pausing before he crossed the little bridge that led to her chambers.

In the cold, he stared motionless at the dark arched doorway framed by yellow and orange leaves. The chambers through the door were his. He no longer needed to ring the wind chimes before he entered.

He stepped through the dark archway to find the study exactly as he remembered it. Silvia, prior to leaving, changed nothing. On the one side of the circular room were yellow couches and a wood coffee table. On the other side was her ornate desk. Walking between the two, Berty saw only one thing out of the ordinary. On the top of her desk laid a note with his name on it.

Opening it, Berty read Silvia's handwriting:

My Dearest Berty,

> *As a former Empress, I would like to give you a bit of advice, like my mother gave me. Do not let anyone sway your mind. Read everything on my bookshelves. And continue to practice and use your magic.*

> *In regards to the house, it knows that you are its owner. When you leave, it will lock itself to everyone else. When you return, it will open for you. Take time to explore the house for there are lots of nooks and crannies.*

> *I will see you soon enough,*

> *Silvia*

The note made him smile. Folding it, Berty tucked it into a pocket of his jeans. With a final look around the room, he walked to the back of the room, climbing up the steps behind the Sages' Seal.

Upstairs, Berty hung his cloak in her empty wardrobe. He walked around the bed to face the tapestry of the stag in the woodland scene. Holding tightly onto the strap of his bag, he stepped forward.

The brief bout of darkness gave way to a brightly sunlit room. Turning around, he saw the fireplace that depicted the same scene in stone. Berty quickly looked around the bedroom, barely registering the dark four poster bed, matching dresser and chest of drawers. He walked through the flanking wing chairs into the paneled hallway, then down the stairs.

Turning away from the stained glass front door, he walked into a hallway where the wood paneling from the foyer followed. Seeing the kitchen door, he opened a paneled cupboard to find a plastic zip bag that held his cell phone and car keys. His cell phone told him that even though he had spent days in the Land of Sages, it was only twenty-six hours later.

Walking out the back door, an autumn chill greeted Berty. In his car, he drove out of the long driveway, away from the old, Victorian house. The tree-lined street eventually gave way to less quaint neighborhoods until he drove onto a highway into the city.

He found a parking space in front of the tall building with a good amount of time left on the parking meter. Inside the building, he swiped his employee badge and opened the inner glass doors. An elevator waited to take him to the offices on the fourteenth floor.

Stepping out of the elevator, Berty passed the main desk where he ignored the lady behind it who said, "Good morning, Mister Chase." He walked straight past cubicles and small side offices. Arriving at a closed wooden door at the end of the hallway, Berty knocked.

"Come in," said an agitated man's voice.

A salt and pepper haired man sat on the large desk, telling a man around Berty's age, "I do not like it. Change it." The younger man began to leave. "And I want it on my desk by the end of the day."

The older man looked at Berty and smiled. "Berty, my boy, close the door." As Berty obliged, the man said, "Sit."

Sitting on an uncomfortable chair in front of the large desk, Berty said, "Mister Hunter, I have something for you."

"Fascinating angle you took," said Mister Hunter, cutting off Berty. "I take it you have another installment."

"Yes," Berty said, "but I haven't had time to type it."

Berty extruded his notebook from his bag, turned it to the proper page and handed it to his editor-in-chief. He noticed a light in Mister Hunter's eyes when he read Berty's words. Although Berty did not want to disturb him, he plucked Silvia's letter out of his bag. Holding it out to Mister Hunter who was still sitting on the edge of his desk, Berty said, "Silvia wanted me to give this to you, Mister Hunter."

Mister Hunter looked up from the notebook and his expression changed. The light in his eyes morphed into a look of concern that encompassed his entire face. Taking the letter from Berty, he glanced at it. Letter in hand, he walked over to his door, opening it. "You, in here now," he bellowed.

A young intern walked cautiously into the office. Mister Hunter picked up the notebook, thrusting it at the intern. "Photocopy from this page until the writing ends, then come back." The intern scurried out of the office with the notebook.

Closing the door, Mister Hunter sat in a chair next to Berty. "The house is yours," said Mister Hunter.

"Yes, Mister Hunter."

"No more of this Mister Hunter business. From now on, you are to call me Martin." Martin shook the letter, saying, "Are you moving everything out of your apartment today?"

"Yes," said Berty, "right after I leave here." There was a knock on the door.

Getting up, Martin answered the door. The intern stood sheepishly with the notebook in hand. "Give me the notebook," said Martin. "You take these copies and type them. As you finish each chapter, email it to me." The intern nodded and Martin closed the door.

Handing the notebook back to Berty, Martin said, "I'll be at the house later today. Don't leave the house without talking to me."

"I won't," said Berty. Placing the notebook back in his bag, he returned to his car.

Berty drove to his small apartment. Leaving the furniture, it took him a little over two hours to pack everything into his car.

When he arrived at the Victorian house, Martin was waiting in his car that was parked on the street. Berty pulled into the driveway, driving around back. He did not want the neighbors to see him moving into the house.

Entering the house, Berty walked down the hallway to the stained glass front door. Opening the door, he let a waiting Martin into the house.

"Let me help you bring your stuff into the house," said Martin as he stepped over the threshold.

Berty led him to the car parked behind the house. It took the two men around a half an hour to unpack all of Berty's belongings. When everything had a spot, they sat on an old, feather cushioned couch in the sitting room.

"Don't worry about a thing," said Martin. "All the house's bills are paid for till the end of the year. Your pay from your story will be more than enough to cover this." He looked around the room at all the antique furniture. "I'll even sublet your apartment for you until your lease is through."

"Thank you," Berty said in astonishment. "Why are you doing this?" He understood why Martin would do things for Silvia, but not for him.

"I grew up in this house," said Martin, smiling. "This house never changes for long periods of time. It is a constant fixture in an ever changing world." Looking at Berty seriously, he said, "In her letter, Silvia told me to tell you everything. So here it goes." He took a deep breath. "Every Empress since the beginning has lived in this house, no matter what form it took. The portal in these nearby woods, the one that Silvia took you through the first time, has always been heavily guarded because of that."

"Has the house always been on this spot?" asked Berty.

"Always."

"I gather that there have been Empresses for more than four hundred years," said Berty. "So does that mean that the first Empress was Native American?"

Martin chuckled. "History, Berty, is not objective." Admitting that Martin had a point, Berty nodded. "A Hunter has always been Empress," continued Martin. "Any Hunter who was not Empress lives on this side of the portal. We protect the house."

"Do your sons protect the house as well?" Berty asked.

"No. The second generation is free from that duty," Martin explained. "They do not know of the world in-between. They do not know that they will never have daughters, only granddaughters."

"Why not?"

"That is the way," answered Martin. "My sister was born when I was two. Yes, Silvia is my sister." Berty opened his mouth to speak, but Martin raised a hand to stop him. Berty seemed to know that Martin had told no one this story. "Until I was five, I lived in the Land of Sages. In order for me to live here, at the age of five, I had to be sent to school. In school, I was known to have an active imagination—sometimes too active for my own good. I soon learned that to get through school, I had to shut my mouth. Therefore, my writing flourished." He flashed a wry smile. "All my time off from school was spent in the Land of Sages, exploring with my sister. Silvia loved to explore. Our mother would get furious because Silvia was neglecting her pre-empress duties and ignoring her lessons. She never liked being cooped up in the Empire Tree or confined to the Sages' Grove." Martin smiled while his eyes saw nostalgic reminisces. "You are probably wondering how Silvia is only two years younger than I, yet looks as if she is around your age. For her, and now for you, time is simply strange like that."

Martin's smile faded as he looked away from Berty. "Your family will not understand. There is not much you can tell them either. They simply will not believe you." He took a deep breath before continuing. "By all means, tell them you live here. They can even visit. But they will never understand the lack of electric or phone. They won't even know why you are gone for long periods of time." Looking at Berty again, he said, "I believe that to be everything. I should be going." Standing, he tried hard to smile. "My sister thinks very highly of you."

Martin walked into the hall and Berty followed him to the front door. "If you can," said Martin with his hand on the doorknob, "keep sending me chapters, even if you have to mail me handwritten pages."

"I'll see what I can do," said Berty.

Martin merely nodded before he walked out the door.

Chapter Seventeen
A Family Tree

Berty looked at his shoulder bag propped up on the stairs and decided to return sooner rather than later. Turning off his cell phone, he placed it with his keys in a small cupboard. Grabbing his bag, he ran up the stairs into the bedroom.

Walking into the fireplace, Berty emerged in Silvia's former bedroom not knowing how long he had been gone. Finding his cloak where he left it, he threw it around his shoulders. He made his way down the steps towards the bookcases. Berty snatched a book off the shelf at random, and placed it in his pocket before stepping out into the cold.

Crossing the bridge to his chambers, he noticed that the sun was not much higher in the sky since he left. Berty was just about to walk through his doorway when Theodore appeared on his platform.

"My Lord," said Theodore, "I am so glad that I caught you. Alfred said that you needed some time alone."

"Let us get out of the cold, Theodore," said Berty as he held his arm out to allow the young Dwarf to enter the study.

Inside his warm study, Berty asked, "What is the problem?"

"Not really a problem, my Lord," said Theodore. "King Elrick's wings are healed and he and Queen Lida wish to leave, but not without your send off."

"Ah," said Berty. "Tell them to ready themselves for leaving. I will see them in the Reception Room shortly. Also, after they leave, I will be spending a fair amount of time in either this or the other study. Therefore, I wish to take my meals in here."

"Very good, my Lord," said Theodore.

Quickly changing into his Emperor clothes, Berty left his chambers, making sure that he had both his wand and the Watcher's locket in his pockets.

When he emerged on the dais from his private staircase, he descended the side steps, hidden from view, in order to greet the Heads more as Berty than as Emperor. Entering the Reception Room, he announced, "Elrick, Lida, thank you both so very much for staying through the trouble."

"Emperor," said Elrick, "noble souls such as ours must stick together in such times."

"We deeply appreciate the hospitality you have shown us," added Lida.

With both Alfred and Declan in the room, Elrick lowered his voice to say, "I wonder if we could ask a favor, my Lord." Lida timidly stood close to her husband.

"Anything," stated Berty.

"As I am sure you are aware," Elrick began, "Fairyland lies on the far northern border, straddling both the Land of Sages and the Dragonlands." He looked at his wife, then back at Berty. "And since we will be sending you a Historian upon our return," the Fairy rubbed his chin nervously, "we wondered if you would be so kind as to let us borrow a few Empire Guards as protection for us to travel home and for her to travel here." Elrick said the last part so fast that Berty needed a few seconds to register what he said.

"Elrick, of course I will send men with you," said Berty smiling. "I want you to stay healthy on your journey home. And there is no way I would allow the Historian to travel alone."

Both Elrick and Lida look relieved. Berty called for Theodore. When the young Dwarf arrived, Berty told him to fetch Alvar. Whilst they awaited the arrival of the Elf, Goscislaw walked over to them.

"My Lord," growled the Dwarf, "I, too, will be leaving today, after lunch. It was an honor fighting beside you."

"The honor was mine," Berty said.

Goscislaw smiled. "I will be sending Colvin soon."

"Thank you," said Berty, shaking the Dwarf Prince's hand. As Goscislaw walked away, a stoic Elf approached.

"You wanted to see me, my Lord," Alvar said.

"The Fairy King and Queen have requested an escort of Empire Guards not only for their journey home, but also for the Historian's journey here," explained Berty. "How quickly can this be arranged?"

"My men will need some provisions," answered Alvar.

"Theodore will help them with whatever they may need," Berty said. Standing in the distance, the young Dwarf nodded.

"Thank you, my Lord," said Alvar. He then turned to the Fairies, saying, "Someone will be up to collect you shortly."

Berty said his goodbyes, then returned to the comfort of his chambers. Finding the book he had put in his pocket, he placed it on his desk. *The Sages' Tales* glowed on the dark leather cover. The glittering letters tempted him to read the book, but his eyes kept glancing at the words *the History of the Empire* that adorned the spine of one of the few books on his shelf. He was not sure which book to read first.

After a quarter of an hour of doing nothing more than shifting in his chair, Berty remembered what Silvia had said about how the job of an Empress was to protect the secrets of the Sages. His mind saw a dark room where he learned to control his magic. Rising out of his chair, he walked to his bookshelf, retrieving the book that kept stealing his attention from the book on his desk. Berty sat in one of his comfortable club chairs, put his feet up, then opened the book. He figured that he could not protect the secrets when he did not know what is already common knowledge.

A few days of keeping to his study, Berty finished the book, *the History of the Empire*. The only person to whom he spoke was Theodore, as the Dwarf brought meals and some news. Berty had finally used his blank book that Silvia had given him a while ago to take notes and express his thoughts. Returning the book to its shelf, he realized that he had learned the details about the Goblin-Troll wars before the Hidden Treaty was drafted.

Hearing the wind chimes interrupted his thoughts and he said, "Come in."

Theodore entered with a tray of food. "Good afternoon, my

Lord. Does the reading go well?"

"Very well," said Berty as he walked over to his small dining table.

"Emperor," Theodore said, "the family of Rowan have returned."

"Please extend them an invitation to the Empire Tree for an audience with me," instructed Berty. "I will see them in the Reception Room. I would like to talk to them first before Leena joins us."

"It will be arranged for this afternoon, my Lord." Theodore finished setting the table, leaving Berty alone to eat his lunch.

As Berty crossed the bridge to the trunk, the autumn chill whipped his face. He had mixed emotions about leaving his chambers. The solitude of his study comforted him. With each step towards the Reception Room, Berty's anxiety rose. He wondered how Silvia managed her solitude with her social appearances.

Reaching the Reception Room, Berty found it empty. He sat on the throne, waiting to greet Leena's family.

Minutes later, Theodore entered the room followed by a young family with two children. "Emperor, the family of Rowan." The young family walked into the center of the room with looks of awe and fear on their faces.

"Welcome to the Empire Tree," said Berty. His anxiety melted. "You are probably wondering why you have been asked to come."

"Emperor," said the man with a worried look on his youngish face, "we wonder if you have news about my mother."

"I do," Berty said. "What is your name?"

"I am Cal," said the man, "and this is my wife, Natalie, our daughter, Alina, and our son, William."

"Cal, it pleases me to tell you that you mother, Leena, is safe," Berty exclaimed. "We brought her to the Empire Tree the morning after your family evacuated the Sages' Grove. We have been taking very good care of her while she awaited your return."

"Thank you, my Lord," said Cal, looking relieved. "We did not

168

want to leave her, but she insisted."

"I understand," Berty reassured. He raised his arm to draw the family's attention to the doorway.

"Grandma!" shouted Alina. She broke free of her mother's arms, running to hug her grandmother. "We camped in the woods! Willie and I got to play in the trees. It was so much fun! You should have come."

Leena glanced at Berty while she held onto the young girl's hand with tears of gratitude in her eyes. Berty knew that Leena feared that she would never see her granddaughter again. "I am glad you had fun in the woods," said Leena. "Did you explore the trees?"

Alina nodded happily. She opened her mouth to say more, but her mother cut her off. "Enough," Natalie said sternly. "I will not have any of this Witch business from you," she said through her teeth to Leena. "I don't care who your great-grandmother was."

Cal looked as though someone slapped him. "Why are you talking to Mom like that?" he demanded.

"Your mother has it in her head that Alina is to be a Witch like her great-grandmother Kalina," snapped Natalie, forgetting Berty was still in the room. "She keeps going on about how Alina has been showing the signs. Signs or no signs, I will not have a Witch in my house!"

"Why not?" asked Berty, calmly. The couple was immediately quiet. Leena simply smiled.

Walking forward, Natalie quietly said, "Witches are nothing."

Berty looked at the disapproving look on the woman's face. His eyes found Cal's insulted expression. Alina was still holding onto her grandmother's hand, but Berty saw disappointment and shame in the little girl's eyes.

"I disagree," Berty said. "A Witch brings honor to her family and is highly revered in her community. It is she who understands the workings of life better than anyone can. Denying fate is one of the worst things that a person can ever do. Tell me, Natalie, are you willing to sentence your daughter to a life without fulfillment and consumed by an inner turmoil?"

Natalie's head turned to look at her daughter. When she faced Berty again, her face was streaked with tears. Natalie shook her head. Cal approached his wife and tenderly held her as she silently cried on his shoulder.

"The family of Rowan," said Berty, "have produced the finest Witches since the beginning of the Empire. I will personally make sure that the woods surrounding the Sages' Grove are safe for Alina to play and explore."

"Thank you, Emperor," said Cal. He looked at his mother and daughter. "For everything."

Berty smiled. "Leena, it has been a pleasure to have you in the Empire Tree," said Berty, walking over to the elderly woman. Grasping her hand, he said, "I will have someone bring you your things. Go home with your family."

Leena kissed Berty on the cheek the only way a grandmother can. Berty smiled as he watched the family descend to the entrance below.

"Emperor," said Alfred, "it is nice to see you around the Empire Tree." Berty turned around to see the elderly Elf strolling towards him. "Before you retire for your evening meal, I would like a moment of your time, my Lord."

"Yes, of course, Alfred."

"First," said the Elf, "there is matter of the Hidden Treaty. Looking at it, there is not much we can do without an Historian."

"One will be arriving soon," Berty said. "You can start on it then."

"Very good, my Lord," said Alfred. "The next is more of a personal matter." He looked at Berty who did not give a response, then continued, "I would like permission to send for my personal servant from Irmingard."

"Have you spoken to Theodore about this?"

"He is the one who first asked me about having a servant, my Lord."

"Since Theodore is Head Tender, he is in charge of staffing the

Empire Tree," said Berty. "If he has no problems with that, then I see nothing wrong with it. It is better to have someone you trust in your employ."

"Thank you, Emperor," said Alfred, looking relieved.

Berty watched the Elf leave the room before ascending the dais. Returning to his study, he began another book while he ate his evening meal.

A couple of days later, the Sages' Grove teemed with life. People were in high spirits as Berty toured the village with his advisors, Alfred and Declan. Business bustled in the streets. Villagers gave Berty cheerful greetings while some gave small gifts. The trio stopped to see how the Rowan family were doing before they returned to the Empire Tree. Berty spent a rare evening eating with the inhabitants of the Empire Tree as it was honoring the return of the Dwarf, Colvin, to the Advisory Council.

After dinner, he called Theodore to his study. Berty was getting ready for a visit through the portal when Theodore arrived.

"I have a question, Theodore, and I hope you know the answer."

Theodore stood curiously in Berty's study.

"I would like to buy a few items from the vendors in the Sages' Grove," Berty explained. "How can I do so?"

The Dwarf's forehead frowned. "I believe you will have to ask Colvin to retrieve the coins for you, my Lord."

"Bring Colvin here after breakfast," Berty instructed.

After Theodore left, Berty walked across the small rope bridge and into the other chambers. Upstairs, he stepped through the tapestry.

Chapter Eighteen
Into the Roots

Darkness enveloped the Victorian house. Thinking about wanting to have light, Berty heard the soft whoosh of gas rushing through the pipes, which sparked to illuminate the house. In the paneled hallway downstairs, he found his cell phone and pressed the on button.

The phone told Berty that it was a few days before Thanksgiving. He sat on the sofa in the elegantly appointed sitting room while dialing.

"Hello?" said a woman's voice through the receiver.

"Hey, Mom," said Berty.

"Berty," she exclaimed, "how are you?"

"Fine, Mom."

"It has been a while since I've talked to you. I have called, but the phone went straight to voicemail. Now, I know you have been busy, but it is nice to call your mother and father every now and then. Just in case you have forgotten, Thanksgiving is this Thursday."

"Mom, I know. I was calling to see...."

"This year it is at Jon and Teresa's, one in the afternoon. Don't be late and bring something nice."

"Yes, Mom." Berty thought it best to agree. "I will see you on Thursday."

"Okay, darling," she answered. "I love you and your father sends his love, too."

"Love you guys, too," Berty said before he closed his phone.

He shut off his phone, placed it back in the cupboard, then walked up the stairs. Standing before the fireplace in the bedroom, Berty thought about turning off the lights. He was thrust into darkness. Stepping through the portal, he arrived in Silvia's old bedroom.

Berty pushed aside his thoughts of bringing Silvia to Thanksgiving dinner while he left her chambers. Hurrying through the cold, he entered his chambers, falling asleep quickly in his warm, cozy bed.

Opening his eyes, Berty saw the late autumn sunlight spill inside his bedroom. Invigorated by the sunshine, he sprang into the shower. Downstairs, he opened his blank book, poised to take notes while he turned the old pages of one of the books off of Silvia's shelves.

Hearing the wind chimes, he said, "Come in."

"Good morning, Emperor," said Theodore, bringing the morning bowl of porridge to the desk where Berty sat.

"Good morning," said Berty as he peered over his notes. "Is Colvin coming to see me soon?"

"Yes," answered Theodore. "He will be here in an hour."

"Great," Berty said as he took a spoonful of porridge. Theodore left him to read a section that stood out from the page.

Not fully understanding why, Berty hastened to copy it into his book. "The clan of Cian is the ruling clan over all the clans in the Dragonlands. Although technically under the Empress, they keep the order in their land as per an agreement with the Empire. If one is a friend of Cian, then one is a friend of all Dragons." He reread it a few more times before finishing his breakfast.

The sound of his wind chimes interrupted his pondering. "Come in," said Berty.

Berty looked away from his notes to see a red headed Dwarf with a long bushy beard. "Colvin," said Berty, rising out of his chair, "good of you to come. Please, sit." Berty extended his arm towards his sitting area.

Colvin sat on the closest chair while Berty sat opposite him. "Let's say I wanted to purchase a few items in the marketplace," Berty said. "How would I go about doing so?"

Smiling, the Dwarf said, "Most on the Advisory Council do not fully understand my role. Mining and Construction translates to metal work. Metal work includes the manufacturing of coins. As you are not from these lands, my Lord, I will briefly explain how the trade system works. The Empire has standardized coins for trading ease. Every village has a coinsmith who keeps the coins regulated. All coinsmiths are appointed by Prince Goscislaw. I am the noble coinsmith for both the Prince and the Emperor."

"How many coins does the Emperor have?" asked Berty.

"Infinite, my Lord."

Seeing confusion on Colvin's face, Berty said, "You will have to pardon my ignorance in these matters and indulge my yearning for knowledge."

"All metal in the Empire is owned by the Emperor," Colvin explained. "When a coin is smithed, on one side is the Empire Tree and on the other side is the individual coinsmith's signature which includes the information of who smithed the coin and when. Every coin that is smithed is recorded in a coin ledger so that every smith has a record of every coin he made and the Empire has a record of every coin ever made."

"Are there a limited number of coins that are allowed to be made?" Berty asked.

"No," Colvin answered. "But you own every coin. Typically, the Emperor rarely touches a coin because most Empresses have never had a reason to do so. For when one does need coins there is a special coin vault. No one but a sitting Emperor can enter."

"How do the Empire Guards and other workers get paid?" Berty's curiosity took over.

"There is a special Empire business vault," said Colvin who clearly enjoyed explaining the intricate workings of the Empire to Berty. "The Empire collects coins from fines, permits and other business conducted in the Receiving Room. We collect enough coins to manage everything."

Impressed, Berty asked, "How do I get to this vault?"

"I can take you," answered Colvin, "but I cannot enter even the antechamber. Before we go, perhaps you would like to know about the coins?"

"Yes, or I will not know how much to take."

Colvin nodded in agreement. "The smallest coin in value is the cop. Next is the ron. A step up is the ver. Lastly, there is the lid." The Dwarf placed one of each coin on the coffee table. "The cop is smithed from copper and thirty-two cops make a ron which is smithed from iron. Sixteen rons are in a ver. Vers are crafted from silver and it takes eight vers to make one lid which is made from gold."

Berty examined the bright orange cop, the dark gray of the ron, the gleaming light gray of the ver and the orangey-yellow of the lid. "How many of each do you suppose I would need?" he asked.

"Hmmm," said Colvin, stroking his beard. "I would only carry about three or so lids, eight vers, two or three dozen rons and a dozen or so cops. The Sages' Grove marketplace is the highest priced in the Land of Sages."

"Thank you for explaining, Colvin. Whenever you are ready to take me to the vault, I am ready as well."

"Is now too soon, my Lord?" Colvin asked.

"Now would be perfect," said Berty, standing.

They fastened their cloaks and raised their hoods before venturing into the cold, morning air. The sun could not warm the morning. Colvin walked into a basket like contraption that met Berty's platform. Berty followed the Dwarf into the basket. Colvin closed the little door. Looking above, Berty expected to see a hot air balloon, but instead saw ropes that connected to a pulley system somewhere.

As Colvin tugged a rope, down they flew. Pulling another rope, they whipped around the Empire Tree so quickly that all Berty could see were blurs of color. Finally, the basket stopped next to a fairly wide bridge. Opening the basket door, Colvin and Berty stepped onto the bridge.

Looking around, Berty was relieved that he was not dizzy. "Does this bridge make a circle around the trunk?" he asked.

"Indeed it does," answered the Dwarf. "This bridge is called Council Circle. It connects every council member's chambers."

They walked off Council Circle onto an intersecting bridge.

When they entered the Empire Tree, Berty found himself in the main corridor outside of the Roundtable Room. Not knowing where he was going, Berty followed Colvin down the stairs and across the floor of the Reception Room. Descending to the Receiving Room, Berty found it busier than ever.

Unnoticed by the people immersed in Empire business, Colvin led Berty to a concealed door in the back of the room. The door was sketched with the Sages' Seal. Berty watched as Colvin pressed the lower circle and the Seal split in two, exposing an inner chamber.

When they entered the inner chamber, the door closed behind them. The chamber's walls were more rough than the smoothly polished wood of all the rooms in the main part of the tree. Berty's stomach jumped as if they were plunging quickly down an elevator shaft.

Before Berty's stomach settled, another door split open. Berty and Colvin walked into a dark tunnel with torches secured onto the walls. In the dancing light of the generous flames, Berty could not tell if the walls were wood or dirt and stone. As they walked deeper into the tunnel, Berty could hear something that sounded like an old wooden roller coaster.

"What is that noise?" asked Berty.

"This tunnel connects to the rest of the underground using mining carts," Colvin explained. "Our cart awaits around this bend."

As they walked in the bend, the tunnel straightened a bit to reveal a niche on the side. At the back of the niche sat a mining cart. The metal cart had the Sages' Seal pressed into what looked like its door.

Colvin opened the door, standing aside to allow Berty to enter the cart first. Stepping into the cart, Berty saw cushioned seats. He sat in a seat while Colvin entered the cart. After the Dwarf secured the door closed, he sat in a seat next to Berty.

"Hold on," said Colvin as he pulled a lever in the front of the cart.

The cart started to roll slowly forward into the dark tunnel. Berty could not see any track ahead of them, but he could hear and feel the metal wheels as they moved along the metal track.

The da-doop sound of the cart rolling along the track started sounding closer together as the cart increased its speed. Moving faster and faster, the da-doop sound disappeared. Berty's eyes adjusted to the darkness, but he still could not see any track.

Suddenly, they rolled out of the tunnel into a huge cavern. Looking over the side, Berty could see more carts zipping in every direction, leaving one tunnel and entering another. The cavern walls glistened with veins of ore as the flickering light of flames around the floor illuminated the cart tracks and wooden supports. Before he was able to see more of the cavern, the cart was plunged into darkness.

After a few minutes of riding in silent darkness, Berty's ears caught the da-doop sound once again. The time between da-doops started to get longer and longer. Berty's eyes registered an increase in flickering light. The mining cart slowed and torches illuminated an even larger niche than the one from which they left.

When the mining cart came to a stop, Colvin unlatched the door before he and Berty stepped into the niche. Berty followed Colvin to a place behind a column of earth where the Empire Tree and circles of the Sages were carved into the rock.

Colvin placed his hand on the center of the tree trunk and the rock swung inward. Berty followed the Dwarf into the next room.

"Welcome to the Vault Room, Emperor," Colvin said. Berty looked around as the rock door closed behind him to see three carved panels of stone. On the left panel, a basic Sages' Seal was carved into the stone with little to no detail. The carving had a very Zen like, modernistic feel. Berty thought that it could grace any modern art museum's wall. The right panel's Sages' Seal carving had more detail, but only in the branches and leaves of the tree. Berty found it odd, but strikingly pleasing to the eye. The center panel had the most intricately carved Sages' Seal. The leaves on the tree were three-dimensional as were the roots. The circles had different designs in them and the whole thing was blushed with color. This was the first time Berty ever saw the Sages' Seal in color or as graphic.

"The door on the left," explained Colvin, "is the Empire Vault. Only the Head Tender has access. The door on the right is the Advisory Council's Vault Room. Each council member has a vault. The center door is how you access your Vault Room. From what I understand, your vault has a dual chamber for added security. On the other side of this door is the antechamber where you will find another door that leads to the vault itself."

Berty walked up to the center door to examine it more closely. Reaching out to touch the intricate carving, the door proceeded to swing open.

"I will wait here for you, my Lord," said Colvin.

Berty nodded, then walked into the antechamber. As he entered the chamber, torches ignited instantaneously. When the door closed, he found himself facing more than one other door. He counted four doors, each with different carvings. There were no trees carved into rock. Instead, he saw simple carvings of scrolls, coins, a trunk, and a ladder.

His curiosity overwhelmed him. Berty wanted to enter every room, but he decided that he could look behind all the doors another time. He walked over to the coin carving, touching it. A blank piece of stone, pretending to be part of the wall, rose into the ceiling. The light from the torches reflected onto the shiny coins inside the vault.

Entering the vault, Berty saw mounds of gold, silver, iron, and copper coins. He began to fill his pockets of his cloak with the different coins. Leaving the coin vault, the stone door descended into its place. He hesitated before leaving the antechamber as the ladder carving caught his eye.

Walking towards the carving, he touched the ladder. Another piece of wall began to move. As the stone slid into the wall, it revealed an old, wooden ladder. Berty walked into the doorway to examine the ladder. He could not see where the ladder ended. When his toe crossed the threshold as he tried to get a better look, another torch came to life. Even in the flame's bright light, he could not see to where the ladder led.

Something in his gut told him that it could lead to a portal. Berty's curiosity took over and he began to climb. Reaching the murky top, the familiar sensation of passing through a dark veil associated with portals washed over him. On the other side of the portal, he found a trap door.

His fingers discovered a metal ring, turning it. He pushed up slowly, not knowing where he was going to be. Peeking through the crack, his eyes found the legs of a couch, a desk and a chair. His eyes distinguished curved bookshelves that followed the curvature of a round room. Pushing the trapdoor open further, Berty poked his head into Silvia's study.

Since Colvin was waiting for him, Berty climbed down the ladder, returning to the Vault Room where the red headed Dwarf stood.

Chapter Nineteen
Necessities

"Ready to head back to the Empire Tree, my Lord?" Colvin asked.

"I am," answered Berty. "Thank you for bringing me."

Smiling, Colvin placed his hand on the door, swinging it open. They entered the mining cart and Berty enjoyed the cart ride as it zipped through the tunnels and cavern.

When they returned inconspicuously to the Receiving Room, Berty thanked Colvin again before he made his way through the crowd, walking out into the cold, autumn day.

A man draped in a light brown cloak walked up the path towards the Empire Tree. "Declan," said Berty, "how are you today?"

"Very well, my Lord," answered Declan. "And yourself?"

"Excellent. What brings you out and about today?" Berty asked.

"I am just returning from having breakfast with the Guild Master."

Berty had an idea. "Do you have anything pressing at the moment?" he asked.

"Nothing," said Declan.

"Would you like to join me?" Berty asked.

Declan looked as though Berty had caught him off guard. "Of course, my Lord," he answered. "What are we doing?"

"This outing is a personal one," said Berty as Declan smiled about being included. "I would like you to help me with a few purchases."

"Okay," Declan said. The two men walked down the winding dirt path to the busy, wooden, vendor stalls. "What do you wish to purchase?" he asked tentatively.

"I need to get a gift to bring to...," Berty said distractedly. "I want to get that," he said as he looked at a hand woven basket hanging from a woman's stall.

Berty and Declan approached the stall. The smiling woman said, "Can I help you with something?"

"May I see that basket?" asked Berty, pointing to the one that caught his eye from the path.

"Of course," she said. The woman carefully removed the basket, handing it to him.

Berty examined the oval, light brown basket with reddish brown accents woven throughout. He held it by its sturdy handle, asking, "How much?"

"Twelve rons," said the lady.

"Did you make this yourself?" asked Berty.

"Yes," the lady said proudly.

"Excellent craftsmanship," complimented Berty. Extracting the coins, he handed them to the woman.

"Thank you, sir," she said. "Have a nice day."

Walking away from the stall, Declan said, "You could have gotten it for ten rons or less."

Looking at Declan, Berty said in a low voice, "I do not feel right haggling as Emperor especially with gold woven into my sleeves." Declan glanced at Berty's gold trimmed shirt, then nodded.

In silence, they passed a stall that sold an array of hand carved wooded items. After Berty looked at the mainly utilitarian items he was ready to move on to the next one, when something tucked in the back caught his attention. An older man sat on a stool nearby, whittling a piece of wood.

"Excuse me, sir," said Berty.

The old man put down his work, walking over to wait on Berty.

"Is that for sale?" Berty asked as he pointed to the back of his stall.

"Yup," said the man. He handed Berty an expertly carved wooden doll. "Two vers for this one and you get to pick its clothes."

Berty examined the doll. It had shiny, dark eyes made from stone and long, sleek, dark brown hair. The arms and legs did not move, but Berty thought it was perfect.

"That is horse hair," said the man. "And I have these colored dresses sewn by my wife." The man laid doll dresses on top of other goods in green, blue, red, brown and muted yellow.

"I'll take it with the blue dress," said Berty, handing the doll back to the man. The man dressed the doll while Berty extracted two vers from his pocket.

After the exchange, Declan asked, "What need to do you have for a doll, my Lord?"

Berty smiled at the puzzled Declan. "It is for my niece."

"Oh," said Declan, laughing.

Meandering through the stalls, Berty bought honey with the comb, beeswax candles, different fruit preserves, a couple of bottles of mead, cheeses made from sheep's, goat's and cow's milk, and an assortment of fall fruits and nuts. Happy with his purchases, he and Declan strolled back to the Empire Tree.

As Berty explained the Thanksgiving holiday to Declan, a passerby walked into Declan, making him fall into Berty.

"Watch where you are going, sir," said Declan in a neutral tone.

The hooded passerby walked up to Declan, saying, "My apologies, Watcher. Tell, me do you feel important cozying up next to the Emperor?"

"Excuse me?" Declan asked, raising an eyebrow.

Lowering his hood, Sean glared at Declan with immense loathing. "All you like to do is feel important, don't you, Declan? Being a part of my elite core and now getting close to the Emperor. You only changed sides because you could hear us losing outside," Sean said.

"Think what you will, Sean," said Declan. "You are nothing but a greedy, pathetic man who is jealous of everyone else's talent."

Full of anger, Sean spat on Declan.

"That was uncalled for," Berty said. "You would think you would have learned some respect by now." The people in the surrounding area stopped to watch the exchange.

"I am simply looking out for your interests, my Lord," said Sean, bowing his head. "You should be aware of the character of the people who surround you."

"I am aware of more than you know," Berty said sternly. "Your ignorance astounds me."

"Oh, don't start this again," whined Sean. "Declan is not a man who can be trusted."

Declan's nostrils began to flare while his hands balled into fists.

"This is the point where I tell you," said Berty, "that although I appreciate your concern, as Emperor, I have many channels from which I collect information, so that I can make the right decision." He surveyed the seething Sean for a moment. "You owe Declan an apology."

Sean scoffed. "What for?"

"I will not tolerate insubordination," said Berty. "Guards, seize him." Two roaming guards grabbed Sean by his arms. "Keep him in a holding cell until it is time to sentence him."

"But I have chores to do in the tree," Sean pleaded.

"I will make sure that the Head Tender knows that you will be detained," stated Berty. "Remember, Seanlaoch, as a servant of the Empire Tree, you are bound by the rules of the Empire Tree and thereby subjected to its punishments." He motioned for the Empire Guards to take Sean away and the captivated audience dispersed.

As the two men entered the Empire Tree, how to punish Sean weighed heavily on Berty's mind. After they climbed the stairs to the Reception Room, Berty said to Declan, "Gather the Advisory Council for an impromptu meeting in the Roundtable Room."

"Yes, my Lord," said Declan before he ran into the corridor.

Berty thought about punishing Sean as he climbed his private staircase. Most of the punishments that crossed Berty's mind were extremely harsh and inappropriate, but they brought a little smirk to his face. Upon reaching the landing, he set the basket full of goods on the floor, then entered the empty Roundtable Room. Before sitting in his chair, Berty called for Theodore.

The young Dwarf entered the room through a side door. "What can I do for you, Emperor?" he asked.

"It seems that Sean has gotten himself in trouble. I would like for you to be present during Sean's sentencing, which will happen after this meeting," said Berty. "Afterwards, I will be taking dinner in my study."

"Very well, my Lord. I will be there."

As Theodore left the room, members of the Advisory Council entered. Berty sat in his chair so that the others would sit around the table. Once everyone was seated, Berty started the meeting.

"Most of you know by now that Sean, a servant in this tree, is being charged with public insubordination," Berty said. "At the moment, he is being held until he will be sentenced. I would like to discuss appropriate sentences."

"My Lord," said Alvar, "my men witnessed the altercation between Sean and Declan. Public disrespect of an Advisory Council member by a servant of the Empire Tree should be publicly punished. I feel that the punishment should fit the crime."

"I agree with Alvar," said Alfred. "But I also believe that we should not forget that this man's servitude is his punishment for attempted murder on the former Empress."

"Not attempted murder, Alfred," Berty said, "actual murder. She died. The fact that she is now alive does not make it not murder."

"My Lord," said Declan, "nothing would make me happier than to see this man punished most severely. For that reason, I must recuse myself from participating in this discussion."

"Duly noted," said Berty. His respect for Declan rose. "Hatcher and Colvin, what are you thoughts?"

"I believe that along with a public punishment," Hatcher said, "should be a private punishment. If I may suggest a full day in the stocks coupled with perhaps a week of confinement."

"That makes sense to me," said Colvin. "We have an underused dungeon, my Lord."

Berty thought about what each person had said for a moment. "Does anyone disagree with a dual punishment?" he asked. No one said a word. "Then it is settled. Alvar, make sure the guards who witnessed his crime are in attendance. It is time."

The members of the Advisory Council dispersed while Berty walked to his private doorway. In the landing, he removed his cloak to hang it on a hook. Taking a deep breath, he proceeded down the steps. He emerged from the hidden entrance behind the Sages' Seal to find Alfred waiting next to the heavy drapes which hung on either side of the dais, framing both the throne and the Sages' Seal.

Seeing Berty, Alfred walked over to him, saying, "An audience is forming. Alvar is stationing guards around the dais and the room, just in case." He peeked out from behind the drape to look at the room. "Looks like everyone is in place, my Lord."

Alfred wandered off the dais as Berty made sure that he was standing up straight. As he stepped out from behind the drape towards his throne, he saw all the members of the Advisory Council, Theodore and Empire Guards standing in the room. When Berty stood in front of his throne, the audience bowed. Berty sat, then said, "Bring the accused."

Escorted by two Empire Guards, Sean entered the room with his wrists and ankles in large, clanging shackles and a look of defiance written across his face.

"Seanlaoch," said Berty, "you are charged with the crime of public insubordination. As a servant of the Empire Tree, this is a most serious crime. Through the ages, punishment for said crime by a servant has ranged from banishment to beheading." A glimmer of fear flickered across Sean's face. "Unfortunately, you can neither be banished nor beheaded. Therefore, you are sentenced to two full days in the stocks and your chore workload will increase by at least double. In addition, you will not be allowed out of this tree and your movement within the tree is limited to the servants' quarters and the Reception Room only, but only when the Advisory Council is not present. These restrictions stay in effect until such time that I remove them. Take him away."

As the guards pulled him away, Berty could see the anger in Sean's eyes. "Wait," said Berty. "Seanlaoch, as much as you think that your special circumstances protect you, all that it really does is buy you time. When your debt to the Empire Tree has been paid, your crimes during your servitude will be weighed and the appropriate sentence will be given. Do I make myself clear?"

Sean looked up and behind his eyes, Berty thought he saw fear swimming in his mind. A spilt second later, Sean said, "Perfectly clear, my Lord."

Berty nodded at the guards and they dragged Sean to his punishment. The crowd stood in silence as Berty rose from his throne, disappearing behind the drape. He quickly walked up his staircase. Pausing on the landing of the Roundtable Room, Berty threw on his cloak and collected his basket. Not being able to walk as quickly with the basket in tow, he only beat Theodore arriving at his study by a few seconds.

"May I set up your meal, Emperor?" asked Theodore.

"Yes, please," Berty said. He placed the basket near the door and hung his cloak. He walked to the back of his study where Theodore was fixing the table for his dinner.

"My Lord," said Theodore as he looked up from the table, "may I discuss Sean?"

"Of course, Theodore. What is on your mind?"

"What you did was very fair," said the young Dwarf, "and I wanted to know if you think that this experience will change him any. I have been getting complaints from the other Tenders about him not doing his share. When I reprimand him, he scoffs at me. He asks if that is the best that I can do."

Sitting in his chair, Berty put his knuckles in front of his mouth. Lifting his head away from his hands, he said, "I hope so.

He tries to use that crystal as some sort of badge of honor. Like it changes anything." He sighed, then said, "I'm sorry that he gives you trouble, Theodore. I wish there was more that I could do about it."

"Hopefully, this will make the realization process come more quickly," said Theodore. "Do you need anything else, my Lord?"

"Yes," Berty said. "I do not wish to be disturbed from the time you leave until I call for you again. If there is an emergency, then Declan knows how to contact me."

"Very good, my Lord." The Dwarf left Berty to eat his meal.

After eating, Berty packed his shoulder bag with the essentials. He made sure it contained his wand, his old notebook and what he called his Emperor's journal. Berty changed into his street clothes, then placed his tray of dirty dishes outside his door for Theodore to take. Making sure the bag's strap was secure across his chest, he fastened his cloak. Grabbing the basket full of goodies, he stepped out of his chambers.

The cold wind whipped his cloak as he walked across the bridge to Silvia's chambers. Although it would make his portal crossings easier, Berty refused to move into Silvia's chambers. Leaving the mass of red and yellow colored leaves empty, Berty had found that it kept his mind from thinking about her, giving him hope that one day she may return.

Walking into her study, he remembered the trap door that he discovered earlier in the vault. His eyes searched the wooden floor for signs of an opening. Berty walked to the back of the study where he believed the trap door to be, but found nothing. He stared at the carved Sages' Seal on the back wall. His mind flashed an image of Colvin pressing a circle. His hand touched the lowest circle on the Seal.

To his right, a square portion of floor opened to reveal the ladder he climbed from the vault. Pleased with his finding, he closed the trapdoor, then proceeded up the hidden stairs to Silvia's bedroom where the tapestry portal hung. Removing the gold locket from his cloak, he placed it into the pocket of his jeans, securing the chain to a belt loop. After hanging his cloak in the empty wardrobe, Berty walked through the tapestry into a sunlight filled bedroom.

Galloping down the stairs of the old house, he opened the panel covered cupboard that contained his cell phone. Berty turned it on to find that it was the afternoon before Thanksgiving.

Placing the cell phone in his pocket, he put the basket on the white tablecloth that covered the dining room table. He artfully arranged the items within the basket so that it looked like a nice gift basket and put the doll on the side of the basket.

With not much else to do, Berty removed both his old notebook and his Emperor's journal from his bag, placing them on the other side of the long, dining room table. Upon opening his notebook, he began to chronicle his time as Emperor in another chapter of *the Adventures of Leigh and Marcus*.

Chapter Twenty
Where the Heart Resides

As the sunlight faded to darkness, Berty was getting hungry. He walked through the gas light illuminated house to the kitchen. Glancing at the big, old-fashioned, gas range, he used his cell phone to call for take out.

When Berty paid the delivery guy, he found it strange paying with paper money. He brought his bag of food into the kitchen and ate at the plank table. After eating, he thought about throwing away the paper containers and chopsticks in the garbage. They disappeared. Berty tried not to wonder where they went.

He wandered into a back sitting room whose entrance was obscured from the main hall. The room was cranberry in color and had a generous fireplace. He looked at the comfortable couch and chairs and wooden writing desk. Berty thought that this room was much less formal than the rest of the house and more like a modern family room minus the television.

On the mantle rested a wooden double clock. Two faces showed the correct time and the time somewhere else. Upon closer inspection of the clock faces, Berty realized that the other face told the time in the Land of Sages. The clock also showed the date for this world and the time of year of the other. Berty made a mental note to try to find one of these dual clocks when he returned to the Empire Tree.

The bookshelves burst with books. He recognized many titles, most of which he was made to read in school. A title-less book caught Berty's eye. The binding looked ancient. Plucking the book off the shelf with great care, he opened its pages.

The pages were handwritten. It looked to be someone's journal. Reading a bit, he learned that it was the journal of an Empress' husband. Berty sat, reading about the man's mundane life within the Sages' Grove. The man enjoyed taking his children around the area. On one trip, the man and his son took a small hunting party to hunt an elusive large deer to help feed the Sages' Grove's inhabitants. Berty put down the book to gather his Emperor's Journal from the dining room. Picking up the book, he read how the man and his son were separated from the hunting party in searching for the deer.

Grabbing a pen, Berty copied the next part in his journal. "In our wanderings, whilst we searched for either the deer or our party, we found a waterfall whose source is unknown. I called this fall, Tears of Beauty. I tasted the water that streaks down the rocks and I found it to be salty. However, the surrounding vegetation was some of the most beautiful that I had ever seen. After rejoining our group, neither I or my son could remember how to find that place again." Berty was not sure why the man's words were important, but he knew that it would come to him in time. Realizing that he was tired, he marked his place and went upstairs to sleep in the large four poster bed that views the fireplace portal.

Berty awoke later than usual the following morning. After he showered and dressed, he strolled into the kitchen to see what was available. Peeking in canisters, he found flour and sugars. He opened cabinets to find plates, glasses, a strange grinding contraption, a ceramic canister and a French press coffeemaker. Excited, Berty opened the canister. The robust aroma of coffee tickled his nose and he smiled.

He placed the beans and coffee making machines on the table. Finding a kettle, he filled it with water, then placed it on one of the burners. He turned the knob on the stove, but there was no flame. Quickly thinking ignite, the blue flames jumped out from underneath the kettle. After Berty turned down the flame, he noticed a box of long matches resting on a nearby shelf.

Chuckling at himself, he measured coffee beans into the grinding contraption. Assuming the coarse setting was correct, he thought grind. The handle turned, rapidly grinding the beans.

The ground coffee flew out of the chute into the small, glass beaker of the French press. He inhaled the intoxicating aroma as he poured hot water onto the grinds. As the coffee steeped, he found himself a mug.

With a mug of hot freshly brewed coffee in hand, Berty returned to the family room to explore more. In the writing desk, he found paper, ink wells, feathers, pens, and ink blotters that spanned the centuries. He felt as though he was living in an extremely well preserved, yet well lived in, museum.

Before he got ready to leave for his family's holiday meal, he brought his empty mug back into the kitchen, thinking the phrase, clean up. All his coffee preparation from earlier was gone. He threw on his wool pea coat, picked up the basket and doll, then walked out the door. In his car, he secured the gifts to the seat before he drove away from his new home.

Although he allotted an hour, it only took Berty forty-five minutes to drive from his new, quaint neighborhood to the other side of the city to Jon and Teresa's new development neighborhood on the outskirts of a typical suburban town.

As Berty drove through their neighborhood, the next house looked hauntingly similar to the previous house. Every lawn was impeccably manicured with unnatural looking green lawns without a speck of multicolored leaves. All of the mailboxes, which were only told apart by the different house numbers, stood firmly next to the driveways.

At last, Berty arrived at Jon and Teresa's. He pulled into the driveway, parking behind a burgundy luxury sedan. Sighing, he figured that it was best to get out of the car before someone had to collect him for they will have heard that someone had arrived.

Grabbing the gift basket and the doll, Berty strolled somberly up the curved sidewalk. Reaching the front door much too quickly, he paused before ringing the doorbell. Hearing the majestic chime ring inside the house, Berty surveyed the front stoop. Looking at the white metal storm door next to the red brick facade, he said to himself, "I do not like homes without porches."

He looked up, muttering, "Not even a cover from the rain."

The front door opened and in the entrance stood a slender man with dark hair wearing rectangular glasses. "Berty," he said surprised. "Teresa expected you to be late. Come in."

Berty walked over the threshold. "Late? Me?" He smiled. The man chuckled while grabbing Berty in a one armed hug.

"Let me take your coat."

Awkwardly removing his coat, Berty held out the basket, saying, "A little something for you and Teresa."

"Wow. She is going to love that," he said as he hung Berty's pea coat in the hall closet. "Just between you and me, Mom is going to love it, too, although I think she was hoping you would bring a girl."

"Jon," called a woman's voice from further inside the house, "who is at the door?"

"Speaking of Mom," Jon said, "we shouldn't keep her in suspense for too long." Berty chuckled with his brother as he followed him to the source of their mother's voice.

Walking down the hall, they entered a large, eat-in kitchen. The modern kitchen completely contrasted with Berty's old kitchen. All the stainless steel appliances shown brightly against the dark cherry cabinets and black stone countertops. A woman with long, brown hair stood at the stainless steel stove, stirring pots and tasting their contents. Sitting on a stool at the lighter kitchen island was a woman with chin length, dark hair with a white streak artfully playing at the side of her face.

"Look who's here," announced Jon.

Berty walked over to the woman sitting at the island, kissed her cheek, saying, "Hi, Mom, happy Thanksgiving."

The woman at the stove turned around, saying, "Berty. You're early."

"Why do you sound so surprised, Teresa?" said Berty with a wry smile as he handed her the basket.

"I... What is this?" she asked, looking at the basket.

"A little gift for you guys," said Berty.

Taking the basket, Teresa placed it on the kitchen table. "Wow," she said. "Look at all this great stuff. Is it all handmade? It is fantastic."

Berty's mother examined the basket. "Where did you find all this, Berty?"

"Just a seasonal, open aired market," Berty smiled.

"Good journalists never reveal their sources," said a man with more salt than pepper in his hair, walking through a swinging door.

"Hey, Dad," Berty said. Walking over, he hugged his father.

A little girl ran through the swinging door, shouting, "Uncle Berty! Grandpa and I set the table!"

Berty bent down, sweeping the girl into his arms. "Did you? I cannot wait to see it." The young girl smiled.

"What is that?" she asked, pointing to the wooden doll in his hand.

"Just a little wooden doll," said Berty.

"Can I see it?"

"Sure you can," he said. He handed his niece the doll while he put her back on the ground.

"Wow," she said softly.

"Do you like it, Hope?" Berty asked.

She stared at him with her big, brown eyes, then slowly nodded her head.

"I brought it for you, you know."

"You did?" Hope asked as her face lit up.

Berty smiled. "Yup."

"You are the best uncle ever," said Hope, hugging him. When she pulled out of the hug, she looked up at her uncle. "Uncle Berty," Hope asked, "what does the word gay mean?"

Berty glanced momentarily at Jon, then said, "Traditionally, it has always meant happy. Where did you hear that word?"

"Aunt Rachel said that she thinks you're gay," answered the little girl. "Are you happy, Uncle Berty?"

"Hope," said Teresa to her daughter, "why don't you come and

193

look at the turkey with Mommy."

"Okay," said Hope as she ran over to the oven with the doll tightly held in her arms.

Berty turned to Jon, asking, "What else does Rachel say?"

"I don't think she means anything malicious, darling," Berty's mother said. "Besides, she will be here soon."

"Yes, she does," snapped Berty. "I still do not know why you allow this woman around your daughter."

"She's my brother's wife," Teresa said.

"Do you ever get to see that little apartment of yours, being so busy?" Berty's father asked.

Glad for a change of subject, Berty said, "No. I have a new place now."

"What kind of place?" asked Jon.

"Just a modest, little house," Berty said. "Nothing special."

"Your father and I will come over tomorrow," said Berty's mother.

The doorbell rang. Jon said, "I'll get it."

Jon was barely gone a minute before he brought two more people into the kitchen. A tall, thin woman with shoulder length, blonde hair walked over to Teresa, giving her a hug and a kiss. A silver haired man walked over to Berty's father. The men shook hands.

"George," said the man, "nice to see you again." He kissed Berty's mother on the cheek, saying, "Kate, looking lovely as always."

"What have you got in your hand, Robert?" George asked.

"Gift for the kids," answered Robert. "Single malt Scotch."

"I love the new kitchen, Teresa," said the woman. "When will you be doing the rest of the house?"

"Thanks, Mom," Teresa said. "Jon and I haven't decided yet."

Teresa's mother walked over to the kitchen table, saying, "This is a nice, little, gourmet basket. Did you bring it, Kate?"

"No," said Kate. "My son brought it, Lillian. I made the pies."

Looking at both women's faces, Berty knew that it was going

to be a long dinner.

The doorbell rang again and Robert said, "That should be Matt and Rachel. They were right behind us." Jon left to answer the door. A few moments later, a woman with long waves of strawberry blonde hair waltzed into the kitchen from the hallway.

"Happy Thanksgiving, everyone," she said with a lurid smile. "Teresa, when will dinner be ready?"

Teresa removed the huge, golden brown turkey from the oven, setting it on the island. "In about twenty minutes, Rachel."

"Fantastic," Rachel said. "I know your kitchen is spacious, but perhaps we should take this party to the living room and have a drink or two." Jon entered the kitchen with another man who had brown hair and a rugged, shadowy beard. "Matt, darling," said Rachel, "be a dear and get me a gin and tonic, heavy on the gin." With a wide smile, she turned to look at Berty. "Berty, gracing us with your presence, I see."

"Every now and then I like to mix with the little people," Berty said. "Helps me stay grounded, you know."

"Are you still hiding behind the printed word?" taunted Rachel.

"Do you still cackle when your maid uses a broom?" Berty retorted.

Rachel smiled, then turned away from Berty, saying, "Where is that darling husband of mine with my drink?"

Walking into the kitchen holding a glass of clear liquid, Matt said, "Here you go, dear." Rachel took it from him, tasted it, then licked her lips.

"Berty," said Matt, after knowing that his wife was satisfied, "are you ready to join us for a little football after we eat?" Rachel snorted.

"I did not know anything about it, so I didn't bring anything to change into," said Berty.

"I have some stuff you can wear," Jon said. Smiling, Berty nodded.

"George," said Teresa, "can you get the wine out of the chiller and pour it? Jon will show you which one. Kate, can you help me with the food? Mom, please bring these rolls to the table. Oh, Jon, you have to carve the turkey." She handed her mother a napkin covered bowl. "Everyone else, please congregate in the dining room."

Berty followed his brother's in-laws through the swinging door with much trepidation. Waiting at the table, Matt discussed his financial business with Robert and Lillian while Rachel thoroughly enjoyed her drink.

George poured the wine, then took his seat while Kate and Teresa walked back and forth, filling the elegantly set table with food. When the last side dish was placed on the table, Kate sat and started to talk to Berty about the location of his house.

Teresa and Jon entered together with Jon carrying the platter of turkey. Placing it on the table, he waited for his wife to sit, then said, "Let's eat."

During dinner, Berty listened to a myriad of conversations about work, Hope's school and Christmas shopping plans. None of the conversations interested him. While he chewed his food, he watched Rachel down drinks like they were going out of style.

When the last morsel was consumed, Jon said, "Berty, Matt, let's go get ready to join the football game." The three men walked up the stairs and through the double doors into Jon's spacious bedroom. Placing his duffel bag on one of Jon's chairs, Matt began to change. Jon went through his drawers, throwing an old t-shirt and a pair of jeans on the sleigh bed for Berty.

Berty removed his sweater, placing it delicately on the bed. He was about to pull the long sleeved t-shirt over his head when Matt said, "Nice tattoo, Berty."

Looking over his left shoulder, Berty saw his back in Jon's large mirror. "Thanks," he said.

"That is cool," said Jon. "How long have you had it?"

"About a month," Berty answered as he pulled the shirt over his head. "Do me a favor, Jon, and don't tell Mom."

"Won't say a thing," Jon said. "When Mom is upset about

something, we all suffer. I am really glad you have a house now. It will keep her from badgering Teresa about fixing you up with a nice girl."

"I do what I can," said Berty. Laughing, they walked out of the house to an open field down the street. Matt, Jon, and Berty met a bunch of men from the neighborhood, either residents or visitors, for a friendly game of football.

After football, the men changed to rejoin their family in the dining room for coffee and pie. Berty sat down in front of his large slice of pumpkin pie and watched Rachel pour something other than cream into her coffee. He was enjoying his dessert while Lillian started a new topic of conversation.

"So, Rachel," said Lillian, "are you guys planning on having a baby sometime soon?"

"Don't concern yourself with my business," Rachel slurred.

"I was just thinking that drinking is not helpful when trying to conceive," stated Lillian.

"The drinking helps with putting up with the likes of you people," said Rachel as she placed a large forkful of pie into her mouth. Lillian did not move a muscle, only stared at Rachel in disbelief. "Oh, don't look at me like that, Lillian. You know that all you and Robert do is pressure me for a grandchild."

"What's wrong with having children?" asked Matt.

"Oh, you are a silly boy," Rachel said, waving a hand at her husband. She addressed her mother-in-law again. "Pressure your own daughter to have another for a change."

Outraged, Matt said, "Stop it, Rachel."

Ignoring him, she continued. "Speaking of your daughter," she took a swig from her cup. "You are not Martha Stewart, Teresa. Stop trying. You give women a bad name."

"That's enough," said Matt sternly while looking squarely at his wife.

"Oh, Matty," cooed Rachel, "did playing football with all the other boys make you feel like you grew a pair?" She smiled, then hiccuped.

"I will not let you talk to my family like that," Matt said. "We're leaving."

Rachel laughed maniacally. "No, we're not. I just got started."

"No." Matt stood. Walking over to his wife, he said, "You're done."

"You don't say no to me, Matt."

Sensing trouble, Berty leaned over to his niece, whispering, "Why don't you go play in the family room with your new doll." Berty watched her brown banana curls bounce as she ran from the room.

"I'm saying no now," said Matt.

Rachel's mouth dropped as she watched her husband grab her arm firmly.

"You are drunk. We are going home."

Rachel quickly finished her alcohol laced coffee.

"Mom, Dad," he said as he let go of his wife's arm to walk towards the door, "I am so sorry. This will not happen again. Teresa, Jon, you hosted a lovely Thanksgiving. I wish we could have been more of a delight instead of a hindrance." Matt barely finished the last word when something whizzed past his ear.

The smash could barely be heard over Rachel's mad laughing and Teresa's shrill shouts. "What are you doing? That's my wedding china!" Rachel's place setting was missing a cup. "I can't replace it," Teresa said as tears trickled down her face. Rachel picked up the saucer while Teresa wildly screamed, "No! No! Stop! Please stop, you crazy...." Her words became mumbled as hysterics commanded her body.

After George wrestled the saucer out of Rachel's hand, he said to Matt, "You had better take her home now."

Jon scrambled to retrieve Matt and Rachel's coats while Matt helped a wobbly, laughing Rachel to the hallway. Teresa collapsed into a heap on the table, sobbing hysterically. Both Lillian and Kate tried to calm her. George decided that it was best to clear the table while Robert hurried after his son.

Seeing the broken shards of china on the dark wooden floors,

Berty quietly walked over to the wall and crouched down, retrieving all the pieces.

"It's no use," said Teresa as she came out of her shocked state. "The set was my grandmother's, Berty."

Gazing at her tear streaked face, Berty said, "I'll take them home with me. Perhaps I can find something." She smiled weakly as Jon returned to her side.

In a small box, Berty's collection of shards sat on the table, waiting for him to bring home. His father wrote down his new address while both mothers contained the leftover food for use another day.

"Your father and I will pick you up for shopping in the morning," Berty heard Lillian say to Teresa as he walked into the kitchen.

He hugged everyone as he said his goodbyes. Teresa thanked him again for the gift basket. Box in hand, Berty followed Jon down the hallway to get his coat. As Jon was removing Berty's coat from its hanger, the sound of little, running footsteps echoed in the hall.

"Uncle Berty," said Hope, "you did not say goodbye to Ashley." Her little hands held out the handmade doll. In the corner of his eye, he saw Jon's smiling face.

"How silly of me," he said, crouching. "Ashley is such a lovely name. From where did she get it?"

"She's made of wood," said Hope as she rolled her eyes. The answer could not have been more obvious to her. "From the ash tree."

"Why didn't I think of that?" Berty said. "Hope, you are getting too smart for your own good."

"Never," she said.

Berty smiled. "Never is right. Bye, Hope," he said, "and bye, Ashley."

Berty put on his coat while Hope held the little wooden doll up to her ear. As he hugged his brother goodbye, Hope tugged on the hem of his wool coat. When Berty and Jon looked down, she said,

"Ashley says, 'look in the roots, and thank you, and bye.'" Smiling, Hope held her doll close as she ran up the stairs. Jon shot a quizzical look at Berty who merely shrugged.

Placing the box on the passenger seat, he drove away from his brother's house. On the drive home, Berty wondered if the doll he gave to Hope was magical without the doll maker's knowledge. Merging onto the freeway, he dismissed that thought. Perhaps, he pondered, Hope was the one with the magic. For the rest of the drive home, Berty kept repeating the words, *look in the roots.* Its meaning eluded him. Arriving home, he went straight to bed, figuring that he would be able to focus his thoughts the following morning.

Berty awoke, reciting *look in the roots* in his mind. Jumping out of bed, he stared at himself in the dresser mirror. His dark hair stuck out in weird ways from sleeping. He scratched the stubble on the side of his cheek, remembering that his parents were coming to visit. As he turned to head into the bathroom, Berty decided to take a closer look at the tattoo resting near his left shoulder blade.

Touching it, it felt as though he had always had it. Three inches in diameter, the surrounding circle was dark black. The multiple shades of green leaves seemed to blow in the breeze when he moved. Even the dark brown bark on the trunk had texture so real that he had to touch it to feel that his skin was still smooth. The muted brown roots looked as though they were burrowing into his skin. Seven vibrant circles jumped out against the dark tree in pink, baby blue, light green, light orange, lavender, pale yellow, and tan.

In the shower, Berty could not remember when he got the tattoo. Wracking his brain, he figured that it had to have happened the day he became Emperor. The only reason why he did not feel it was because he was intent on saving Silvia. It bothered him that he had not seen it before.

Getting dressed, he realized that he had never noticed the tattoo because he had been preoccupied with re-establishing order in the Empire. As Berty attempted to grab the Watcher's locket that he left on the dresser, he saw that it glowed brightly. Opening it, he read, "People keep inquiring at the Empire Tree wanting to know why the magic keeps disappearing and how they can get magical solutions to their problems. What shall we say? — Declan."

Holding the clasp's rod like a pen, Berty replied, "Tell whoever asks that we are aware of this problem and are actively working on a solution. Also, tell them that they need to be patient and just live their lives as they have been." He read it over twice before signing it 'E.' Although he thought that he sounded like a generic recording that plays when he calls the electric company during a power outage, he sent it anyway.

On his way down to the kitchen, he knew that there was nothing else he could say. He had no idea why the magic was vanishing.

In the kitchen, Berty stared blankly at the cabinet doors. He had nothing to offer his parents when they came. Awaiting their morning arrival, Berty figured he could at least make coffee. The coffee equipment flew out of the cabinets and coffee was starting to be made. He wished that he could offer some sort of coffeecake, since that was something his parents really enjoyed. Off a shelf, a book flew at his head. Catching it, the book opened to a page with a coffeecake recipe. Never making anything not originating from a can or a box, he looked at the page with the utmost curiosity. On the top of the page, it said, "Do not speed bake. You may speed cool."

Following his gut, Berty read the recipe aloud. As he read, ingredients flew around the kitchen. Flour and sugar measured into bowls. Eggs flew out of an old icebox Berty had not yet noticed and cracked into the sugar. After the batter mixed itself, it poured into a pan. As it baked, Berty smiled, knowing how Silvia made all those cookies for when he first arrived.

He walked around the house, wondering if its hiding places held answers. Magic flourished in the house. A buzzer in the kitchen interrupted his thoughts.

Returning to the kitchen, the beautiful coffeecake rested on top of the stove. While he allowed the cake to speed cool, he thought about how he would serve everything. Remembering the tray and coffee carafe Silvia once used, the items along with plates, cups and utensils arranged themselves on the plank kitchen table. With the cake on a stand and everything else on a tray, Berty ushered everything onto the dining room table. As he admired his magic, the doorbell rang. He hoped the cake tasted okay.

Berty opened the door and saw his mother and father admiring the porch. "Mom, Dad," he said, "come in." Kate and George stepped into the wood paneled foyer as Berty said, "Let me take your coats." As they removed their coats, they peered at the dark wood walls and the brass chandelier. They noticed the throw rugs and antique furniture. While Berty hung his parents' coats in the closet that Silvia once made him leave his bag, their silence bothered him. "Did you find the place okay?"

"Yes," said George, finally stopping taking inventory. "The directions that you gave were great."

After his mother had seemed to catalogue everything in her photographic memory, she smiled, hugging her son. "Did you sleep well after last night?"

"Fine," Berty said. "Would you guys like some coffee?"

"Love some," said George. Berty escorted his parents through beveled glass pocket doors into the dining room where he had coffee and cake ready.

Berty held the chair for his mother. Her eyes scanned the room as Berty poured coffee into cups for his parents. Cutting the cake, he placed a piece in front of each of them with a fork.

"Where did you get the cake?" asked Kate.

"Made it."

"A man of many talents," George said while taking a bite.

"This is quite a hidden gem," said Kate. "Did all of this come with the house?"

"All of what?" asked Berty as he took a bite of cake. He was pleased with his magical baking skill.

"The furniture," Kate answered, "with its table cloth and the china and the silver."

"Everything," said Berty. "All I did was move in my clothes."

"Well you didn't have much else," Kate said.

"Turn key house," George stated. "Probably cost you a pretty penny."

"It wasn't too bad," said Berty. Seeing his mother give him an I am going to get to the bottom of this smile, he held his breath, dreading what she might be thinking.

"Once we are finished with coffee," said Kate using flamboyant hand gestures, "why don't you give us the grand tour."

"What a good idea," Berty said, returning the smile.

After they drank the last drop of coffee, Berty showed his parents the sitting room in which his editor-in-chief, Martin Hunter, spoke of family matters.

"These antiques are in excellent condition," said Kate while she walked around the room.

"How many bedrooms?" George asked.

"Four."

"Let's see those next," said Kate as she walked out of the sitting room.

Berty led them up the stairs where George felt the wood paneling. The first bedroom had two single beds, a small dresser and a chest. It shared a bath with the second bedroom, which held a brass framed double bed, a chest of drawers and a small writing desk. When they explored the third bedroom, George walked past the four poster bed, asking, "Do all the rooms have fireplaces?"

"Yes," answered Berty, "except for the kitchen where it was converted to the gas stove." Watching his father examine a mantle clock, Berty walked over to join him.

"Look at this," said George. "I've seen this sort of thing on TV—on that British show where they rummage through people's homes to sell stuff at auction. I forget what they are called, but they hold pocket watches and double as a clock." Berty had never seen his father so excited in a long time. "That show never mentioned a double clock before. This must be rare."

Looking at the mantle clock, Berty realized that it was the family room's clock in pocket size. On the one side was a normal watch face with inset dials for month and day. On the other side, the face showed the time of year and sunrise and sunset hours. Berty was relieved to finally have a watch to bring with him to the Land of Sages, so he could know the time on both sides of the portal.

After a quick peek inside the adjoining bathroom, Kate and George wandered into the last bedroom—Berty's bedroom. The large four poster bed anchored the room on one side while the fireplace with its carved relief of a stag in the woods anchored the other side.

Admiring the wing chairs in front of the fireplace, Kate said, "Now this is a master bedroom." She smiled at her son who was standing in the doorway. "I would like to see the kitchen."

Berty led his parents back down the main stairs and down the dark paneled hallway. Standing in the kitchen, Berty held his breath until his mother said, "Charming."

"Kate, dear," said George, "we should get going if we want to make lunch."

"You are leaving so soon?" Berty asked. He was surprised, yet hopeful.

"*We* are leaving," corrected Kate, motioning to the three of them. "A new Indian restaurant opened and we wanted to treat our eldest son to lunch."

"Thanks guys," Berty said, smiling. "Can we stop by the copy store? I have something to copy for my editor."

"Absolutely," said George as he followed Berty out of the kitchen. "If you show me where the closet is, I can get the coats for your mother and me."

Berty opened the closet masquerading as a panel for his father before he ran up the stairs to retrieve his notebook. Running downstairs, Berty's parents were buttoning their coats and he quickly put on his coat. Opening the stained glass door for his parents, he followed them onto the porch, closing the door behind him. As he walked off the porch, he heard a soft click as the door locked itself.

Sitting in the back seat of his parents' car felt strange, but he did not mind. Before arriving at the restaurant, George dropped Berty off to make copies of his newly written chapter of *the Adventures of Leigh and Marcus*. He was able to mail them to Martin Hunter without much fuss.

At the restaurant, Berty had a view of some Indian artwork of which he admired the bright colors. When the drinks arrived, George raised his glass, saying, "To Berty's new house." He and Kate raised their glasses as well and all three of them took a sip.

A server placed their food in front of them. Berty listened to his parents compliment the food as seasoned rice was being passed around the table.

"So," said Kate as she ripped off a piece of naan, "who is she?"

Berty watched his mother grab some food off her plate with her bread. Swallowing the chunk of paneer in his mouth, he said, "I do not understand."

"The woman who has stolen your heart," said Kate. Tearing another piece of bread, she continued, "The reason why you have the house, there must be a woman behind it." Kate shrugged. "That is what your father and I have been talking about all night. There is a woman, is there not?" his mother said with a smile.

Flashes of short, dark red hair, brown eyes, and soft lips popped into Berty's head. "Yeah... no."

Putting down his glass, George said, "So there is the possibility of a woman, but you are not together yet?"

"Right."

"When will you be getting together?" Kate asked.

Never, Berty thought. "It's complicated... because she is away... right now... traveling... for her job... gone for a long period of time."

"Oh," said Kate. "What kind of work does she do?"

"Education." Berty could feel himself sweating while his stomach turned and a burning sensation rose in his chest. Wishing that he had not ordered extra spicy, he said, "She travels to teach special life skills."

Kate's kind face softened. "How noble. What is her name?"

"Silvia." Berty watched his mother's eyebrow raise as if to say, no last name. "Silvia Hunter," Berty added.

"You weren't planning on bringing her for Christmas were you?" asked George.

"No. I was not," Berty said.

"Good," said George, "because your mother and I are going away for Christmas."

"Where are you going?" asked Berty.

"On a Caribbean cruise," Kate answered.

"We got one of those last minute deals," said George.

"Your brother and his family are going to Teresa's parents house," Kate said as she put her hand on Berty's arm. "I hate the thought of you being in that big house all alone on Christmas." She extracted a phone from her purse. "I'll call Lillian to have you invited over there."

"Mom, no." Berty placed his hand on her phone. "I will be fine, better than fine. You guys go have fun and have a piña colada for me."

Kate smiled at her son. "Are you sure?"

"Absolutely."

Kate nodded, then said, "Aren't you boys glad that I found this place? What a great lunch."

After lunch, Kate and George dropped Berty off at his house. He waved from the porch as his parents drove away. As he crossed over the threshold, the gaslights came to life, illuminating the darkening house.

Berty made sure that everything was clean and put away. Walking past the plank table in the kitchen, he saw the box of broken cup shards. He placed his hands over the box and thought about seamlessly repairing his sister-in-law's cup. When he

206

removed his hands, the cup returned to its pre-Rachel's outburst state.

He delicately picked up the cup, examining it. Teresa would never know that Berty had repaired the cup. Smiling, he tried to decide where to keep it for a month. Walking into the dining room, he placed the cup on the middle of the table, saying, "I am going to place the cup here for safe keeping." Berty had no idea why he spoke aloud, but it made sense to him.

Gathering his things from around the house, he walked into the third bedroom. Berty walked over to the mantle where the dual pocket watch was kept, saying, "This, I need." The white metal pocket watch popped out of its holder like a piece of toast from a toaster. Closing the watch, he placed it in his pocket.

With his bag secured across his shoulder, Berty walked into his bedroom. He took a moment to turn off the lights, then he stepped through the fireplace, returning to the Land of Sages.

Chapter Twenty-one
The Acceptance of History

He walked through the tapestry into Silvia's dark chambers. As a lantern lit nearby, he extracted the pocket watch from the pocket of his corduroys. Looking at it in the steady oil fueled light, he realized that it was three hours till sunrise. With no intentions of falling asleep, he carried the lantern down the stairs, wandering over towards Silvia's collection of books.

As Berty perused the book titles, *the Order of the Empress* caught his eye. Opening to the first page, he began to read by lantern light. He read the story that Silvia had told him on his maiden journey through the Land of Sages. As he read, his memory recalled sitting around a fire with strangers and ultimately Sean, listening to Silvia's voice tell the story of how the first Empress was chosen by the scepter. Silvia's tale sounded as if the scepter chose just any first child born from any family within the Empire. The book told a slightly different story.

Berty sat on the couch as he read the book's version. The book told of ancient nobility who escaped to the Land of Sages. After the scepter was created, it chose the first born child of the noble escapees to be Empress. Each succeeding Empress was chosen from within the noble bloodline of the original Empress.

Turning the page, Berty found a tidbit that Silvia had not divulged. The nobility anointed their children not too long after birth. A person's fate was set in stone during the child's anointing ritual. The ritual was performed to protect babies from illnesses and other maladies. Usually performed by a Witch or Wizard, the baby was placed in a circle of candles as special oils were rubbed onto the baby's body. Hands were passed over the baby's forehead four times and the baby's hands and feet were dipped in blessed water. After anointing, the child's fate was revealed during the age of discovery. A future Empress, during that time, would have a vision that would lead her to the place where she would begin the age of learning. That place would influence the type of Empress that she would become.

Berty set the book, opened to its page, on the coffee table. Looking out the window, his eyes registered black fading into blue. His mind recalled the woods of which Silvia was so fond. He wondered what those woods said about her. "Old and wise, like the trees," he muttered.

From his reclined position on the couch, his eyes could still read the word, *bloodline*, on the open page. He closed his eyes, but the word did not fade from his mind. Opening his eyes, Berty looked anywhere, but the coffee table.

"Did you know that we were related?" he asked the room. Leaning over, Berty slammed the book shut. Without hesitation, he picked up the book, returning it to its place on the shelf.

Pulling another book at random off the shelf, Berty blindly placed it in his bag before he secured his cloak. He extinguished the lantern, then walked into the cold, pre-dawn air.

The walk across the short bridge was brisk. His nostrils could smell the onset of winter, but his heart did not care. Let the cold come, he thought as he entered his study.

In the warmth of his study, Berty threw his cloak over a chair and allowed his bag to slide onto the floor. With an upward flick of his hand, he lit a lantern as he proceeded up his spiral staircase. The light followed him while he carelessly peeled his clothes from his body. He looked at the shower, but the temptation of drowning enticed him, so he turned away.

Throwing open the doors of his wardrobe, he found yet another gold trimmed garment. Finishing dressing, he stepped down his stairs into his study. Cold, early morning sunlight flooded through the window. Pausing on the last step, Berty looked around his study. He thought it was too neat and tidy. Before he could think about spreading clutter on top of his desk and having it spill onto the floor, he heard his wind chimes.

With a swipe of his arm, his cloak hung itself on the rack and his bag rested neatly near the side of his desk. Stepping off the last step, he said, "Come in."

"My Lord," said a short bundle of green crossing the threshold, "I am so sorry to disturb you. Thank you for allowing me to call on you."

"What is it, Theodore?" asked Berty.

"The new Historian's party has been sighted on the road from Fairyland. They are expected to arrive this afternoon. Shall I prepare for a welcome feast after breakfast?"

"Absolutely," said Berty. "Make sure the entire Advisory Council is in attendance as well."

"Of course, my Lord," Theodore said. "Will you be taking breakfast in your chambers this morning?"

"I will. I have some reading that I need to do before I have to entertain the Historian." Walking to his desk, Berty opened his bag as the well-bundled Dwarf left.

Extracting his next borrowed book from his bag, Berty opened the book, without looking at its title. He sat at his desk and began to read. Only the sound of the wind chimes that announced Theodore arriving with his breakfast made Berty tear his eyes from the page.

As Theodore set the food on the table behind his desk, Berty still glanced at the black words on the yellowed paper. When black blurred with yellow, Berty marked his spot on the page, then stood.

Walking towards the table, Berty said, "Thank you, Theodore. Alert me when the Historian arrives."

"Of course, my Lord," Theodore said, bowing. "Hatcher and I seek your permission to open the Empire Tree for Wassail this year."

"Wassail?" Berty looked at the Dwarf's hopeful face.

"Yes, my Lord. We will need this much time to prepare."

In the back of Berty's mind, a tune played to the words, *here we come a-wassailing*. Not to sound like a completely ignorant Emperor, he chose his words carefully. "How much of the Empire

Tree is usually opened for Wassail?" he asked.

"After the prophecy was made to the former Empress, they thought it best to only open the Receiving Room. Prior to all that, the Reception Room was opened as well," answered Theodore.

Berty understood 'they' to mean Leif, Silvia's former advisor. He watched Theodore alternate between swaying from side to side and rocking slightly on the balls of his feet. Berty took a deep breath before saying, "You will have to forgive my ignorance, Theodore. Could you explain Wassail?"

"Of course, my Lord." Theodore's eyes sparkled. "Over the next few days, the apples will be gathered to be made into cider. On the first day of Wassail, everyone gathers to watch the apples get pressed and the first sip is taken. As the week wears on, the vat of cider is heated and different things are added. People come from far and wide to drink. The Empire Tree usually provides the travelers with a place to sleep and some food. On the last day of Wassail, the surplus of large animals that were hunted in the forest for the Empire Tree are divided and given to the people along with the used wood. The week of Wassail," Theodore explained, "starts the Winter Festival. It is the best time of the year."

"How many people come for Wassail?"

"A plethora," answered the young Dwarf. "However, if I may speculate, I think that many more will come because of you and not just because the Sages' Grove is the only Knownot free Wassail in the Land of Sages."

"No one will be allowed beyond the Reception Room?"

"No, Emperor."

"Then," said Berty, "open the Empire Tree for Wassail."

A wide smile spread across Theodore's face, making him look even younger. "Yes, Emperor." The young Dwarf rushed out of the room, leaving Berty to eat his breakfast in peace.

However, peace did not find its way into Berty's mind. As he chewed, he pondered his family tree. Focusing on his ancestors, he realized that none of them were Hunters. Nothing made sense to him. According to the book, the scepter only chose from a certain bloodline. Exhausting his memory as he ate, Berty came to the conclusion that he simply did not know enough about his ancestors. But, he thought, there is someone who does.

After breakfast, Berty returned to his desk, continuing his reading. It took him the rest of the morning to finish the book. Berty secured his cloak, then carried the book back to Silvia's study. Plucking more books from her shelves, he floated a stack of books into his study, making a pile on his desk.

He pulled the top book off the pile. As he cracked its spine, he heard his wind chimes. "Come in," he said.

"Emperor," said Theodore, running inside, "the Historian is arriving at the gates of the Sages' Grove as we speak."

"Have the Historian escorted to the Reception Room. I will greet he or she there." Theodore bowed, then ran out the door.

Gathering his cloak, Berty stepped out of his study into the cold, late autumn air. Looking around, he half hoped to see a vision cloaked in light blue, but instead all he saw were almost bare branch bundles as more and more leaves fell with each passing breeze. Remembering that he had to greet the Historian, Berty walked across the bridge into the trunk.

On his way down the stairs, Berty lowered his hood and threw the sides of his cloak onto his shoulders to make a cape. It billowed behind him as he emerged onto the dais from behind the Sages' Seal. Berty acknowledged his Advisory Council with a nod of his head while he walked to his throne.

Two Fairies draped in dark purple and periwinkle traveling cloaks entered the Reception Room followed by four Empire Guards.

One of the Fairies stepped forward, approaching the throne. A small hand lowered the dark purple hood to reveal a young woman with long, curly, dark hair, light skin and piercing, violet eyes. Looking directly at Berty, she bowed her head, saying, "Emperor, I am Princess Delyth. My mother and father, Queen Lida and King Elrick, have spoken very highly of you and send their highest regards." Delyth spoke in the manner of the extreme well to do with the best education. "It is their greatest desire and a great honor for me to become the Empire Historian."

"Your mother and father have my greatest respect," said Berty. "It would be an honor to accept you as our Historian."

Delyth smiled a smile that only magnified her beauty. "Thank you, my Lord," she said with a bow.

Berty nodded to Theodore who stood off to one side. The young Dwarf approached Delyth, saying, "Allow me to show you to your chambers, Princess." As Theodore magically gathered Delyth's things, Berty's eyes scanned the members of the Advisory Council. They found Declan standing slack-jawed and bug-eyed. It was apparent to Berty that Declan found Delyth to be quite the beauty.

As his ears heard Delyth introduce her maid to Theodore, Berty's eyes moved onto Alfred's face. His expression changed from intense concentration to abject horror as he observed Delyth. Berty also quickly looked at Delyth. The Fairy Princess was standing in front of one of the guards with her hand opened in front of her mouth as if she were blowing a kiss. She closed her hand as if she captured something, then seemed to empty her palm into a small pouch.

"You used Fairy Dust on Empire Guards?" asked a horrified Alfred.

Delyth turned to face the Elf, saying, "Yes. And now I am removing it."

"Fairy Dust and Elves are not a good combination," said Alfred.

"They are fine," Delyth said before she moved onto the next one.

"It can have adverse effects on an Elf for the rest of his life," protested Alfred.

"That is why only the nobility are allowed to use Fairy Dust in this manner. I know what I am doing," Delyth said defiantly.

Berty watched the guards as they snapped out of a trance-like state. "Delyth," said Berty calmly, "while you reside within the

Empire Tree, I am going to ask you to not use Fairy Dust on anyone without my permission."

The Fairy threw Alfred a scornful look before looking at Berty, saying, "I would not dream of it, Emperor." She and her maid followed Theodore out of the Reception Room.

When Delyth was out of earshot, Alfred approached the dais. "Thank you for disallowing the free use of Fairy Dust, my Lord. It is a most dangerous substance."

"Walk with me, Alfred," said Berty as he stood. "Enlighten me on its uses and its dangers."

They climbed the stairs as Alfred explained. "Fairy Dust is a powerful weapon for a Fairy to have in his or her arsenal if attacked. It renders the recipient useless in both mind and body. If inhaled in small doses, it can have a mild, mind controlling effect. When it is used in this form for a long period of time, it can have lasting mind-numbing consequences. Fairy Dust has also been used as a mind-altering device for both magical and recreational purposes. For this, it is either ingested or injected, both of which are banned in Irmingard. It seems to affect Elves in the worst way."

Stopping by the door of the Roundtable Room, Berty said, "Thank you for telling me."

"You are welcome, Emperor," said Alfred. "If I may suggest," Berty nodded, "that you advise Delyth to keep her pouch under lock and key so that someone does not try to steal it."

"Good advice. Thank you, Alfred." Berty shook the Elf's hand, then walked into the room.

Alfred followed Berty into the room. "My Lord, what is troubling you?"

Berty turned to see the concern in the elder Elf's eyes. Not realizing that he wore his heart on his sleeve, he said, "I am fine."

"I did not ask how you are," said Alfred, taking a couple of steps closer. "I can see that something troubles you."

Berty's mouth opened, but no sound escaped. Taking a deep breath, he said, "What I tell you does not leave this room."

"Never," said Alfred.

"Why is it that the people are still complaining about the magic still being missing, yet I see it everywhere?"

"You have the power of the scepter within," reasoned Alfred, "which makes it easier for you to recognize magic, unlike others."

Berty sat in his chair at the Roundtable while Alfred sat next to him. "I traveled to the other side of the portal to see my family. I brought my young niece a wooden doll. Now I know that children have active imaginations, but this doll spoke to her and she to it. Did I cross a boundary? Should I have not brought her this doll?"

"How old is the child?" Alfred asked.

"Almost six."

Alfred looked at Berty inquisitively, tilting his head to one side. "Without meeting the girl, I cannot say for certain. Do you know if she has shown this behavior before?"

"I do not."

"No," said Alfred. "Children do not usually share these things and sometimes if they do, we do not pay proper attention." Alfred placed his thumb sideways on his lips in deep thought. "I think that a wider opinion is needed."

"I do not wish to tell the rest of the Advisory Council that she is my niece," said Berty.

"You do not have to," Alfred assured. "We can make it seem as if she is any young girl."

Berty slowly nodded.

"Out of curiosity, what did she tell you?"

In a corner of his eye, Berty saw his brother's foyer with Hope delicately holding the doll in her arms. "Something about looking in the roots."

"The doll wants you to see a seer? There are not any seers left in the Land of Sages," said Alfred.

"Why do you think that it meant a seer?"

"Seers have also been known as root workers," Alfred explained.

A door opened, and in walked Theodore, interrupting their conversation. "I am sorry to interrupt, my Lord," the Dwarf said, "but the feast is ready."

"Thank you," said Berty.

The click of the door told both Berty and Alfred that Theodore had gone.

Berty rose from his chair. "There will be an Advisory Council meeting tomorrow. We can discuss it over lunch."

"I will inform Council, my Lord," said Alfred, rising from his chair.

"Good," Berty said. "Let us go to the feast."

When the two men entered the Reception Room, the other members of the Advisory Council and ranking members of the Empire Guard were already seated at the long table in the center of the room. The dinner guests stood as Berty walked towards his chair at the center of the table. Standing in-between his chair and the table, Berty glanced across the room to see a dainty vision of beauty. "Our guest of honor," he said, extending his arm, "the newest member of the Advisory Council, Princess Delyth."

Delyth glided across the room in a deep purple gown like the ones Silvia wore except the Fairy's trim was silver. She took her seat directly across from Berty. As soon as Berty sat, the rest of the table followed.

Once drinks were poured, Delyth said, "Thank you for this warm reception. I know it is not protocol, but I would like to make the toast." Berty graciously nodded, motioning for her to do so. When she lifted her glass, everyone followed her lead. "To our new Emperor, may the sun always shine on his reign." Smiling, Berty nodded in acknowledgement. She bowed her head slightly, then continued, "And to unity. Though we may come from different places, may our honor and our ideals unite us." Everyone took a sip from his or her glass.

People placed their glasses on the table as the food started to arrive. "How have you found everything, Delyth?" asked Berty.

"Very satisfactory, my Lord," she answered. "You are very

generous."

Berty smiled, then turned his attention to his plate of food. As he ate, conversation flowed around him.

"How is your father doing?" Declan asked Delyth. He could not hold his gaze with the Fairy.

"Very well, thank you, and very busy," said Delyth. Berty thought he saw her blush. "My brother is in line to be king and my parents are having difficulties with finding him a suitable wife."

"Why is that?" Colvin asked.

"My parents are the last of the ancient noble Fairy families," explained Delyth. "Since they married each other, my brother has to marry someone from a lesser noble family. The problem is that many of them have lost their honor. My parents will not settle for a less than honorable queen. Needless to say, it is a very daunting task."

"Then they have to do it all over again with you," Colvin said.

"Oh, no," said Delyth. "They do not have to go through all of that for me. I get to choose who I want." Delyth quickly looked away from Declan. "As long as he is honorable, I need not marry someone with a noble bloodline."

Declan looked at a wall, smiling. Berty and Alfred exchanged looks, then continued eating.

The evening wore on with Delyth displaying her knowledge of the history of the Empire. Sometimes Berty thought she was showing off to prove her worth and other times to try to impress the men who surrounded her. Every so often, Berty would find Declan stealing a glance in Delyth's direction. For most of the evening, the Watcher effectively ignored the Fairy's direct contact. Berty would have found it amusing, if both Declan and Delyth were not a part of his Advisory Council. At the end of the feast, people bode each other well while Alfred let the council members know about the next meeting.

Morning broke with a soft, cold light inching through Berty's window. Getting out of bed, Berty paused to look at the gray sky though his window, thinking that finally the outside reflected the inside. After he showered and dressed, Berty walked downstairs to sit at his desk.

Opening a book, he began to read. A chapter into the book, Berty realized that it was yet another book that not only described different places within the Empire, but also chronicled someone's journey through it. "You could not travel yourself," muttered Berty aloud, "so you filled your study with books about people who did." Theodore ringing his wind chimes interrupted his pondering about how lonely and confining Silvia's life must have been.

"Good morning, Emperor," said the young Dwarf.

"You are cheerful today," Berty said.

"Getting ready for Wassail," said Theodore. "This is my first Wassail as Head Tender. I am so excited."

Berty could not help but smile as Theodore placed his breakfast on the table. After Theodore left, Berty ate. His mind wandered more and more with each chew. Taking a sip from his goblet, he lowered it slowly to the table, saying, "I did give you my life—I set you free." He closed his eyes and could feel her limp cold hand beneath his as he wrapped her fingers around the metal of the scepter. Opening his eyes, a single tear rolled down his cheek.

Chapter Twenty-two
Magical Ties

Wiping his cheek with his cuff, he stood, shaking his body a little from head to toe. Berty took a deep breath, then sat down at his desk ready to continue reading. The book described the Dragonlands as a place where the trees were huge and far apart from each other. The forest canopy was so vast and so thick that the forest was dark even in midday. Berty did not understand why anyone wanted to go to such a dreary place.

After reading the next sentence, he dug into his bag, pulling out his Emperor's Journal. He copied, "Deep within the darkness of the Dragonlands lies an even darker place. This place seems to be a cursed area where nothing lives. The dragon clans refer to this section as the place where nothing dies. In a forgotten corner of this dreadful place is a forgotten hut. Around and inside this hut are the remnants of a life. Who lived in this hut? When was it occupied? What happened that it seems to be abandoned? The clans give no answer. Either they do not know the whole story or they hide some secret."

Berty did not understand why those words held meaning for him. Perhaps, he thought, answers lie within the Dragonlands.

He finished reading the book just before he had to leave. Placing the book off to the side, he looked at the rest of the pile that he needed to read when he returned. Closing his journal, Berty secured his cloak. He quickly crossed the bridge, hurrying into the warmth of the tree.

At the landing near the Roundtable Room, he hung his cloak on the hook next to the door. Upon entering the room, he saw Theodore ordering Tenders with food. "Emperor," said Theodore and all the Tenders bowed, "we will be out of your way in a moment."

"No need to rush on my account," Berty said with a smile.

As the workers finished, Theodore ushered them out of the room, then bowed to Berty before following them through the door. Leaning on the back of his exquisitely carved chair, he did not regret his decision to set Silvia free. He was simply returning the favor.

A door opened, interrupting his thought and he stood up straight. Alvar and Hatcher entered the room, bowing to Berty before walking to their chairs. They were quickly followed by Alfred, Colvin and Declan who also bowed upon entering. Delyth sauntered into the room, a few steps behind, walking towards the empty seat between Alfred and Hatcher.

As Berty sat in his chair, everyone followed. "Delyth, I would like to officially welcome you to the Roundtable."

"Thank you, my Lord," she said.

"The first thing that I would like to discuss is the violation of the Hidden Treaty," said Berty. "I understand, Hatcher, you have recused yourself from these dealings."

"Why?" asked Delyth. "Would it not be better to have a Troll involved in the process?"

"Not without having a Goblin involved as well," answered Berty.

"But they are the ones who violated the treaty in the first place," Delyth exclaimed.

"The Empire Tree," said Berty, "of which you are now a part, is completely impartial. We do not take sides. It is not our job to judge what is right and what is wrong. It simply is not that simple."

Delyth cocked her head to one side, allowing her dark curls to hit the tabletop. "I do not understand. My Lord, if the treaty was violated, then is that not wrong?"

Berty looked into her searching violet eyes before he pulled his wand from his pocket. With a quick upwards flick, a three dimensional holographic model of a tree, complete with leaves and roots, appeared above the center of the table. "As it is above, so it is below. They may be different, but they are connected. One cannot live without the other. Like light and shadow, take away one and no one could recognize the other." Berty put away his wand and the image disappeared.

"Now, I can trust that this matter will be dealt with diplomatically," said Berty.

Those seated around the table collectively nodded, saying, "Yes, my Lord."

"I think that we should all take some food, then we can continue," Berty said as he gestured at the spread in the middle of the Roundtable.

Berty watched everyone take some food. Theodore knew everyone's favorites, placing it in front of him or her. Berty finally fixed a plate for himself, then resumed the meeting.

"Something has come to my attention," said Berty, "and I would like to hear your opinions." The council members chewed silently. "There is a little girl who was given a wooden doll. The girl acts as if the doll can speak to her. I am well aware of a child's imagination, but I believe this to be something different."

Looking around the table, he saw Declan's jaw drop. "A Listener," said the Watcher. Berty stared intently at him. "I have only heard stories about Listeners. The Guild Master teaches us Watchers about all things magical. Listeners are very rare."

"Especially a Wood Listener," said Delyth.

"There are different types of Listeners?" Berty asked.

"Oh, yes," she answered. "There has not been a Wood Listener for a very, very long time. In fact, most people have forgotten that that type of Listener even existed."

"This girl must be found," Colvin said. "Do you realize how much she could tell us?"

"Yes, I agree," said Alvar. "The knowledge bestowed upon her by the trees could be both invaluable to us and yet dangerous in the wrong hands. What if Seanlaoch had that knowledge when he tried to invade."

"Perhaps it would have prevented the invasion," added Alfred.

Through the chatter about Hope, Berty noticed Hatcher's

221

triangular face had gone pale and his eyes were heavy with concern. "Hatcher," he said, "do you have anything to add?"

The Troll's pale eyes gazed at Berty. Concern turned to fear. "Emperor, you know that I am a faithful and loyal member of the Empire Tree." Berty nodded. "I do not know how a Wood Listener got through the portal."

"Please explain," said Berty.

"The Trolls keep track of every being that comes or goes through every portal in the entire Empire," Hatcher explained. "The reason why there has not been a Wood Listener in more modern history," he said with a glance at Delyth, "is because the last of the Wood Listeners walked through the portal an extremely long time ago and never returned."

"How do you know kin did not return?" asked Colvin. "Do you know how many generations have passed since then?"

"I know what I know," Hatcher snapped.

"Perhaps you don't know as much as you think," Colvin muttered under his breath.

Ignoring his comment, Hatcher continued, "Since the scepter's establishment of the Empire, unifying the different lands, only one without prior Empire ties has traveled through any portal."

"But would not the Listener have ties to the Empire?" Alvar asked.

"After that many generations, a person would register tie-less," explained Hatcher.

"Are you sure?" Berty asked his Advisor.

"Absolutely, Emperor," said the Troll.

Berty slowly nodded, then his eyes found Alfred's face. "The point," said Alfred, "is that this Listener is even more proof that the magic is not dying."

"Magic may not be dying," said Declan, "but I feel that it is being siphoned."

"Siphoned?" Berty asked.

"I have not experienced this myself, but I have heard of other Watchers who find a small, yet lingering, magical trail," Declan explained.

"Where does this trail lead?" asked Berty.

"I do not know," said Declan. "I fear that there is more than one trail. I will need more time to investigate."

"Very well," Berty said. "We will meet again after the Winter Festival and you can discuss your progress."

"Thank you, my Lord," said Declan.

Berty looked at each face around the table. "Anything else?" he asked. They all shook their heads. "Then we are finished with today's meeting." Standing, he walked away from the Roundtable as the Advisory Council began to hurriedly whisper.

Fastening his cloak, Berty raced up the stairs and across the bridge, pausing only to raise the hood of his claret cloak. Back inside the cozy solitude of his study, he plucked another book from the pile on his desk, burying his head within its bindings.

Darkness was beginning to take over earlier in the evening, but Berty barely noticed the lanterns come to life through the words on the pages. He was reading yet another book about someone's travels through the Land of Sages.

Looking up from the open book, he began to imagine Silvia journeying across the land, enraptured in all she saw. His lips curved upwards thinking about her happiness. The smile was short lived when he began to wonder if she thought about him as much as he thought about her. He wondered if she missed him or if she yearned to feel his hand in hers.

Berty shook his head. "Snap out if it," he said to himself. "We are related." His mind slowly recalled what Hatcher said about only one person without ties traveling through a portal. "Then we cannot be related or else I would have registered as having a tie." His smiled returned as his heart leapt.

Berty's ears heard the wind chimes as Theodore entered with his dinner. Seeing the smile on Berty's face, Theodore said, "The anticipation of Wassail is exciting."

"How are the preparations coming along?" asked Berty.

"Very well, my Lord. Everything will be finished tomorrow,

just in time for the start of Wassail the day after," Theodore answered.

"Excellent." Berty rose from his chair, walking towards the table as the young Dwarf set out his meal. For the first time in a while, Theodore left Berty to eat his solitary meal in much higher spirits. Although Theodore probably thought that Berty was excited about Wassail, Berty's thoughts did not wander towards big vats of mulled cider and singing. He imagined Silvia sitting across the table in a gold trimmed gown while her dark red hair reflected the flickering candlelight. Swimming in his imagination, Berty barely heard the young Dwarf leave.

He paid no attention to what he ate. He yearned to see her smile, to gaze into her warm, brown eyes, and to run his hand through her soft, dark red hair. Reaching out his hand, he grasped only air. "Someday," he sighed, then returned his focus to his dinner.

After he ate, Berty spent the rest of his evening at his desk, reading Silvia's books. When his eyes could no longer see the words clearly, Berty decided to go to bed. Walking up his spiral staircase to his bedroom, he reflected on the books that he had been reading recently. Silvia's love for exploration and of the Empire truly showed itself through the books that she kept, Berty thought. As he climbed into bed, he knew that there had to be a connection between what was written in the books and the magic fading from the land. However, he could not fathom what it was. Tackling it in the morning, he thought, was his best bet as he drifted off to sleep.

Berty awoke as the morning sun peeked through gray clouds, illuminating the circular bedroom. Smiling, he bounced out of bed into the shower. After getting dressed, Berty descended the stairs to his study, removing the final book in the pile from the top of his desk.

The aged leather binding had a soft, well-worn feel. His fingers outlined the embossed silver letters that said *Magical Beings Found within the Land of Sages.*

Still standing next to his desk, Berty opened the book to the first page and read, "The very essence of magic flourishes within the Land of Sages. Sleeping under the stars, one can feel it pulsate between the trees."

With the book still open to the first page, Berty sat down retrieving his Emperor's journal. After copying both sentences into his journal, he continued reading.

It is said that if a child is born when the magic pulsates, then this child will capture some of the passing magic. During a child's age of discovery, the magic will develop into one form or another.

Berty placed his finger on the page, saying, "But Hope was born in a hospital."

Questioning the book's validity, Berty read more.

However, there are some who believe that magic only stays within certain families. Believing the former or the latter gives one a very limited scope of magic. Magic is omnipresent and by nature is neither inclusive nor exclusive. How one first acquires magical skill is uncertain. Yet, magical signs can be seen in children during the age of discovery. The skill is then honed in the age of learning.

The sound of wind chimes interrupted Berty's reading. "Come in," he said.

"Good morning, Emperor," said Theodore, carrying a breakfast tray.

"Good morning," Berty replied while marking his place on the page.

"The grand Wassail kettlebarrel is being constructed today," said the young Dwarf. Walking over to the table, Berty saw excited anticipation in the Head Tender's eyes.

"Wassail starts tomorrow?" Berty asked as he sat.

"Yes," answered Theodore. His whole body shook with excitement. "There are only a few things left to do."

Berty could not help but smile at Theodore as he hurried out the door. Chuckling, Berty sprinkled sugar on his porridge.

When his bowl was empty, Berty leaned back in his chair, tapping his fingers on his lips as his eyes cast towards the book on his desk. Taking his fingers away from his mouth, Berty opened his palm and the book flew into his hand. With a swipe of his other hand, the table before him was cleared of all dishes.

Placing the book on the table, Berty opened it to continue reading.

> While some manifestations of magic, like Witches, seem to stay within bloodlines, other manifestations, such as Watchers, do not. Magical manifestation is indeed a mystery. However, it is certain that magic manifests in categorized specialties. Each category has certain traits or skill sets that define a manifestation. It should be noted that varying degrees of skill level are found within each specialization.

Berty shook his head. "This is like reading a scientific journal," he muttered. He flipped through the pages to find that a good chunk of space had been dedicated to each magical category.

As the pages passed through his gaze, Berty's eyes caught the heading of Listener. Opening the book to that section, he read, "Listeners are ones who can listen to things that most people cannot. This particular manifestation is extremely rare and can skip multiple generations, making it seem random. The types of Listeners are Cattle, Horse, Sheep, Hawk, Sparrow and Lark. Rumors of Wood Listeners have been found in old records. These Listeners supposedly could listen to a specific type of tree. Evidence of such a Listener has never been found."

Berty turned the page, but there was nothing more written about Listeners. Closing the book, he placed it on his shelf. After securing his cloak, Berty picked up the pile of books that he had read, then walked out into the cold, late autumn air. Taking a deep breath, he whispered, "Winter is on its way."

With the smell of threatening frozen water vapor in the air, Berty stepped across the short bridge, entering Silvia's study. Adding to his finished section, he looked at the books that he still needed to read. "Less than half," he said.

Berty pulled books from the shelves. He carried the rather large stack back to his study, dropping the pile on his desk. Free of books, his hands grasped the clasp of his cloak, but did not unfasten it. Glancing at the pile of books, he walked out the door.

After crossing the long bridge, Berty stood inside the trunk of the Empire Tree. He lowered his hood before turning right. At the end of the dark hallway, he came to a door. Berty paused for a breath, then stepped through it into the wide, well lighted passageway.

He walked a familiar path and remembered following a light blue cloak into an arc shaped room. Looking around the room, he found it devoid of life. In the center of the room, he saw the miniature model of the Sages' Grove. Smiling, Berty walked towards it. Taking a deep breath, he bent over the model, breathing into the miniature Empire Tree.

The mini Sages' Grove sprang to life with people's likenesses scurrying to and fro. Berty summoned a chair from near the wall and sat to watch as people readied for Wassail.

Carts of apples arrived like clockwork, being placed near a construction site. The Dwarf foreman conducted his workers, as if he were the conductor of a symphony orchestra. Each section of workers played their part in perfect harmony with the other sections. Berty leaned in closer to try to hear the waltz of Wassail preparation.

Listening intently, Berty heard a faint giggle. Confused, he sat back from the model, studying the people. Then, he heard a quiet unlatching. Looking away from the model, Berty saw the door slowly swing open. Moments later, two stunned faces stared at him.

"Emperor, I, we," stammered Declan, "I did not mean to disturb you. I was just showing Delyth around."

"He was bringing me to a good spot to watch the Wassail preparations," explained Delyth.

Berty smiled, suppressing a laugh. "Come in."

The two stumbled into the room, red faced, and Declan closed the door behind him. Delyth awkwardly walked to the window.

"You will not see as much from there as you can from here," Berty said. Repeating Silvia's words that she had said to him brought a smile to his face and a growing warmth inside his core.

Walking over to the model of the Sages' Grove, Delyth gasped. Declan waited to see where the Fairy stopped, then chose a spot across from her.

"That is amazing," Delyth exclaimed. "I thought such magic was lost."

"Not in the Empire Tree," said Declan. "The scepter creates a shield that keeps magic inside."

Berty looked at Declan. "How do you know?"

"I can see it," Declan answered.

Nodding, Berty turned his attention back to the Sages' Grove in miniature.

"Look at the size of the kettlebarrel base," said Delyth. "I have never seen one so big before."

Out of the corner of his eyes, Berty watched Declan smile at Delyth's excitement. He knew that he had seen that smile before. His brother wore it when Jon watched Teresa help decorate the Christmas Tree at their parent's house before they got married.

For the first time, Berty realized that he would be spending the holidays alone. The growing warmth in his core shrank slightly. Quickly, he cast that thought aside. He did holidays solo before, therefore he thought that this holiday season would not be much different. Thinking that it might be his last solo holiday brought back the inner warmth.

Berty's mind registered a change in Declan's expression from happiness to concern. Looking over at Delyth, Berty saw a tear leak from her violet eyes and roll down her cheek. "What is the matter, Delyth?" Berty asked.

"Being away from home—my family—is harder than I thought it would be," answered Delyth as she wiped her cheek dry with her silver trimmed sleeve.

"If you wish to return home for the holidays," said Berty, "I would completely understand."

Delyth smiled brightly at him, saying, "Thank you, my Lord. But I will stay. I want to experience as much as I can here in the Empire Tree." She glanced quickly at Declan. "This is where I belong."

Berty smiled. "I am glad you feel at home here. Perhaps sending a holiday greeting home would make you feel better."

"I think I'll do that," said Delyth full of smiles. "Thank you, Emperor." She placed a hand on Declan's arm, saying, "I will only be gone a short while." She looked at both men, then at the miniature before she ran out the door.

Berty debated with himself about whether or not he wanted to know for a few moments, then said, "You two seem to be bonding."

Declan stared at Berty. The deer caught in the headlights look faded after a couple of seconds to reveal a bursting at the seams expression. "We are close in age," he said finally. "Plus, I can understand her trying to find a real place in this world. It was never meant for her to be Historian, but it is something she loves and she has a gift for it. I know about fate throwing one off course."

Berty nodded. He never expected to be living a world in-between, let alone be Emperor. Keeping his thoughts to himself, his gaze wandered back to the people preparing for Wassail.

Declan pulled over a chair to watch the people's likenesses craft the kettlebarrel. "I have always watched this from the Watcher's Guild. Never in my wildest imagination did I gather that this," he gestured toward the model of the Sages' Grove, "is what was meant by a Watching Room."

Chuckling, Berty said, "Neither did I."

The two men watched the construction, commenting on the

work that was being done. Declan explained the process to Berty. "The apples get placed into this smaller barrel." He pointed to the wine barrel next to the carts of apples. "The stone slab presses the apples and the juice will flow through a tube into the kettlebarrel. After all the apples are pressed, the juice is tasted. Then they light a fire under the kettlebarrel. It is stirred throughout the night until it is all uniformly warm. The next day when the fire goes out, the juice is left untouched. On the fourth day, the top is skimmed and the fire is rekindled. After stirring all afternoon, the first addition is made that evening."

"What is added?"

"Barks and roots, I believe. The actual ingredients are a secret. On the fifth day, it is tasted again. And again that evening other additions are made. Of course, different Cider Masters do things differently from year to year. On the last day, the Wassail is rationed and drunk by everyone. The day after, the kettlebarrel and press are deconstructed. The wood used to construct it all is given away for firewood and the Empire Tree shares its excess bounty. Everyone then leaves and takes a week to make final preparations to their homes and for their families for the winter. Then, the Winter Festival begins."

Before Berty could ask about what the Winter Festival entailed, Delyth returned with a broad smile that reached from ear to ear. "Thank you so much for the suggestion, my Lord," she said. "I feel much lighter, as if a weight has been lifted off my chest."

"I am so glad," said Berty with a smile.

For a few moments, the three of them watched the people in the model continue to prepare for Wassail. "My Lord," said Delyth, finally sitting in the chair that Declan brought for her, "may I ask a personal question?"

Slightly taken aback, Berty answered, "Of course."

"Does the Emperor have family to miss?"

Declan's eyes widened as he quickly glanced at both Delyth and Berty.

Berty smiled to let Delyth know that her question was not

completely out of line. "Of course, I do," he said. "My parents—"

"Must be proud," interjected Delyth.

"Know nothing of this world," Berty said, "and neither does my brother."

Delyth's jaw dropped slightly. "I had no idea," she said softly. "That must be terrible."

"It works out okay," said Berty. "They have full, busy lives and I would not want to be anywhere but here." He looked at Delyth and Declan. "This is our home now and we have to be there for each other, like a family."

Declan looked at Berty, nodding while Delyth said, "I agree, my Lord."

Sitting in silence once again, Berty wondered if Silvia would have approved. Thinking back to Silvia's former Advisor, Leif, and his solo decision making, Berty knew that at least with the two Advisors which sat with him, he would not have to deal with such betrayal. However, he thought, as he watched them steal glances, other issues might form around his Roundtable.

"My Lord," said Declan. Berty focused his gaze on him. "Thank you for allowing us to watch. It has been most exciting."

"You are leaving?" Berty asked.

"Yes," answered Declan. "Lunch is soon."

"Ah, so it is," said Berty.

"Will you be joining us, Emperor?" Delyth asked.

"Not today," said Berty. "I am devoting the afternoon to a final read before Wassail."

Nodding, Delyth rose out of her chair. Declan grabbed both chairs, returning them to their places along the wall. With a small bow and a smile to Berty, both walked out the door.

After waiting a few moments to make sure that they were gone, Berty stood. He waved his hand, sending his chair against the wall. Bending over the model of the Sages' Grove, he breathed into the representation of the Empire Tree. All movement disappeared. Turning away from the miniature, Berty opened the door, stepping into the passageway.

Solitude pressed into him from every angle, but somehow Berty no longer felt so alone. Smiling, he walked through the wall and down the hallway, finally crossing his bridge to his chambers.

Inside his study, Berty picked up the top book from the pile on his desk. Cracking the old spine, he sat in his chair and began to read. Another story of travel enveloped him as his eyes absorbed the words on the pages.

Halfway through the book, Berty heard the wind chimes ring. As soon as Berty said, "Come in," a Dwarf scurried inside, suspending a large tray in front of him.

"I am sorry for being late with your lunch, my Lord," Theodore said, frazzled.

"Preparations for Wassail not going well?" asked Berty.

"Quite the contrary, my Lord, everything is in place." The young Dwarf silently set Berty's table. "I am simply having staff issues."

"Will we be understaffed during the holiday?"

"No."

Berty walked over to his table, looking at Theodore. "Who?"

"Seanlaoch, my Lord." Bowing his head, Theodore closed his eyes.

"What has he done now?"

"It is more of what he will not do," Theodore said, raising his eyes. When Berty did not say anything, he raised his head, then continued, "He does not feel as though he should be doing washing during Wassail. He wants to be in the Reception Room. At least he has accepted the fact that he serves the Empire Tree. Now, if he would stop serving himself...." Theodore glanced over the table. "My Lord, you will be needed in the Reception Room by midmorning to start Wassail. Will you be taking breakfast here or in the Roundtable Room with Council?"

"In the Roundtable Room."

"Very well, my Lord," Theodore said, bowing.

After the Dwarf was gone, Berty picked at his food while somehow feeling guilty about Theodore's hassles with Sean. "I do not have the power to set him free, Theodore," he muttered. Taking a sip from his goblet, Berty willed the book to his spot to continue his reading.

As he read, Berty took notes about quirky little creatures called wood sprites. "Wood sprites," he jotted, "abundant in the Land of Sages, care for the trees and help to keep the balance of the forest. With their ability to change into trees, they will not always make their presence known, but they are there, watching and keeping." Berty placed his pen in the vacant space made by the book being open in his Emperor's Journal. His eyes continued to read latter paragraphs about how graceful and playful wood sprites were. When the section on wood sprites ended, Berty was disappointed that the book did not describe what one looked like.

Rising from his chair, Berty walked over to his bookshelf. Standing in front of it, his eyes quickly perused the titles. His hand extracted a large leather bound book entitled, *Magical Creatures of the Empire*. Opening the book, the pages whizzed past his face until he found the chapter on wood sprites.

Scanning the words for information, he only slowed to read, "Wood sprites are shape shifters. Only the Master Woodsman can force them to take their true form."

Somewhat satisfied, Berty replaced the large book on the shelf, then returned to his reading.

Chapter Twenty-three
Wassail

The flame of the lanterns flickered brightly as evening came. Berty had strolled to his desk where he changed books. The next book brought him out of the Land of Sages on a return visit to the Dragonlands.

Sitting in his chair, he followed the adventurer of the story in his mind. The adventurer was more daring, more brave and even a bit more reckless than others in previous books Berty had read. Placing his finger in between the pages, he closed over the book to examine it. The leather binding was newer. The book was much more recent than the rest. "The Dragonlands are now feared," he said, remembering how Silvia told him that people feared Dragons although not one Dragon had been seen in ages.

"I wonder what changed," muttered Berty. His glance wandered out the window. Realizing that it was late, his question would have to be answered another day. Marking his place, he proceeded to bed.

Overcast skies greeted Berty through the window when he woke. Staring at his brown ceiling, he said, "First day of Wassail. This should be interesting." Berty jumped out of bed and into the shower.

Berty's feet stepped lightly going down his private staircase. His cloak floated behind him while he entered the Roundtable Room.

Alfred caught sight of Berty and walked towards him. "Emperor, good morning. I see that I am not the only one who is early."

Berty smiled. "Good morning, Alfred. I did not want to miss the start of Wassail. It might look bad," he chuckled.

"Indeed." Alfred walked with Berty towards the table. "Will

this be your first Wassail?"

"It will," Berty answered.

"There was a time," Alfred began thoughtfully, "where people on both sides of the portals were more in synchronization. We dressed the same. We ate the same." He looked away from Berty. "We celebrated the same." Alfred sighed. "I suppose," his gaze found Berty again, "Wassail is no longer?"

"It is known only as a warm drink that people rarely make during the fall and winter," said Berty.

Berty's words cast a shadow of sadness on the Elf's face. "Magic is gone from there, too?" Alfred asked.

"Mostly," answered Berty. "It survives in forms that you would not recognize."

Alfred stood in silence. Berty saw his mind working behind his blue eyes. "We cannot let what has happened there to happen here. It would be a travesty." He looked at Berty in his kind, fatherly way, saying, "I am lucky to call you Emperor. You know the horrors of a world run amuck without the boundaries of magic." Alfred clapped Berty on the shoulder when a door opened and Tenders walked into the room, carrying trays of food.

Another door opened. Berty turned his head to see Colvin emerge through the door. "Just in time," he said to himself. "Good morning, Emperor," the Dwarf said more loudly.

"Good morning," Berty replied.

"Word in the Sages' Grove," said Colvin, "is that this should be the best Wassail the Land of Sages has ever seen."

"Not to mention the biggest," said Hatcher as he walked through the door. "I am glad that I sent for extra help at the gates. The line started to form late last night."

Alfred smiled as Berty watched his three Advisors gather food on their plates. Oblivious to the others, a vision of long, dark curls resting on small shoulders draped in dark blue and silver glided towards the Roundtable caught the corner of Berty's eye.

"Good morning, Emperor," Delyth said softly.

"Good morning," replied Berty. "Where is Declan?"

"Is he not here yet?" Delyth asked, not making an effort to look around the room.

Berty smiled. "How is everything today?"

"Not as difficult as I first feared," she answered. She glanced at the three men eating their breakfast. "Thank you, my Lord." Lowering her voice to a whisper, she said, "Sometimes we are not always as strong as we would like to portray." Delyth smiled.

Berty returned her smile while nodding. She turned to take some food. As he waited for her to sit, Berty heard Alvar and Declan enter the room having an in-depth discussion about the subtle differences between bow and arrow styles.

"The arrows you were crafting," Alvar said to Declan, "do you shape them specifically for your bow?"

"I have never crafted arrows for anyone else," Declan answered.

"And you have never used another bow?" asked Alvar. Declan shook his head. "Where did you learn to make that shape?"

Out of the corner of his eye, Berty watched Declan scrunch his face. "I do not remember my grandfather making arrows like that," Declan muttered. "I guess it is just a technique I developed. Makes for a nice, smooth release," he said, smiling.

Not knowing anything about weaponry, especially bows and arrows, Berty ignored the rest of their conversation to focus on his breakfast.

At the table, conversation flowed around Berty like a gentle breeze. His Advisors were filled with anticipation. Berty had to admit that the excitement was contagious. His face mimicked theirs, showing a warm smile. Resting an arm on his ornate chair, Berty wished that Silvia were celebrating with him.

Closing his eyes, he saw her light blue cloak covering her dark red hair and draping her body well, even hiding her shoes. She stood at the edge of the woods, facing a large, stone wall many yards away. A small door inside large, curved, wooden gates offered a tiny glimpse of stone buildings and a cobbled street. Lanced guards flanked the little opening. Berty could not tell if they were to keep people out or to keep people in the stone walls. Silvia took a deep breath before she stepped onto the path towards the door.

The sound of wood scraping against wood made Berty open his eyes. "We had better get downstairs and take our places," said Colvin, rising from his chair. Berty heard a general murmur of agreement around him. He took a deep breath before he followed Alfred through the door.

At the bottom of the stairs, Berty allowed his Advisory Council to file through the door before him. Without instructions, he knew exactly what role he played. He spread his arms to ready his cloak, then stepped into the Reception Room. As his cloak floated around him, his arms naturally fell to his side. Berty could only imagine what airs he gave as he looked into the wide-eyed, dropped-jawed audience of regular people.

Walking across the dais, Berty stood in front of his throne. The audience bowed simultaneously. When every pair of eyes rested on him, Berty opened his arms wide, saying, "Welcome, friends."

The crowd parted. A short, rotund, Human woman and a tall, thin, Elf man approached. The two bowed in front of Berty.

"My Lord," she said, standing upright, "may I present the Cider Master."

Berty nodded. The Elf took a step forward. "Everything is ready, Emperor," he said.

Looking at this man, Berty said, "Let it begin."

The crowd cheered. He allowed the Cider Master to lead while Berty followed with Alfred and Delyth on his sides. Behind him, the rest of his Advisors and the crowd followed.

The procession walked down the steps and out of the Empire Tree. Down the dirt road, they marched until they found the giant kettlebarrel.

"Start the fires and load the press," the Cider Master bellowed. A cascade of dull thuds filled the silence, then multiple crackles joined to create a strange, autumnal symphony.

When liquid hit the bottom of the kettlebarrel, the crowd cheered. Berty allowed himself to get caught in the happiness. The kettlebarrel filled rather quickly with freshly squeezed apple cider. Berty watched the Cider Master climb to the top of a platform surrounding the mouth of the kettlebarrel. He stirred the liquid with a large wooden paddle. The Elf watched his ward carefully. He stirred and sniffed every so often until the faintest wisp of steam escaped from the cider.

Reaching the ground, the Cider Master grabbed a shallow wooden bowl, then turned the spigot near the bottom. Filled with dark golden liquid, he took a sip. Carefully, he carried the bowl to Berty and held it towards him. Berty took the bowl with both his hands. Lifting it towards his mouth, Berty could smell the sweet apples. Taking a sip, tart and sweet exploded in his mouth. He had never tasted apple cider like that before.

Nodding, Berty held the bowl in front of him for the Cider Master to take. As soon as the Elf touched the bowl, the crowd cheered once more. The Advisory Council took their turns tasting the cider as well. Knowing that his role was finished for the day, Berty returned to the Empire Tree.

Too many people lingered in the Reception Room for Berty to feel safe using his private staircase. Instead, he used the common stairs, ducking into the Roundtable Room for a respite.

Noticing that the Tenders left some food, Berty took a chunk of bread to help destroy the sweetly tart aftertaste. Sitting in his chair, he wondered if Silvia used to do the same thing. He chuckled as he ripped off a piece of bread, placing it in his mouth.

As he chewed, his mind replayed the morning. Berty closed his eyes. Instead of seeing the dirt road and white cob buildings he passed in the village, he saw cobbled streets and tall stone buildings. In the midst of all the gray, a figure in shining light blue glanced at wooden signs that hung into the street from the buildings. Brown eyes found the target and the blue figure stepped quickly.

Stopping in front of a heavy studded wooden door, the brown

eyes paused to read the wooden sign once more. "Nelson's Fine Goods and Collectibles," said the sign. A delicate hand reached for the door handle, then pushed. The act of opening the door made a bell ring. Both delicate hands lowered the light blue hood, revealing dark red hair slightly longer than Berty had remembered. She did not pause to look at any of the exquisitely made items. Walking to the back of the store, she stopped at the counter where she was greeted by a well-dressed man who was walking out of a back room.

"How may I help you today, madam?" the man asked.

"I hear your family is in need of a teacher," said Silvia.

"You will need to speak to my wife," he said. "Wait here." The man disappeared through a door behind him.

A moment later, hurried clomping as if someone was running down stairs preceded a flushed faced woman, also dressed well with her blonde hair pinned up, walked through the doorway. "Are you the teacher?" she asked.

"I am," said Silvia.

The woman smiled. "I did not know there were any teachers left in this world, especially ones who would help." She took a breath. "We will gladly pay any price."

"That will not be necessary, Mrs. Nelson," Silvia said. "I only ask for a place to sleep and something to eat in exchange for my services."

"Done." Mrs. Nelson smiled. "I'm sorry," she shook her head. "In the excitement, I didn't even ask your name."

Silvia let a little laugh escape. "Leigh."

"Would you like to see her now, Leigh?"

"Yes, please."

Mrs. Nelson opened the flip-up counter for Silvia to walk through. "I should warn you that others have deemed her hopeless."

"I specialize in hopeless," Silvia said with a smile as she followed Mrs. Nelson through the door.

A creaking noise made Berty open his eyes.

"I see we have the same idea," said Alfred as he walked into the room, taking a chunk of bread.

Berty nodded, placing another piece into his mouth.

"I always hated taking sips before it was complete," Alfred continued while he sat. "The aftertaste is just awful."

Berty laughed. "I am glad that I am not the only one who thinks so."

"Wait, the others will be joining us soon."

Berty smiled. Any thoughts of sharing with Alfred what he saw when he closed his eyes crept out of his mind. Standing, Berty said, "Might as well finish some reading before the start of the feast."

"Those were my plans today as well," said Alfred.

The two men walked in opposite directions. Berty stepped through his private door. Stopping on the landing, he closed his eyes.

Mrs. Nelson stood between Silvia and a closed door. She smiled tentatively at Silvia, then opened the door. The room was full of exquisite chairs, a settee, writing desk and exotic bowls, vases and figurines.

"Estelle," Mrs. Nelson called, "I would like you to meet your new teacher."

Across the room, sitting on a cushioned window seat, a young woman turned in the direction of Mrs. Nelson's voice. Her expensive, midnight blue dress showed signs of neglect. Framed by lank, light blonde hair that obviously had not seen a comb in a long time, her pale blue eyes searched into Silvia's brown eyes.

"Stjarnan, Ellri, fortelte þu koma," Estelle said in a soft voice.

Smiling, Silvia said, "You can tell me all about it later. I am going to speak with your mother first. Okay?"

Estelle smiled at Silvia while nodding. Silvia looked at an astonished Mrs. Nelson and followed her out the door.

Berty opened his eyes, then sprinted up his staircase and across the bridge. Inside his study, his cloak flew off his shoulders as he sat on one of his chairs. Promptly, he closed his eyes again.

In what looked like a formal sitting room, Mrs. Nelson and Silvia were sitting on chairs, facing each other with a tray of food and drink on a coffee table between them. Silvia had shed her light blue cloak, revealing her once bright gold gown had changed into light brown. Berty was not sure if the color had been darkened on purpose or not.

"I am so glad that you have decided to still take Estelle as your pupil after meeting her," said Mrs. Nelson.

"I should warn you that progress will be slow," Silvia stated, "but I do think that I can help her."

"I hope you can, Leigh," Mrs. Nelson said. She looked away, muttering, "All these years and never getting any better...."

"If I may ask," Silvia grabbed Mrs. Nelson's attention, "has she always communicated like that?"

Mrs. Nelson's blue eyes began to get moist. "If she says anything, it is always gibberish."

Silvia nodded. "How long has she been like this?"

"Since she was a small child." A tear escaped from Mrs. Nelson's eye, trailing down her cheek. "The day she was born, I knew she was more intelligent than most. My bright, little star. She learned very quickly and was always very curious. Her favorite pastime was to go to the central gardens and lay in the grass, observing the world around her. On rainy days, she would sit at the window." Her cheeks were wet with tears. "It was raining that day...," Mrs. Nelson placed her hand over her mouth, then closed her eyes, sobbing quietly.

"I am so sorry, Mrs. Nelson," Silvia consoled. "It must be so difficult to watch your daughter in this state."

Mrs. Nelson looked into Silvia's kind, caring eyes, then managed to say, "Thank you." She took a deep breath. "I do not know what happened to have changed her. I was told once that intelligence is fickle and her mind turned on her. I wish I knew why." She pulled a handkerchief from a well-hidden pocket to dry her face.

"Excuse me, Mother," said the voice of a young man. Walking

towards Mrs. Nelson was what looked like a blond haired, blue eyed boy in men's clothing.

"Thomas," said Mrs. Nelson, "have you met Leigh, your sister's new teacher?"

"Not yet," Thomas said. "How do you do, Miss Leigh?"

"Very well, Thomas, thank you. Please do not let my presence interrupt what you had to ask your mother."

Nodding, Thomas turned to Mrs. Nelson. "Father wanted me to ask if you knew when the next shipment was going to arrive."

"Not until next week."

"That's what I told him," said Thomas as he walked out of the room.

Opening his eyes, Berty thought that reading a book would be a better use of his time. He summoned the book from his desk and began to read.

By the time the lanterns began to flicker, Berty was already halfway through another book. Deciding that it was time to get ready for the feast, he marked his place before heading to the trunk.

His Advisors were beginning to gather in the Roundtable Room when Berty joined them. After waiting a few minutes for everyone to assemble, Berty proceeded down the stairs behind the Advisory Council. He waited for all of his Advisors to climb the back steps to the dais before he followed.

As he stepped out from behind the drape, all the dinner guests stood. He approached his throne where it sat in the middle of a long table spread on either side. Below the dais, the Reception Room was crammed with tables and chairs. When Berty sat in his chair, all the guests sat as well. Noticing drink in his and every goblet, he lifted his goblet, saying, "For a good Wassail and a good feast." Everyone in the room raised their goblets as well, drinking when Berty drank.

Only after the food began to arrive, did Berty notice who besides the Advisory Council sat at the long table. He saw Lieutenant Edwin, Theodore, the Cider Master, the Watchers' Guild

Master, and Alina, the girl who was slated to become the Sages' Grove Witch.

The feast was exceptional with its many courses and good conversation. After all the plates had been cleared, Berty thanked everyone for coming, then the guests were ushered down the stairs.

"Nothing like a good meal to make a man sleepy," said Colvin, patting his stomach.

"Yes," Hatcher agreed. "I am glad that there is not another big meal for a while."

Berty watched as the two men walked out of the room, continuing their conversation. He also noticed Delyth catch Declan's eye as he talked to his Guild Master before she sauntered through the door. Alfred and Alvar were deep in conversation about the next round of recruits from Irmingard. Only Edwin stayed silent, also watching everyone who remained in the room.

After shaking hands with the Watchers' Guild Master and wishing him a good night, Berty excused himself, trudging up his private staircase. Being so tired, he fell asleep as soon as his head hit the pillow.

Berty awoke to see another gray sky morning out his window. After walking downstairs, he realized that he had to take all his meals in the Reception Room for the rest of week. Berty placed the book he had been reading in his pocket before heading to the Reception Room.

Choosing his food from the buffet table in the Reception Room, Berty was literally rubbing elbows with people from all walks of life who all greeted him with versions of "Good morning, Emperor." He smiled, wishing everyone a good morning.

After eating breakfast at the same table where he ate the feast, he strolled around the Sages' Grove, watching residents and visitors share stories, food and drink. Walking by the kettlebarrel, he noticed that workers were taking turns keeping the cider constantly stirred. Berty even saw a chart of names with how many revolutions they were to take the paddle around the inside of the kettlebarrel.

Chuckling at all the happiness he saw, Berty retreated to the Roundtable Room to read. He placed his opened book on the Roundtable, but could not seem to read a word on the page. His eyes were resisting the words, so he closed them to get a better focus.

The focus that came was Silvia, dressed in maroon, entering the same room that he saw before with that same girl sitting on a cushioned window seat. The girl still wore the worn, dark blue dress and still no one had bothered to comb her light blonde hair.

"Hello again, Estelle," said Silvia.

Estelle turned and looked kindly at Silvia with her piercing, pale blue eyes, saying, "Ellri."

Silvia sat in an upholstered chair near Estelle. "Are you glad that I am here?"

Smiling, Estelle nodded.

"Good," said Silvia. "Then, I need you to help me help you. While I am here, you should not refer to me as Elder. Do you understand?"

Estelle's untidy blonde locks bounced fervently as she nodded.

Silvia smiled. "I would like to know how you have come to know this ancient tongue."

Estelle quickly glanced out the window. "Stjarnan."

"The stars taught you?"

The girl nodded again.

"Have you ever seen it written anywhere?"

She shook her head. Berty wished that he knew what was going through Silvia's mind as she looked at the strange girl.

Silvia did not grant Berty's wish, but continued her questioning. "You understand the modern tongue. Do you speak it?"

Again, Estelle shook her head.

"Can you speak it?"

"Yes," Estelle replied. "Lopt tala til mig."

"I understand that you are not comfortable using the modern

tongue," said Silvia. "The sky speaks to me," she translated.

"No, El—Leigh."

Silvia smiled kindly, saying, "Although I can understand this ancient tongue, I would prefer if we conversed in the modern. I know it will take some getting used to, but I will work with you." She placed a hand on Estelle's hand. "You will have to trust me."

Estelle looked at Silvia's hand on hers. Berty could not read what was going through her mind. She slowly nodded.

Berty heard footsteps on the stairs and quickly opened his eyes. A few moments later, Berty heard, "Emperor." Declan walked past the table with a large sack. "Would it bother you if I added feathers to my arrow shafts in here?"

"Not at all," answered Berty. "Too many people outside for you?"

"Yes. I cannot get my work done properly. Strangers like to watch and ask questions. It is very distracting."

Berty began reading his book as Declan sat off to the side on the floor, digging into his bag.

Hours later, as Berty finished his book, his stomach began to growl. He looked over at Declan who was still on the floor securing feathers to the end of an arrow shaft. Declan raised his head when Berty stood.

"I am going to get some food," Berty said.

"May I join you?" asked Declan.

"Of course."

Declan placed his finished arrow in a pile before getting off the floor.

"Why so many arrows?" Berty asked as they walked down the stairs.

"It gives me something to do while I cannot practice," answered Declan.

"I was not sure if you had planned on going hunting or expecting a fight," Berty joked.

Declan laughed. "I only hunt when need be. But like my grandfather said, 'you can never have too many arrows.'"

They joined the line around the buffet table, filling their plates with food. After lunch, Berty and Declan decided to take a stroll around the Sages' Grove. They greeted all sorts of people and watched the workers as they kept stirring the cider in the kettlebarrel. With their lungs full of fresh air, Berty and Declan returned to the relative quiet of the Roundtable Room.

Declan sat back down on the floor to finish his arrows and Berty pulled the book from his pocket. "Looks like I need a new book," he said. Berty walked into his private staircase to his study. He placed the read book on his finished pile, then gathered two small books from the other pile. Putting them into his pockets, he quickly returned to the Roundtable Room.

Berty entered the room to find Declan still on the floor. Walking towards the table, he noticed two chairs occupied. He sat in his seat, pulling a book from his pocket. Next to him, Alfred looked at Berty over his half moon spectacles, smiling. Smiling back, Berty saw that the Elf was reading as well. Seemingly oblivious to almost everyone in the room, sat Delyth on Alfred's right. Her small frame bent over her part of the table. Her dark brown curls cascaded onto the reflective tabletop creating a curtain between her and the world.

Ignoring her, Berty began to read. The book was about a traveler who visited Irmingard. Berty read with interest as the author described the white stone fortress in which the Elves lived. Berty's only distraction was when his eyes registered a parting of the dark curtain.

Delyth sat back in her chair with the end of her pen clenched in her teeth. In front of her were eight inkbottles and a thick piece of paper on which she seemed to have been drawing. Each inkbottle held a different color ink and she was utilizing each color in the way she captured the second day workings of Wassail. After a moment's pause, Delyth dipped her pen in an inkbottle before drawing her curtain closed once more. Berty returned to his book.

The adventurer in his book was having dinner with the High

246

Elf as Delyth finally rested her pen on the table. The clinking sound of the young Fairy securing the metal lids onto her inkbottles made Berty, Alfred, and Declan look up from what they were doing.

Seeming to realize that she was no longer alone, Delyth said, "I am sorry. I did not mean to disturb all of you."

"Quite all right," said Alfred. "I do believe it is getting to be somewhere around dinner time. Shall we all go?"

"Let's," Berty answered. He placed a bookmark in-between his pages, then stuffed the book into a pocket.

"I have run out of arrows to finish," remarked Declan as he got off the floor. "Whatever am I going to do for the rest of this week?"

"You can always find a new hobby," Alfred joked.

Delyth observed Alfred putting his book away. "Reading is always in fashion," she said with a sly smile.

Ignoring her comment, Declan joined Alfred and Berty on the staircase landing. "I guess I will find something."

As Berty walked down the steps, he wondered if he really wanted to know what had transpired between Delyth and Declan to cause such tension. They seemed to have been getting along really well, perhaps rather too well, Berty thought.

At the dinner table, Declan and Delyth were forced to sit next to each other as everyone came to dinner at the same time. They did not speak to one another and avoided any eye contact.

After dinner, everyone congregated outside to watch the removal of the stirring oar ceremony. Carefully, Fairy workers lifted the oar out of the kettlebarrel and flew it to its secure clasps on the side of the stairs and platform. The audience clapped before they dispersed into social gatherings. Declan strolled towards his fellow Watchers from the Guild while Delyth almost ran back inside the Empire Tree.

"Clever ruse or lover's tiff?" asked Alfred, walking up the dirt path with Berty to the door of the tree.

"Do you really want to know?" Berty asked in return.

"You do have a point," conceded Alfred.

"Tell me, Alfred, is such a romance common?"

"Between the different peoples? No. A few may have some sort of infatuation with each other, but usually that is as far as it goes. Relationships that go beyond friendship are highly discouraged and often times taboo. I would suspect that if they are having feelings for one another, then they are keeping them well-hidden."

"From us, each other, or themselves?" Berty asked.

"Could be all three."

While they ascended the stairs to the Roundtable Room Alfred continued, "I think that it might be best to not say anything to either of them. Let it die out on its own." He was silent for a few steps. "At least for now."

When they entered the room, they found Delyth's drawing missing, but Declan's arrows still in piles on the floor. Sitting on their chairs, they continued their reading.

Berty had just finished his book when Declan walked into the room. Without saying a word to anyone, Declan picked up his arrows, carefully placing them in the bottom of his bag. All his extra feathers he dumped on top as he stood to draw his bag closed.

With a jolt of surprise, Declan immediately thrust his hand into his cloak, retrieving his gold locket. Opening the locket, Berty assumed that Declan was reading a message. Declan ran his hand through his sandy hair, then replied using the rod of his clasp. Returning the locket to his pocket, he glanced at Berty.

"Emperor," said Declan while walking over to the table, "I have some not so great news." Sitting in his chair, he looked from Berty to Alfred. "Remember when I told you about stories of magic siphoning?" Berty nodded his head. "Well it seems that not one Watcher recalls hearing about magic streams nor knows anything about them. I swear that they are not figments of my imagination." He sighed. "I would like your permission to leave the Sages' Grove through the holiday. I will return when I have something."

"If you feel that this is something that you need to do in order to get to the bottom of it, then go ahead," Berty said.

"Very necessary," said Declan. "Thank you, my Lord." Grabbing his bag, he hurried out of the room.

Berty turned to Alfred, saying, "Not a word to anyone until Declan's return."

"Of course not," answered Alfred. "Silence is paramount."

"We should get some sleep," Berty said casually as he rose from his chair. "See you in the morning."

"Good night, Emperor," said Alfred also rising from his.

Chapter Twenty-four
Watcher of the Prophecy

Berty awoke, knowing that Declan had already left under the cover of darkness. Once in his study, he made sure that he had a book in his pocket before leaving for breakfast. On the landing before the Roundtable Room's entrance, Berty paused to peek.

"That boy was sure in a hurry last night," said the voice of Hatcher. "'Hatcher,' he said, 'quickly, let me through.' 'What's the hurry?' I asked him. So he answered, 'I am running an errand for the Emperor.' As I opened the door, I asked if he would be back for the end of Wassail. All he said to me was, 'Thanks,' before scurrying off into the night."

"Perhaps he was trying to evade the spell of a vixen," Colvin's voice said. The two men laughed.

Deciding that it was safe to enter without them knowing that he had heard anything, Berty walked into the room, joyfully saying, "Good Morning."

"Good morning, my Lord," said Colvin. "Are you enjoying Wassail so far?"

"What is not to enjoy?" Berty replied.

Colvin nodded, saying, "So true, so true."

"I hope the Cider Master brews a strong Wassail," said Hatcher. "I fear that winter will be much colder and wetter this year."

"You fear too much," said Colvin, laughing.

"It is easy not to fear when you spend most of your life underground," Hatcher retorted.

Smiling, Berty followed the bickering pair to the buffet table in the Reception Room. As he sat with his plate of food, Alfred and Delyth quickly joined him. Both Berty and Alfred watched Delyth out of the corner of their eyes as she glanced around the room every few bites. She barely finished her food before almost running from the table, looking as if she wanted to cry.

"Wassail usually makes people happy?" asked Berty.

"Usually," replied Alfred.

"I had better go talk to her," Berty said.

Berty walked up the main staircase to the Roundtable Room, going through the door that led to the Advisory Council's chambers. After crossing the bridge from the trunk, he walked along the circular bridge until he came to Delyth's cluster of branches. He rang her wind chimes and waited.

"Come in," said a weak voice.

Berty entered Delyth's study. "Have a seat. I will be right down," Delyth called from the floor above. He figured she was trying to dry her eyes so that it did not seem like she was crying.

Delyth's study's walls were awash with books and scrolls. One large, curved, plain wooden table almost encircled her center spiral staircase. On the inside curve of the table was one large, upholstered chair. On the outside of the curve were straight backed, cushioned chairs every so often. Her study offered no other seating, so he chose the middle chair.

A minute or two later, tiny, dark blue, heeled shoes emerged from the top of the stairs. Slowly, a silver hem was revealed followed by a dark blue gown. Finally, Berty saw the puffy, violet eyes whose sadness filled the room.

"Emperor," said Delyth in surprise. When she reached the last step, Berty stood. "Please, sit. What can I do for you?" She sat in her large chair that seemed to envelop her small frame.

Berty sat again, saying, "I am here to check to see if you are okay."

"My Lord, you do not have to do that." She smiled weakly.

"Delyth, I saw you at breakfast. Please tell me what is bothering you." His voice resonated with kindness and warmth.

The Fairy's eyes welled with wetness as she squeaked, "I thought, I thought." She looked at some papers on her table. "I thought we had." Picking up a pen, she fiddled with it through her

251

fingers. "I thought we had a friendship." Putting down the pen, she looked at Berty while absent-mindedly twirled her curls with her fingers. "We were close."

"You and Declan."

Delyth nodded, causing tears to escape from her sad eyes. "Then he disappears without saying a word to me this morning."

"I am afraid that is my doing."

"Your doing?" She stopped twirling her hair. "I did not think...."

Before she could finish, Berty said, "I sent him on an errand that could not wait. He could not tell anyone and had to leave as soon as he could."

All the muscles in her face relaxed.

"I am sorry," he said.

Delyth let out a little laugh. "I am just being silly. Over emotional. Wassail without my family. Thank you for coming, Emperor." Shaking her head, she laughed again.

"There is no sense in you locking yourself in your chambers all day," said Berty. "Alfred and I will be sitting at the Roundtable, reading. Come and join us. We should also be strolling around the Sages' Grove later. Walk with us."

She smiled. "Yes, I will. Let me collect my things. I will join you shortly."

Berty returned her smile. "Great, then I will see you soon." Rising from the chair, he walked out her door.

When he returned to the Roundtable Room, he found Alfred reading at the table.

Looking up from his book, Alfred asked, "Is everything copesthetic?"

"Yes," answered Berty as he took his seat. Wanting to keep Delyth's indignation private, he said, "It turns out that she is just over emotional this time of year not having any family or friends around."

"That would do it," nodded Alfred. "Will she be joining us?"

"So she said." Berty opened a book that he extracted from his pocket as Alfred turned his attention back to his book.

A quarter into his book, Berty was distracted by Delyth sprawling out a big piece of thick paper on the table. She looked over at him, smiling. Her eyes were no longer red and puffy. He smiled back while she strategically placed her inkbottles around her paper.

"What are we sketching today?" asked Alfred.

"I am not sure yet," Delyth answered. "I will know once I have been meandering through the Sages' Grove."

"I could stretch my legs at the moment," said Alfred. "My Lord?"

"Yes, and my eyes could use a rest." Berty closed his book.

The three of them left the Roundtable Room to begin their journey, strolling out of the Empire Tree.

"You read a lot, Emperor," observed Delyth.

"I have a lifetime of learning about the Empire and I need to play catch-up," Berty replied.

"Is life much different on the other side of the portal?" she asked.

"Very much so."

"The Fairies and I imagine the Elves as well," she glanced at Alfred, "went into hiding on the other side of the portals during the Invasionary Period. After the wide spread acceptance of the 'New Way,' we were banished. Any who stayed were captured in secret and made to do the most horrid things. The ones who were our friends were burned at stakes while we watched. If we did not do as we were told, we were stuffed in sacks with rocks and drowned. The few who survived, escaped to the Land of Sages, telling their horror stories."

"Witch hunts," Berty muttered.

Delyth looked at him with her eyebrows scrunched.

"They were called Witch Hunts, during that period. Many people were burned at the stake or drowned because they were accused of being witches. Mostly the accusations were false," Berty explained. "Witch hunts like those do not happen anymore." Berty never knew how intertwined the histories were. Lost in his thoughts, Berty took a few steps into the chilly autumn air before realizing that he should raise his hood.

A wind wafted the aroma from the kettlebarrel towards him and Berty wrinkled his nose. Alfred laughed. "What is that smell?" Berty asked.

"Today is the day of still," Alfred explained.

As they walked closer to the kettlebarrel, Berty noticed that the workers were resting while the Cider Master merely observed. With each passing breeze, the sour smell strengthened in his nose.

"Oh," said Berty. "It is fermenting. Do they use wild yeast?"

"The top is left open to collect the magical strands," Alfred answered.

Berty laughed at the usage of magical strands. He guessed that yeast would be considered magical because of how it converts sugar to alcohol or how it makes bread rise. Walking with his Advisors around the village, he noticed how the people were still excited and anticipated the drinking of the Wassail.

Returning to the Empire Tree, Berty and Alfred read their books while Delyth busied herself blending colors on the paper. For the remainder of the day, spirits were high even when there was an empty chair at the table during dinner. The mood was still cheerful when the three of them retired for the evening.

Back in his study, Berty placed the finished book on the pile and sat in one of his chairs. Feeling good about how Wassail had been going, he smiled, closing his eyes.

He saw a candle flickering inside a glass hurricane sitting on a small, ornate dressing table. The mirror reflected the dim light into the rest of the room. Against one wall was a double sleigh bed. The sheets were turned down and a white nightgown was draped across the dark covers. Berty's eyes wandered to a large, dark shape that he guessed to be a wardrobe. Near a small heater, disguised as a fireplace, were two occasional chairs. A figure draped in forest green stood, looking out the long window. A soft knock at the door made her head full of dark red hair turn.

"Come in," she said.

The door opened slowly, then a blond haired boy's head poked around. "I am sorry to disturb you, Miss Leigh."

"It is okay, Thomas," said Silvia.

His head disappeared for a few seconds, then he squeezed inside, softly shutting the door behind him. As he stood at the door, he asked, "I wondered if I could talk to you for a minute."

"Yes, of course," Silvia said as she moved away from the window. "Have a seat."

"Thank you," said Thomas. He scurried to sit in a chair.

Silvia sat in the other chair facing him, saying, "About what would you like to talk, Thomas?"

"My sister." Thomas spoke softly, leaning towards Silvia. "Estelle seems to be really taking to you well and your presence is bringing life back to her. There is a light in her eyes that I have not seen in years. These are good things, of course. However, there is something that you need to know."

He fidgeted with his hands, looked around the room as if the walls could listen before he took a deep breath. "One day, when we were really young, in order to celebrate the expansion of Father's business, we were supposed to have a picnic on our rooftop terrace. Estelle suggested to Father to have the picnic inside, because she said that it was going to rain. Father would not hear of it because picnics were held outside. It was a beautiful, clear day and he was not going to hear that it was going to rain.

"We were sitting on the roof, on a blanket, when father held up his glass to make a toast. The warm stillness was suddenly chased away by blustering winds and raindrops the size of coins fell on our heads. By the time Mother got everything inside, we were drenched. Mother was busy getting us towels and dry clothes when I overheard Estelle telling Father about some shipment that was going to be late. I did not hear everything that was said, but Father got very angry. I hid, but not before I saw Father drag Estelle by her hair into another room and close the door. Wrapped in a blanket, I peeked through the keyhole."

He glanced down at his fidgeting hands, then began to rock on the chair. "He threw her across the room, repeatedly. He told her to never say anything to anyone again. The one time, I did not think that she would get up off the floor." He looked off into the distance while saying even more softly, "I can still hear her screams begging him to stop."

Tears welled in his light blue eyes and the image of the scared little boy was reflected in his face. "Mother thought that Estelle had slipped and fallen in all the wetness, for that is what Father led her to believe." A tear streaked down his young face. "Estelle was never the same again after that."

He looked away from Silvia for a minute before continuing. "With each passing year, it gets worse. Please, don't tell anyone. Father does not know that I know. It is better that way. I care about my sister and I want her to get better. However, she cannot do that while she is around Father." His hands stopped fidgeting. "Please, Miss Leigh, I beg you, take her. Take her from this place. This house, this town, is no place for her. Take her far away so that she can be what she is meant to be, what she was born to be." Thomas broke his gaze with Silvia, then jumped off the chair. Quickly wiping his eyes, he softly left Silvia's room.

Still sitting in her chair, Silvia gazed at the closed door. "I will see what I can do, Thomas." Slowly rising from the chair, she walked over to the bed, picking up her nightgown.

Berty quickly opened his eyes. He wondered if what he saw was real or contrived by his imagination. "There is only one way to find out," he said. "Unfortunately, I cannot seek her until after the holidays and after I have finished reading all these books." With a yawn, Berty climbed his stairs.

Poking through breaks in the clouds, sunlight found the backs of Berty's eyelids. He moved his head to the side before opening his eyes. Sitting up, Berty began to remember bits of his dream. He was running for his life through the trees with Silvia. "But that already happened," he said to himself. Then he remembered that the blonde girl who is Silvia's pupil in his visions was running with them. "This vision thing or whatever it is has to stop," said Berty. He moped out of bed and straight into the shower.

The water running down his face and body helped clear his mind. After he got dressed, Berty walked downstairs. Picking up the last book from the pile, he resolved to focus on what was tangible in his life at the moment. Pushing the dream and the visions into the back of his mind, he went into the trunk for breakfast.

A joyful mood permeated the Reception Room during breakfast because people were excited about another tasting day. Before leaving for the grounds, Berty made sure that he tucked a roll into one of his pockets in case he needed to cleanse any aftertaste.

He walked into the Sages' Grove behind his Advisory Council. Alvar had suggested that Lieutenant Edwin take Declan's place during the tasting to which Berty agreed. A few feet away from the kettlebarrel, Berty and the Advisory Council formed a semicircle behind which the crowd gathered.

When the Cider Master appeared on top of the platform, the crowd cheered. He dipped a Y-shaped wooden contraption that held a cheese cloth type mesh within the vacant space of the Y into the kettlebarrel. Carefully, he moved the contraption across the top of the cider. When he finished, workers helped the Cider Master lift the contraption out of the kettlebarrel. Berty could see a frothy like scum substance in the mesh as the workers removed the mesh from the wooden Y. Another set of workers secured a new mesh to the form, then the Cider Master repeated the skimming process.

The crowd watched intently as workers removed the wooden Y before the Cider Master inspected the surface. When the Cider Master finally stood, bellowing, "Rekindle the fires," the excited crowd cheered again. Seemingly oblivious to the crowd, the Cider Master climbed down the platform to inspect the fires. Satisfied with his inspection, he addressed some workers. The Elf climbed back onto the platform, watching his workers lower the wooden paddle into the kettlebarrel.

While onlookers' eyes followed his every move, the Cider Master stirred and stirred. Finally, a faint wisp of steam escaped. He handed the paddle to his workers that waited off to the side. Climbing back down the platform, he grabbed the shallow wooden tasting bowl.

Filling it at the spigot, the Cider Master took a sip. Smiling, he carried the bowl to Berty. The watching crowd silenced when Berty touched the bowl. He lifted it to his lips and tasted. This time, he could taste the change in the cider from a mere juice to an alcoholic beverage. It held onto the fruitiness of the apple, yet it became much more complex in his mouth. Liking what he had tasted, Berty gave an approving nod to the Cider Master as he passed back the bowl. The crowd cheered once again as the Cider Master allowed the Advisory Council plus Edwin to taste the cider as well.

When the tasting was over and the crowd started to disperse, Berty and most of the Advisory Council walked back into the Empire Tree. "That must be the finest cider I have ever tasted," Colvin exclaimed. "What a Wassail it will make." Colvin did not join Berty on the staircase to the Reception Room. The Dwarf separated from the group, heading to the tunnels under the tree.

"I think Colvin is quite right," said Alfred, walking up the stairs. "It has been a long time since a Cider Master that talented has been around. It makes me want to make sure that I have my Wassail Stein."

"Your Wassail Stein?" asked Berty.

"Oh, yes!" Alfred answered with a sparkle in his eye. "Mine is about two feet long and made out of the finest silver." Alfred had a dreamy look in his eye as they climbed another set of stairs to the Roundtable Room. Reaching the landing, Alfred said, "I think I will go look for mine." Smiling, he walked through a door and across the bridge leading to his chambers.

"My mother sent me my Wassail Stein," said Delyth as she entered the Roundtable Room. "It arrived the other day."

Following her into the room, Berty watched her sit at the table, getting ready to start another day's drawing. "Mine is silver as well, mixed with crushed stones and nowhere nearly as big as Alfred's."

Berty stood transfixed on the notion that he did not have a Wassail Stein of which he was aware.

"It is good that Alfred is looking for his now," Delyth said, dipping a pen into an inkwell. "We will be needing them in a few days."

Berty felt the book in his pocket, saying, "I need to check something. You will be okay by yourself?"

Delyth looked up at Berty. "Oh yes. I am fine."

He smiled at her, then walked into his private staircase. As he climbed, Berty wondered from where he would get a Wassail Stein. Sure that Silvia had one, he did not want to have to use hers. He could not use her chambers as his own although she said that they were his.

Walking across the bridge, Berty wondered why he was so reluctant to use her things in the Land of Sages when he already had taken possession of her family's house on the other side of the portal. "I had to," Berty rationalized, "or it would have been lost. No one else can live in that house except those with ties to the Empire Tree."

Entering his study, Berty hung his cloak, then sat in one of his club chairs. Face in his hands, he thought about asking Theodore about how to obtain a Wassail Stein. He pushed that thought to the back of mind, muttering, "Last resort." His eyes peeked through his fingers at the Sages' Seal that was carved into the front of his desk. Lowering his hands from his face, he continued to stare at it as if it were going to give him an answer. After a moment, Berty slid off his chair onto the floor, crawling over to his desk.

Up close, he examined the carving of the tree with seven circles. Gently he ran his fingers over the carved wood, feeling every raised piece and carefully carved gully. Berty thought about how he got thrown into his life without preparation, without any prior knowledge, and how he still had so much to learn about living the world in-between. His right hand paused on top of one of the branches. Rising frustration and anger from deep inside caused him to put pressure onto the front of his desk where his hand rested in a subdued attempt to punch it.

Berty's ears heard a soft click. Surprised, he looked to the right of his hand. A panel on the front of the desk had gently opened. Prying the door open with his fingers, he found a secret compartment. Inside the compartment was a gleaming, tall, silver stein. Berty's hand reached in, grabbing the curved bone handle.

Pulling the stein into the light, he examined it. It vaguely reminded Berty of German beer steins with its tall stature and hinged lid. His hand slid down the handle feeling the concentric ribbing of the bone. Wondering how it was made, he looked closer. The base of the handle was wider than the top where it curved inward.

"It's a horn," exclaimed Berty, "from a ram, perhaps."

Tearing his eyes away from the horn handle, he inspected the embossed scene that encompassed the entirety of the stein's outside. Two thirds of the tall stein was covered with trunks, branches and leaves of a dense forest. Above the silver forest canopy, majestic birds of prey like eagles, owls and falcons flew in all different directions that made them seem as if they were soaring into, out of, and above the forest.

Grasping the stein with both hands, Berty lifted it off his lap, placing it on his desk. Wondering from where it came, he knew it was not Silvia's Wassail Stein. Hers would have the stag in the woods scene on it like the tapestry in her chambers and its corresponding fireplace in the house.

Berty sat in the chair of his desk, staring at the stein. "Can I use it?" he asked aloud. "Should I use it?" His eyes found one of the birds on the stein and he noticed that it clutched a mouse or something similar in its talons. "Of course, I should use it," he said. "The tree has yet to steer me wrong."

Elated over the fact that he has his own Wassail Stein, Berty wanted to rejoin his council members in the Roundtable Room. He left the stein on his desk, then closed the door to the hidden compartment before fastening his cloak. Checking his pocket for a book, Berty crossed the bridge and descended the stairs.

At the Roundtable, Delyth sat immersed in her sketch. Berty tried to peek through her dark curtain of hair as he sat in his chair. Extracting his book, he thought it best not to bother her, so he began to read.

Before lunch, Alfred entered the room, carrying a book of his own. "I found it, finally," he said as he sat next to Berty. "It took me forever. I do not know what that servant was thinking when he packed my things." Alfred placed his book on the table. "The Cider Master is ready to make the first addition," he continued. "We should be heading down to watch."

Berty marked his place in his book, then stood. "I could use a walk about now anyway." He noticed that Delyth was concentrating on adding shadows. "Delyth, are you coming?" She did not look away from her work. "Delyth?" Berty walked over and tapped her on her shoulder.

Startled, she looked up at Berty. "Sorry, my Lord," she said. "I can get a bit focused." Berty noticed that her eye color was fading from a deep purple back to their usual violet shade as she spoke.

"We need to head outside to witness the first addition," said Alfred.

"Is it that time already?" Delyth smiled at the two men as she threw on her cloak.

Outside, the three of them joined the rest of the Advisory Council as they gathered around the kettlebarrel. Excitedly, the crowd found their places to watch as well. The Cider Master appeared on the top of the platform as an anxious hush fell over the people. Silently, the Cider Master waved his hand over his area of the kettlebarrel to coax the aroma in his direction.

Workers brought mystery ingredients to him in wooden buckets. Before scooping amounts of ingredients into the cider, the Elf smelled the contents of each bucket. For ten minutes, the Cider Master scooped, dropped and sniffed. After he dismissed his workers with the buckets, the paddle was lowered into the cider, then he began to stir. He smelled the cider once more before he passed the paddle to his workers. From the platform, the Cider Master caught Berty's eyes and nodded. The crowd cheered. As the Elf descended off the platform, people broke away from the gathering to go about other business.

Delyth, Alfred and Berty climbed the stairs of the Empire Tree to return to the Roundtable Room. On the landing, Alfred stepped aside to allow Delyth to enter the room, then turned to Berty. "My Lord, a word if you please." Nodding, Berty followed Alfred onto the bridge that leads to the council member's chambers.

Halfway across the bridge Alfred stopped, then said, "I am concerned, Emperor."

"About?"

"Before we left the tree, did you notice Delyth's eyes changing color?"

"Yes."

"I do not know if you had realized, but she was using Fairy Dust," said Alfred.

Berty said nothing so, Alfred explained, "She is using it to improve her concentration. The darkening of her eye color is a tell-tale sign."

"That she was using Fairy Dust?"

"Precisely."

Berty looked into Alfred's worried eyes. "You are concerned about the use of Fairy Dust?"

"Yes, my Lord."

"And what would you propose to be done about it?"

"Ban its use, my Lord," said Alfred, bowing his head.

Taking a deep breath, Berty said, "But she is a Fairy using Fairy Dust on herself."

"You are not grasping the scope of the danger that this imposes," Alfred exasperated.

Remembering Alfred's initial gripe about Fairy Dust, Berty chose his words carefully. "If you would illuminate the scope for me."

"Certainly, my Lord." Alfred looked relieved that Berty was taking his issue seriously. "Fairy Dust is a highly dangerous substance to all peoples. The fact that it exists within the Empire Tree poses a danger to all those living not only in the Empire Tree, but also in the Sages' Grove itself, and even beyond."

"Are you trying to tell me that Delyth will use it on everyone in the area?"

"No, but people can steal."

Berty nodded. "Alfred, I appreciate your concern. I already had a talk with Delyth about keeping her stores of Fairy Dust hidden under lock and key. Until her personal use of it causes a disturbance, I am afraid that I cannot ban it." Alfred opened his mouth to protest, but Berty continued, "Delyth is the Princess of the Fairies and the Historian of the Empire. If we cannot trust her judgement to use Fairy Dust responsibly for she grew up using it, then the Empire has much bigger problems. Do you agree?"

Alfred's tense face softened. "Yes."

"Good. Is there anything else that you would like to discuss?"

"No, my Lord."

Berty and Alfred returned to the Roundtable Room to find Delyth focused on her sketching. Alfred studied her for a moment, then sat in his chair to read. For the remainder of the day, Alfred did not bother Berty again about Fairy Dust. Berty was almost able to finish his book between meals by the time they all said goodnight.

A warm orange glow cast by a few lanterns softened the designs on the Wassail Stein as Berty entered his study. Hanging his cloak, he could not help but wonder if he had made the right decision about Delyth and her Fairy Dust. A candle on his desk flickered to life as Berty walked towards his bookshelf.

His hand automatically reached for the thick, leather bound spine of his magical reference book. Flipping through the pages, he had found his desired subject. The book said, "Fairies create Fairy Dust using a secret process. Fairies use the dust in a wide array of applications. Medicinally, it is most commonly used as a remedy for headaches. It is also used as a stimulant, which can improve concentration. Abuse among Fairies is rare.

"Fairy Dust is also a powerful weapon against non-Fairies, rendering the victim incapacitated for an extended amount of time. Depending on the dose and the method of use, Fairy Dust use on non-Fairies can be used as a mind-controlling agent. Recreationally, non-Fairies use the dust as a mind-altering hallucinogen."

Feeling settled, Berty returned the book to its shelf before climbing the spiral staircase to go to bed.

Berty awoke to find another gray sky out his window. After he showered and dressed, he made sure that he had books in his pocket before walking out under the blanket of gray clouds. Crossing the bridge, he looked at the gray above him and sniffed the air. Not smelling any moisture in the air, he continued into the trunk, then down the stairs to the Roundtable Room.

The members of the Advisory Council were chatting together when Berty entered the room. Everyone greeted Berty with cheery good mornings.

On the way down to breakfast, Berty turned to Alfred who was walking beside him, asking, "What happens if it rains during Wassail?"

Alfred gave Berty a puzzled look, then answered, "It will not rain."

"But what if it does?"

"It will not rain."

"Why not?"

"It does not rain during Wassail," interjected Colvin.

"What do you mean?" Berty asked as he walked onto the dais.

"It has never rained during Wassail," answered Delyth.

Berty wondered if someone was pulling his leg. "Ever?"

"Never, ever," said Delyth, "in Empire history has it rained immediately before or during Wassail. Or snowed for that matter."

"How?"

"The magic of Wassail," Alfred explained, "is highly protected. Its secrets are only passed from Cider Master to Cider Master. And they are bound by an oath never to tell anyone but another Cider Master."

"So even though the skies are gray," began Berty as he sat at the table.

"It will not rain," finished Alfred, sitting in his seat beside Berty.

Berty took some food onto his plate. "Fascinating."

After breakfast, the crowd inside the Reception Room filtered outside to take their places for another midmorning addition. Walking down the dirt path to the kettlebarrel, Berty glanced at the increasingly graying sky, pondering the Cider Master's achievement.

Gathered around the kettlebarrel, a hush fell upon the crowd as they watched the Cider Master take a whiff of the would-be Wassail and add more mystery ingredients from wooden buckets. When the Cider Master was finished, he gave Berty a nod. The crowd cheered before dispersing.

Back in the Roundtable Room, Colvin joined Berty, Alfred and Delyth around the table. While Alfred cracked open a book and Delyth began another sketch, Colvin unrolled a large, double rolled scroll. Berty opened his book, but could not help to notice how the Dwarf scrutinized every detail on the scroll. Every so often, Colvin would stroke his long, bright red beard, making annotations next to blueprint like drawings.

Finishing the little amount he had left to read, Berty looked around the table. Alfred turned a page. Delyth hid behind her long, dark hair. Colvin studied detailed cross sections of what Berty thought looked like a Christmas Tree, complete with decorations.

"Hmmm," said Colvin as he ran his fingers over the drawings.

He looked up. "My Lord, concerning this year's Life of Light Tree, I would like to make a change, with your permission."

"A change?" asked Berty.

"Yes," Colvin answered. "Traditionally, it has been decorated in gold. But I thought it appropriate to mark the new era under the Emperor. I only have a week and a half to get this ready. May I?"

Hiding his ignorance about the Life of Light Tree, Berty asked, "What sort of change?"

"I was thinking about adding red decorations," said Colvin excitedly. "They would symbolize your color." Berty realized that Colvin was talking about his claret cloak. "Plus, the color of the crystal as well. Red would go well, I think, with the gold decorations and the green of the tree."

Berty understood the Life of Light Tree to be the Empire's version of a Christmas Tree. "Where is the Life of Light Tree?"

"I forgot that you would not know, my Lord," said Colvin. "The Empire Tree uses the same fir every year. We erect it in the center of the Reception Room. People from all over the Empire come to see it and to make offerings to be burnt in the Sages' Grove Yule fire. Somehow, people think that our fire is better or stronger than their local fires."

"I think they believe that the journey makes it better," interjected Alfred, "not the fire itself."

"Maybe," Colvin said. "Either way, they come." He glanced at his plans. "Is red acceptable my Lord?"

Berty pondered for a moment. "Alfred, your thoughts?"

"I do not see a problem, as long as they are only additions and nothing is subtracted from the traditional tree. People do like their traditions," said Alfred.

"I agree with Alfred," Berty said. "Add, but do not subtract. I do not want it to look like the Empire Tree has completely changed."

"Yes, of course, my Lord," said Colvin, taking notes. "Thank you."

"Is there anything else?" asked Berty.

Colvin shook his head.

"Good, then let's all head to lunch," Berty suggested.

Sitting at the table in the Reception Room, Berty tried to imagine a large fir tree, covered in decorations, shining in the center of the room, but found it difficult amongst the people sitting and eating at the crowed tables.

After lunch, Berty saying that he needed to replace his book excused himself from the Roundtable Room. Walking to his chambers, he wondered if Silvia would approve of such additions to their Life of Light Tree. As he entered his study, Berty hoped that she would.

He hung his cloak, then cast his book into the read pile. As he sat in his chair, he pondered how Silvia thought. Wishing that he could pick her brain, he closed his eyes.

Silvia sat at a long, highly polished table, finishing a meal. Across the table sat a blond haired boy in a gray three-piece suit, who, Berty thought, was named Thomas. At the head of the table, a man, also blond and wearing a similar suit except in dark brown with an ascot tied at his neck, swirled a brown liquid in a small glass. He sniffed, then took a sip. A woman with a large, blonde bun on top of her head entered the room. She adjusted her high necked, dark blue, bustled dress before sitting in the chair at the other end of the table. The woman smiled.

The man placed his glass on the table, saying, "I must thank you, Leigh, for coming. You have made my wife very happy."

"You are welcome, Mister Nelson," said Silvia.

"Estelle smiled today," Mrs. Nelson said almost in tears.

Mister Nelson smiled at his wife. "I don't know how you do it, Leigh." His smile disappeared, being replaced with a look of concern. "Do you think that she will make a full recovery?"

Silvia looked at Mister Nelson carefully. "I cannot guarantee a full recovery. I have only been here a short time. It really is too early to tell. If after some time of working with Estelle, my only achievement is keeping a smile on her face, then I think that we would have taken great strides."

"If you can keep her smiling," said Mrs. Nelson, "then I will be eternally grateful."

Silvia smiled at the three of them. Where Mrs. Nelson look elated, the other two looked worried. Mister Nelson's worry seemed to stem from inside while Thomas' worry seemed to stem from his father at whom he kept casting nervous glances.

Mister Nelson finished his drink, then said, "Well it is time to tend to the store. Thomas, are you coming?"

"I will be down in a minute, Father," Thomas answered.

"Very well." Mister Nelson rose from his chair. "Angelica?"

"Yes, James, I am ready." Mrs. Nelson stood, smoothing the skirt of her dress before she left the room with her husband.

Thomas' pale blue eyes stared intently at Silvia. "Please, Leigh, don't forget." He lowered his voice to a whisper. "The Governor does not approve of magic and therefore father will not tolerate it either. I hope you can find a way." He rose from his chair, then hurried from the room.

Berty opened his eyes. Sighing, he wished that he knew how he was spying on Silvia and he wondered if she knew when he was watching.

Standing, he took the last book from his desk. As he fastened his cloak, he tried to push his vision to the back of his mind. Instead his mind recited, *Empress watches over all / High in the Empire Tree / Finding the time, four will fall / Watcher watches over thee.* At one time, Berty wondered if the Pixie Priestess, who made the prophecy to Silvia, meant Declan instead of him. He reached the landing to the Roundtable Room sooner than he had anticipated. Pausing before entering the room, Berty muttered, "She meant me."

Thoughts about being Silvia's Watcher consumed him throughout dinner. After dinner, Berty returned to the Roundtable Room in hopes of losing his thoughts in his book. Opening the book to the first page, he began to read. He turned the page, realizing that he had read the book before.

As Berty rose from his chair, Alfred looked up, saying, "Is there a problem, my Lord?"

"I picked up the wrong book," said Berty with a smile. "I will see you in the morning." Alfred bowed his head, then returned to his reading.

When Berty entered his study, he saw that he had read every book on his desk. He gathered all the books and walked across the short bridge to Silvia's study. After placing all the read books on the shelves, he pulled every unread book left. Berty examined the small pile of books. He could not believe that he had read everything else so quickly. Grabbing the last of the books, he returned to his chambers.

He deposited the books onto his desk before he removed his cloak to sit in the chair. Staring at the new pile of books, Berty decided that he would not start reading until tomorrow. Automatically, his one hand grabbed his old notebook while the other hand grabbed a pen. Opening the notebook to where he last wrote, he began to pen new chapters in the Adventures of Leigh and Marcus.

Chapter Twenty-five
A Feast for the Fall

The morning greeted Berty with bits of sunlight peeking through the gray. After getting ready, he grabbed a book, then left his chambers to head to the Roundtable Room. As he crossed the bridge, the cold morning air whipped his face and the smell of winter reached his nostrils.

"I'm telling you, winter is going to be harsh this year." Berty could hear Hatcher's gruff voice carry into the staircase while he descended.

"Since when does being Gatekeeper give you any credence in predicting the weather?" asked the voice of Colvin.

Berty entered the room to see Hatcher inch so close to Colvin that their noses almost touched. "I spend a lot of time outside," said the Troll as he poked a knobby finger into the Dwarf's chest. "It makes one aware of things."

Colvin snorted. "You are just getting soft in your old age."

Hatcher's nostrils flared. Berty thought it best to diffuse the situation. "Good morning," he said in a cheerful voice.

The two quarrelers stepped away from each other, then greeted Berty with, "Good morning, my Lord."

"Is there a problem?" asked Berty.

"No, not at all," Hatcher answered.

"Just a friendly disagreement," said Colvin.

Berty chuckled, walking past them. Reaching the door on the other side of the room, Alfred was waiting for him on the landing.

"Good morning, my Lord," greeted Alfred. "Another addition to witness this morning. I do hope the fires under the kettlebarrel will be able to keep the people warm as they gather."

"Can we not put fires around the village to help keep the people warm?"

"Oh, no. That could disturb the Wassail making process."

"Yes, yes. You are quite right," Berty agreed, not really knowing why as they descended the stairs to breakfast.

At breakfast, the spread of foods set on the tables was considerably smaller than the previous days. "Why do we always have to starve before the Wassail meal?" complained Colvin as he bit into a sweet roll.

"Tradition," Alfred answered.

"Bah," said Colvin as he poured hot liquid into his cup. All those around the table laughed.

When breakfast ended, everyone headed down the stairs into the cold.

"I do hope this addition will be quick," said Delyth. She shivered while pulling her dark purple cloak around her slender frame.

Gathered around the kettlebarrel, the crowd huddled as close to one another as possible. The Cider Master appeared on the platform seemingly unaware of both the crowd and the cold. The Elf began with a stir and a sniff. He called to his workers who immediately brought him buckets of mystery ingredients. In-between handfuls of this and that, he did more stirring and sniffing. People huddled closer together as they watched with bated breath.

After many additions, the Cider Master finally had a satisfied look on his face. Smiling, he gave a sharp nod to Berty, then wiped his hands. As he climbed down the platform, the crowd cheered. They quickly disappeared into the warmth of the surrounding buildings. Berty and some of his advisors returned to the Roundtable Room.

Both Berty and Alfred opened their books, beginning to read while Delyth sat in her chair, shivering. Berty glanced up from his book to see her shaking violently. "Delyth, are you okay? Would you like a blanket or something to wrap around you?"

"No thank you, my Lord," she answered. "Kayla is bringing me...." A door opened and Delyth's servant entered, carrying a silver tray that held a silver carafe and mug. "Here she is." Kayla poured steaming liquid into the mug, then handed it to Delyth. Delyth took a sip of the warming liquid and smiled.

"Id tere anyting eld you be needing 'ighnid?" asked Kayla.

"No, Kayla," said Delyth. "Thank you, I will be fine. You may finish your chores." Kayla curtsied, then left. Delyth quickly finished her mug. She stopped shaking enough to pour another. "As soon as the shops officially reopen," she said between sips, "I am going to have my cloak lined with fur."

Returning his gaze to his book, Berty's mind wandered to his own cloak. His cloak was never too warm or too cold. After figuring it had something to do with the magic of being Emperor, he continued to read his book.

Eventually, Delyth became warm enough to sketch another day's scene. At lunch, Colvin griped about there being even less food than there was at breakfast. After lunch, Berty returned to reading his book while Kayla brought Delyth another carafe of warm drink.

During dinner, an excited mood electrified the Reception Room. Even Colvin did not complain much about the lack of food.

"The fire is starting to die," said Hatcher with a sparkle in his eyes. "It won't be long before we all have full steins of Wassail."

"And we get to eat," Colvin added. Those around the table laughed.

Climbing the stairs, Alfred asked, "My, Lord, shall we take some Wassail for Declan and set it aside in case he does not return tomorrow?"

"Excellent idea, Alfred," said Berty. They entered the Roundtable Room to read some more before retiring for the evening.

Berty awoke to the sound of wind rustling through the tree. Looking out the window at the mighty wind, he muttered, "This will be fun." Leaving his chambers, he stepped into the windy morning. The long plank and rope bridge swayed ominously. Grabbing hold of the ropes tightly, Berty crossed the bridge quickly.

In the Roundtable Room, Delyth was already sitting at the table, bundled in her cloak, shaking. Kayla brought her a warm drink, saying, "'Ere you go, 'ighnid, tat dould warm you."

"Thank you, Kayla," said Delyth taking a sip. "The blasted wind. Keep them coming."

"Are you feeling well?" Berty asked as he sat with her at the table.

Delyth took a long drink. "I will be. Thank you for your concern."

"Perhaps you should have warmer clothes made," Berty suggested.

"I think I had better," conceded Delyth. "I do not remember being so cold in Fairyland. The shops will not reopen for another week or so. May I ask Theodore for the Empire's clothes maker?"

"Of course, you may."

"Thank you, Emperor." Delyth smiled before pouring herself more hot drink.

By the time they went to breakfast, Delyth was warm. Colvin complained about what was waiting for them on the table. "Toast! Who in their right mind thinks that toast is a meal?"

"If you're not going to eat it," said Edwin with his hand reaching towards Colvin's share.

"Don't you dare touch my toast, boy!" Colvin said. Everyone laughed.

After breakfast, everyone but Delyth ran to get his Wassail Stein. Kayla brought the Wassail Stein to a barely shivering Delyth.

Berty and his advisors sat around the Roundtable with the Wassail Steins gleaming in silver, pewter and bronze. The excitement was so contagious that Berty could not concentrate on reading while waiting for the Wassail to be ready. Only one thing distracted him from the collective excitement. Delyth started to shake more violently than ever.

"Theodore," called Berty.

"Yes, my Lord," he said as the Dwarf entered the room.

"I am sorry to bother you during the excitement," said Berty. "Could you quickly fetch a warm blanket or something to wrap around Delyth?"

"Of course." Theodore hurried out of the room.

The Dwarf returned momentarily with a woolen fleece, which with the help of a little magic, wrapped around the shivering Fairy.

"Thank you," said Delyth. "Oh, that is so warm." Immediately her shivers subsided. Theodore bowed, then disappeared out the door.

Berty did not know for how long they sat in silence. All he knew was that he kept reading the same page over and over again. Finally, he closed his book, placing it on the table. His council smiled at him and he smiled back.

Through the main door flew a beautiful blue jay. He landed in the middle of the table, facing Berty. Opening his beak, it said, "Emperor, Wassailing is here." As the bird flew out of the room, everyone cheered.

Grabbing their steins, the Advisory Council began to sing as they walked to the kettlebarrel. "Here we go a-Wassailing, a-Wassailing we go. Come with me, down the tree and through the grove to the kettlebarrel we all go."

Everyone who joined them sang the song over and over. Even Berty hummed along for he knew the melody. When everyone arrived at the kettlebarrel, the singing stopped. The Cider Master stood before them with his hand on the tap. In the excited quietness, Berty realized that the wind did not blow within the grounds of the Sages' Grove.

"Good men and women," said the Cider Master, "the harvest has been good to us. The gifts from the trees will allow us to have good health, not only through the darkness, but throughout the entire year." He paused. "Emperor, your stein, if you please." Berty walked to the kettlebarrel and handed the Cider Master his silver stein. The Elf filled it. While handing it back to Berty, he said, "To your good health."

Berty raised his stein, saying, "And to the good health of the Empire." Taking a small sip, his tongue elated in the warm, spicy drink. Giving a nod to the Cider Master, Berty stepped aside. The Advisory Council formed a line to have their steins filled. Next in line were the Empire Guards. Theodore followed, then so did everyone else.

With his Advisory Council in tow, Berty returned to the Reception Room to await the start of the feast. As soon as Theodore appeared on the top step, the room immediately became more crowded with tables and chairs.

As many people as possible crammed into the Reception Room for the feast. When the room was full, Theodore climbed onto the seat of his chair at the head table and announced, "Let the feast begin." Food appeared on the tables and people grabbed what they could and ate.

The Reception Room buzzed with merry conversation and laughter. Berty thought he heard singing from a table in the back of the room. The Wassail was just the right drink to wash down all the rich foods.

Darkness enveloped the sky and the chandelier shone brighter than ever. Berty looked at all the food still on the tables that people were eating, then he asked, "How long does the feast last?"

"Until all the Wassail is finished," answered Alfred. "Each vessel filled by the Cider Master will magically refill until the contents of the kettlebarrel are gone."

Every so often, Berty would watch Delyth. She would involuntarily shudder once in a while, but otherwise seemed okay.

After many hours of drinking and eating, the merriment mellowed to a sleepy contentment. No more new food appeared on the tables and the last drops of Wassail were being drunk. The crowd was beginning to disperse, even the singers in the back of the room were singing their way home.

Berty looked around the table at his content guests. Delyth caught his eye and smiled weakly. Her eyelids were heavy. "I am going to call it a night," she said. "I cannot keep up with all you men."

"Good Wassail," cheered Alfred.

Delyth nodded happily. Berty watched her as she laboriously got off her chair. His eyes followed her as she trudged to the stairs, Wassail Stein in hand. Before she reached the first step, her stein clanged as she collapsed to the floor.

Berty rushed to her side and picked up her wrist. From across the room, he heard a familiar voice shout, "Delyth!" Declan knelt by her side, examining her. "She's alive, but barely," he said.

"Her pulse is weak," confirmed Berty. He bent over, carefully picking her up off the floor. Her limp body looked like a purple cloth wrapped in wool draped in his arms. "Get her stein," he instructed.

Colvin grabbed the stein that rolled away from where she fell. Declan walked beside Berty in silence, as Berty carried her up the stairs. Following closely behind were Colvin, Alfred, Alvar, and Hatcher.

In the Roundtable Room, Berty laid her on the table. As he fixed the sheared wool around her body, Hatcher asked, "What's wrong with her?"

Seeing the small jeweled silver stein in Colvin's hand, Declan held his hand out for it. The Dwarf obliged. Sniffing the inside, Declan declared, "Poison. She's been poisoned." He placed the stein on the table.

Picking it up, Alfred smelled the stein also. "I do not recognize the poison." The Elf glanced at the Fairy, then back at the stein. "The amount of poison in this thing should have killed her."

"How is she not dead?" asked Colvin.

"The Wassail must contain the antidote," Berty deduced. Looking at Alvar, he said, "Find Delyth's servant, Kayla, and question her." He looked back at Delyth. "Someone, fetch the Cider Master." Alvar and Hatcher ran down the steps. "We will need blankets and some water." Alfred and Colvin hurried from the room.

"How could this have happened?" asked Declan while he

tenderly held her hand.

"We will find out," Berty reassured.

Hatcher returned with the Cider Master as Alfred and Colvin brought blankets and water. "How can I be of service to you, Emperor?" asked the Cider Master.

"Do you recognize this?" Berty asked, handing him the stein.

The Elf took a whiff. "This is not in my Wassail."

"We know," said Berty. "Do you know what it is?"

"I do. Without divulging my secrets, I can tell you that it is a poison which is derived from a very rare herb that is only found on God Mountain."

"The Wassail contains the antidote to this poison?" asked Berty.

"It does."

"Do you have any of the antidote left over?"

The Cider Master looked over at the sick Fairy. "I do, but it will need to be extracted. Where can I set up?"

Berty saw a long table against the wall. "Will that do?" He pointed to the table.

"Very well, my Lord." As the Cider Master left, audible shivers came from the table.

"Let's get these blankets on her," said Alfred. Colvin helped Alfred tuck the blankets around the frail Fairy.

Declan inched close to her ear, saying, "Hang on, Delyth, hang on." He stroked her face. "She's really hot."

Berty felt her forehead and cheek with the back of his hand. "What a fever. Start putting a wet rag on her forehead."

Dipping a rag in water, Declan placed it on her head. "She is making this rag too hot, too fast," he said. He pulled the rag off her head, dipping it back into the bucket of water.

As Declan pulled the rag out of the bucket, Berty said, "Wait." Berty lunged his hand towards the rag and it froze. "Now try." Declan placed the frozen rag on her forehead. It stayed cool longer.

The Cider Master returned with his gear and began his work

making the antidote.

After a while, Berty and Alfred wandered towards the Cider Master. "How long will it take?" asked Alfred.

"Hours," the Cider Master replied.

Gazing toward the table, Alfred said, "She may not have that long."

"Where is the Wassail that we saved for Declan?" asked Berty.

"Yes, of course," Alfred said. "That should buy some time." He ran out of the room.

"You did not have to save me any Wassail," said Declan. "I had some in a nearby village." He looked at Delyth's pale skin. "I am glad you did."

When Alfred returned, Declan began to administer small doses of Wassail to the Fairy. Berty watched as Declan alternated between the frozen rag and spoonfuls of Wassail. Awhile later, Declan said, "The color is returning to her cheeks." He continued his administrations in silence.

After a couple of hours, Declan approached Berty. "Her temperature is coming down, but we are running out of Wassail."

"Do not worry," said the Cider Master. "All it needs to do now is stew for a half an hour, then she can take it."

"Thank you," Berty said.

"My Lord," said an out of breath Alvar as he entered the room, "we have captured Kayla in the woods. She was running away. She has been detained and questioned." He took a deep breath. "Kayla has admitted to putting something in her drinks, but not to poisoning Delyth."

"Excellent work. Keep her detained. If she says anything else, listen. I would like to speak to her once I know that Delyth is okay," said Berty.

Bowing, Alvar said, "Very good." His cloak floated out behind him as the Elf left the room.

Tired of pacing, Berty sat in his chair to wait. He could not remember a longer half-hour. Looking around the room, all was quiet with the exception of splashing sounds as Declan kept dipping the rag and wiping her forehead.

Finally breaking the silence, the Cider Master said, "It is ready." Both Berty and Alfred watched the Cider Master pour a cup of milky liquid out of a large glass contraption. Handing the cup to Declan, he said, "Give her a little." Declan tipped the cup to her mouth. Within seconds of swallowing, color rushed back to her skin. "Good," said the Elf. "A little more now." Declan followed his instructions carefully.

Four doses later, Delyth opened her eyes. She looked at everyone standing around her. Smiling, she said, "I feel so drained. What happened?"

"Shh," said Declan as he placed a finger to her lips, "don't speak now. Save your strength." He took her frail hand in his.

Berty turned to the Cider Master, asking, "How fast does it work?"

"I do not know for how long she was being poisoned or how much she was given. It could take a while before her health is fully restored." The Elf handed Declan a small hourglass like timer. "Keep giving her a dose each time the sand empties." Declan nodded. "She should be strong enough to move soon. I will make another batch. The good thing is that she is responding well."

"Thank you for your help," said Berty. Looking at Declan, he asked, "You will stay with her?"

"Of course."

"Hatcher," said Berty, "you stay here, just in case." The Troll nodded. "Colvin, have Theodore help you do a thorough search of both Delyth's and Kayla's chambers."

"Will do."

"Alfred, come with me." Berty led Alfred out of the room and down the stairs until they reached the Receiving Room, where they met Alvar.

"Are you ready to see her?" Alvar asked.

"Yes," answered Berty. "Lead the way."

Chapter Twenty-six
Clarity

A lvar called to Edwin to accompany them. He led them to another hidden Sages' Seal in the room. Touching the second to bottom circle, the Seal split in two, revealing a long, dark set of stone steps. Once all four men began to descend, the door closed behind them and torches illuminated the way. When the stairs ended, they traveled down a long stone corridor. The corridor eventually gave way to a large, chamber where a handful of Empire Guards were stationed.

"We are here to see the prisoner," said Alvar.

"Yes, Captain," one of the guards said. He led the men down another dark corridor.

In an iron barred cell sat a forlorn Fairy who raised her head at the sound of the men stopping outside.

"Emperor," said Kayla with a bow.

Through the bars, Berty said, "I want to know what you have been giving Delyth."

Fear shown in the Fairy's eyes as she spoke. "A powder in 'er drinkd."

"What sort of powder?"

The look of fear in her eyes morphed into a dreamy look. "To take ud 'ome."

"Home," said Berty incredulously. "You were willing to kill to go home?"

"Kill?" The fear returned. "Not kill my 'ighnid. Make her dick, tat'd all."

"Where did you get this powder and when did you start giving it to her?"

"A woman in te market. I put a little in 'er evenin' cup of tea every night. Tose were tee indrucktond."

Berty could not believe his ears. "What instructions?"

"From te woman," answered Kayla.

"What did this woman...?" Alfred began to ask, but Berty tapped his arm to stop him.

"Then what?" asked Berty as calmly as he could.

"I 'ad to up it. Te woman paid me more to put it in every drink tat I could during Waddail. And I wad to get a bonud atter tonight."

"Who was this woman?"

"A Fairy," answered Kayla. "Alwayd wearing a cloak wit a 'ood." Berty and Alfred exchanged looks. "Dee daid tat if I gave it to 'er eggdackly ad told, ten I would get to go 'ome." New tears streaked down her face.

Berty took a deep breath, then said, "Kayla, you are charged with the attempted murder of the Empire Historian, Delyth."

"No!" Her sobs echoed throughout the dungeon. Berty and Alfred began to walk away from her cell. "Wait," she cried. They returned. "Te Fairy 'ad drawberry blonde 'air and freckled. I never knew 'er name."

"Thank you, Kayla," said Berty. As he walked away, he could hear her crying.

Alvar led Berty, Alfred and Edwin up the stone steps to return to the Receiving Room. The four men walked in silence. At the top of the stairs, the door split open and they walked into the empty room.

"Thank you, Alvar, Edwin," Berty said. Leaving them, Alfred followed him up the stairs into the Reception Room. At the base of the main stairs, Berty turned to Alfred, saying, "It is time to inform Elrick and Lida of all that we know."

Bowing, Alfred hurried into a corridor. About to climb the steps, Berty heard, "My Lord." Turning, he saw Colvin approaching with Theodore behind him. "We found powdery residue everywhere in Delyth's chambers," Colvin reported, "and a stash of coins much greater than servant's pay in Kayla's room."

"Colvin, trace those coins," instructed Berty. "Theodore, can you put all the powdery residue into a bottle with a stopper?"

281

"Yes, my Lord," they said in unison. The Dwarves left, going different directions.

Berty returned to the Roundtable Room, finding Delyth awake. "How are you feeling?" he asked, walking towards the table.

"Achy, but better than before," replied Delyth. "Emperor, will you please tell me what is going on? They will not."

"I am glad you are feeling better. As soon as Theodore cleans your room, you will be able to rest in your own bed." He looked at her, measuring her strength. "I am afraid that you were being poisoned."

"Poisoned?"

"By Kayla," said Berty. "Your parents have been informed and she is being detained."

"Kayla," she breathed. "They never thought that it would be my own servant."

"What do you mean?" asked Berty.

"My parents asked for Empire Guards as my escort to the Empire Tree for the sole purpose of me being able to use Fairy Dust on them. It was so I could control them. That way, they could protect me and be loyal to me," she explained.

"But why?"

"I am not entirely sure. All I know is that they were fearful of my journey here."

"I know why," said Alfred, joining Berty at his side. "On the way to the Empire Tree to answer the former Empress' summons, Elrick and Lida overheard...."

"Millicent," Berty finished.

"Yes," said Alfred.

"Who?" Declan asked.

"She used to be Historian," answered Berty.

"Millicent," Alfred continued, "was not alone. She was with Leif, the former Scholar. They were plotting the demise of the Empress together."

"Millicent knew that she would no longer be Historian," Berty said.

"Your parents thought that with your own servant, that once you got to the Empire Tree, you would be safe from her reach," Alfred said to Delyth. "But it seems that Millicent bought Kayla."

"Colvin and Theodore found a lot of coins in Kayla's room," said Berty. "Last I heard, Leif was heading to God Mountain. I do not think that it is a coincidence that the poison originated from there."

"How do you know that was where Leif was going?" asked Hatcher.

"He was seen in the Dragonlands, heading in that direction."

"Goblins," said Hatcher in disgust. "As much as I don't like them, they do know just about everything. Nosy little buggers."

"Emperor," Alfred said, "the Fairies wish to deal with Kayla themselves. They want to know if we can hold her in the dungeon until they can retrieve her."

"Fine," said Berty. "I would want to deal with her myself, too, if it were my daughter."

Alfred bowed his head. "I will let them know."

Berty sat in his chair while Delyth fell asleep with Declan beside her. Returning to the room, Alfred quietly sat in his chair. No one said a word. The Cider Master made the only movement in the room as he brewed another batch of antidote. The rhythmic stillness of the night was broken when Theodore entered the room.

Walking over to Berty, he said, "It is done, my Lord." He held out a glass phial no larger than a perfume bottle. "Here is all the powder residue found in her chambers."

"That was the amount of powder residue?" asked the Cider Master, his face full of shock.

"Yes," Theodore answered. "All from her study. There was none in the upper chambers."

"A lot of poison," said the Cider Master, "especially for a Fairy." He shook his head. "She is lucky to be alive."

"Thank you, Theodore," Berty said. "Put that in a place where no one but you can get it and tell no one where you put it, not even me."

"Yes, my Lord."

"I also want you to find a loyal... an extremely loyal Tender for Delyth."

"I will, Emperor. In the meantime, I will tend to her myself."

"Excellent," said Berty. "Declan, when do you think we can move her?"

Taking his eyes off the sleeping Fairy, Declan turned to Berty, saying, "Now would be good. I am sure she would rest better in her own bed."

Berty nodded in agreement. "If you would carry her." Declan began to pick her up off the table. "Theodore, you will have to open her chambers for us."

"Here, I will take that," said Alfred to Declan whilst grabbing the antidote and the timer.

"Thank you," Declan said. Delyth opened her eyes a little. "Go back to sleep, we are just taking you to your room." She closed her eyes, resting her head on Declan's shoulder.

"Hatcher," Berty began.

"I will stay with the Cider Master in case he needs anything," finished Hatcher.

Berty gave the Troll a sharp nod, then said to Theodore, "Lead the way." Declan followed the Dwarf with the Fairy sleeping in his arms. Alfred and Berty walked behind as Theodore led them all out of the trunk onto Council Circle.

"Do you really think it was Millicent who gave Kayla the poison?" asked Alfred.

"I know it was," Berty answered. Alfred raised his eyebrows. "As soon as Kayla mentioned strawberry blonde hair and freckles." He gave Alfred a sad smile. "Millicent was not very fond of me. Leif was even less fond, to put it mildly."

They arrived at Delyth's bundle of bare branches and waited as Theodore unlocked the arched entrance. Inside, Declan carried Delyth up the spiral staircase. Theodore said to Berty, "My Lord, I will... return." Berty nodded, knowing that the young Dwarf was going to hide the bottle of powder.

Berty followed Alfred up the spiral staircase to Delyth's bedroom. She slept on the short bed peacefully while Alfred placed the antidote on her nightstand. With one eye on the timer, Declan walked over to Berty. "Emperor, I have news," he said.

"What is it?" asked Berty.

"I found them, lots and lots of them," Declan said. "Streams of magic. And they all lead to one place."

"Where?" asked Alfred.

"The Dragonlands," Declan answered.

"Do you know where within the Dragonlands?" Berty asked.

"No, my Lord," answered Declan. "I dare not cross the border. I am no match for a Dragon, let alone many Dragons."

"Thank you, Declan." Berty looked around Delyth's room. "Our first priority is to get her well. You will need to administer another dose soon. There is only one chair up here, Alfred and I will be downstairs." Berty led Alfred down the steps. They sat in chairs around Delyth's room filling, curved desk.

After sitting awhile in silence, Alfred said, "Do you think they know that you are now Emperor?"

"Leif and Millicent," said Berty. "Most likely."

"Then why try to disparage you?"

"Leif is good at undermining," Berty answered. "Being Scholar for three Empresses has given him a lot of practice. He has honed his skill well."

"You are saying that that is all he knows?"

"There is that." Berty looked unfocused at the back wall as he remembered Leif's tirade in the Roundtable Room before Silvia dismissed her Advisory Council. "But do not forget that Leif thinks that I undermined his authority and usurped his power within the Empire Tree. He felt that he was the most important advisor and therefore irreplaceable. How very wrong he was." Berty sighed. "Which makes him all the more dangerous."

"All right," said Alfred. "How does Millicent fit into the picture? How can she go along with it all?" Alfred showed a look of utter disgust on his face. "How does she conspire to kill one of her own? A member of her royal family in fact?"

"How indeed, Alfred. How indeed." Berty shook his head.

"Loyalty means different things to different people," Declan said as he descended the steps. He looked at their faces and answered their unasked question. "Delyth is doing really well. She is sleeping again."

"Good," said Berty.

"I would like to stay here tonight," Declan declared. "To watch over her. She should not be left alone."

Berty nodded. "I agree."

The wind chimes rang and Berty said, "Come in."

Hatcher led the Cider Master into Delyth's study. "My Lord," said the Cider Master, "I have finished the second batch of the antidote."

"Thank you," Berty said. "Please, address everything to Declan. He in charge of Delyth's recovery."

The Elf bowed, then walked around the table to speak with Declan. After thanking the Cider Master, Declan ran back upstairs with the new batch of antidote. While walking around the curved table towards the door, the Cider Master said, "It has been an honor to be able to be of greater service to you, Emperor."

"We were honored to have you."

He bowed his head, saying, "By my estimates, the Fairy's health should be fully restored within a couple of days. I am no Wizard, so I can only rely on my cider mastery."

"And we are very grateful," said Berty.

"My Lord," the Cider Master said while taking a deep bow.

"I will see to the Cider Master, my Lord," said Hatcher.

"Thank you, Hatcher, then I would suggest retiring for the evening."

Hatcher bowed, then followed the Cider Master out of the room.

"This is not exactly what one expects at the end of a festive occasion," Alfred said. "One of your own getting poisoned."

"No," agreed Berty.

"I am guessing that we will need to have a serious meeting before the Winter Festival begins," remarked Alfred, looking concerned.

"Yes, and Delyth needs to be a part of that meeting."

Alfred nodded and the two men sat in silence. The aged Elf began to nod off to sleep when the wind chimes rang again.

Theodore walked into the room, saying, "My Lord, everything is secure. Declan's bag that he dropped has been retrieved and placed in his chambers. What do you need me to do?"

Berty smiled at the young Dwarf, saying, "Thank you, Theodore. Go get some sleep. I will see you in the morning." Barely noticing the Dwarf's bow, his eyelids became heavy and he fell asleep in the chair.

Morning arrived sooner than expected. Berty awoke with pains in his neck and back. Getting off the hard wooden chair, he stretched and saw Alfred open his eyes.

Berty and Alfred climbed the spiral staircase to find a smiling Delyth. "You did not have to stay," she said.

Berty smiled at her. "How are you feeling?"

"Much better, thank you," she said as she sat up in bed.

Declan walked over to help adjust her pillows behind her. "You should not try to do too much. Today should be spent in bed," he told her.

"Theodore will be tending to you," said Berty. "I will return to check on you later, Delyth."

"As will I," Alfred said with a smile.

While Berty and Alfred walked out the door of Delyth's chambers, Theodore entered, carrying a tray of food for Delyth and Declan. Leaving Alfred on Council Circle, Berty returned to his chambers. After his shower, he walked down the steps to find his Wassail Stein sitting on the top of his desk, clean. He returned it to its hiding place in his desk.

Remembering what Declan had told him about where the magic was going, Berty quickly perused his notes. "Dragonlands," he muttered. Fastening his cloak, he ran out of his study.

Arriving in the Roundtable Room, he found Colvin waiting for him. "My Lord, I have finished researching the coins," said Colvin.

"Good," Berty said. "Walk with me and tell me your findings." He led the Dwarf out of the trunk towards Delyth's chambers.

"All the coins originated here, except two. This one," Colvin held up a dull ron, "comes from a small town that lies near the border of the Dragonlands. And this one," he showed Berty a tarnished ver, "was made a very long time ago by a Dwarf named, Halvard. Halvard smithed coins that were distributed to a cluster of coastal villages." Berty rang the wind chimes, then they both entered Delyth's study. Alfred was sitting at the curved table while Colvin continued talking. "It was rumored that Leif was raised in one of those coastal villages. No one would have that long of a memory to be certain."

"There could be someone who knows," said Berty. "How is she?" he asked Alfred.

"Sleeping," Alfred answered.

Berty nodded. "Thank you, Colvin."

"A delegation from Fairyland will be arriving soon," said Alfred. "I do not know if they will send a new servant or if they will just collect the girl for sentencing."

"I do not think that they will try to poison Delyth again," Berty said as he sat in a chair.

The wind chimes rang and Theodore entered with a tray followed by Alvar and Hatcher. Theodore placed the tray on the table, then left.

"Emperor, we need to discuss Sages' Grove security," said Alvar.

"Delyth, where are you going?" Declan's voice carried into the study.

"Downstairs. I do not want to stay up here," said Delyth's defiant voice.

"Fine," conceded the voice of Declan, "but let me help you."

"Declan, I can walk! Put me down!" Declan emerged on the

spiral staircase, carrying a feisty Fairy in his arms. "Hello, everyone," said Delyth, her voice lowered a few decibels. "You can put me down now," she said to Declan.

"Okay," he said. He continued to carry her to her chair. Finally, he placed her feet delicately on the ground next to her chair and stood near as she sat in her chair. Declan found an empty chair, keeping the Fairy in his view.

Berty looked around the room, saying, "Since everyone is present, shall we discuss a few things?"

Consent resonated around the room. "I believe you wanted to discuss security, Alvar."

"Yes, Emperor, thank you." Alvar looked at everyone. "Hatcher and I were discussing searching each person as they enter the gates of the Sages' Grove."

"How many people enter the Sages' Grove daily?" asked Berty.

"Thousands," Hatcher answered.

"Do you have the means and the man power for such an operation?"

"Well, no," said Hatcher.

"We need to keep dangerous substances out for all of our safety," Alvar implored.

Berty looked at his men. "I know we are all shaken and perhaps a bit fearful. We cannot be certain that they will try something similar again."

"Those traitors must be stopped," bellowed Alvar.

"I agree with you, Alvar," Berty said calmly. "But encroaching the people's freedoms is not the answer. Leif is a highly intelligent man and Millicent should not be underestimated either. They will find a way around such roadblocks. People bent on destroying often do. Yes, we need to be vigilant, but our first defense against them is our trust in each other."

"But Delyth trusted Kayla," said Colvin, "and look where that got her."

Delyth blushed.

"Misplaced trust. She is not the first person to be forced to

289

trust someone," Berty said. "I trust every one of you, implicitly. I trust the Empire Guard and I trust the Head Tender of the Empire Tree. We must trust each other. Theodore will replace Kayla with a more trustworthy candidate. Kayla was not subjected to his screening process. Alfred's servant from Irmingard...."

"Was approved when he first arrived," finished Alfred. "'As long as it was okay with Theodore,' you said."

Berty took a sip of juice, then said, "Trust. Respect. Honor. These are the threads that bind us together. United, we are strong and solid. Divided, we crumble. Without trust, we have nothing."

The room was silent for a moment. Each advisor began to nod his or her head. Berty could feel a strength between them all.

"Now," said Alvar, breaking the silence, "what are we to do about Leif and Millicent?"

"I have no choice but to declare them enemies of the Empire," Berty said. "They are to be imprisoned, for now."

"What about the magic that is being siphoned into the Dragonlands?" asked Delyth.

"Perhaps it has something to do with the one with no prior ties," Hatcher said. "She entered through a portal in the Dragonlands." He screwed up his triangular face in confusion. "But that was a very long time ago."

"Before or after the lost Dwarves?" asked Colvin.

"Before. Well before."

Declan finally took his eyes off of Delyth for a moment to ask, "What lost Dwarves?"

"Generations ago," answered Colvin, "the Dragons asked for some of our finest craftsman to build something for them. They would not tell anyone what it was beforehand. So we sent six workers and a foreman. Supposedly they built whatever needed to be built, but got lost on the way back home."

"I thought that was a legend," said Delyth. "There is no record of anything being built in the Dragonlands."

"No legend," Colvin said. "One of the Dwarves was a relative of mine."

"Delyth," said Berty, "what do you know of the Dragons?"

"Well," she answered, "they are reclusive and very wise. People used to travel to seek the wisdom of the Dragons at one time. The clans used to maintain the forests there and the top clan would keep order within the land. But this is no longer. The clans fight each other. Clan warfare has made it difficult to travel through the Dragonlands."

"I wonder what they are hiding," muttered Berty.

"If anyone can find out, it is you, my Lord," said Alfred. "They must respect the Emperor."

"It is not as if he can just walk over there and ask them if clan warfare is rampart," Alvar said. "Dragons are not known for being able to control their tempers."

"Magic is fluttering away from here," Alfred explained. "The Emperor has to go."

"How?" asked Alvar.

"I must seek her," said Berty. "The one who knows." Berty saw the blank expressions on his advisors' faces. "Elder Hunter."

"When?" asked Alfred.

"As soon as I can."

"After the Winter Festival," Alfred stated.

"That will give me time to prepare my men for the journey," said Alvar.

"No," said Berty. "I do not need an army of escorts."

"My Lord, I must insist that you are traveling well protected," Alvar exasperated. "There are two potential killers on the loose."

"And traveling with such a large party, even if they are guards, makes me a much bigger target," said Berty. "It is best if I travel incognito. No one needs to know that I am gone."

"Very well," conceded Alvar. "May I suggest you take Lieutenant Edwin with you?"

"Excellent idea," Berty said. "Have him moved into the Empire Tree immediately, so it looks as if we are increasing security within and no one will have to know that he left. Do not tell him about our journey until he has been inside for a week."

"My Lord?" asked a confused Alvar.

"Perceptions are everything," Berty answered.

"Yes, of course," said Alvar.

"Now," said Berty with a smile, "let us get ready for the Winter Festival."

Chapter Twenty-seven
Flightless of the Fairy

Everyone except Delyth and Declan dispersed from Delyth's chambers going his separate way. Berty decided to return to his study, thinking that he would be able to read. As he walked up the stairs, his mind recalled Hatcher's words about the one without ties to the Empire entering through a portal in the Dragonlands. "That was not me," he breathed. On the landing at the top of the stairs, Berty paused. Deciding not to cross the bridge to his chambers, his feet took him down the narrow hallway and through the door at the end.

Emerging into the wide passageway, he followed his feet into the familiar Watching Room. To escape his mind before it wandered too dangerously into thoughts of being related to Silvia, Berty blew life into the miniature model of the Sages' Grove. He watched workers dismantle the kettlebarrel, then dry the pieces of wood over a fire before stacking them into a pile. Another set of workers handed the dried wood to people waiting in line. People either disappeared past the gates or into their homes, carrying bundles of wood, animal hides, and wrapped pieces of meat that were being distributed in different areas of the village.

Mesmerized by the movement of the miniature people, Berty was startled when Theodore entered the room. "My Lord, I do not mean to disturb you, but will you be taking your meal in the Reception Room or elsewhere?"

He stared at the young Dwarf for a moment. "In the Reception Room," he said. Berty thought it best to be with people. "Is it that time already?"

"Yes, Emperor."

The Dwarf left as Berty blew into the small tree. He used the main passageways to the Reception Room where he found a small table. Around the table sat Hatcher, Alfred, Alvar and Edwin. The four men stood as Berty approached the table. When Berty sat, they sat, then everyone began to eat.

Hatcher discussed the mass exodus out of the Sages' Grove post Wassail with Alfred and Alvar. Edwin stayed silent, obviously not used to dining with the select few.

When the Troll finished his conversation, Alvar said to Berty, "Where would you like the Lieutenant to be stationed?"

"This week while preparations abound," began Berty, "I would like for you, Lieutenant, to be ever so observant without interfering. Constantly walk throughout the tree, including the Tenders' areas. Dine with us. At the end of this week, we will evaluate."

Nodding, Edwin looked more relaxed. For the rest of the meal, he ate as if he belonged at the table. Berty, on the other hand, slumped into thoughts of fate's cruel betrayal because he felt that he must be related to Silvia.

Berty's funk lasted for days until he walked into the Reception Room and saw greenery being secured around the room. When the strong, woodsy smell of freshly cut pine hit his nose, childhood memories flooded into his mind.

His father parked the car in the parking lot of the shopping center. Large white lights strung around the area reflected on the snow, illuminating the section where the Christmas Trees were being sold. He and his brother ran to the trees, trying to find the best one. After his parents selected the tree, the tree lot workers helped secure the tree to the roof of the car and they drove home. His mother and father positioned the tree perfectly in front of the window. They all stayed up late, decorating and drinking hot chocolate. The memory made Berty smile. He decided that it was best if he just accepted his fate and enjoyed the holidays.

The end of the week found Berty in higher spirits as he waited to meet Edwin in the Roundtable Room. He sat in his chair while the young Elf entered the room. "I am here to make my report, my Lord," Edwin said with a bow.

"Thank you for coming, Edwin," said Berty. "Shut the door

and please have a seat." Edwin did as he was instructed. "Captain Alvar is not joining us. Tell me, what have you observed?"

Surprise in Edwin's face melted, then he said, "The inhabitants of the Empire Tree are extremely diligent. They look after each other."

"Do you feel that we need more security?"

"More security would only be excessive, my Lord. Our resources would be best used throughout the Sages' Grove."

"I can see why your Captain thinks so highly of you, Edwin." The Elf sat up straighter in the chair. "Now," continued Berty, "it is time to reveal the rest of my plan to you. I regret that we were not able to tell you everything from the beginning, but security was paramount. I do hope you understand."

"I understand."

"Captain Alvar recommended you for my personal security." Edwin's eyebrows raised. "Not within this tree of course. You will be my sole accompaniment as I travel through the Land of Sages." Comprehension drew on Edwin's face. "You realize that you being stationed here now is part of a ruse. I have no intention of alerting the Empire of our departure. We will be leaving after the Winter Festival. I would suggest that you make your presence scarce within the tree. There will be no need to patrol as often. I wish to share with you the two things that I do not know. Where exactly we are going and for how long we will be gone. Any questions?"

Edwin looked as though he wanted to ask why they were leaving, but he answered, "No, my Lord."

"Very well," said Berty as he stood. He smiled at the lieutenant, saying, "It is a quest for knowledge and perhaps we will have some wisdom thrown in." The Elf's body relaxed. "I believe Colvin wishes me to inspect the tree before it is decorated. Join me, won't you, Edwin."

Smiling, Edwin rose from his chair to follow his Emperor to the Reception Room.

"A little more to the left," instructed the voice of Colvin. "A little more. Keep going. Stop! Emperor," said Colvin as he walked over to greet Berty at the bottom of the stairs, "come and see what you think."

Berty allowed Colvin to lead him into the room where a mass of green stood in the center. Looking up, Berty saw a beautiful pine reaching from floor to ceiling. His hand reached out and felt the soft, long, pine needles. He smiled. "I love this time of year," he said quietly.

"May we begin to decorate, Emperor?" asked Colvin.

"Absolutely," Berty answered. Colvin clapped his hands and people started to rush around the room.

Berty turned to climb the stairs when Theodore called, "Emperor." Turning around, he waited for the Dwarf to approach. "The Fairy delegation should be arriving soon."

"Bring them to the Roundtable Room," said Berty. "I do not wish to disrupt Colvin's work here."

Colvin approached Berty, saying, "It is no bother, my Lord. We can continue later."

"Very well," said Berty. "I will meet them here. At least Alvar and Alfred should be in attendance. Delyth is in no way obligated to meet them, I will leave that choice up to her."

"Yes, my Lord," Theodore said as he bowed.

Berty looked at his Lieutenant. "You will greet them as well, Edwin."

"Of course."

Berty walked up the side steps of the dais, then sat on his throne. He watched Colvin usher the Tenders out of the room. As Edwin stood to the side, members of the Advisory Council took their places near the dais. Delyth stood strong with Declan by her side.

Sounds of men climbing the steps caused Berty to stand. Emerging from the floor below came a line of pearlized, purplish-blue metal. The first in line removed a helmet to reveal a hardened lined face and flecks of gray through dark hair.

Separating from the pack, he walked towards the dais, pausing to bow to Delyth. When he reached Berty, he bowed low, then said, "Emperor, I am Colonel Gwron. I come on behalf of King Elrick and Queen Lida to collect the traitor, Kayla. In accordance with Empire law, I must reveal to you, my Lord, our methods and manner of sentencing before it is released into my custody. I would like to request a more private audience for this formality."

"That can be arranged, Colonel," Berty said. "Captain Alvar, kindly show Colonel Gwron to the Roundtable Room."

"Yes, Emperor," said Alvar. He extended an arm towards the staircase and Gwron ascended the stairs beside Alvar.

Berty looked at Alfred before he stepped behind the drape. At the entrance to the stairs, Alfred joined Berty. "Emperor," said Delyth, running over, "I wish to join you."

"Are you sure?" Berty asked.

"Yes," she said with a determined look in her violet eyes.

"Let us go then." Berty led Alfred and Delyth up the stairs to the Roundtable Room.

Upon entering the room, Gwron approached Delyth, saying, "Your Highness, their Majesties did not want you to be exposed to such things. They felt that you have been through enough."

"With all due respect to my parents, Colonel, this is a decision which they cannot make for me," Delyth defied.

Gwron bowed his head, then looked imploringly at Berty. "Please," said Berty, "sit down." They took their usual seats around the table while Gwron chose a seat directly across from Berty.

"Emperor," said Gwron, "the King and Queen have given me the task of investigating the poisoning so that the traitor can be sentenced properly. My methods are simple questions of any witnesses. After I have finished my investigation, the traitor will be transferred from your dungeon to our traveling cell. This cell will be draped in a cloth during the journey back to Fairyland. It will then be transferred to our dungeon while I report all that I have found to the King and Queen. Their Majesties have already charged the prisoner with attempted murder of the Princess.

Once they have made their decision, the prisoner will appear in front of the full court and be sentenced. Punishment will duly follow."

"What punishment awaits her?" Berty asked.

"If found guilty of its crimes, the punishment for a Fairy is worse than death."

Delyth gasped, then closed her eyes. Upon opening them, she nodded slowly. Berty looked confused. "Dewinged, my Lord," answered Gwron.

"It has always been believed that our wings give us the very essence of Fairydom," explained Delyth. "Removing them is a punishment saved for only the most heinous of crimes. And in doing so, it is said to zap the Fairy of its very life force, leaving the dewinged Fairy to live a cursed life. I believe Millicent will be sharing Kayla's fate," she turned her head to look at Berty, "if she is not killed first."

"Rest assured, Princess," said Gwron, "Millicent will be dewinged, dead or alive."

Delyth gave the Colonel a sharp nod. Berty noticed a cold, hard look in her usually vibrant, violet eyes.

"Alfred," Berty said, "why don't you give Colonel Gwron your first hand account of what happened."

"Yes, my Lord," said Alfred, standing. "Colonel, if you will follow me." Gwron followed Alfred out of the room.

"Captain," Delyth said, "I would like to be taught the art of combat."

Alvar looked surprised of the Fairy's request. "But you have Fairy Dust."

"Which is completely useless against another Fairy," stated Delyth. "I wish to be fit with a sword and trained in how to use it."

Stunned, Alvar gazed at Berty. "If she wants to learn, then I think it is a good idea," Berty said.

"I will bring the smith tomorrow," said Alvar. He gave Berty a calculated look, then added, "Perhaps, Emperor, you should be fitted as well."

"Great idea," Berty said. "Delyth and I can learn together."

"I will arrange it," said Alvar as he stood.

Just before he reached the door, Delyth said, "Thank you." Alvar gave her a nod, then disappeared onto the landing. Standing, she gave Berty a fleeting smile, then she, too, walked away.

Wondering what he should do, Berty sat in his chair, taking a deep breath. He wanted to keep his spirits uplifted and occupy his mind so that it did not wander.

Distraction came in the form of a young Dwarf entering the Roundtable Room. "My Lord," said Theodore, "shall I give Colonel Gwron the bottle of poison?"

Berty thought for a moment. "No. By all means show him the amount which you retrieved. If he wishes to have some, then give him a sample. The bottle must remain here. Tell him that the bottle of poison is needed for evidence against another. He will understand."

"I will bring it to the interview, as I am on his roster," Theodore stated.

As the Dwarf was leaving, Berty thought of a great preoccupation. "Theodore," he said, "I have a conundrum of a personal matter." Theodore looked at him with curious eyes. "I have confined myself within the Empire Tree, unfortunately, before I was able to buy a present for my niece. If I gave you some coins, would you be able to buy a cloak for her and one for her doll?"

"It would easier to have them made, my Lord," answered Theodore.

"All right. When do you think they will be ready?"

"In about two days."

"Thank you, Theodore," Berty said. The Dwarf bowed, leaving Berty alone again. Sitting in his chair, the quietness of the room unnerved him. The smells of freshly cut pine wafted through the tree, finding his nose. Emptying his mind, he concentrated on the smell. It was so warm and woodsy. It made him think of pies and lights, eggnog and snow. He longed for a time that was simpler. A time where he did not have a heavy weight resting on his shoulders. Trying to forget about finding the lost magic, the possibility of being related to Silvia, traitors, poisonings, dewingings, interrogations, and Dragons, he created a void that the pine smell was not filling. Berty began to hum to fill the void. Deciding to do something useful, he ascended his private staircase whilst singing, "Fa la la la la, la la la la."

Entering his study, the humming continued. He sat at his desk and wrote another installment of *the Adventures of Leigh and Marcus.*

As he placed his pen on the desk, the wind chimes rang. Theodore entered with food. "Ah, Theodore," said Berty rising from behind his desk, "you never told me how much you need for my niece's present." He opened a box where he kept his sack of money.

"Nothing, my Lord," Theodore said as he set the table. Berty threw him a puzzled look. "The cloaks are not purchases from a stall or a store. They will be made from material you already own. I hope that is okay."

"Perfectly fine," said Berty with a smile as he sat down to eat his food. Theodore left him chewing and staring at more unread books that he had been neglecting to read.

After dinner, Berty cracked open a book. He read until sleep wanted to take over his body. Marking his spot, he went to bed.

The sound of rain lashing Berty's window made him open his eyes. Remembering that he was getting fitted for a sword, he groaned as he dreaded the bridge crossing in the rain. After he showered and dressed, he fastened his cloak and raised his hood. Stepping outside his study, Berty did not face a long, narrow bridge that swayed ominously high off the ground wet with cold rain. His narrow plank and rope bridge was covered in sleet. Berty watched the long, icy rain crash into the wood and ropes sideways. Hearing his stomach growl, he took a deep breath before he walked into the cold, wet slickness. His eyes focused on the opening into the warm, dry trunk while under his breath he repeated, "Get there. Get there. Get there."

Inside the trunk, he breathed a sigh of relief, then proceeded down the steps. Hanging his cloak before entering the Roundtable Room for breakfast, he noticed that his cloak was bone dry as if he never walked through buckets of sleet crashing into his body. Berty smiled in spite of himself while walking into the room.

Sitting as if she were a mannequin, Delyth did not acknowledge Declan crouched by her side. "Delyth, please talk to me," he begged. "I want to know what is wrong."

A single tear streaking down her cheek broke her stillness. "You would not understand."

"Help me understand, Delyth."

Her head turned to look at Declan who was almost kneeling on the floor as he leaned towards her imploringly. Her violet eyes welled with tears. She sprinted out of her chair so fast that all Berty saw was a blur of sliver and green.

Declan caught Berty's gaze, saying, "Gwron questioned her last night." Berty jerked his head towards the door and Declan ran from the room, screaming her name.

Berty sat in his chair while Alfred entered the room, sitting next to Berty. Tenders entered the room, filling the table with food and drink. When they left, Alfred asked, "Do you think it was wise to allow Delyth to have a sword?"

Thinking of his sister-in-law's desire to take self-defense classes after her friend got mugged, Berty said, "If it will make her feel safer, then yes."

While Colvin, Hatcher and Alvar entered, talking about the weather, Delyth and Declan sneaked back into the room in silence. After eating, everyone except Berty, Delyth and Alvar busied themselves in other parts of the Empire Tree.

"I should return shortly with the smith," said Alvar.

After Alvar left, Berty asked Delyth, "Did Gwron ask you something...?"

"I trusted her," Delyth began. "To be betrayed by one of your own. I never saw it coming."

"It was not your fault."

"All my life, I was taught that all Fairies held us in the highest of reverence. Fairyland was our Fairy utopia. We trusted each other without question. It was always assumed that all Fairies were pure of heart. We never needed to be in fear of our own. Non-Fairies were the ones who would do us harm, if harm was to be done. They are the ones to be feared. Against them, we have our weapons. Fairy Dust. We needed nothing more in our arsenal. Our wings made us different from them in more ways than just having the ability to fly—it made us nobler than they. And, of course, being royal raises us above all. We had no worries from anyone, but from them. Only they could corrupt the lessers. That was so wrong. They saved me." She looked up at Berty with sadness looming in her eyes.

"Not that you are really part of them, Emperor. You have true nobility, old blood, running through your veins as do Alfred and I. Though, we still were taught that we were superior, being Fairies. The noble Fairies against the common world that surrounded us." Tears began to form in her eyes. "How wrong. How wrong." She paused as the tears began to stream down her cheeks.

"Declan, without a drop of nobility in his blood but noble in his soul, took care of me as if I were one of his own. Theodore tended to me, making sure that I had everything I needed and then some, as if I were *his* princess." Her cheeks glistened with wetness. Berty extracted a magically made handkerchief from his sleeve, then handed it to Delyth. Taking it, she continued, "I was taught a lie." She wiped her face dry. "I will repay her, someday."

Before Berty could inquire further, Alvar entered the room with the smith. The smith was a Dwarf with a short, scruffy, light brown beard, carrying a large, black leather case. "Emperor," said the smith, bowing, "this is an honorable day to be able to fit you and select members of the Advisory Council." He looked at Delyth, then back at Berty. "Shall we begin?"

"Yes, of course," said Berty.

The Dwarf placed his case on the floor, opening it. "Who will be first?"

Berty motioned for Delyth to go first. Nodding, she tried to hand Berty back his handkerchief. Shaking his head, Berty mouthed, "Keep it." A smile lit up her face as she walked over to the Dwarf.

While the smith was busy with Delyth, Alvar joined Berty at the table. "I will have Edwin train you both," he said.

"Your turn, Emperor," said the smith, "if you please." Berty nodded to Alvar as he rose from his chair, walking towards the Dwarf. "Stand here." Berty stepped onto a metal two foot by three foot rectangle. "Now, hold this." The smith handed Berty a hollow, metal, pipe like object while jotting onto a piece of paper. "Thank you, my Lord." Handing back the pipe, Berty stepped off the metal sheet.

The smith walked over to Alvar, saying, "The dummies will be ready first. The swords will take longer. I will let you know when everything is ready."

"Very good, thank you," said Alvar.

"Excuse me, Emperor," Theodore said, entering from the servant's door, "but Colonel Gwron would like a word."

"Send him in," said Berty.

The Dwarf left while Alvar asked, "Shall I leave?"

"No. You may stay."

Theodore opened the main door through which Gwron entered. "My Lord," the Fairy stood extremely straight, "I have finished the investigation. With your permission, I would like to escort the prisoner to Fairyland."

"Have a seat, Colonel," said Berty. Gwron took a seat across the table from Berty and Alvar. "Did our Head Tender give you a sample of the poison?"

"Yes. Thank you for allowing us to have some."

"I will be sending word to the King and Queen, telling them that you will be arriving with the sample so that they can prepare for its arrival." Gwron nodded sharply. "Captain Alvar will conduct the transfer."

"May I empty the Receiving Room now?" Alvar asked.

"Yes," answered Berty. "The sooner before nightfall they leave, the better." The three men stood. "Safe journey, Colonel Gwron."

"Thank you, Emperor," said Gwron with a bow. "May your reign always be noble." The Fairy turned to follow Alvar out of the room.

Berty walked onto the main landing where he saw Delyth entering the trunk from the bridge. When she lowered her hood, he asked, "I am heading to the Watching Rooms, did you want to join me?"

"Yes, thank you, Emperor." As they climbed the stairs, Delyth continued, "I want to thank you, my Lord, for not treating me like a child. Others have been trying to shield me or protect me from some further horrific situations. You allow me to make my own decisions." Berty saw her violet eyes brimming with wetness.

"You are welcome," said Berty. "What kind of advisor would you be if you did not have your own mind?"

When they entered the room, Berty closed the door behind them. Delyth walked over to the table covered with the miniature Sages' Grove. Joining her at the table, Berty blew into the center of the tree and movement spread throughout the model.

Not far from the doors of the Empire Tree waited two horses harnessed to a cart holding a cage. Fairy guards surrounded the cage as people exited the tree. Delyth blinked furiously as if she were trying to hold back tears.

"I know what has to happen," said Delyth, breaking the silence, "and I know that she deserves it." Her eyes looked imploringly at Berty. "Why does it make me so sad?"

Berty gazed into her searching, violet eyes. "That is what makes you a person. Complex, rational and emotional, all things that I think are needed to make one whole. Fairness and justice do not come without their difficulties."

"Yes, I suppose you are right," said Delyth. "Look, the doors are opening."

Out of the doors marched four Empire Guards followed closely by two Fairy Guards escorting a dejected Kayla. Her ankles and wrists were shackled as her head hung low. Behind her walked Alvar and Gwron. The Fairy Guards locked her into the cage, then covered it completely with a cloth. The Captain and the Colonel shook hands before the Fairies rode out of the Sages' Grove.

After Berty blew into the tree, he looked up to see that Delyth had succumbed to her tears. Pulling a handkerchief out of her sleeve, she wiped her face, then took a few deep breaths. Composing herself, she said, "Thank you again, Emperor." Regally, she walked out of the room.

Leaving the Watching Room, Berty walked down the hall and stepped through the wall. The narrow passageway brought him to the bridge, which he crossed despite the sleet, to enter his study. Once inside, he sat at his desk, continuing his reading. As he finished the book, his wind chimes rang.

Theodore entered, carrying food. "My Lord," he said, "Colvin is asking for meals to be taken in the Roundtable Room, so he can finish decorating."

Berty nodded and Theodore left him to dine alone.

Quickly eating his lunch, Berty returned to his desk to read another book. A chapter into the book, Berty opened his Empire Journal and poised his pen to take notes. The book explored the beginnings of the Dragon clan wars. He copied into his journal the author's words that said, "None of the Dragons will discuss it, so I will name it. Since it travels like the mist and reaches every crevice, I will name it Misty.

"Misty spreads her sadness and discord like a disease. She has sickened this land like a plague. There must be a source."

Pages later, Berty read, "I wish I could find Misty and come to terms with her. Perhaps I could heal her sickness."

As Berty continued to read, he realized that the author's task had gone from daunting to impossible. "The Dragons and their stupid territorial skirmishes," wrote the author, "make finding anything extremely challenging."

The book concluded with, "All the land's a flame. I have doubled back more times than I wish to admit. For the safety of my remaining team, I will end this crusade to find Misty and cross the border never to return to the Dragonlands."

Closing the book, Berty wondered what the Dragons were hiding and if they were still hiding it. When the lanterns around his study flickered, he realized that he should be going to dinner. Crossing his bridge, he noticed that the sleet had subsided some.

As Berty entered the Roundtable Room, conversation was light—mostly pertaining to the weather. Tenders had just finished placing food on the table when he sat. While they ate, the conversation drifted from weather to winter decorations. Berty's eyes found Delyth keeping to herself, not conversing with anyone. Her eyes were hard and calculating while the rest of her stayed soft and feminine. Declan kept glancing at her as if she were a bomb on a timer that was about to explode.

When dinner ended, all the men rose from the table, leaving Delyth still seated. Declan walked over to her, crouching beside her chair. If he had said anything to her, Berty could not hear it, nor did Delyth acknowledge him.

Berty had almost reached the door when Delyth finally sprang from her seat. Approaching Berty, she said, "Emperor." A hurt Declan stood near the table. Berty turned to fully face her. Looking at him squarely in the eyes, she asked, "Am I doing the right thing?"

Even though Berty's eyes never removed their gaze from Delyth's, he knew that everyone in the room stopped to listen. "Taking responsibility for oneself is never wrong," he said.

"Thank you, Emperor. Goodnight." Holding her head high, Delyth turned. She walked out of the room, ignoring everyone staring at her.

"Goodnight." Berty's words echoed slightly in the almost still room. Not wanting questions, he stepped through his door, ascending his stairway.

Worry crept further into his mind with each step he took. He wondered if Delyth taking up arms would cause a rift in his Advisory Council. "I don't see what the big deal is," he mumbled. "What is wrong with learning how to fight?" Berty paused to raise his hood before he crossed the wet bridge. With no sleet to distract him, his mind continued to look for possible issues that might plague his Advisors.

By the time he entered his study, all he had thought was that she is a Fairy and a Princess. Sitting in his chair, he wondered if they thought that she was not in a proper mindset to learn how to fight because they felt that all she wanted was revenge. Berty ran his fingers through his hair, sighing.

Summoning a book from his desk, Berty decided to read a little before bed.

Morning greeted him with a sense of uneasiness. Outside his door, a beautiful glistening bridge hung still. "Ice," said Berty with disdain. Searching his pockets, he found soft, fur lined, leather gloves. After pulling them on his hands, he carefully stepped forward onto his ice coated platform. His boots had surprising traction.

After walking across the bridge with ease, Berty descended the stairs. A feeling in his gut told him to wait on the landing before entering the Roundtable Room for breakfast.

"Do you think that she will ever recover?" asked Hatcher.

"If she is permitted to defend herself," Declan answered.

"What good would that do?"

"Gives her a sense of control," said Declan to the Troll. "She needs that desperately."

"Yes, but," Colvin said, "she's a woman."

"I think we've noticed that she is a woman," said Declan.

"Who can make decisions for herself," Berty added as he walked across the room.

"Surely you would not allow her to enter a combative fray?" asked Colvin.

"Who am I to stop her?" Berty stopped walking when he

reached his chair.

"The Emperor," answered Hatcher.

"You know as well as I," Colvin said, "that women do not belong in combat."

Berty looked at the three men and the silently uncomfortable Edwin, then said, "Where I come from, women fight in many combative situations. I think you will find that women can be much more protective and defensive than we men could ever hope to be."

Hatcher nodded. Declan grinned, while Colvin said, "Let us eat, shall we?"

Chapter Twenty-eight
Light of Life

After Breakfast, Berty returned to his study to continue reading. As soon as he opened the book, he heard his wind chimes.

Theodore entered Berty's study, carrying two cloth wrapped bundles. "Finished earlier than expected, my Lord," said the young Dwarf.

"Excellent." Berty leapt out of his chair, taking the bundles from the Dwarf. "Thank you, Theodore."

Theodore smiled. "It was an honor. Colvin wants to show you the decorations tomorrow after breakfast so that you may approve them. Once approved, we will open the Empire Tree for the Yuletide and begin distribution of faðbra. I think he wants to change the location of that, but he'll talk to you about it tomorrow. Also, the practice swords will be ready tomorrow, so Alvar wants Edwin to begin training. Edwin asked me about a suitable place for training inside the tree. One of the Watching Rooms is set for training. All I would have to do is remove the coverings. May I?"

Berty barely registered that Theodore had stopped talking. He looked at the Dwarf for a minute while Theodore's words caught up to him. "Tomorrow. Right." His hand felt the thick cloth wrapping. "You may. And I do not wish to be disturbed for the rest of the day."

"Very well, my Lord," said Theodore as he bowed.

As soon as the Dwarf stepped out of Berty's study, Berty's cloak draped his body. With bundles in hand, he hastened into Silvia's chambers and through the tapestry.

The house was bright. Berty checked his dual pocket watch. It said three in the afternoon. He brought the bundles into the dining room, placing them on the table next to the repaired cup. Back in his bedroom, he changed his clothes.

Finding some paper, he wrapped the cup, then magically constructed a box out of more paper. Berty carefully placed the wrapped cup into the box. He brought it along with the bundles into the kitchen, placing them on the table, ready to go. Gathering his coat, keys and phone, Berty picked up the gifts, then left through the back door.

Singing along with the carols on the all Christmas music radio station helped to make the trip to his brother's house seem shorter. Berty pulled into the driveway with a smile on his face. Getting out of the car, he grabbed the packages and walked to the front door. The chill nipping the tip of his nose invigorated him as he pushed the round button, causing an electronic belled Christmas carol to chime.

A few moments later, the door opened. Teresa greeted Berty with a warm smile. "Berty. What a surprise. Come in."

"Thanks, Teresa," Berty said as he stepped into their holiday themed foyer. "I wanted to bring these over before Christmas."

"That's sweet," replied Teresa. "Hope is in the family room and Jon should be home soon." She led him into a plush carpeted room with a big puffy couch dominating the space. In front of the large screen television, which was off, Hope played with her wooden doll, Ashley. Towering over Hope was a large, undecorated Christmas Tree.

As Berty put his packages on the square coffee table, Hope looked up, saying, "Hi, Uncle Berty."

"Hey. Having fun?"

Smiling, Hope nodded her head full of brown curls. "Yup."

Berty smiled. Hope returned to playing while Teresa said, "Take your coat off and stay a while." Removing his coat, Berty laid it over the couch. "Please, sit down," she said. "Would you like anything to drink?"

"I'm fine, thanks," he answered while he sat on the couch.

Teresa sat near Berty, watching her daughter play. "She loves that doll," she began in a low voice. "Wherever she is, the doll is with her. Of course, there are a few exceptions. She won't bring it to school. And when her friends come over, she will share all her toys with them except that doll. Jon and I asked her why, and she told us that she doesn't want anyone to break it. Which, of course, I understand." Her eyes moved off of Hope and onto Berty. "She treats it like it is her best friend. You know how some children have imaginary friends?" Berty nodded. "Well, that's how she is with the doll except," Teresa paused, "it's different." She looked at Hope again. "She accepts that it is only a piece of wood."

Berty did not know what to say. Guilt bubbled inside of him and he began to feel very uncomfortable. Looking from Teresa to Hope, he knew that he could not tell his sister-in-law the truth about Hope being a Wood Listener. Fortunately, the sound of the garage door opening saved him from saying anything at all.

"Daddy's home," Hope exclaimed. Picking up her doll, she ran from the room. Teresa smiled, seemingly lost in her own thoughts, until Hope returned to the room followed by Jon.

"Hey, honey," Jon said as he bent over to kiss his wife. "Berty, what brings you over today?" He looked at the packages on the coffee table, then unbuttoned his suit jacket before he sat on the couch next to Berty.

"Early Christmas presents," answered Berty as he looked at Hope. Reaching across the table, he grabbed the small, square box from the pile on the table, placing it in front of Teresa. "That one is yours and the other two are for Hope."

Hope's eyes opened wide. "Do we have to wait till Christmas to open them, Mommy?" she asked.

Teresa looked at Jon, then said, "No, I think we can open them while Uncle Berty is here."

"You first, Mommy," said Hope.

Smiling at her daughter, Teresa picked up the small box, opening it. She put her hand inside, plucking a wad of paper out of the box. Peeling back the paper, her eyes began to well with tears as her smashed cup sat in front of her whole once more.

"How did you?" was all Teresa managed to say before her cheeks became wet.

"I've got connections."

"Thank you," she breathed.

Hope waited for her mother to place the cup on the coffee table before carefully untying the smaller of the two bundles. Unfolding the cloth wrapping, her eyes lit up as she lifted the dark brown, doll-sized cloak. "Ooh, Uncle Berty, Ashley's outfit is complete now. Thank you."

"You're welcome."

Her fingers smoothly untied the string on the larger bundle. Hope folded back the cloth to uncover a dark magenta cloak. "I got one, too," she said excitedly. Twirling the cloak around her, she draped it over her shoulders, fastening it so expertly it was as if she had always worn a cloak. With a gleam in her eyes, she cloaked her doll. "Thank you, Uncle Berty." Carefully walking around the table, she gave Berty a hug.

"I'm going to put this in a safe place," Teresa said, picking up her cup.

After she walked out of the room, Jon said to Berty, "Bringing her that cup was the best thing. I've been going crazy trying to find one. Matt has been getting the second degree from her, which he does not need right now. Rachel is putting him through the ringer, that woman. It's about time Matt finally, you know. Christmas is going to be a wonderful Rachel free zone." Berty chuckled. "Why aren't you coming for Christmas? Lillian and Robert would love to have you come."

"I can't. I am so busy," Berty replied.

"Well, I hope you aren't too busy to stay for dinner." Berty looked up to see Teresa walking towards them.

"You never know," said Berty with a sly smile. "Whatcha having?"

Letting out a little laugh, Teresa answered, "Tonight, we're having Jon's favorite. Food."

"Well, in that case, I'll clear my schedule."

Jon laughed, asking, "Do you mind watching Hope while I change out of my work clothes?"

"Not at all," Berty replied.

As soon as Jon and Teresa left the room, Hope sat on the couch next to Berty, still wearing her cloak. He looked into his niece's big brown eyes gazing up at him and knew she had been thinking.

"Will you take me someday?" she asked.

"Take you where?"

"The place where Ashley is from. The Land of Sages."

Berty's insides dropped.

"Ashley told me," Hope continued, "that she was carved from a branch that broke off an ash tree not too far from the Sages' Grove. She wants me to visit the tree and introduce myself." Berty looked at Hope in disbelief. "Please, Uncle Berty?"

Finding his voice, Berty asked, "Do your parents know that you want to visit the Land of Sages?"

Her face fell. "Mommy and Daddy don't know anything about the Land of Sages."

"Have you asked them about it?"

"They don't listen," she answered in a small voice. "I know you know about it. How often do you go? Can I go with you sometime?"

Hope's eyes were filled with pleads and wonderment. Berty knew that Hope's trip to the Land of Sages was inevitable. "Someday," he said to her. Her face lit with happiness.

When Teresa called them for dinner, Berty suggested that Hope remove her cloak before eating. Sitting around the kitchen table, Berty shoved a forkful of macaroni and cheese into his mouth when Teresa asked, "So what are you so busy doing that you can't come to my parents' for Christmas dinner?"

"I'll be away," replied Berty, "taking lessons."

"What kind of lessons?" Jon asked.

"Sword fighting," answered Berty as nonchalantly as he could. Jon stared at him in disbelief. "Why?"

"It seemed like a good idea," shrugged Berty. "You never

313

know, it might come in handy."

Jon let out a hardy laugh. Seeing Teresa's I wonder what you are up to look, Berty joined his brother in laughter.

When the plates were empty, Jon cleared the table. As he loaded the dishwasher, Teresa asked Berty, "What's happening with you and the mystery woman?"

Berty sighed. "I don't know. After the holidays, I am heading out to visit her." Teresa's eyebrows raised as if to ask, how do you not know what is going on if you are going to see her. "Silvia is currently staying with this family—the Nelson's—while she helps their special needs child."

"So everything is kind of on hold?"

"Kind of, yeah." Sitting at his brother's kitchen table, Berty was beginning to feel uneasy about being away from the Empire Tree. When Jon offered Berty some coffee, he declined, explaining, "I have a long day tomorrow and I should be getting home."

"Sword fighting lessons?" his brother asked.

"Among other things."

"I'll make it decaf then."

"No, I really should get going." Berty stood. "Thanks for dinner, Teresa. It was great."

"Thank you for the cup," she said, hugging him.

"Have a nice Christmas, guys." Berty hugged Hope goodbye, grabbed his coat, then drove home.

Returning to his study, Berty flopped in a club chair, holding his face in his hands. Hope and her trees remained a mystery to Berty. Not helping the uneasiness in this stomach, his mind drifted to his family tree. He got as far back as his great-grandparents, then realized that he did not know enough about his lineage to be sure of his relation to Silvia. Walking over to his desk, he returned to reading books for the rest of the day.

Berty got a better night's rest after returning the once smashed cup to his sister-in-law. In the shower however, his stomach began to feel queasy, knowing that he was going to start to learn how to use a sword.

After a breakfast that did not settle well, Colvin brought Berty and the Advisory Council to the Reception Room. The room sparkled in gold and glittered with red amongst the green. Berty looked at the spectacular tree covered in shiny gold and red balls. Boughs and wreaths covered the room as golden and red icicle like decorations dripped down from greenery. Not being able to contain his smile, the amazing affect of the decorations infected him, and from what he could see everyone else as well.

"Do you approve, my Lord?" asked Colvin excitedly.

"It is fantastic," Berty answered.

Colvin smiled wide. "I was thinking about bringing the faðbra up here so that everyone would see our tree."

"I think that is a bad idea," interjected Hatcher.

"You would," Colvin grumbled.

"Less and less people make faðbra anymore," continued Hatcher, ignoring Colvin's grumbles. "They come here and grab our version."

"Empire bread is the best faðbra ever made," Colvin mumbled.

"This brings lots and lots of people," said Hatcher. "They would interfere. We should setup Light of Life Tree viewing times while people can get their faðbra during Empire Tree hours."

"I agree with Hatcher," Alvar stated. "It would make security much easier."

Colvin looked tentatively at Berty. "Sorry, Colvin, I think we should keep it downstairs."

Nodding, the Dwarf said, "Fine. It was just a suggestion." He walked away, mumbling to himself.

A tender walked over to Alvar. The Elf disappeared down the stairs while Alfred admired the décor, saying to Declan and Edwin, "Irmingard never made Yule look this nice."

Delyth stood off by herself until Alvar quickly returned, carrying a package. "They are here," Alvar said to Berty and Delyth. "I think that it is best to start as soon as possible." Berty nodded.

"Edwin," called Alvar, "you are needed." Edwin joined them and they climbed the steps to the Roundtable Room.

On the landing in front of the room's entrance, Alvar passed the package to Edwin. "Time to start," he said to Edwin.

Edwin looked at Berty, saying, "Theodore knows where."

Chapter Twenty-nine
Taking the Blade

"Theodore," called Berty. Theodore arrived on the landing and without a word led them up the stairs. Passing the Scepter Room, they ascended to the level with the Watching Rooms. Theodore strolled past the door Berty usually entered, opening a door that Berty barely noticed existed because it blended so well with the wall.

"All ready, as requested," said Theodore. "Changes of clothes are in that trunk for you and behind that door is a changing room." Closing the door behind him, Theodore left the three admiring the room.

All sorts of medieval looking and some ancient looking metal and wood equipment adorned the walls. Straw stuffed practice dummies hung from the ceiling. Berty recognized maces, axes, and spiked balls attached to chains. In an inconspicuous corner hid strange stone contraptions that Berty had no idea what they did.

Placing the package on a table against the curved inside wall, Edwin said, "Well, better get changed so we may begin."

Both Berty and Delyth changed into thin cotton shirts and pants that breathed well. Edwin told them that they did not need the padding or leather coverings to start. On the table laid two swords of different lengths. Pointing out which was whose, Edwin had each pick it up and hold it.

"I thought we were not starting with real swords," said Delyth.

"You are not," Edwin explained. "They are wood covered with tin."

Allowing Berty and Delyth to get comfortable with their swords, Edwin chuckled. Berty did not know what struck as funny in Edwin's mind as the Elf inspected their grips.

Unsheathing his sword, Edwin spent the rest of the morning teaching them basic moves and counter weight placement.

After lunch, Edwin made them demonstrate what they had learned. Delyth had internalized Edwin's every movement and every word. Berty wished that he had not been as clumsy as he was.

"I must admit, my Lord," sheepishly Edwin stated, "I thought that you would have had some sword or weapon experience."

"I chose the pen," said Berty.

Edwin gave Berty a puzzled look. "A pen is not a weapon."

Smiling wryly, Berty answered, "It has been said that the pen is mightier than the sword."

"Only if it has a very sharp point," said Delyth facetiously.

Berty laughed a little, then explained, "Swords, from where I come, are archaic. Though some use knives as weapons. Fighting with swords is more of a theatrical performance."

Edwin's eyebrows raised at Berty's words. Composing himself, the Elf said, "Let's keep practicing moving until dinner, then we will continue after breakfast tomorrow."

After dinner, Berty returned to his chambers with his body screaming in pain. Every muscle hurt, even muscles he was not aware of having. "Who knew I was such a weakling in such bad shape," he said as he drew himself a warm bath. The warm water helped his body relax so well that as soon as he dried himself, Berty crawled into bed, then drifted off to sleep.

The morning found Berty in the Watching Room, holding his practice sword. A dummy dangled in front of him.

"This morning," said Edwin, "we are going to practice our moves that we learned yesterday on the dummies in front of you."

Looking over at Delyth, Berty saw a wild focus in her eyes as they stepped towards their respective dummies.

"Begin," Edwin instructed.

Methodically, Berty attacked his dangling dummy. "Good," remarked Edwin. As if Edwin's words unplugged a drain, Delyth began to attack her dummy with fervor. She thrust her sword wildly until she let out a final scream of frustration, then fell to her knees. Dropping her sword beside her, her body shifted to the other side as she deflated onto the floor. Berty watched Delyth's body shake and he knew that she had begun to cry.

As her sobs grew louder, Edwin stood transfixed, a look of shock frozen on his face. Clearly, Edwin had never experienced such a meltdown. Putting down his practice sword, Berty knelt on the floor besides the Fairy, putting his arm around her. Eventually, the crying stopped. Through her hands Delyth said, "Sorry. I need a minute." Berty recoiled his arm, then without showing her face, she ran into the changing room.

Finally moving, Edwin said, "Taking a break would be good."

Thinking about all Delyth had gone through, Berty sat in a chair against the wall. Kayla must have arrived in Fairyland already, he thought. Closing his eyes, he saw Fairies lining the walls of a glistening blue and gold hall. On a dais, stood Lida and Elrick, wearing jeweled crowns.

"Bring in the accused," Elrick bellowed.

Kayla was escorted into the hall in a shackling contraption that even held her open wings still.

"You have been charged with the attempted murder of Princess Delyth," said Lida with the utmost contempt and coldness in her voice. "What do you have to say for yourself?"

Kayla looked around at the Court of Fairies before addressing her King and Queen. "I am only dorry tat dee did not die."

The Fairies in the hall gasped.

A wicked smile slunk onto her face. "I haff been derfing you for doe long, but I aldoe been derfing anoter. I haff done my part. Oterd will continue ta work."

"What work?" Lida asked.

"Royal downfall," answered Kayla. As Lida's face fell, Kayla began to giggle.

Stopping the laughter, Elrick bellowed, "By your own admission, you have been found guilty of attempted murder. You have also admitted, in front of the full court, to a crime for you had not been formally charged—treachery. I hereby charge you also with treason. And, of that, too, you are guilty." Elrick paused. "For the charge of attempted murder, your sentence is thus: in one hour from now, you will be publicly dewinged." His own purplish-blue wings fluttered. "For the charge of treason, you are sentenced to death. The time, date and method will be determined later." Looking at Colonel Gwron, he said, "Take her away."

Berty opened his eyes. His shock must have shown on his face.

"My Lord," said Edwin, "did you have a nightmare?"

Berty shook his head while Delyth knelt before him. "What did you see?"

"What?" asked Edwin, looking confused.

"Emperor, I know you had a vision. Please," Delyth pleaded.

Looking at them both, Berty said, "You are both sworn to secrecy." They nodded. He looked directly into Delyth's searching, violet eyes. "Kayla. Treason. Death."

"I do not understand," said Delyth. "I thought she was charged...."

"Official word will come and explain." Still looking in her eyes, Berty told her everything that had just transpired.

Resolutely, Delyth stood, saying, "My parents will have to conduct an inquiry." She picked up her sword. "Edwin, I am ready to continue."

For the next hour, Edwin corrected their moves until Delyth stopped. She said, "My Lord, can I ask you...?"

Berty looked at her. He knew that she needed to know, but he was not sure if he could watch on command. "No promises," he said as he closed his eyes.

"Are you ready?" Elrick asked Lida. She gave her husband a slow nod. He took her hand while they walked through double, golden, stained glass doors onto a balcony that overlooked a square full of Fairies dressed in their winter cloaks. In the center of the public square was a stage set with a wooden stool and a table full of objects. Guards surrounded the stage.

320

Kayla was escorted onto the stage in a simple, cream colored dress with her light brown hair pinned on top of her head. Her wings sparkled in the daylight. They sat her on the stool, then anchored her hands and feet to hooks in the stage floor. A hooded person grabbed a very sharp device with a gloved hand. As he worked, cries of discontent escaped from Kayla's lips. The crowd flinched with each cry.

Lida held her husband's hand tightly. Kayla's wails of pain increased in frequency and strength. With one final cry of anguish, Kayla's wings were separated from her body. The sparkled died as they carried the wings away. As they unshackled her, Kayla's wail filled the square with despair and destitution. When they unpinned her hair, streaks of white cascaded alongside light brown.

The watching Fairies turned, abandoning the wingless Fairy. Falling onto the floor of the stage, Kayla curled into the fetal position in her blood stained dress and cried with a pain that Berty had never heard.

Elrick tugged on his wife's hand. "Come, darling," he said soothingly. Looking away from the stage, Lida stared into nowhere. "Lida?" Elrick continued with his soothing tone. "I know it was not pleasant."

She turned to face Elrick with a stony expression, then said, "Time to start the inquisition."

Berty opened his eyes. "It has been done," he said.

Nodding, Delyth turned to face her dummy. For the rest of the day, Delyth seemed to have found a new determination, grasping new moves faster than Berty.

At dinner, Alfred mentioned that they had received news from Fairyland. After relaying the news, Alfred turned to Berty. "She lied to us in that dungeon."

"Perhaps," said Alvar, "she thought that it would save her from being turned over to the Fairies. I cannot begin to imagine how horrific having your wings amputated would be."

"But why admit to treason?" Hatcher asked.

"Gwron said it was worse than death," answered Berty who could not scratch the image of a dejected Kayla of out his mind's eye. "What else did she have to lose? I am sure she delighted in the horrified looks on their faces when she told them."

The table sat in silence until Tenders brought dessert. "This year's faðbra," Theodore announced.

As a Tender placed a slice in front of him, Berty studied his piece. It looked like it contained a great amount of dried fruit and chopped nuts that were just held together by some form of batter. If the fruits had been brightly colored, he would have thought that he had something his grandmother always served at Christmas. Not believing his eyes, Berty said, "Fruitcake? People come from all over the Empire to get fruitcake?" From his experience, fruitcake was one of the most disgusting things he had ever eaten.

Everyone around the table gave Berty a puzzled look. "Nowadays most people call it Empire Bread instead of faðbra, but I have never heard it called fruitcake," said Colvin. "And our faðbra is believed to be an original faðbra recipe."

Berty's stomach churned as he watched everyone enjoying the fruitcake. Breaking off a corner of his slice, he thought it best that the Emperor at least try faðbra. He popped it into his mouth. Chewing slowly, Berty was surprised to taste a moist bread, like the consistency of banana bread, filled with soft, sweet fruit and nuts.

"Faðbra," Alfred explained, "is a relic of the old and that is why so many call it Empire Bread now. The word is from the ancient tongue, meaning father bread. The old lore said that the mother, after having bearing and rearing her fruit all three seasons, slept during winter, and that is when the father took over. Hence, father bread is made using the mother's gifts."

Alfred's explanation made Berty think about how some call Santa Claus, Father Christmas. His mind connected that to Old Man Winter and even to Father Time. He began to wonder if they were all names for the same thing.

Abandoning his pondering, Berty climbed into bed after

dinner, falling asleep. When he arrived in the Watching Room in the morning, Edwin instructed them to wear their padding and leather coverings.

Standing in their practice positions, Berty watched Edwin crank the dummies to the wall. The Elf then unsheathed his sword and placed it on the table. Picking up a practice sword, Edwin said, "Your real swords have arrived. Before I can allow you to touch them, I must be sure that you are ready."

Stepping into the practice circle, the Elf said, "Delyth, attack me." Her grip on her practice sword tightened as she stepped into the circle to face Edwin.

The fact that the Fairy was at least two and half feet shorter than the Elf did not seem to matter to her. Berty watched as Delyth fought with gusto. Despite Edwin blocking her every move, Edwin commended Delyth's attempt.

When Berty stepped into the circle, he noticed how much bigger Edwin was than he. Although the height difference was not as great, Berty focused on how Edwin held his practice sword with great strength and without effort. Berty began to attack the way that Edwin had taught him. From watching Edwin and Delyth spar, Berty anticipated Edwin's counterattacks. Changing his moves slightly made Edwin smile.

After the allotted sparring time, Edwin commented, "That was very good. You were watching. I hope you were paying attention, Delyth." He took a sip of water before saying, "Your turn again, Delyth."

The sparring sessions lasted all day. With each subsequent spar, both Berty and Delyth improved. At the end of the day, Edwin was really pleased with their progress.

When Berty entered the Watching Room the next morning, Edwin greeted him with a smile. His eyes noticed two gleaming swords on the table next to the Elf. "You have earned your swords," said Edwin. "Your sword is more than a mere weapon. It is a companion whom you can trust implicitly. When it is in your hand, it becomes one with your arm, an extension of your appendage. The more you practice with your sword, the more fluid your movements will be. Please, you may pick up your swords."

Berty grabbed the handle of his sword, lifting it off the table. Holding it in his hand, he expected it to be heavier. Surprised, he swung it a couple of times. He enjoyed the balance and the slight ringing the metal made in the air.

Edwin turned the crank for the dummies to swing towards Berty and Delyth. The dummies wore chainmail while the two of them wore padding and leather.

With each passing day, Yule edged closer. Berty began to hurt less. His exhaustion dwindled enough that he was able to read in the evenings after dinner. Two days before the Yule log lighting ceremony, Fairyland sent word that they had eradicated a potential uprising against the Fairy elite. The news made Delyth work harder than ever.

The morning of Yule, Berty dressed in clothes that he knew he was not going to have to change, for Edwin told them the previous evening that there would not be anymore training sessions until further notice. Stepping out of his study, Berty strolled across his bridge between the snowflakes. He felt that the holiday season needed snow and he was glad that it finally arrived.

"The snow is going to greatly diminish our number of visitors past this first day," Hatcher said during breakfast. "They'll stay tonight, but in the morning, they will leave."

Before entering his study to finish his last book, Berty called Theodore. He told him to bring Edwin to his chambers. Sitting in his club chair, he waited to hear his wind chimes.

When Edwin entered, Berty said, "You, too, Theodore." The Dwarf entered the room, looking unsure of why he was there. "Please sit." Both men sat in chairs across from Berty. "Tomorrow, after breakfast, we are leaving," he said as he looked at Edwin. "Theodore, I want you to have supplies ready for us. I know not where we go or for how long we will be gone."

"Will you be taking your sword, my Lord?" asked Edwin.

"Only if you feel that I should and am ready for such a step," Berty answered.

"I feel that you should," said Edwin. "Not that I expect that we will have to draw our swords."

"Very well," Berty said, then dismissed them. For the rest of the morning, Berty finished reading his book.

Before leaving his chambers for the evening, he returned the books to their shelves in Silvia's study. In the Reception Room, Berty emerged from behind the Sages' Seal. He stepped off the front of the dais to join the gathering of Advisors and Edwin. Theodore ran into the room, saying, "The log is ready. Sunset is fast approaching."

Berty, his Advisors, Edwin and Theodore walked the familiar path to the village square. The snow still fell at a soft, steady pace, slowly whitening the Sages' Grove. In the middle of the square where the kettlebarrel once stood, laid a huge log which more closely resembled a felled tree. The gathering around the log was much smaller than the one for Wassail, consisting mainly of residents and only some visitors.

Although he had some idea what a Yule log entailed, Berty watched with wonderment as people checked the sky. When it was dark enough, but still before the darkness of the evening had settled, an elderly man emerged from one of the houses, carrying a small torch. The man lit a small bit of kindling, then handed the torch to a young boy, no older than twelve, to light the rest around the large log. Once the kindling was completely lit, the boy returned the torch to the house.

The sun had firmly settled on the other side of the earth for the evening before the log began to burn. As the flames found their consistency, people dropped pieces of paper into the fire, one by one. Hatcher followed a woman from the village, and then Berty's eyes found Delyth extracting a folded paper from inside her cloak. While she waited her turn, her wings unfolded. The large, bluish-purple wings sparkled in the dancing firelight. As she strolled to the fire, her wings fluttered slightly with every step. Standing in-between Berty and the fire, Berty noticed how the fire illuminated the outline of Delyth's body like a silhouette on a shade through her wings.

With her wings still open, she turned away from the fire, walking towards Declan who stood not too far from Berty. The glow from the fire gave Delyth an ethereal, lavender colored essence that emanated around her body. By the time she reached Declan, her wings returned to their folded state.

Snowflakes swayed silently to the ground while the flames engulfed the last paper, sending puffs of smoke into the charcoal sky. Families and friends departed in groups to partake in their Yule meals.

A small, lavish table set in gold and silver waited for Berty in the beautifully decorated Reception Room. Joining Berty at the table were Declan, Alfred, Delyth, Edwin and Theodore.

"Are we it?" asked Berty as a steaming bowl of golden orange squash soup was placed in front of him.

"Colvin was complaining about having to go to his sister's," said Declan.

"And Hatcher and his wife are spending the evening with their one daughter," Delyth added.

"Alvar's daughter and son-in-law arrived from Irmingard today. He and his wife are spending some quality time with them now as the boy is being considered for Low Elf," said Alfred. "I have to say, Declan, that I am surprised to see you here. I thought you would have spent tonight at the Watchers' Guild."

Declan sipped the soup off his spoon before looking up at the aged Elf. "While the Guild doors are always open to me, not all the guild members share the Master's partiality towards me. I rather spend my time where I am welcome." He glanced at Delyth before dipping his spoon back into his soup.

"My parents do not want me traveling in such tumultuous times," Delyth stated. "But what about you, Alfred?"

Alfred smiled, "My grandson is High Elf now. He must stay in Irmingard for Yule. Young as he is, he understands his responsibilities and performs his duties with honor."

Berty could see the pride in Alfred's eyes and it made him smile. "Do they not have Yule on the other side of the portals?" Delyth asked Berty.

"Christmas is similar," answered Berty. "It is not for a few days yet."

Conversation flowed merrily around the table throughout the many courses for the remainder of the evening. After dinner, Declan and Delyth indulged in some glogg around the Yule log while Berty and the others retired for the night. Before heading to bed, Berty perused his notes to keep everything fresh in his mind.

With some trepidation, Berty went through his morning routine. Dressed, he descended his spiral staircase to find bags of supplies lying on his table along his sword securely in its scabbard. The hilt glistened as Berty fastened his sword to his belt. Securing the supplies to the inside of his cloak, Berty's eyes took a last sweep around his study before leaving for breakfast.

Walking across the bridge and down the steps with a large piece of metal dangling on his left side felt strange, but he figured he would get used to it soon enough. Breakfast was a small affair like dinner was the night before. After eating, Berty and Edwin quietly said their goodbyes before heading towards the stairs.

At the top of the stairs, Berty raised his hood. Edwin mimicked him, then they proceeded down the steps. Before they reached the Receiving Room, Berty had magically transformed their colorful red and green cloaks to dark gray and Berty's clothes had changed from bright blue to brown without any gold trim.

Stepping out of the doors of the Empire Tree, a snow filled Sage's Grove greeted them. White covered everything. Only the dark wooden doors of the buildings punctuated the wintry scene. Soft, delicate snowflakes continued to fall steadily from the light gray sky as the two men strolled towards the gates.

As his body passed through the gates of the Sages' Grove, Berty felt a jolt in his stomach. He immediately checked to make sure that his magic was still working. Satisfied with still seeing gray, he realized that he had never walked through the gates before. The memory of Silvia walking through the gates as he looked on surfaced. Edwin had slowed when they reached a crossroads at the edge of the forest. Instinctively, Berty said, "This way," as he led Edwin into the snow covered trees.

Chapter Thirty
Snow Trodden

They walked in silence for hours. The snow softly blanketed the forest floor and piled on the branches above them. Out of the corner of Berty's eyes, he saw Edwin's astonishment as the Elf finally glanced at their cloaks.

"How does?" Edwin began, but Berty silenced him with a sharp look.

The lack of snow in places unnerved Berty. "We are not alone, Eddie."

Edwin suddenly stiffened. His right hand grabbed the exposed hilt of his sword.

"I wouldn't do anything too hasty now, Eddie," said a squirrelly looking man as he stepped out from behind a tree while brandishing a long blade.

While keeping an eye on the man, Berty became aware of two men positioned in the trees and a few more still in hiding around them.

"You see," said the man, "I've staked claim to this part of the woods. In order to pass, you have to pay my toll."

"And if we refuse?" asked Berty.

The man laughed. "You'd never win a fight against me," he said.

Berty smiled while ignoring Edwin's ever increasing look of concern. "How about just you and me? We choose our weapon. If I lose, then my friend and I pay your toll. If you lose, then you and your friends pay."

"Very well," said the man. "I choose this weapon." He flashed his blade. "And you?"

A crossbow bolt fell at Berty's feet. "An honorable man would abide by the rules to which he agreed. Obviously, you need some help with that. Lucky for you that I am in a very helpful mood today," Berty said with a smile, not knowing what had gotten into him. "It must be the holiday spirit. Gets me every year." Another crossbow bolt fell to the ground. "Let me show you my weapon of choice." Berty reached his hand into his cloak pocket, plucking from its depths his smooth, wooden wand. A pair of newly shot crossbow bolts hovered in place inches from Berty and Edwin.

The smile slunk off the man's face. "A Watcher," he said as he took a few steps backwards.

"Giving up so soon?" taunted Berty. The man looked horrified. "I'll take that as a yes." The man tried to back further away, but Berty stopped him with magic. "Where do you think you are going? You did agree to pay." With a flick of Berty's wand, sacks of coins headed towards Berty and Edwin from every direction. Berty thought about returning the coins to the people from whom the thieves stole it. Instantly, the money was gone.

"We best be on our way or we won't make it to granny's house on time," said Berty casually.

They began to walk away from the would-be thieves when a large man ran towards them, carrying an axe raised over his head. "Give me back that money," screamed the man. Berty gave him a fleeting look and the man fell on his face. When he raised his head off the forest floor, the snow and mud could not hide the look of fear.

After walking for another hour or so in silence, Edwin said, "My...?"

"Please, address me as Marcus," said Berty.

Nodding, Edwin said, "If you could do that, why learn to use a sword?"

"Every weapon has its limitations," Berty answered. "Do you not use both a sword and a bow?"

"Yes, but."

"No buts. Besides, I take the advice of those who know better than I."

Berty navigated through the unfamiliar snowy woods as if he had always known the way. They traveled in more silence, constantly keeping an eye open for another band of thieves. They came across no one. Finally Edwin broke the silence, saying, "We should find a place to camp. It will be dark soon."

Agreeing, Berty found a secluded spot. While Edwin pitched the two-man tent, Berty built the fire, lighting it with his hand. The snow continued to fall around them as they ate, drank and laughed a little about the day's events.

More snow greeted Berty as he crawled out of the tent in the morning. After a quick snack, the tent was packed, then Berty led Edwin through more unfamiliar woods.

"I have never been through this area before," Edwin exclaimed.

"Not even during patrols?"

"We do not patrol the entire forest. Forest patrol in a greater area around the Sages' Grove recently started," explained Edwin.

"And by recently," Berty asked, "you mean since me?"

"Yes." Berty could tell that Edwin was thinking. "A greater patrol area would stave away things like we encountered yesterday."

"You should mention that to Alvar when we return," suggested Berty.

Edwin walked more proudly through the forest as he followed Berty's lead. Instinct led Berty through the snow-laden trees. Berty and Edwin kept their eyes peeled in case they ran into any more undesirables.

For hours, they walked cautiously in the forest. Finally, they stopped to take a break. As Edwin swept snow off a rock, a faint giggling reached Berty's ears. He knew that Edwin heard it, too, for the Elf froze as his eyes roved around in their sockets.

The giggling grew louder. Edwin slowly straightened while clutching the hilt of his sword. Edwin's hood fell off his head and the giggling turned into raucous, high-pitched laughter. A nearby tree began to shake, showering Edwin with snow. Through uncontrollable laughter, a high-pitched voice said, "Elfie. Snowy on Elfie."

Edwin slowly backed away from the tree.

"Where you go-y, Elfie?" asked the voice. "Come back, Elfie." The tree morphed into a very tall, thin, girlish woman or womanish girl. Berty noted her messy, dark brown hair, smooth, brown skin and bright, green eyes. As she walked towards Edwin, her torn, dark brown clothes bounced with each step. "Hello, Elfie." She bent over to be face to face with Edwin.

Berty was not sure whether to laugh or to pull Edwin away. Suddenly, the female's head turned sharply and she took a few steps backwards. She threw her arms out as if to become a tree, but she never transformed. "Uh-oh," she said. Trying to run away, she froze on the spot. Only her eyes could move. Berty watched as they darted from side to side.

"Miradelle, what are you doing?" asked a bellowing man's voice. Walking into view was an old man with a long, white beard. He wore a white belted cloak with his hood raised and carried a long staff. "Miradelle," he said when he reached her, "you know better. I am disappointed in you."

He twitched his staff and she unfroze. "Don't be maddie. I was only having funnie with the Elfie."

"Unacceptable and unbecoming of a wood sprite," said the old man.

"Peeze, peeze," the wood sprite pleaded.

With another wave of his staff, she stiffened. "I am sorry, Emperor, that you had to see that," the old man said to Berty. "I am the Master Woodsman and Miradelle is my only charge," he said with a bow.

Berty remembered reading about wood sprites. "Only?"

"I am sad to say, yes," answered the Master Woodsman. "Some years after the sprite wars, the remaining wood sprites...." Pausing, he wiped his ice blue eyes with his hand. "Petrified. All of them petrified except Miradelle here. I have no idea how she survived petrifaction, but she did not survive unscathed. Somehow, her mind has been addled, making her quite a handful. I apologize for the trouble she has caused you and your guard, my

332

Lord."

"It is quite all right," Berty reassured.

"You are far from the Empire Tree, Emperor," stated the Master Woodsman. "What is it you seek?"

"Counsel," Berty answered.

"Ah, yes. Elder Hunter." The old man waved his staff and Miradelle moved again. "I must get her to a more remote area. Do you mind if we walk with you for a ways?"

"Of course not."

Miradelle smiled at Edwin who periodically looked up at her as they walked. The Master Woodsman pointed out different trees while nostalgically musing about bygone eras.

As the sun fell in the sky, the Master Woodsman said, "An ideal camping spot for you, my Lord." He pointed into a thicket. "Miradelle and I must keep moving. You should reach your destination in the morning. It has been an honor to meet you, Emperor. Perhaps our paths will cross again one day." He bowed, then beckoned Miradelle to disappear into the darkening woods with him.

Berty and Edwin followed the Master Woodsman's advice and walked into the thicket. The tall pines sheltered the little clearing from the snow, which made it feel warmer. After setting up camp, they sat around the fire, eating some warm food.

"Strange creatures those wood sprites," Edwin remarked.

"She seemed to have taken a liking to you," chuckled Berty.

Edwin laughed. "She would have gone over well with my mother and father."

"Do they live in the Sages' Grove?"

Shaking his head, Edwin said, "Irmingard. My brother is being considered for Low Elf. When we were children, he went into training as an Irmingard Warrior and I chose to be an Empire Guard. I was not going to follow my older brother. And I think it made it easier on my parents, too." He smiled.

Returning his smile, Berty sipped his magically brewed coffee, thinking about how glad he was that Edwin accompanied him on this journey. Some of the barrier between Emperor and Lieutenant had been lowered, making them more of equal traveling companions. Watching the dancing flames brought the Master Woodsman's words to the forefront—they will find Silvia tomorrow.

"Edwin, about tomorrow," Berty began. "While we will be seeking Elder Hunter, I do not think that we should let on that we are searching for her." Edwin slowly sipped his warm infusion as he listened. "I will be asking for Leigh, an alias Elder Hunter uses. Marcus is the name that I will be using and I think continuing to call you Eddie will be imperative to the charade."

The Elf nodded. Berty felt a mixture of excited anticipation and a touch of dread. He wanted to see her. His eyes longed to look into hers. However, the words he feared the most were the ones that confirmed their relation. "I need answers," Berty breathed. Finishing his coffee, he fell asleep in the tent.

Berty awoke with a renewed energy and determination to speak with Silvia. Packing up the campsite, Berty led Edwin through the woods for a few hours. Finally, Berty and Edwin emerged from the edge of the forest. Berty found himself on a path that led to a large, stone wall with an arched wooden door that was flanked by lanced guards.

Taking a deep breath, Berty said, "She's behind those walls." He stepped fully onto the path that directed them to the town.

Each step heightened the anticipation. The desire to see her intensified inside of him. But what if, he kept thinking. Trying to distract his mind, he focused on the surroundings. Small, handmade signs popped out from the snow at Berty. *Magic users beware. Turn around now. They do not like you. If they find you, they will kill you.* "Great, a place that hates magic," he whispered.

The next sign he saw was an official, chiseled, stone sign that said, "Welcome to Calledin." Beside the stone was a wooden sign that said, "All visitors will be subject to a weapons search upon entering."

Plunging his hand into his pocket, he held his wand until it turned into a sheathed blade. As they approached the small wooden door, Berty could see a mass of gray stone kissed with white snow through the opening.

When they passed under the arch, a gray metal armored man stopped Berty and Edwin, saying, "Raise your arms, please." Berty held out his arms as another armored man searched his pockets.

"One sword," said the second man as the first man wrote on a clipboard. "And one hand blade," the man added when he found the transformed wand. Edwin showed no sign of shock as the man returned the blade to Berty's pocket. Searching Edwin, the man said, "One sword, one bow and a quiver of arrows."

"Thank you," said the first man. "Enjoy your time in Calledin." Berty felt uneasy as he watched the man walk away without a hint of a smile on his face. Edwin shot Berty a furtive look before they started down the cobblestone street.

They approached a building whose sign said that it was an inn. Edwin and Berty glanced at the grimy windows and worn wooden door, then kept walking. Turning down another street, Berty saw a sign, saying, "Nelson's Fine Goods and Collectibles."

"She's in there," Berty said.

Edwin looked around. "I'm going to find us lodging. Meet you back here."

Berty nodded, then pushed open the large wooden door. As he stepped over the threshold, his ear heard a bell ring and his appearance tidied. Walking past objects he had only seen in museums and old home tours, he found his way to the counter at the back of the store.

A well-dressed blond haired young man greeted Berty with a cheery, "Hello, I am Thomas. How can I help you today?"

Berty gave the boy a warm smile, saying, "I hope you can. I am looking for a teacher named Leigh. I understand she is staying with your family currently."

"Yes," he said. "She is in session presently. If you would wait here a moment, who may I say is calling?"

"Marcus. I am an old friend of Leigh's."

His blue eyes gleamed as he turned away, disappearing through a door. After watching people walk along the street through the multiple paned windows, an older woman wearing her blonde hair in a bun came through the door. "Marcus," she said warmly, "I am Angelica Nelson. Leigh is so happy that you are here. She will be finished with my daughter's session soon. Please, come upstairs and wait for tea."

"Thank you very much, Mrs. Nelson," said Berty with a smile. She returned his smile warmly while she lifted the counter for him to step through to the back. He followed her up the bright, narrow steps into an old fashioned sitting room. Sitting in the ornate, cushioned chair to which she pointed, Berty watched as she poured hot water from a sliver kettle into a floral decorated teapot.

Mrs. Nelson sat in a chair opposite Berty while Silvia entered the salon, wearing a high-necked, cranberry dress with a small bustle similar to the dress Mrs. Nelson wore. Berty stood to greet her.

Silvia walked towards him with a warm smile, saying, "This is a pleasant surprise." Berty could not help but smile as he kissed her cheeks in greeting, inhaling the familiar berry pie smell that he missed.

As they sat, Mrs. Nelson placed cakes and cups of hot tea on the small tables in front of them. "It is so nice to meet one of Leigh's friends," said Mrs. Nelson. "Have you traveled long, Marcus?"

"Two days," Berty answered.

"That's a fair journey," said Mrs. Nelson. "I take it that this is not merely a social calling."

"I wish it were," Berty said as he sipped some tea. "I am looking for some advice," he looked at Silvia, then at Mrs. Nelson, "and Leigh is the best."

"I can attest to that," said Mrs. Nelson. "She is working miracles with my Estelle. Is it for your own child, Marcus?"

"No, I am here because of my brother's child," Berty answered.

"It is... a delicate situation and he does not know where to turn. Naturally, I came to seek your advice, Leigh."

"I am glad you did, Marcus," said Silvia. "Today, I have another session with Estelle, then I will seek you at your lodging. Did you travel alone?"

"Eddie accompanied me." Berty looked poignantly at Silvia, hoping that she knew that he meant Lieutenant Edwin.

Silvia smiled through the steam of her teacup, saying, "Then I'll know where to find you."

After their brief tea, Berty thanked Mrs. Nelson for her gracious hospitality, then left. Outside the shop, Edwin waited for him. Giving the Elf a sharp nod, Berty proceeded to follow Edwin down the streets of Calledin. Walking along the sidewalk, he noticed horse drawn carriages passing on the cobblestone streets. The more he looked around at the surrounding gray town, the more he thought it looked like something out of a Charles Dickens novel.

Edwin opened a large, studded, wooden door preceding Berty into the building. Walking into the large room filled with round wooden tables and chairs where people were eating lunch, Berty realized that he was the shortest person in the room. He understood why Silvia would know where to find him.

A young, dark blonde woman with dark blue eyes approached Edwin, saying, "Your room is ready. If you gentlemen would follow me." The Elf's voice was clear and relatively high. She led them up a side staircase and down a hallway. Extracting a key from her pocket, she unlocked the last door down the hall. Letting the men pass her into the room, she held the key in her hand, saying, "My mom needs a deposit of eighteen vers." She blushed as she looked away from Edwin.

Counting the coins, Berty deposited them into her hand. She placed the key on the nearby table, then said, "Lunch will only be served for a little while longer. I would suggest coming down as soon as you get settled." She smiled at both of them. Locking eyes with Edwin, she looked away quickly before walking down the hall.

Accommodations in the room were modest, but adequate. Two single beds flanked a small nightstand on which stood an oil lamp. Edwin and Berty removed their cloaks and their weapons, storing them in the trunk near the wall. Berty locked the trunk magically before they proceeded down the steps to have lunch.

Elves were finishing their meals while Berty and Edwin made their way towards a small table in the corner of the room, which faced the door. The young woman who showed them to their room was clearing tables while a slightly older woman approached them, asking, "Two?" After Edwin nodded, she disappeared behind a pair of swinging doors.

When the woman returned with food and drink, most of the dining room had emptied. Berty and Edwin ate slowly. By the time they had finished their food, everyone was gone except for the Elf family who operated the inn. An older Elf, who Berty assumed was the father of the two ladies, walked over to them after watching his younger daughter exchange quick glances with Edwin.

"How are you two finding everything?" the man asked.

"Very well, thank you," answered Edwin.

"I didn't catch your names," he said. "I am Thaddeus, owner of Violet's Inn."

"My name is Eddie," explained Edwin, "and this is Marcus."

"Nice to meet you," Thaddeus said as he took a seat. "Where are you two gentlemen from?"

Berty thought it best to tell the Elf part of the truth. He answered, "The Sages' Grove."

"What do you do there, and what brings you to Calledin?"

"We do work for the Empire," answered Berty. "We are here seeking some advice from the teacher, Leigh."

"Is she the one working with Estelle the mad?" asked his youngest daughter as she inched closer to the table.

"Lark," Thaddeus exclaimed. "The girl is not mad, she simply had a mishap." He looked at his daughter. "Don't you have any chores?"

338

"No," replied Lark, "Cesare finished everything. I have nothing to do until dinner." She tried not to blush as she glanced at Edwin. Berty noticed that Edwin tried not to look at Lark at all.

"Perhaps you can help your mother," Thaddeus suggested. Lark disappeared through the swinging doors. "Do either of you have children?"

"No," replied Edwin.

"Yes, well," Thaddeus said, lost in his thoughts. "Enjoy your stay with us." Standing, he walked through the swinging doors after his daughter.

"When will you be meeting with her again?" Edwin asked Berty.

"All I know is that she will be coming to us sometime later today," answered Berty.

They returned to their room. When Edwin opened the door, he looked around, then said, "Someone was in here, searching."

"Are they gone?"

Edwin motioned for Berty to stay near the door while he checked the room. Locking the door, he answered, "Yes. We should check the trunk."

Magically unlocking the trunk, Berty checked its contents. "Everything is in order." Edwin grabbed his sword from the trunk before Berty closed the lid. When magically locking the trunk again, Berty also magically locked the door.

With a sword by Edwin's side, they sat on their beds, discussing who could have been inside their room and for what was being searched. When possibilities turned endless and fruitless, Berty said, "You know, I am the only person who is not an Elf in this establishment."

Looking puzzled, Edwin asked, "What does that have to do with anything?"

"Prejudice," replied Berty.

"Against you?"

"And I am sure that there is some suspicion of you."

"Utter lunacy," Edwin remarked.

"You must remember that here, I am not an emperor and you are not a lieutenant," explained Berty. "We are outsiders lodging in what seems to be a safe haven for Elves. I speculate that they see an unlikely friendship, one of which to be wary."

Berty saw calculations running behind Edwin's eyes. "The guards at the gate," Edwin began, "the uneasy feeling I had while walking through town, the strange anti-magic attitude... of course. Why didn't I see it?"

Before Berty could answer, he heard a knock on the door. Edwin clutched the handle of his sword while silently walking towards the door.

Berty asked, "Who is it?"

"It's Leigh," Silvia's voice answered. Magically unlocking the door, Berty nodded to Edwin to open it. When the door was opened, Silvia stepped into the room. Her eyes glanced at Edwin positioned behind the door before walking towards the lone chair in the room which Berty had placed for her between the beds. Edwin closed the door, then Silvia said, "Let me guess, your room was searched?"

"How did you know?" asked Edwin.

"Because," Silvia replied as she removed her cloak, "the Elves and Dwarves of Calledin are not treated with the same level of respect. Naturally, the two of you would have raised some suspicion. That being said, this was the best choice of lodging. Perhaps you should be your cheerful Elf self downstairs with the owners and some of the patrons to dispel any doubts or rumors."

Sheathing his sword, Edwin left the room.

Berty magically locked the door, then began, "Silvia...."

"Did you come all this way to talk about your niece, Berty?" asked Silvia.

Smiling at the use of his nickname, Berty replied, "Among other things. Please sit."

Sitting, Silvia listened to Berty tell her about how he discovered that Hope was a Wood Listener. When he got to the part about the tattoo of the Sages' Seal on his back, Silvia interrupted.

"Your Empire Mark proves that you are the Emperor. May I see it?"

Shocked that she asked to see it, Berty nodded slowly. Turning around, he lifted his shirt over his head. Almost immediately, he felt her soft, gentle fingers grazing his shoulder blade and a chill ran up his spine as he closed his eyes.

"I have never seen one like that," she remarked. "Martin knew what he was doing."

As she sat back down, Berty pulled the shirt over his head. Turning, he asked, "What do you mean?"

"My mark, as well as every Empress before me, was only in black, brown and dark green. Yours has an array of colors that I have never seen. It's beautiful." She looked at Berty with tender eyes and a soft smile on her face. "Oh, Berty, I had thought that Martin had made a mistake." Berty was completely puzzled, but let her continue. "I could not see how he would have, but nothing else was making sense to me. It never occurred to me that the scepter would choose another. You were under the same assumption as well, were you not?"

"Which assumption?"

"That we had to have been related somehow."

"And we are not?"

"No," she said with a wide smile. "We have different Empire Marks. We are different families." She laughed a little.

Berty's insides melted into a pool of happiness. He wanted to hug her, kiss her and not let her out of his sight.

"Now, tell me what else has happened," Silvia said with a lift in her voice. "You and Edwin are incognito for a reason. And I am sure that there is no horde of Empire Guards waiting in the woods outside the gates for your return."

His elation deflated a little as he told her the story of Delyth's poisoning. Silvia stayed silent as Berty recounted every detail until he mentioned Declan's findings.

"Magic is being siphoned into the Dragonlands?" She looked

away from Berty for a moment, then said, "Then into the Dragonlands you must go. Find the Clan of Cian and speak to the First Dragon."

"The First Dragon?"

"It is what the Dragons call their clan leader," Silvia answered.

Berty asked further, "Do you feel that they are hiding something?"

"Perhaps. But only you can find the truth," said Silvia. "Is there anything more?"

Knowing that he should tell her, but not know how she would react, Berty took a deep breath, then said, "I can watch you when I close my eyes."

"Only me?" Her expression showed curiosity.

"At first," he answered, "but recently I saw Lida and Elrick."

Smiling, she said, "The Pixie Priestess was right about you." Silvia leaned in towards Berty, saying softly, "Now, I have a favor to ask."

Chapter Thirty-one
Favors

Leaning towards Silvia, Berty waited to hear what she wanted.
"I need you to make sure that Edwin is on board," Began
Silvia, "because you two are going to help me smuggle Estelle out
of Calledin."

Looking into her warm, brown eyes, he asked, "When?"

"Tomorrow night. You have a whole day of planning ahead
of you." She sat back in the chair. "Hope will have to come
through the portal someday. Do not concern yourself with Leif
and Millicent as of yet. They will expose themselves
eventually." Looking towards the other bed, she said, "When
you go to see the Dragons, take more than just Edwin with
you."

Berty said, "Okay," as he watched her head turn towards him.

Taking a deep breath, she stood, saying, "It is time for me to
go."

Standing also, he said, "I will walk you out."

"I'll be taking Estelle to the park in the afternoon," Silvia
stated as she waited for him to open the door. "I will be watched."

Nodding his head, he opened the door, saying, "After you."
Walking beside Silvia down the semi-dark hallway reminded him
of walking with her throughout the Empire Tree. His thoughts
made him grin as he followed her down the stairs.

While he escorted Silvia to the door, Berty noticed Edwin
chatting with Lark and a woman Berty guessed was her mother.
At the door, Berty gave Silvia a hug while he said, "Thank you,
Leigh, for everything."

"You are welcome, Marcus," Silvia replied. "I am all too happy
to help." She smiled warmly at Berty before she disappeared
through the door.

With the feeling of the hug still a fresh memory on his body,

Berty turned around and saw Edwin wave him over. When Berty approached the bar, Edwin introduced him to Lark and Charlotte, Lark's mother.

"That Leigh is the nicest woman I have ever met," remarked Charlotte. Smiling warmly, she looked fondly at her daughter and Edwin. "Dinner is almost ready. Why don't you two gentlemen take a table. Lark, get these men a pint while they wait for their supper."

Edwin followed Berty to a small, out of the way table. When they sat, Lark brought them each a glass of dark beer. "How long are you two staying in town?"

"Just until tomorrow," Berty answered. "Our work bids us back."

Looking crestfallen, Lark said, "Oh," and walked away.

Edwin looked at Berty. Berty answered his unasked question, whispering, "Nighttime, plus two."

Taking a long drink of his beer, Edwin gazed longingly at the swinging door behind which Lark had disappeared.

Knowing what was going through Edwin's mind, Berty said, "You do not have to choose. She could help." Berty watched a light turn on behind Edwin's eyes and his face lifted.

When Lark brought two plates of food to their table, Edwin jumped at his opportunity. "Lark," he said excitedly, "would you like to spend some time with me this evening, perhaps after dinner, we could go for a walk, you could show me your town, I know it is a bit dark and cold, but I was thinking that perhaps, maybe, it would be nice to spend some time together?"

Trying his best not to laugh, Berty saw the happiness in Lark's eyes when she said, "Let me see what time I can get off tonight." She almost floated back into the kitchen.

Finally letting out a small chuckle, Berty said quietly, "Smooth. Haven't you ever asked a lady out before?"

Edwin turned a bit red. "Not like her. She's...." He stopped talking when he noticed that she was coming towards him.

"Give me a bit," Lark said. "I should be ready to go after you have finished your meal."

"Great," Edwin exclaimed. Smiling, she walked away. With a lovesick smile on his face, he whispered to Berty, "She said yes."

"So I heard," said Berty. Figuring he might not see Edwin again for a while he asked, "What were you discussing while I was upstairs?"

"Lots of things," Edwin said. "Lark's great-grandmother was the Violet for whom this inn was named. Violet's parents were part of a group of Elves who relocated to Calledin during the huge population boom in Irmingard. Anyway, at that time, Calledin was a much more tolerant place. The town is run by a Governor named Manfred whose ancestors have always been in charge. After everything was well established and looking pretty much the same as it does now, the Governor at the time's wife took ill. The town's resident Wizard tended to her. And while he did everything he could for her, he could not save her life. The Governor accused him of murdering his wife. So, he rounded up all the magic users in Calledin, most of whom defended the Wizard, then he executed them all. Needless to say, Manfred inherited this hatred. He's the one who established the weapon search at the gate as an excuse to search people and find magic users to torture and kill. This intense hatred of magic keeps all the residents on edge and fuels the distrust between the peoples." He paused and a grin spread on his face. "Charlotte also expressed that she would be fine with Lark leaving Calledin."

Berty smiled, saying, "Well you better finish eating, so you can spend as much time as possible with Lark this evening." Smiling, Edwin finished his meal, leaving Berty alone in a room full of Elves.

Finishing his second glass of beer, Berty felt many pairs of eyes follow him across the room to the staircase. As soon as he shut the door to his room behind him, he realized that he needed to get a bit of air. Donning his sword and cloak, he stepped into the hallway when a side door opened.

"Marcus," said an Elf that he saw working in the inn, "my

name is Cesare. I'm married to Thaddeus' daughter, Violet."
Cesare shook Berty's hand with a strong, friendly grip. "I thought
that maybe you would like to avoid being seen by the general
crowd."

"Thanks," Berty said.

"Follow me," said Cesare. He led Berty into a dark, narrow
back staircase. Small landings dotted the staircase with a few
doors at each one. As they descended, Cesare continued, "I hope
the Empire does not look at Calledin too poorly. We are not all
against those who are different than we." At the bottom of the
stairs, Cesare opened the door to the cold, wintry night. "Rap
thrice on the door and it will open for you."

"Thank you," Berty said. The door closed behind him as he
stepped into a cobblestone alley.

Sounds of people scurrying in and out of stone buildings
throughout the town reached Berty's ears. As he wandered
through the dimly lit streets, his leather soled boots barely made a
sound on the pavers. The tall, stone buildings and walls
suppressed the sounds of the surrounding forest while magnifying
the sounds of the streets. Crunching snow under his feet alerted
his eyes to the opening of a park in the middle of all the gray.
Bare, brown branches were buried under white lines. Paved paths
cut through the expanses of snow that were punctuated by dark
metal benches half covered in snow.

The snow muffled the clomping sounds of horse hooves on
pavement. Berty found the park peaceful enough to begin to think
of what awaited them tomorrow. Excited giggling interrupted his
thought. Under a nearby tree, shielded from the park light, two
tall figures embraced. Knowing they were Edwin and Lark, Berty
walked the other way.

On the way back to the inn's rear door, Berty took note of the
dark shadows the poor street lighting cast. He was not sure if they
would need them, but he thought it best to be prepared for
anything. Knocking three times, the door opened automatically.
Berty smiled at the defiant use of magic.

Returning to his room, he readied for sleep. Before he slipped into bed, he glanced out the window, seeing a view of the dark alley. In the shadows, he noticed Edwin and Lark strolling arm in arm towards the back door. Before Berty could turn away, he caught Edwin turning Lark towards him and Edwin's head lowered to Lark's. Happy for Edwin, Berty climbed into the long narrow bed, falling asleep before Edwin returned to the room.

Waking before Edwin, Berty proceeded to get ready for the day quietly. When Edwin finally stirred, Berty asked, "How did you find it last night?"

"Lark was a huge help," answered Edwin, getting out of bed. "In addition to showing me around, she helped me find all the dark spaces." Edwin blushed.

"They'll be in the park in the afternoon," Berty said, pretending not to notice. "See you downstairs."

Charlotte greeted Berty with a cheery hello in the dining room, asking, "Pot of breakfast tea this morning?"

"That would be great," he answered with a smile. He was glad to have tea and not risk using magic for coffee. Charlotte brought him a teacup and saucer decorated with a fuzzy blue print and matching teapot. She placed a silver strainer over his cup, then poured the tea. After taking a sip, the tea reminded him of Sundays with his grandmother. He said to Charlotte, "I have never had tea like this anywhere else in the Land of Sages."

She glanced at her near empty dining room, then took a seat at the table with Berty. "Back when magic was still accepted," she began, "people would travel through the nearby portal. The city on the other side was the epitome of sophistication, style and civility. Our lives were modeled after theirs, except we were better. We had real magic while theirs was merely flashes and bangs. During that time, we had imported, then later, copied many things. Some of us still do." Charlotte threw him a rebellious look before she walked into the kitchen to retrieve his breakfast.

Joining Berty at the table, Edwin grinned from ear to ear.

Berty knew that he had just seen Lark. Edwin said as he sat, "We are going to spend as much time as possible together before we leave today."

Berty smiled partly because he knew that he was going to see Silvia soon. When he saw Lark approaching, he finished his food quickly. "I am off to stroll the shops. You kids have fun," he said. As his hand brushed his moneybag, magically he transferred some money to Edwin's pocket before he walked through the door.

Wind blew fast through the streets, swirling the falling snowflakes. Berty gazed into shop windows whilst familiarizing himself with the town's layout. As he walked, part of him wished he had at least one more night to prepare and another part wanted to leave right then.

After a solo lunch at another establishment, Berty strolled through the snow filled park. Shortly after entering the park, a light blue cloak shone amongst the white. Next to her was a midnight blue cloak. Light blonde hair blew out of the hood in the wind. Beyond Silvia and Estelle, Berty spotted men in dark clothes hovering and watching. He meandered through the park, then returned to his shopping so as not to raise suspicion.

Returning to the inn, Berty found Edwin asking Cesare for supplies. In their room, Berty waited for Edwin. As soon as Edwin closed the door, Berty said, "There are at least a half dozen men following Estelle."

"At least three more were watching Elder Hunter," added Edwin.

Berty nodded, for he saw them also. "I doubt they will be able to shake all of them before we meet them."

"Lark will take us to the back door to leave," Edwin said.

"Good," said Berty, "that is where they will meet us."

Someone knocked quietly on the door. Opening the door, Edwin let Lark into the room.

"It's almost dark," she said. "Here are your supplies." She handed them both sacks. As they secured them to their cloaks, she said, "Let me come with you."

348

"No, Lark," said Edwin.

"Please," she pleaded.

"I can't take you," exasperated Edwin. "I'll come back for you. I promise."

"How about continuing this downstairs," Berty suggested.

Lark led them into the staircase hidden behind a door. As they descended, she said, "I know you're an Empire Guard, Eddie."

"How do you?" Edwin began.

"It is just who you are. I don't have an issue with being a guard's wife," Lark said.

"Lark, it's not that," explained Edwin. "I want to do everything properly. Have my family come for you."

She smiled as a tear escaped her eyes.

"I know that we haven't spent a lot of time together, but I love you, Lark, and I want to spend forever with you," Edwin proclaimed. "Leaving you right now is one of the hardest things I've ever had to do. However, if you came with us now, it would cause your family harm. And I don't want that to happen. Please, you have to understand."

Opening the door to the dark, cold evening, comprehension dawned on Lark's face. She remarked, "Oh."

Edwin looked at Berty. Berty nodded. Turning to Lark, Edwin said, "You are sworn to secrecy." He took her hand. "It is the only way I can keep you safe until I return."

"Yes, of course," she said. "I have a secret for you as well." She whispered, "I'm a Listener." Berty sharply turned his head towards her. "Larks. I'll send one to you, to know you're safe."

Berty returned his watchful eye on the dark alley while Edwin and Lark embraced. "I think I see them coming," Berty said. When Edwin did not respond, Berty continued, "Be ready to go, Edwin."

Berty hoped Edwin's, "Mm-hmm," was a response to him.

The shapes in the distance became clearer. Berty knew that they were Silvia and Estelle. "Time to go, Edwin."

"I'll write when I can," Edwin said to Lark. "I'll miss you."

"I'll miss you, too," said Lark.

Edwin still held Lark's hands. "Lieutenant," Berty scolded.

"Ready, my Lord," said Edwin. Lark's eyes opened wide. "I love you," he said to her with a kiss, then he joined Berty in the alley.

In a dark corner of the alley, they met Silvia and Estelle. Wasting no time, Silvia said, "They're going to realize that she's missing soon. Thomas could buy us only so long. We can't use magic. If we do, the Nelsons will burn."

"I'll take point with the girl," said Edwin. "You two should follow closely behind." Like someone flipped a switch, Edwin locked arms with Estelle while keeping his hands on weapons hidden under his cloak.

Trying not to obsess about how far away the gate was from them, Berty gave Silvia his arm. They pretended to stroll through town like they were two happy couples.

A couple of blocks away from Violet's Inn, Berty heard the hurried shuffling of feet, then a muffled voice said, "I see her. Get her!"

Edwin pulled Estelle down another alley. Berty and Silvia ran behind them. Shuffling morphed into running. Berty whispered to Edwin, "The gate. Where's the gate?"

Zig zagging through the streets, Edwin navigated them through the maze of buildings, finally leading them to the main street where Berty could see the opened gate ahead.

Whipping her head around, Silvia ordered, "Run!"

From behind, Berty heard a man shout, "Lower the lock!" Loud clinking noises preceded large wooden beams lowering over the gate on thick metal chains.

"Edwin," said Silvia looking at the pulley system, "fire an arrow through an upward moving chain link. It will buy us some time."

Handing Estelle to Silvia and Berty, Edwin raised his bow, releasing an arrow. Out of the corner of his eye, Berty saw the arrow make its target. The beams stopped dropping as the arrow hit the pulley. However, unready men with swords scrambled to block the exit.

Both Berty and Edwin pulled their swords from their scabbards, charging the unarmored men. Shocked, the men allowed themselves to be knocked aside. With the way clear, the four ran below the lock. As they escaped through the opened gate, Berty thought he heard a faint snap as though the arrow had broken. Without stopping to look back, they continued down the path to the trees.

"Lift the lock! Lift the lock," someone shouted from behind the walls.

"They're coming," said Berty.

"Quick, into the forest," Silvia instructed. "Get off the path."

They wove in-between the trees as fast as they could. Berty watched Estelle's hood fall off her head, exposing her light blonde hair that glowed in the night. Reaching a small clearing, Silvia stopped running.

"This is far enough," said Silvia.

"But they're not going to stop chasing us," Edwin exclaimed.

"I know," answered Silvia. "Edwin, give me your bow and quiver." He handed them over to Silvia without question. "Estelle, raise your hood." She covered her light hair with her dark hood. "Hide behind those trees," Silvia added, pointing behind her. Opening her right hand, the walking stick that the Empire Tree had given her before she embarked sprouted from her palm. "Berty, undo your magic."

His and Edwin's cloaks returned to their original dark red and green. "Undone," he said.

Silvia raised the staff to the sky, saying, "From the stars above, to the depths below, Great Tree protect us, so your seeds we sow." Encircling her head with the staff like a lasso, a wavy sphere of magic grew from the staff's edge, enclosing the clearing. When the haze cleared, tents erected behind them, a fire sprang to life before them and Edwin was dressed like an Empire Guard with a helmet.

"Estelle, get in a tent," instructed Silvia. Estelle did as she was told. Silvia rested Edwin's bows and arrows on one of the logs surrounding the fire. Turning to Berty, she said, "Stick your sword in the ground near that log." She pointed to a log on the opposite side of the fire from the bow. As Berty forcefully stuck his sword in the ground, Silvia addressed Edwin, "Guard the opening and do not walk beyond the first trees. You will be speaking to them when they come, which should be any moment. We will be in the tent." Edwin nodded. Berty followed Silvia to the tent opening.

Before entering the tent, Silvia tapped the ground once with her staff. Multiples of Berty's sword and Edwin's bow and quiver appeared around the campsite. Clones of Edwin sat around the fire and stood by different trees on guard duty. Inside the tent, they sat on cots. Berty whispered to Silvia, "You never cease to amaze me." Smiling, she placed a finger to her lips and they waited.

Sitting made Berty tense, but he trusted Silvia. Glancing at Estelle, she seemed to be oblivious to what was happening. Berty watched curiously while she inhaled deeply with her eyes closed. Her breathing was slow and rhythmic as if she were meditating.

Estelle's eyes snapped open, then Berty heard Edwin bellow, "Halt." The familiar sound of metal ringing reached Berty's ears. He knew that Edwin had withdrawn his sword. "It would be wise for you to put away your weapons and state your business in these woods."

"We don't mean to trespass into your camp," said a man's voice. "We are merely a search party from Calledin."

"For whom or what are you searching?" Edwin asked.

"A girl," the man answered.

"You have a lot of weapons for one girl," Edwin observed.

"She was kidnapped," said the man angrily.

"When?" Edwin asked.

"Just now," the man exasperated. "If we could go, perhaps we could still find her. They could not have gone far."

"We have been patrolling these woods all day," said Edwin. "If anyone was around we would have found them. Give me a description of this girl, we will find her."

"Her name is Estelle Nelson," the man said. "She has blonde hair and light blue eyes. A woman with dark red hair kidnapped her. This woman was helped by two unidentified men."

"Is she a very young girl?" asked Edwin.

"Not exactly," the man answered.

"An older girl?" Edwin asked further.

"She's more of a woman," said another man.

"A woman?" Edwin sounded annoyed.

"But she has the mind of a child," the first man said.

"Go back to Calledin," dismissed Edwin. "You have no authority here. The Emperor has charged us with making the forest safe for hunting and traveling. If this woman was kidnapped, as you claim, we will find her and contact her family in Calledin."

"Come on," said a new voice, "we don't need to incur the wrath of the Empire on us."

"Thank you," the first man said.

Berty, Silvia and Estelle sat motionless in the tent, waiting for Edwin. The minutes passed like hours until Edwin poked his head through the opening, saying, "They are long gone. It is safe to come out now."

Berty followed Silvia and Estelle out of the tent. Tapping the ground twice with her staff, all the clones disappeared, leaving one tent, the fire and surrounding logs, and Berty's and Edwin's weapons. Edwin returned to his original clothing.

"I am not sure if they will return to Calledin right away," said Edwin, sitting on a log.

"They do not have to return right away. They will not be back this way," Silvia replied.

Estelle stayed quiet through dinner while Edwin kept looking for intrusions. Silvia assured him that the staff's magic hides them completely and that nothing could pass through the magical barrier.

To relax a little after their long evening, they sat near the fire, sipping warm drinks. Berty watched Estelle close her eyes, breathing like she had never breathed fresh air before. When his eyes glanced at Edwin, Berty realized that the Elf was reminiscing about his time with Lark.

Berty smiled at Silvia, asking, "Can we ever walk peacefully through the forest?"

Laughing, Silvia answered, "Someday, I am sure." Her eyes met his for a moment, then she asked, "Speaking of walking through the forest, who are you planning on bringing with you to the Dragonlands?"

Berty had not had much time to think about it, but he knew. "Declan and Edwin."

"Those are good choices," Silvia approved, "but you need to bring one more."

"Only one more?"

"When it comes to Dragons," explained Silvia, "three people constitute a scouting party, four is a delegation and five is an act of war."

Berty looked at her in disbelief. "I read nothing about this in those books. How do you know?"

Silvia raised her eyebrows as if to say, I am Elder Hunter after all. She then suggested, "Take Seanlaoch."

"Sean? Why Sean?" Berty's stomach turned over at the very thought.

"You need someone who you can trust."

Raising his eyebrows, Berty wondered if she was not thinking straight.

Silvia explained, "You cannot bring both Alvar and Edwin. One or the other must stay behind. And just any Empire Guard should not go. Could you really trust one of them to keep secrets?"

A whole battalion could, but just one, Berty was not so sure. Realizing that she was right, he shook his head.

"Sean is bound by his crystal," she added. "Plus, he can use a weapon."

Visions of a silver dagger flying through the air flashed in Berty's mind. "So I recall."

Briefly touching her abdomen, Silvia continued, "The crystal forces him to protect you. Use him. Besides, he may say something interesting."

Reluctantly, Berty nodded his head. Silvia had never steered him wrong.

Chapter Thirty-two
The Empire Delegation

B erty awoke to crunching noises. Poking his head outside the tent, he saw that it had snowed overnight. Silvia's footsteps crunched the snow as she walked from the tent to the fire.

"Good morning, Berty," Silvia said with her warm smile that Berty cherished. As he approached the fire, she asked, "Coffee?" He returned her smile while she poured him a cup. "I am sorry if I woke you," she said.

Sitting next to her with his cup of coffee, Berty shook his head, saying, "I was wondering how long we should stay in the area. Estelle needs to be far out of her father's reach."

"You have been watching."

"Enough to know that his abuse caused her *madness*."

Silvia looked at the woods past her magical barrier. "There is only so much I can do." She turned to Berty, then said, "You and Edwin need to return to the Sages' Grove. There is something Estelle needs to find."

Her words deflated Berty, but he understood and nodded his head. The tent stirred. Soon Edwin and Estelle joined them by the fire.

After everything was gathered, Silvia made a circle above her head with her staff. The magical barrier disappeared along with the tent and fire. It looked as if no one was ever there. Berty magically changed his and Edwin's cloaks back to gray.

"Ellri," said Estelle to Silvia, "wait here for me." Estelle disappeared in-between the trees.

Berty was about to ask Silvia if they should wait with her when he heard a bird chirping. A small brown bird flew to Edwin.

"A lark," Edwin exclaimed. Raising a gloved hand, the bird rested on his fingers. Berty noticed a rolled piece of paper tied to its leg as if it were a carrier pigeon. After Edwin's other hand untied the paper, the bird flew onto Edwin's shoulder. Opening the rolled paper, he said, "It's a note from Lark." He began to read the note. "Her family is okay," he told Berty and Silvia. "The men who chased us returned last night. There seems to be some sort of meeting in town today. She will write again when she knows more, but some of them do not like the presence of the Empire Guard so close to their borders." Edwin smirked. He placed the note into his pocket, then addressed the bird. "We are fine. Thank you for the letter. Keep me posted, but do not get caught. Off you go." The lark took flight into the snow-covered trees.

Estelle emerged from the forest clutching something in her hand. "I found it, Ellri, where it was supposed to be." She opened her hand to show a large, smooth, grayish-blue gemstone surround by a silver starburst with pointed radials. The pendant was attached to a delicate, silver chain.

Standing where the fire once burned, Estelle removed her dark blue cloak, handing it to Edwin. Her midnight blue dress still showed signs of prolonged wear while her light blonde hair was still listless and unkempt. Berty watched as she secured the chain with both hands behind her neck. When her arms returned to her side, strong winds rushed into the clearing. They encircled Estelle, gently blowing her dress and hair. At the center of her personal tornado, Estelle raised her arms above her head and looked towards the sky. A column of bright white light enveloped her. Berty caught Edwin's jaw drop out of the corner of his eye.

The wind and light disappeared at the same time, leaving Estelle standing like nothing happened. Berty studied Estelle as she took a few deep breaths. Her once tattered dress had been mended with silver thread. She looked as if she twinkled like the night sky. Her long, light blonde hair had life breathed into it. It was as if she had finally made the transition from girl to woman that she had been waiting to do for a long time.

She approached Berty, saying, "I want to thank you, Emperor, for helping us escape. It would have been much more difficult without you and your Lieutenant."

Smiling, Berty said, "You are welcome."

Edwin helped Estelle put on her cloak, then asked, "How are we going to find our way back to the Sages' Grove?"

"Our travels take us north as well," answered Silvia. "I want to keep her away from the southern villages. We will travel together."

For the rest of the day, the four of them kept to the lesser used paths, encountering no one. Before it became dark, Silvia crafted a magically barricaded campsite using her staff.

Once they were settled around the fire, Berty asked Silvia, "What did you mean when you said that you thought Martin had made a mistake?"

"Martin's a Matchmaker," she answered matter-of-factly.

"A Matchmaker?"

"Did he not tell you?"

Berty looked at her, shaking his head.

"It is his gift," Silvia explained. "He knows our family tree better than I, and he knows the best matches, not just with two people, but with anything. That is what makes him a good newspaper editor. You were sent on the interview as a blind date." She blushed.

In a way, Berty felt a little hurt. "I guess he wasn't impressed with my writing skills."

Smiling warmly, she whispered, "He doesn't send me just anyone. You had to be deemed worthy and that is a tall order as far as my brother is concerned."

Feeling more uplifted, he smiled. Looking into her soft, brown eyes, he said, "Who would have expected this?"

A little laugh escaped her lips and Berty yearned to be closer to her.

"I'm taking her to the tent," announced Edwin with a sleeping Estelle in his arms. "She fell asleep by the fire."

Silvia nodded, saying, "We should all get some sleep. It is getting awfully late."

Knowing the moment was lost, Berty left the warmth of the

fire for the warmth of a camp bed.

The clear, blue, morning sky motivated them to move through the snow laden trees at a good pace. As they traveled north, Berty knew that Silvia could not come beyond the gates of the Sages' Grove, but he wondered how close she would go.

A little after midday, they stopped for a break. Before they continued their journey, Silvia said, "This is where we part. You and Edwin should reach the Sages' Grove by evening, continuing on this path. Estelle and I are heading east."

"Would it not be safer for Estelle to stay in the Sages' Grove?" Edwin asked.

"Perhaps," answered Silvia, "but she would not learn all she needs to learn there."

Edwin glanced at Estelle, then nodded.

"Berty," Silvia said, "to help you on your way, ask the scepter for a map of the portaled Empire. One will appear on the wall and will need to be copied from that."

"Silvia," said Berty. He stood there not knowing what else to say.

She gave him a warm hug, then said, "Until we meet again, good luck." Before he could answer, Silvia and Estelle had departed down another path.

Just after nightfall, Berty and Edwin emerged from the woods, facing the treed wall of the Sages' Grove. Before they entered the gates, a lark landed on Edwin's shoulder. With a smile on his face, he followed Berty into the Empire Tree and up the stairs to the Reception Room.

Walking across the floor of the empty Reception Room, Berty removed his magic from their clothes, saying, "Tell Declan we leave in the morning. Rest well." After Edwin disappeared up the staircase, Berty called for Theodore.

When the young Dwarf arrived, Berty instructed, "Take me to see Seanlaoch."

Berty followed Theodore across bridges that he had never crossed down to the lowest level of the branches to the Tenders' quarters. They stopped at a bundle of bare branches. Theodore rang a bell before they entered. Inside the circular room were chairs of different sizes some with men lounging, napping or reading. In the far end of the room, Sean laid across the arms of a chair, staring at the ceiling above.

"Sean," said Theodore.

Without looking away, Sean replied, "What did I do now, Head Tender?"

"You have a visitor," said Theodore.

Sean's eyes glanced at Berty. Sean sprung from his chair. He said with a bow of his head, "My Lord, what an honor for you to visit me."

Trying to suppress his loathing, Berty said, "We need to a have a word in private."

"Of course, my Lord. This way," said Sean. He led Berty up the spiral staircase. At the landing were six doors. The stairs continued spiraling upwards. Sean opened a door, saying, "My chamber." Berty entered, seeing a small bed and a wardrobe. "Please, have a seat."

Surprised by Sean's politeness, Berty sat on the end of his bed, then asked, "How would you like an opportunity to leave this tree?"

"I would like that very much, my Lord," answered Sean. "Thinking can be done outside as well as inside."

"Thinking?"

Sean sat on the other end of his bed, answering, "About where my great-grandfather's staff is."

Remembering something that Estelle had said in the forest, Berty asked further, "It was not where it should have been?"

"Nowhere remotely nearby."

"What did you do?"

"Looked for answers," Sean explained. "I came here and secured an audience with the scholar at the time."

"Leif," said Berty. "What did he tell you?"

Sean's gray eyes looked away, losing focus. "He told me to

secure lodging in the village and that he would look into it. A couple of days later, he told me that the scepter was to blame and the Empress, I don't remember his exact words anymore, was the only one privy to the powers of the scepter. Then the Fairy came to me and told me that magic had been fading from the Land of Sages for years except from the Sages' Grove. She said, 'It's no wonder why you can't find the staff that should be rightfully yours.' Then I traveled and found what she said to be true." He sighed.

Berty studied Sean for a moment, then asked, "Would you like to find the truth?"

With a look of surprise, Sean answered, "I would."

"Would you be willing to be a part of a truth finding journey outside these walls?"

Sean tried to downplay the excitement on his face. "Yes."

"We leave in the morning," Berty said, standing. "Be in the Reception Room."

"Yes, my Lord."

Downstairs, Berty saw that Theodore was waiting for him. "Everything all right, my Lord," Theodore asked.

"Yes, Theodore." Berty walked with the Dwarf onto the bridge. "I will take dinner in my study tonight. Supplies for four will be needed in the morning. Sean is coming with me. He will need his traveling clothes and his sword. However, put his sword in the Reception Room with the supplies."

"It will be done, my Lord."

Berty climbed his private staircase to his chambers where he ate his dinner and took a bath before enjoying a long sleep in his big, comfortable bed.

Before the sun rose above the horizon, Berty descended his private staircase. Peeking into the Scepter Room, he wondered if it was not too early to wake Delyth. Reaching the Reception Room, he realized that it was not too early at all. She sat next to Declan at the breakfast table, not eating a thing.

"Delyth, just the person I need right now," said Berty as he approached the table.

"You need me?" She sounded pleasantly surprised.

"Can you sketch something for me?"

"Of course, my Lord."

"Bring your things to the Scepter Room," Berty instructed. "I will be right there." She left the room in a hurry, leaving Declan eating alone, looking terrified. "We will be fine," he said to Declan. Declan nodded while Berty climbed the stairs to the Scepter Room.

Delyth stood by the doorway of the main steps when Berty arrived. He walked into the inner circle, beckoning Delyth to join him. "Are you ready to sketch?" he asked her.

"Just tell me what," she answered.

Facing the scepter, Berty looked at the glowing red crystal, asking, "Could you please show us a map of the portaled Empire?"

The crystal glowed brighter for a moment, then shot a beam of light onto the opposite wall. "Thank you," said Berty. They walked over to the glowing wall. Borders, roads and villages were illuminated on the wood. "Sketch at least the Land of Sages and the Dragonlands," he said to Delyth, "before it fades."

"I will do my best," said Delyth, beginning to draw. "These labels are written in a very ancient tongue. Eat something before you go. I will bring it down to you."

Leaving Delyth, Berty returned to the Reception Room to find that Edwin had joined Declan. "My Lord," said Edwin, "Lark's note said that Mister Nelson is now saying that Estelle left willingly so that she could see the world. I have the Empire Guard sending a note in a few days about her saying something similar when we found her."

"Good work, Edwin," Berty said while choosing some food. "Delyth is drawing a map for us as we speak."

"My Lord," asked Declan, "for whom is the sword?"

"The fourth man on the journey," Berty answered as he sat at the table.

"Who—?" Declan cut off when he heard footsteps.

"My Lord," asked Sean, "am I late?"

Declan silently seethed while Berty answered, "Not at all. Have you eaten?"

"I have," replied Sean, keeping his distance from the breakfast table.

"I do not want to question your judgement," Declan began quietly.

"Then do not," interjected Berty firmly. "He has to be given a chance to redeem himself." Berty knew that it had something to do with the crystals. Silvia understood better than he.

Finishing the little food on his plate, Berty walked over to another table, saying, "Let us ready ourselves." Picking up Sean's sword off the table, he called to Sean while holding out the sheathed sword towards him.

"I get my sword back?" Sean looked scared to take it.

"You may need it," said Berty. "No one travels unarmed."

"Emperor," Delyth said as she entered the room, "it is done." She lowered her voice so that only Berty could hear. "The roads through the Dragonlands may or may not be there. The Dragon wars could have burned everything beyond recognition."

"Thank you, Delyth."

She hugged Declan meaningfully. When she let go, she said to all of them, "Good luck."

After securing their supplies, they descended the steps as Delyth watched. Berty did not bother to disguise them, for he wanted people to know that their Emperor was trying to restore the lost magic.

Walking through the gates of the Sages' Grove, nothing shielded them from the bitter, morning wind. "Lead the way, Declan," said Berty. Declan took them on a path around the wall.

Once in the shelter of the trees, Sean commented, "At least the trees give some protection from the cold."

"We will not have to worry about the cold in the Dragonlands," remarked Declan.

"We are going into the Dragonlands?" Sean asked with terror

in his voice and on his face.

"Scared?" asked Edwin.

"Me? No," Sean responded unconvincingly.

Declan smiled with satisfaction while he led them deeper into the woods.

After walking nonstop most of the day, Declan stopped to explain, "Many smaller streams merge here to form one of the larger streams." He pointed above them, but no one knew what to see.

"Does it merge with other large streams of magic?" Berty asked.

"I do not know," replied Declan. "My best guess would be that it does. I am inclined to think that they all converge to a single point eventually. This one leads into the Dragonlands. We are not far from the portal road."

"We do not have much daylight left," Edwin said.

"There is a place to camp near the border," said Declan.

"Let's keep going then," Berty suggested.

Chapter Thirty-three
A Match Made of Fire

The portal road was still as derelict as Berty remembered with the forest encroaching well into parts of the road. Looking up and down the road, only animal tracks disturbed the snow. On the other side of the road, Declan led them to a secluded area, perfect for a campsite.

Sitting around the fire, Sean said, "This part of the forest is creepy."

"That is because we are so close to the Dragonlands," replied Declan.

Berty extracted the map, saying, "Where are we?"

The four men examined the map. Sean said, "Wow, this is confusing. What are these blobs that are labeled *area*?"

Declan gave him a dirty look while Berty answered, "She could not interpret the ancient words."

"Great," exclaimed Sean. "A bunch of areas that we do not know what they are. Why bother marking them?"

"At least we have a general idea," Edwin said.

"What a waste," said Sean, then he walked away.

Scowling, but otherwise ignoring Sean's comments, Declan said as he pointed to a place near the border, "I believe we are here."

Studying the map, Berty said, "I think we should follow the magic to its end, then go looking for the Clan of Cian."

"Makes sense," said Declan. Looking up, he pondered, "I wonder from where all this magic is coming."

"Does not all magic originate from the scepter?" asked Sean.

Declan threw Sean a dirty look as he sat on the opposite side of the fire.

"No," Berty answered.

"That's what the scholar told me," said Sean.

"Alfred knows better than that," Declan said.

"Not Alfred," corrected Berty. "Leif."

Sean nodded.

"Magic is a mystery," Berty explained. "Why some have it and others do not, I have no idea. Magic is the mysterious force that the scepter uses. However, magic is independent of the scepter. The scepter was crafted using magic." Pausing, he looked at each man. "Like energy, never created nor destroyed, just changing shape, it is probably tied to life itself."

"I don't get it," said Sean. "What does that have to do with the scepter being at the center of all things?"

Looking at Sean in disbelief, Berty said, "She was right, you are woefully ignorant."

Declan and Edwin snickered while Sean asked, "She who?"

"The last Empress," said Berty.

Sean shifted guiltily in his seat and looked elsewhere.

"Looks like we have a long day ahead of us tomorrow," said Edwin, changing the subject. Berty and his men extinguished the fire, falling asleep in the tent.

Berty awoke to the howling wind whipping past the tent. The morning was still dark, but when he sat up, he was able to see that the others were also awake.

"I thought this place was sheltered," Sean complained.

"It is," said Declan through gritted teeth. "A major storm must be blowing through."

"Don't think we should risk a morning fire," Edwin said while getting out of his bedroll.

"Great," whined Sean. "So we either trek through dangerous lands hungry or eat nearly frozen food."

Berty stepped outside the tent. The wind lashed his cloak around him. Closing his eyes, his cloak fell still and the howling stopped in his ears. When he opened his eyes, he saw the wind violently blow the snow off the trees outside the magical bubble he had created. Extending his right hand, a fire roared to life in front of him, instantly warming the area.

Edwin peeked out from the tent, saying, "I'll get breakfast."

"It's not light enough for breakfast," Berty heard Sean say inside.

Declan walked out of the tent behind Edwin, looking above him. Standing next to Berty, he said quietly, "You cannot see. Does being Emperor cloud your vision or have you never been able to?"

"Never," answered Berty. "How did you know?"

"No Watcher could do this, even with all the magic in the stream above us," Declan replied. "That, and I saw you from the tent."

Berty took a hot cup from Edwin, changing it into coffee.

Wrinkling his brow, Declan asked, "What did you do to your root tea?"

"Made coffee," said Berty. He was not sure if Declan even knew what coffee was, but he had other questions in his mind. "I though Watchers could only see magic in constant use."

Taking a cup from Edwin as well, Declan answered, "Most do, but not me. I see magic big or small, constant or fleeting. My gift, or curse, since birth."

Berty wanted to ask him what he meant, but Sean finally staggered out of the tent over to the fire. "So warm," Sean said.

After the campsite was packed, Berty said, "Brace yourselves." He looked at the trees blowing in the wind, clutched his cloak around him, then removed the bubble of magic that protected them. The wind had increased in veracity. Declan's mouth moved, but the words never reached Berty's ears. Edwin pointed at his ear while he shook his head. Understanding his pantomime, Declan pointed into even darker woods so dramatically that Shakespearean actors would have been proud.

They followed Declan silently into the ever thickening forest. As it became darker, the wind lessened. "If you take one more step," warned a gruff voice from a nearby bundle of sticks, "you will be leaving the Land of Sages and entering the Dragonlands."

"Thank you," Declan said, then he stepped over the border.

"You have been warned," said the Troll with his large, dark eyes full of fear, peeking through the branches.

Berty, Edwin and Sean stepped over the boundary as well. Immediately, the forest felt more mysterious.

As they walked deeper into the Dragonlands, they changed directions, following the magical stream. Declan commented, "I thought it would have picked up or merged with at least one other stream by now."

The further inside they went, the more Edwin kept looking around. Berty felt as if they were being watched. In a large clearing, Berty saw remnants of burnt trees. A bad feeling bubbled in his gut.

"I lost the stream," said a worried Declan, stopping and looking around.

"How?" asked Sean annoyed.

"Too much magic," Declan answered. He turned around in a circle. "Oh, no."

Sean looked at him in disbelief, asking, "What do you mean, oh, no?"

"Magic is everywhere," Declan replied, sounding scared. "We are completely surrounded by magic."

"Oh, no," mimicked Sean.

Declan squinted while scanning the area. His eyes became big and round while screaming, "Duck!"

A ball of fire barreled straight for them. Scattering, they lunged to the ground.

Berty lifted his head to ask, "Is everyone all right?"

A couple of yards away, Berty saw Edwin pushing himself off the ground. Out of the corner of his eye, a line of fire began to descend on the Elf.

Berty cried, "No," while throwing his arm up to push the fire away. He breathed a sigh of relief until his ears heard a grunt of disgust. An unhappy Dragon, he thought. Picking himself off the ground, he said, "Hurry, everyone stay close to me."

As Berty stood in the direction where he thought the Dragon

368

was, Declan, Edwin and Sean gathered around him, weapons in hand. Waiting for the next strike, Berty could hear his men's hearts beating fast. The soft whoosh that gas makes as it travels through pipes before igniting reached Berty's ear. With both arms spread high over his head, he thought, *no fire reaches us.*

A spilt second later, fire shot towards them. The reddish orange flames flattened, dispersing around them as if they were the bottom of a pan on an open flame turned on high. A bead of sweat trickled down the side of Berty's face. Closing his hands, the fire concentrated. He pushed his hands hard away from him and the fire retreated back up its path. Smoke rolled in, surrounding them.

With trepidation, Berty waited. The smoke cleared to reveal a black, serpent like creature with a very large, boxy head hovering before them in the sky. Berty made out its big, golden eyes and thin, gold mustache under very large nostrils. Further down its slim body were four muscular legs with claws. Its spiny back ended in a pointed tail.

The square jaw opened, exposing large, pointed teeth. "Sorcerer," the Dragon said to Berty, "a truce for we are equals."

"Put your weapons away," Berty whispered to his men.

"I am Tong, Guardian of the Dragonlands." Tong's big eyes rested on Berty, waiting for him to speak.

"I am Hubert," said Berty, "Emperor of all that surrounds us."

The Dragon let out a laugh that sounded like a roar. "You are a great Sorcerer, Hubert," he said, "but you cannot be Emperor. The Empire is overseen by Empresses."

"So it has always been, but not anymore," said Berty.

Tong scrutinized Berty with his globe like eyes. "If you are the Emperor, then you will have suffered the mark."

Berty understood the Dragon to mean his Empire Mark. Removing his cloak, he handed it to Declan. He turned around, lifting the back of his shirt to expose the multicolored Sages' Seal on his left shoulder blade.

After a moment of deliberation, Tong announced, "A new

family has been chosen. A new era is upon us."

Berty fixed his shirt. Turning around, he retrieved his cloak and fastened it.

"An honor to meet you, Emperor, and be your equal," said Tong. "What brings your delegation to the Dragonlands?"

Deciding to change the direction of his plan, Berty answered, "We seek an audience with the Clan of Cian."

"Allow me to escort your delegation, Emperor," Tong said proudly. Flying slowly, Tong led them deep into the dark forest completely devoid of snow.

"Tong," Berty asked, "if you knew that we were a delegation, then why did you attack us?"

"I have my orders, Emperor. Being a clanless Dragon, Cian allows me to be a Guardian, which has kept me out of the clan wars ever since... well, it is not my tale to tell. As a Guardian, I have one order—keep out men, except for lone travelers.

"Then why are you escorting us now?" Berty asked.

"Law of equals trumps their orders," explained Tong. "So does the Emperor's wishes."

After traveling for hours, Tong stopped and emitted a high pitched coo, which sounded like a bird's call to Berty. As soon as he heard a return call, Tong led them into a large, rocky clearing with gigantic boulders that could have rolled down from the hill a couple of hundred yards away.

The ground shook for a moment, then Berty saw a large, broad-bellied, green Dragon with an elongated, rounded snout stomping towards them with huge, muscular, scaly legs. "What is wrong with you Tong? You bring men into our lair," the Dragon said angrily. "Can you not follow simple orders?"

"Cool your fire," said a similar shaped, brown Dragon, walking into view. "Give Tong a chance to explain."

"Explain? Keep men out, what is to explain?" Smoke rushed out of the green Dragon's nostrils. "You are getting soft in old age, Emdellion." The green Dragon spread its leathery green wings, then soared into the sky.

"I am awaiting your explanation, Tong," said Emdellion sternly.

"Clan of Cian," said Tong as he landed awkwardly on some rocks, "may I present the Emperor."

Emdellion closed her eyes for a moment. Her expression was hard to read. "Emperor," she addressed Berty, "allow me to welcome you to the Dragonlands and to the lair of Cian. I apologize for Tanguy. Youth tend to be short tempered. Why have you come all this way?"

"We need to speak to the First Dragon of the Clan of Cian," Berty answered.

"I thought you might," said an elderly female voice whose body was hidden in the shadows of the boulders.

Berty waited as a lustrous gray Dragon emerged from the shadows, carrying her long snouted head high. The Dragon perched on a high, throne like rock, then said, "Emdellion, leave us."

The brown Dragon bowed her head, stretched her wings, then flew above the trees.

Once Emdellion disappeared, the gray Dragon said, "I am Angana, the First Dragon of Cian. Emperor, it has been a long time since an official Empire delegation has visited. Please, have seats." Berty and his men sat on small rocks. "Tell me, why have you come to see me."

Choosing his words carefully, Berty said, "There is a tale."

"What sort of tale?"

"A Sage's Tale."

"There are many Sage's Tales, Emperor," said Angana cautiously.

"The one about which I am inquiring is about a boy who stumbles upon a clan of Dragons and later grows up to be a king," Berty explained.

Angana looked at Berty with a mixture of curiosity and fear on her old, reptilian face.

"Years later, the king returns to the clan only to leave his young daughter with them," continued Berty. "Is this true?"

"Why does it matter?" Her nonchalant manner did not convince Berty.

"I need to know what happened to the girl," Berty pushed further. He knew that the girl in the tale Silvia had told him on his first foray through the portal had something to do with the siphoned magic.

The Dragon took a deep breath and sighed. "That happened well before your time, Emperor." Pausing, Berty thought he saw a twinge of guilt on her face. "But, if you must know," Angana conceded, "then I will tell you."

Berty nodded for her to tell the story.

"The king never returned for his daughter, Eirawen. Not that I believed he would when I made the deal with him. We brought her to the Dragonlands and this is where she was raised.

"The girl was raised in our ways and with our traditions. Through the years, Eirawen never forgot from whence she came. I can only imagine that being a person living among Dragons was not easy for her. Although she had to learn to do many things on her own, we helped her the best we could.

"When Dragons come of age, we leave the clan for awhile to find ourselves. Naturally, when Eirawen came of age, she was encouraged to go and live among the people. She was always welcomed to return if that life did not suit her, but we felt it best that she at least try.

"Eirawen was gone through two sun cycles. When she returned, she was very upset and we did not know why. Per our customs, we do not pry into other's personal journeys. She did not confide in us. Eventually, she sunk into a deep depression and left the clan. Eirawen never returned."

Angana took another deep breath as if the unpleasant part was still to come. "Within twenty sun cycles after she left us, Goblins visited the clan. Knowing everything as they do, the Goblins told us that Eirawen was living in the place without death. Her misery, they relayed to us, seeped everywhere. The Goblins believed that given time, she would suck all the happiness out of the world. They told us that since she was our charge, we needed to do something about her.

"After much deliberation," she said quickly as if she did not want Berty to think about how long they deliberated, "some of the clan were chosen to talk to her. When they found Eirawen, she was living in a cottage that she built. Before they could convince her to come back with them, she did the unspeakable." Closing her eyes, she continued, "Because, Emperor, you ask, I will tell you what happened. What she did is against our ways. Eirawen turned a weapon on her own body."

Completely rapt in the story, Sean looked shocked, asking, "She killed herself?"

Opening her eyes, Angana looked aghast, "We do not speak of it!"

"I'm sorry," Sean said sheepishly.

Calming herself, Angana said, "Yes, that is what she did. Or I should say attempted. Since she was in the place without death, she could not die. Yet, she was not really alive either. It was as if she were in a deep sleep.

"We could not leave her there, so we enlisted the help of Dwarves. Six Dwarf workers and a Dwarf foreman constructed a crystal and gold box in which she were to lay. They were instructed to place her somewhere no one would find her and never tell anyone where she is, including us. To the best of my knowledge, the Dwarves kept their end of the bargain."

The once proud Dragon looked dejected. "Thank you, Angana," said Berty.

"I am sorry that you must do what we could not, Emperor," she said. "I hope she returns all that she has taken. Tong will take you to her cottage from here."

"I understand," said Berty, standing.

As they turned to leave, Angana called, "Emperor." Berty faced the aged Dragon once again. "After you encounter Eirawen, it may serve you well to seek the one who has the eyes hidden in the folds of God Mountain. Good luck to you, my Lord." The Dragon hopped off her rock, returning to the shadows.

"This way, Emperor," excitedly said Tong. He rose to the sky, leading them into an even darker part of the forest.

"My Lord," Declan quietly said, "I thought we were looking for the source of the magic siphoning."

"We are," answered Berty. "Now we know who is behind it."

"Eirawen."

"Yes," Berty explained. "Maybe we will find something useful where she once lived."

The Dragon finally stopped in a dark, dank and desolate part of the forest. "Here we are," said Tong, "the forest where nothing dies."

Berty looked at the bare branches of the trees. He did not think that any buds would form on them in the spring. Everywhere he looked had a distinct lack of vegetation.

"This should be named the forest where nothing lives," Sean said.

"Life needs death," said the Dragon Berty recognized as Emdellion while she landed. "Since nothing dies here, nothing can be reborn. Eirawen's little cottage is just beyond those trees. It would be wise not to linger. Tong will make sure you camp outside of this forest. When I found her, Emperor, she was not in her right mind. I can only imagine that time has made it worse." Not waiting for a response, she spread her wings, then flew away.

They cautiously explored in the direction that Emdellion had told them. Berty rounded a dead looking tree and saw a poorly constructed shanty.

"Cottage was a bit of an exaggeration," Declan commented.

Agreeing, Berty thought a cardboard box would make a better shelter.

"She must have been extremely depressed," said Sean. "Who would want to live here?"

The shanty's door was partially opened, so Berty stepped inside. It would have been completely dark inside if the gaps between the boards were not wide, letting in some light. Against one wall was a small bed that looked like someone had recently slept in it. At the back of the shanty rested a small writing desk. Noticing a small drawer that seemed to have been haphazardly closed, Berty tried to open it, but it was stuck. Instead of trying to force it, he used magic to open it. Inside the drawer, he found a small book and a quill with ink dried on the tip.

"My Lord," called Edwin, "come see this."

Taking the book, Berty left the shanty.

"Is that blood?" Sean asked.

"Don't touch it," scolded Edwin.

Joining Edwin, Berty saw a short, bronze blade laying on the dirt. He crouched down to see that dark stains clung to the sharp edges. "Well," said Berty as he stood, "we now know how. I think we have been here long enough. Let's go."

Tong led them to a spot far enough from the forest where nothing dies to make camp. They were erecting the tent when Edwin stopped to pick up his bow and load it with an arrow. Berty listened hard to hear the cracking of twigs. Declan also had an arrow ready to fly as Sean unsheathed his sword. Putting his hand on the hilt of his sword, Berty decided not to be so hasty.

"Hold your fire," called Silvia's voice. Recognizing her voice, Edwin lowered his bow.

Silvia and Estelle emerged from the trees. Berty asked, "How did you know where we were?"

"Goblins," answered Silvia. "May we join you?"

"Of course," Berty replied.

Flying overhead, Tong said, "I think I have enough wood." He placed two giant claws full of wood in a pile on the ground some ways away from the tent.

"Tong is in charge of the fire," explained Berty as Tong blew fire on the woodpile, causing a bonfire like blaze. Silvia looked at the Dragon with curiosity. Berty added, "He is my equal."

"Dragon matches," Silvia, "of course." Berty threw her a puzzled look. "Estelle was reading the stars," she clarified, "and she said that you would meet your match. Anyway, I had to check."

Berty smiled, knowing that she came out of concern for him.

With her fears quelled, the wild look in her eyes, which Berty remembered from the first time that she brought him to the forest, had returned. Silvia asked, "Is it the girl? Or did the First Dragon tell you something different?"

"The girl."

"I knew there was something. What have you discovered?"

Telling Silvia about their day in the Dragonlands reminded Berty of the book he took from the shanty. They sat on a log together, opened to the first page and began to read by bonfire light.

"She seemed to have started this diary only after leaving the Dragons," remarked Silvia. "The first thing she did was to return to her father's kingdom."

"He told her that she was dead to him," Berty said disgusted. "I would be hurt and angry, too."

"She discovered a younger brother by the king's new wife who is inline for the throne," said Silvia.

"It looks like she and her father had a nasty argument," Berty said. "I am not really sure what it was about. Perhaps her birthright."

"She is very angry," commented Silvia. "I cannot even read the intricate details where she plots her father's murder."

Berty made a face, saying, "Utter heartlessness. She watched her father die a slow death and relished in it. And she wants more."

Turning the pages, Silvia exclaimed, "This is sick. She devoted years to plotting the death of her brother. After starting a war, she stood, untouched, on the battlefield, watching the man whom she had hand picked as a boy, destroy her own brother. Ugh. She goes on for pages about her victory."

"She sabotaged the kingdom until it was completely decimated," said Berty further in disgust.

"When she finally returned to the Dragonlands, her thirst for power consumed her," Silvia said. "It was like a drug to her. I think this is when Eirawen began to absorb other's magic. I am not sure if it was intentional, but it seems that after her first taste, she could not stop."

"She talks a lot about her insatiable thirst for the magic," agreed Berty. "Is this the last page of entry?"

"Looks like it," Silvia said while flipping through the pages. "Listen to this, 'After all these years, vindication alludes me. All the wrongs have not been righted. More needs to be done. I wonder why I cannot motivate myself to leave this forest. The Goblins are meddlesome. Did I seed enough to re-ignite the war between them and the Trolls? I am afraid that it is taking too long for my liking. The current generations are awfully careful not to break their silly treaty. Future generations will take the bait and war will be inevitable. Doing more would show my involvement. That, I cannot risk. It is much more gratifying to watch my well planted seeds grow into sometimes more that what I have imagined.' It abruptly stops there." Silvia closed the book.

Looking at the leather bindings, Berty was too disgusted to talk. He knew that the Dragons interrupted her written ramblings. Even seeing it in her own words, he could not believe how one person could be so destructive, but then he thought that if he had learned anything from history it was that it only took one person or idea to be pivotal.

Interrupting his thoughts, Silvia asked, "You know where she is?"

"Tears of beauty," he answered.

"There should be a cave where the waterfall begins," said Silvia, deep in thought. "That is, if the books were accurate."

Berty had also read those books and he hoped that the authors wrote accurately. Nodding his head in agreement, he looked around the campsite. Declan and Edwin had their heads together in a deep discussion. Estelle was having a conversation with Tong while Sean sat quietly on a rock, glancing nervously in their direction.

Knowing what they must do when the morning came, Berty called Declan over. When he arrived, Berty asked him, "Will you be able to find the streams of magic easily again?"

Declan sat with concern on his face. "I am not sure. The Dragon might throw off my wand because he exudes magic." Studying the Dragon for a moment, he said, "Actually, I think the Dragon is bleeding magic. Eirawen is draining the Dragons of magic, too. We can follow his stream."

Nodding, Berty said, "Then we should get some sleep."

Chapter Thirty-four
Out of the Cave

When laying on a bedroll in a strange forest with a sleeping Dragon curled around the campsite, the only thing scarier than facing the unknown was facing the known. Berty mulled it over in his mind until the restlessness forced him to leave his bedroll earlier then he had wanted. Leaving Sean's snores in the tent, Berty walked outside to find Silvia tending a small fire.

"Couldn't sleep?" she asked quietly while looking at him approach.

"Had enough," answered Berty. "You?" Sitting next to her, he watched the flame light flicker in her eyes and hair and knew she had been thinking.

"Since I was a little girl," Silvia began. "I always wanted to go on a Dragonlands adventure. The girl in the story intrigued me." She turned her gaze to the dancing flames. "I have to admit that I am disappointed in Eirawen. I thought she would be different. Guess I was still holding on to a girl's imagination."

"Perhaps there is something we are missing," said Berty trying to comfort her.

Silvia looked at Berty for a moment. "Perhaps." She searched into his eyes. "Something seems wrong with her diary. It is like there is a major omission. I don't know." She looked into the fire again.

People in the tents began to stir so Berty and Silvia ended their conversation. Getting an early morning start, Declan led the group into another part of the Dragonlands.

Changing directions slightly, Declan pointed to the gray sky in front of him, saying, "A bunch of streams are merging here. We should be getting close." They walked further while Declan remarked, "An unbelievable amount of magic is being siphoned."

Going down a slight hill, they rounded a bend, then Declan

stopped. Stopping with him, Berty surveyed the scene a little further down the hill. Lush green foliage accented with red, white and pink flowers surrounded a lake that was being fed by a small dual waterfall.

"It is winter?" Edwin asked.

"Tears of beauty," said Silvia. "The magic must keep everything green all year round."

"Wait," Declan said with a confused look on his face. "You can see something?"

"Yes," answered Berty, Silvia and Edwin in unison.

Silvia looked at Declan, asking, "What do you see?"

"Mist," Declan replied, "nothing but mist." His eyes darted wildly trying to see something.

Tong landed behind them, saying, "Emperor, I cannot go any further with you. Mists usually aid Dragons, but this mist is sinister. I fear it would weaken me rather than strengthen me. If you wish to explore this mist, I will wait here for your return."

"Thank you, Tong," said Berty.

"Can Estelle wait with you?" Silvia asked Tong.

Smiling, Tong answered, "Yes, of course."

Estelle stayed with the Dragon while the rest of them continued towards the small lake. The ground turned from brown to green.

A couple of steps further made Declan freeze. "I can't see," he said with panic in his voice. "I thought it was just a barrier, but it is like walking into the thickest fog."

"I'll guide him out," said Edwin as he grabbed Declan's arm. When Edwin returned, he said, "He's fine. Worried, but fine."

Berty did not like losing Declan, but they pushed onwards through the tropical like lushness.

"Is it me," asked Sean, "or is it really warm?"

The wet, sticky heat was the furthest thing from Berty's mind as he replied, "Look for an entrance to a cave."

Exploring the steep hill, Berty felt frustrated until Edwin called, "I think I found something."

Behind overgrown vines was a narrow crack of an opening just wide enough through which a person could squeeze. The opening barely let any light into the cave. Trickling water echoed as Berty tried to see further into the cave, but saw nothing in the pitch black. However, over to the side his eyes made out something leaning against the rock wall.

Walking over, Edwin saw them, too. He said, "Dwarf torches."

"Only three of them," said Sean.

"Better than nothing," Berty said, picking them up off the ground. He handed one to Edwin and one to Sean while keeping one for himself. With a wave of his hand, all three ignited.

Berty led the group down the narrow passageway with Silvia behind him. The passage opened into a larger cavern with two streams running through the cavern floor, carving an island in the center.

Something on the island glistened in the torchlight. "Is that Eirawen?" Sean asked.

"I believe so," answered Berty.

They stepped over the small stream that separated them from the island. On a stone altar laid the crystal and gold box, which encased Eirawen. Berty's mind had been filled with strange visions from the stories of his childhood. Peering thought the crystal he recoiled.

"What is the matter?" Silvia asked.

"I expected something different," replied Berty. "Where's the ebony hair and the blood red lips?" He looked at her extremely light skin and colorless hair. "She's an albino." Her red dress gave her a very disturbed look, even with her eyes closed.

Silvia gazed at Berty with understanding, saying, "Many people have crossed through the portals over the years. I am sure someone stumbled upon the Dwarves that encased her. You have to remember that many tales were only known orally. Storytellers would embellish or change certain aspects to suit their audiences. Some of these tales through the years combined with others or split, creating new tales. By the time the brothers Grimm finished retelling them, the stories had morphed into something completely different. But obviously," she glanced at Eirawen sleeping in the casket, "some have a hint of the truth woven within the fabrications."

"She is really creepy," remarked Sean. "Should we open it?"

"I think we are going to have to," Silvia replied.

Edwin crouched to be eye level with the encasement while moving his torch along the bottom, asking, "How does it open?"

"There should be," Silvia began as she ran her fingers along the gold, "latches to release it, if it is indicative of Dwarf construction." Walking alongside the box, Silvia kept feeling for invisible latches. Finally, she exclaimed, "Found one." As she fiddled with a latch, Berty heard a click. On the other side of the box, she found the latch more quickly. Berty heard another click. "It should lift off now."

Edwin and Sean handed their torches to Silvia and Berty. Placing their hands on the bottom, they lifted the lid. Berty heard the sound of gases escaping. Placing the lid to the side, Edwin and Sean retrieved their torches. With trepidation, the four of them watched Eirawen, not knowing what else to do.

The cavern echoed with the sound of an intake of breath. Eirawen's colorless eyelashes flickered. Her eyelids opened revealing, light colored eyes with a pinkish hue. She blinked, then sat up, causing everyone to take a step backwards.

Turning her head towards them, she squinted. "Who are you?" she demanded. "Where am I?" She looked at her own body while she ran her hands over her stomach. "The Dragons sent you. Cowards." Her knees bent. Turning her head, she attempted to look at them again.

"Eirawen," said Silvia calmly, "why did you have your father killed?"

A smile slunk across her face. "Another coward. He needed to be punished."

"For leaving you with the Dragons?" Berty asked.

"That was the best thing he ever did for me," Eirawen said,

dangling her feet over the side. "Although he did it for himself and not me at all."

"I do not understand," said Silvia.

"He would refer to me as unnatural," Eirawen explained. "Blamed my mother. Before I was given to the Dragons, I watched him kill her for producing such an offspring. He tried to pass it off as an accident, but I knew better. I vowed my revenge. When I got my opportunity, I took it."

"Then why kill your brother, too?" asked Silvia, trying to stay calm.

Eirawen stood, holding onto her encasement. "We were at war," she said nonchalantly.

"Do you realize that you are taking other's magic?" inquired Silvia further.

Closing her eyes, Eirawen inhaled deeply. "So much power," she relished.

Silvia and Berty exchanged looks before they took another step backwards.

"You ask too many questions," Eirawen said. "Tell those meddling Dragons that I will not stop. I will not give up anything." She breathed deeply again as if she were gathering strength.

"Run," said Silvia.

As they ran, stalactites exploded above them, causing Sean to drop his torch in the water. Running through the dark passageway, her maniacal laughter traveled with them.

"We need to lure her away from the lushness," panted Silvia. "Get her away from all the magic."

Outside the entrance of the cave, they caught their breath. Extinguishing the remaining torches, Berty heard echoing footsteps coming towards them. "She's coming," Berty said. They backed away from the cave, taking shelter in the vegetation.

When she emerged, a wild look of enjoyment played on her face. With an extension of her arm, Edwin ducked as a tree behind him exploded. They ran past the lake while she followed, screaming, "Everyone gets what is coming to them."

Back on the brown, bleak ground of the Dragonlands, they heard her laugh. "Silvia, get back," Berty ordered. "Weapons men."

Silvia's eyes opened wide, but she stepped behind the men. Berty, Edwin and Sean drew their swords and waited for her.

Eirawen slunk out of the lush green. She stopped a few feet in front of them, laughing. Opening her arms wide, Berty felt weakened. His sword became heavy in his hand and his vision began to blur. Behind him, Silvia collapsed, holding her head. Dropping his sword from the weight, he fell to the ground.

Sean screamed in terror, "Distract her." Berty barely saw Sean charge Eirawen.

Crawling to Silvia's side, Berty could just make out Sean and Edwin taking turns attacking Eirawen. "Silvia," called Berty weakly.

"I'm here," she said just as weakly. "She's draining our magic."

Berty took her hand. Raising his head, he thought he saw an arrow fly out of a tree. In a breath, his eyesight cleared and he began to feel stronger. He was able to see Declan climb out of a tree. He joined Edwin and Sean who stood over a body lying on the ground.

Helping Silvia to her feet, they walked over to find Eirawen's body sprawled before them with an arrow firmly stuck through her heart. Her red dress had various slashes.

"We stabbed her multiple times," explained Edwin while he returned Berty's sword, "but our blades had no effect."

"Because, that is how she originally tried to kill herself," Silvia said.

Declan looked around, then said, "All the magic is returning to wherever it came and the mist is dissipating."

"Why did you take so long to shoot her?" asked Sean annoyed.

"You two kept getting in the way of my shot," Declan retorted.

"At least it is over," said Sean as he sheathed his sword.

"We need to inform the Clan of Cian," Berty said.

"I will," said Tong, approaching them, "as soon as I know you are safely on your way back to the Empire Tree, Emperor. The Dragonlands might be in a state of disarray once word spreads."

"Can we leave her here?" asked Edwin.

"Do not worry," Tong answered.

They followed Tong to a wide road that looked rarely used and badly charred. "Follow this road west and it will return you to the Land of Sages," the Dragon said. "Good bye for now, Emperor. Equals will meet again." Tong turned, then sped across the sky as a black streak.

As they walked, heavy snow began to fall. "If the stolen magic," began Berty, "returned to its proper places, then does it mean everything has been restored?"

"Only time will tell," Silvia stated as she glanced at Estelle.

"Still do not know why I cannot find my staff," said Sean.

They made camp right over the border. As they sat around the fire, Estelle looked at Sean, saying, "What you seek takes you far beyond here. Forced to serve another, but not to its full potential."

Gazing at Estelle, Sean waited for her to say more. When she did not, he quickly looked away. Estelle, however, continued to watch him curiously.

While Edwin received another note from a visiting lark, Declan sat near Berty and Silvia. The Watcher said quietly, "My Lord, please forgive me for questioning your decision to bring Sean with us. When Eirawen was stealing both of your magic, Edwin would not have been able to distract her alone. As both attacked, the flow of magic slowed to only a trickle and because of Sean's help I was able to take my shot." He hung his head a little. "But I still do not like him."

"Thank you, Declan," said Berty. "You do not have to like him."

Smiling, Declan gave a sigh of relief.

"Delyth should be given Eirawen's diary," Silvia said to Berty, "to aid in creating the new Hidden Treaty."

Feeling the book in his pocket, Berty agreed.

Declan glanced over at Edwin who wore a sappy smile and a lark on his shoulder as he read. "What... how does love work?"

Smiling, Silvia responded, "I will not pretend that I understand love. What I do know is that love exists on multiple levels and has varying degrees. But the love of which you are asking has evaded our comprehension since the inception of rational thought. However, my advice I will gladly give. Love is to be felt and not thought." She quickly glanced at Berty. "Although there may be obstacles, if love is true, then a way will be found."

Declan smiled wide. Berty knew that his heart had been lifted. "Thank you, Elder Hunter," said Declan.

As Berty watched Declan enter the tent, he felt that perhaps Silvia was not speaking only to Declan.

After a better night's sleep than he had in a while, Berty left the tent to find a new blanket of snow covering the forest. The brown of the dormant trees contrasted beautifully with the white snow. Breathing in the cold, morning air made him feel alive, ready to begin his journey home. Gazing into the trees, a bright red cardinal perched on a branch in front of him. As Berty looked at the bird, the bird looked at him. The cardinal appeared to bow to Berty, then flew away.

"A good sign," said Silvia, standing next to him.

"Good morning," Berty greeted.

"Estelle and I must be off soon," said Silvia.

Searching into her warm, brown eyes Berty said, "I thought you might." He caressed her soft hands. Lowering his head towards her, he inhaled the smell of berry pie that he adored. "Be safe. I am sure we will see each other again soon."

Smiling, Silvia stood on her tiptoes and kissed Berty on the cheek. "Of course, I will be safe. You are watching." With a squeeze of his hands, she let go. Joining Estelle, they said a final goodbye to the men, then trekked into the snowy woods.

After watching her light blue cloak disappear into the white, Berty said, "Good work men. Time to head home."

About the Author

IE Castellano is an American author and poet living in the Eastern United States. Falling in love with the mechanics of the English language at an early age, she started writing poetry before venturing into fiction. With her propensity to ask, what if, she writes speculative fiction—authoring the dystopian sci-fi novel, *Tricentennial*, and the contemporary epic fantasy series, *the World In-between*.

Continue Reading the World In-between Series
Book Two:
Bow of the Moon

Also by IE Castellano:
Tricentennial

IE's blog: http://iecastellano.blogpost.com

Contact IE: iecastellano@zoho.com

JosDCreations: http://JosDCreations.com

www.ingramcontent.com/pod-product-compliance
Lightning Source LLC
Chambersburg PA
CBHW030806260626
47169CB00001B/206